THE
MAGIC
COLLECTOR

CHESNEY INFALT

THE MAGIC COLLECTOR

The Magic Collector
A Gothic Fantasy Romance

Published 2023 by BookDragon Publishing. All rights reserved.

No part of this book may be reproduced in any form or by any electronic or mechanical means, including information storage and retrieval systems, without written permission from the author, except for the use of brief quotations in a book review.

This is a work of fiction. All names, places, and events are created by the author or used fictitiously. Any ties to real life are coincidental.

Cover Design by Lydia Russell.
Interior Design and Formatting by Nicole Scarano Formatting & Design.
Character Art by @stephydrawsart_ & @wintermaiden11

CONTENTS

Books by Chesney Infalt	ix
Author's Note	xi
1. Pardon Me, but I'd Rather You Not Help	1
2. Am I Not Merciful?	13
3. What Are You Doing Here?	25
4. No One Can Help You	33
5. I Do Not Know What I Was Expecting, But It Was Definitely Not a Broom Closet.	43
6. It Is a Temporary Fix	51
7. Hungry Again, Are You?	59
8. Ghosts, Monsters, and a Little Boy with a Wild Imagination...	69
9. Can I Show You a Trick?	77
10. You Never Quite Get Used to It	89
11. What Exactly Did She Say to You?	97
12. I Hate This Part	107
13. He Won't Tell Me, but I Think Mother Knows	115
14. Ghosts and Ghouls and Spirits, I'd Imagine	123
15. Stay With Me	131
16. To Help Someone	137
17. I Didn't Know You Were a Barber	147
18. I'm the Idiot	157
19. Where is Yours?	167
20. At Least We Go Together	175
21. Not Without You!	185
22. I Would Like to Paint You	193
23. That Might Have Bought You Twenty Minutes	203
24. That is Not a Question for Anyone Else to Answer	211
25. The Only Person Stopping You is Yourself	219
26. You Hate to Lie, Don't You?	227
27. What Fun Is Life Without a Little Frivolity?	237
28. I Could Never Hate You	249
29. Stifling Your Emotions Only Stifles Who You Are	259

30. If It Means Anything to You, I Promise I Have Not
    Taken Advantage of Your Sister   265
31. While It Was a Tragedy...   277
32. You Did What You Had To, for His Safety   285
33. Not as Selfless as You Might Think   293
34. I Never Even Got to Hold Him   299
35. He Was My Friend...   307
36. I'm Just Like Bash!   319
37. It Would Be So Much Easier if You Were Nosy, Just
    This Once   327
38. He's Come for Me!   335
39. I Cast the Wrong Spell   345
40. I'm Here   353
41. There's That Word Again...   363
42. We Have to Pick the Right Material   375
43. Do You Not Like Kissing in Books?   383
44. I Wish I Would Have Said Something Sooner   393
45. You Loved Well   403
46. I'm Slightly Terrified, Not Knowing What That
    Expression Means   411
47. I Am Glad to See That You and I Are of a Similar Mind   419
48. I Was Afraid I Hated You   427
49. You Cannot Hide Forever   435
50. Is He Going to Let Her Out?   445
51. You Don't Have a Bad Side   455
52. What Foul Price Did You Require of Him for This?   463
53. Ah, More's the Pity   473
54. And Beyond That, if It Is Possible   481
55. It Is Done   489
56. Not Without Me   497
    Epilogue   503

    Acknowledgments   507
    About the Author   509

*To all who are dealing with hurt and trauma:
The journey of healing is difficult but worthwhile.*

BOOKS BY CHESNEY INFALT

Once Upon a Reimagined Time

-The Heart of the Sea

-The Fox and the Briar

A Different Kind of Magic

-A Different Kind of Magic

Standalones

-The Magic Collector

AUTHOR'S NOTE

The Magic Collector is a gothic fantasy romance, so it delves into some heavier topics that the characters work through. I recommend ages 16 and up. If you would like to go into this book blind, feel free! But if you would like the CWs, read on below.

This book contains scenes of fantasy violence, a brief implied love scene between a married couple, and flashbacks of a birth, death, and physical and verbal abuse. SPOILER—there is a loss of limb.

CHAPTER 1

PARDON ME, BUT I'D RATHER YOU NOT HELP

"Polite society does not go looking for magic," Grand Duchess Katarina Lestat said for what felt to Aveline like the thousandth time since yesterday. The old woman glared out the window, at the children excitedly gathering around a street performer. He stood in front of one of the less busy shops; surprisingly, instead of shooing him away, the flower shop owner just watched from the doorway, her attention fixated on the man as much as the children's was. His clothes were brightly coloured, easily drawing the eye amongst the sea of neutral tones, and the sparks at his fingertips enraptured the growing crowd.

No, polite society just relies on magic users to do its dirty work, Aveline wanted to retort, but stuffed it down with the rest of her commentary that the old woman would harrumph at. After all, if she wanted to make it in polite society and keep her disguise as Princess Gwendoline Allard, she had to watch her speech, act properly, and dress fashionably. And Aveline did not intend to just make it—no, she was going to win the game. She would marry Prince Alexei tomorrow, ensuring the survival of her family. King Charles had promised that when she had agreed to the ruse, and she would make sure he kept his end of the bargain.

Instead of taking a motorcar, the prince's great aunt had insisted they take a carriage—which Aveline truly did not mind, other than the fact that the Grand Duchess's favourite carriage was ancient and went along so slowly, Aveline was certain passersby were walking faster than they were riding. The more the old woman prattled on, the more tempting walking became, but Aveline did not entertain the idea in all seriousness: she would not show up to the royal celebration sweaty and exhausted.

At this rate, she hoped they showed up before the celebration ended.

"We can trust Our Majesty's wizards to do what we need," Lady Beatrice chimed in, her voice a touch too shrill for Aveline to believe it was how she truly sounded. Like most everyone in high society, Beatrice upheld her image by following the latest trends and agreeing with those in power—although when two figures disagreed, she tended to go silent. "There is no need for us to go looking for magic."

"That is not true magic, just parlour tricks." The Grand Duchess's glare soured further—at this point, Aveline thought it might be the woman's natural expression.

Aveline shifted slightly, enough to keep the dark-haired man in sight. He lifted his left hand dramatically, his gold and silver rings glinting in the sunlight. His fingers spread wide to reveal a lotus flower blooming on his palm, its petals an iridescent pink, making the others seem dull in comparison. The crowd gasped and murmured. There were no lotus flowers on the shop display, nothing he could have snatched while the crowd's focus was elsewhere.

Just before the carriage passed by the scene, a man ducked down to scoop up his child, and the street performer locked gazes with Aveline. Striking, rich brown, his eyes were full of life. He tilted his head, his wide smile slipping for the briefest of moments.

Grand Duchess Katarina thumped her cane on the floor of the carriage, snapping Aveline's attention back. "A frivolous use of magic." She *tsked*.

Aveline straightened. Of course, she wouldn't point out that the woman had just said it wasn't *real* magic. But it looked real enough to her. Despite her homeland being known for its mines of a magic-conductive metal known as nickerite, there was little magic left to be found, the country too small and impoverished to be able to pay for the protection court-bound wizards could offer. Her king, King Charles, only had the one wizard left, and he was the punchline of many jokes, most of them having to do with clumsiness; a far cry from the ones she had seen so far in Salise, who strutted about the castle as if they were in charge. No one would dare say a disrespectful word about any of them.

"Arrest him!" someone ordered. Aveline gritted her teeth to keep from reacting. What had he done wrong in giving the children some entertainment? Surely, the officers had worse people to imprison, ones who were actually a danger to society. But it was none of her business, especially when stepping in would put her reputation on the line.

"Frivolous, indeed," Princess Lucille concurred with a sniff, as if she did not hear the scuffle outside. "Although I would rather they do silly parlour tricks on street corners than become monsters like The Heart Thief."

"Or The Magic Collector." Lady Beatrice shuddered.

"No one has seen him in ages," said Princess Lucille, shaking her head. "He must be dead by now."

Lady Beatrice leant forward, lowering her tone. "I heard that his castle reappeared near the edge of the city. It—"

The Grand Duchess thumped her cane again, this time with more force. "That is quite enough!"

Silence reigned. Aveline fought the urge to look back at the street performer, knowing full well that he was out of sight by now anyway, unless she wanted to make a fool of herself by sticking her head out of the window.

With a snap and a jolt, the carriage toppled at an odd angle, throwing the occupants into one another. Aveline grunted, Lady Beatrice's elbow finding her side, the brim of her wide hat crumpling against Aveline's cheek. The carriage shuddered as it was dragged across the ground, until the coachman called to the spooked horses in soothing tones that convinced them to stop.

"Help! Help us!" demanded the Grand Duchess. Aveline clenched her fist to keep from reaching for the door: she, a lady of high status in society, was never to open her own door, not even in situations such as these. However, she drew the line at wailing like the others did, no matter how hard her heart hammered against her ribcage. Calm and collected, calm and collected...

The footman came to their rescue. "Our deepest apologies for the fright, Grand Duchess. It seems one of the wheels broke."

"Did you not check them before we left?" she spat, accepting the help.

The footman mumbled apologies and continued to aid the women out of the carriage. Aveline was the last one out, not wanting to get shoved out of the way by the others. Soon enough, they would make way for her, when she was their princess. Until then, they could be as petty as they wanted to be. Prince Alexei had chosen *her*, and King Byron himself had agreed to the match.

"Just what are we to do? We cannot wait here until help comes; that could take ages!" The Grand Duchess retrieved a handkerchief from her handbag to dab at the sweat already beading upon her brow.

"My father will hear of this," Princess Lucille declared, snapping open her lace fan.

"Perhaps someone has a carriage we could borrow," suggested the coachman.

Grand Duchess Katarina's heated response was cut off by an officer pulling his simple carriage alongside theirs. "Grand Duchess, Princess, what can I do for you?"

As the old woman vented, Aveline's focus drifted towards where another officer was ordering the people to scatter and leading the now cuffed street performer towards his motorcar. Not stylish like the ones the royal family owned, the officer's had an open area in the front with room enough for a driver and passenger, and the back was enclosed like a carriage, only the windows were small and barred. The street performer did not struggle, keeping his head high as the officer locked him in the back.

The crowd dispersed, their protests dying out. Reluctantly, the flower shop owner stepped back inside, holding the pink lotus close to her heart. The other colourful flowers on display shimmered, bright-ening as their revitalised petals opened like they were embracing the sun.

"We can escort you back to the castle," the first officer said with a bow. "Although I am afraid I do not have room for all of you."

Before she could stop herself, Aveline said, "I can ride with him."

That struck them speechless, all looking to where Aveline gestured. Feeling awkward, she lowered her hand. What had possessed her to suggest such a thing? She didn't think the man was a criminal, but others did, and that could soil her reputation, riding along in the prison motorcar, even if it was in the passenger seat.

"He is taking a prisoner—"

"To the castle," Grand Duchess Katarina interrupted the officer. "A perfect solution, Gwendoline."

The officer floundered. "Your Grace, I would not recommend—"

"Nonsense!" She tapped her cane on the ground to emphasise her statement. "The culprit is already apprehended and his magic is blocked by the handcuffs, yes? I am sure Gwendoline will be quite safe."

Not giving him a chance to argue, she stepped into his carriage, the Princess and Lady behind her. With a sigh, the officer whistled to get his comrade's attention. They argued for a few moments, and then the second one beckoned for Aveline to follow him.

"If I may, I'd suggest you keep your hands to yourself and do not talk to him, Princess Gwendoline," he warned as he helped her into her seat. "All magic-users are cunning, and those who are not bound by oath to the King are never to be trusted."

"I am sure I am safe in such capable hands," Aveline said, smoothing her skirts. The officer's expression softened, and he dipped his head, hurrying to take his own seat. A turn of the key, and the motorcar rumbled to life. Within minutes, they passed the other officer's carriage, even though they had gotten a head start. The wind tugged at her hair, so Aveline put a hand on her hat to keep it in place. Hopefully, she would not look too much of a mess by the time they arrived. Hanna would be certain to help her; the handmaiden seemed to have a magic of her own, the way she could quickly fix anything that might go wrong, from a torn hem to a stained glove to a missing button.

Why did I suggest this? Aveline lamented again. Despite the wall separating them, she could feel the strange street performer, the *wizard*, like he was somehow drawing her to him. *Absurd. That is just your curiosity, which will only get you into trouble.*

Still, she couldn't help wondering what would happen to him once they reached the castle. Nothing good, she guessed, all things considered. Would they force him to take the oath? What was his reasoning for not taking it in the first place? While they did not seem particularly happy, the wizards in the King's service had everything they could want, all of their needs met.

It is not a matter of the head, Aveline, she could hear her sister Edith say, *but of the heart.*

Her chest twinged. *Your matters of the heart forced me to take on your responsibility,* she thought bitterly. *No one should be forced into anything.*

Aveline shook her head. There was nothing she could do for him, even if she wanted to. She wouldn't use force to take the keys, and there would be no explaining her way out of setting him free. It would be obvious that she was the culprit, which would ruin all of her plans, and hurt her family in the process. No, that would not do. She had to press down the guilt, if not for her own sake, then for theirs.

They passed by the shops, and the streets carried them closer to the castle, where the buildings were fewer, albeit much bigger and more grandiose, with gilded signs and cobblestone pathways leading up to the doors. Most were homes of nobles or expensive shops that only the upper class could afford. The first time she had stepped inside one, she'd had to press her lips together to keep her jaw from falling open. Such intricate craftsmanship—in perfect condition, no less—was nowhere to be found in her homeland. Whatever was once beautiful had fallen into disrepair many years ago, indicative of the current state of their once-thriving country.

Warily, the officer glanced up at the darkening sky. Aveline did the same, seeking out the storm clouds encroaching on their sunny afternoon. She'd welcome a cool breeze, but rain... Imagining herself arriving at the castle completely drenched made her grimace.

Jaw clenched, the officer pressed the gas pedal to the floorboard. The motorcar sped up slightly, engine whining as they continued uphill. "Sit back, Princess Gwendoline," he ordered tersely. "We should make it to the castle before they arrive."

Aveline stared at him. "Who?"

A siren blared, wailing repeatedly. She clapped her hands over her ears, and the wind snatched her hat. More dark clouds appeared, spreading across the sky like a layer of fog. People scattered, rushing inside, bolting doors and closing curtains. The wretched sound continued, rattling her head and chattering her teeth. She screwed her eyes shut, telling herself they would reach the castle soon, where it was sa—

She heard the high-pitched whistle before the explosion hit. The earth shuddered violently, throwing everything in its path. A split second of weightlessness, then Aveline collided with the ground, stars bursting in her vision, debris raining down atop her.

For one horrible moment, she could not move, could not breathe, could not think, could not feel. Then she gasped, her aching lungs spasming as they sucked in the smoky air. Coughing, she pushed herself onto shaky legs, falling against a semi-blackened tree. Flames licked at the ground, catching on what bits of vegetation it could find between the buildings. The motorcar had toppled and skidded across the ground, leaving scrapes not nearly as deep as the scorch-marked gouge on the other side of the street.

More balls of fire streaked across the sky, their muffled collisions drowned out by Aveline's roaring heartbeat. What was happening? She thought she had done her research and knew what she was getting herself into...

She had to leave, to find some sort of shelter. A groan caught her attention; the officer lay a few paces away, his leg bent at an awkward angle. His eyes moved restlessly behind closed lids, blood trickling down his temple. At his hip was a ring of keys.

Aveline whirled around to stare at the motorcar. From what she could tell, it was still locked, the street performer trapped inside. Before she could overthink it, she snatched the keys.

From the direction of the castle, there was a hum overhead, and something translucent spread across the sky to form a shimmering canopy, shielding the city from the dark clouds and their raining fire.

The sirens cut off abruptly, replaced by a crackling voice stating, "Royal wizards are handling the situation. Do not leave your homes until we have made the announcement that it is safe to do so."

The magic dome remained, undeterred by the barrage of blazing strikes from the dark clouds. Bright light arced above the dome, splintering into the heart of the attacks, dispersing the clouds.

Ignoring the ringing in her ears, Aveline raced to the back of the motorcar. "Sir!" she called, fumbling with the keys, which all looked more or less the same. "I'm going to release you. You'd better hurry before the officer comes to."

It was too dark to see much of anything through the small barred slot in the door, so when the street performer's face appeared suddenly, Aveline dropped the keyring in surprise.

"I would advise you not to help me." The bright lights cast a myriad of reds, yellows, and oranges on his pale skin. This close, she could see the hint of stubble at his jawline and the long, dark lashes framing his brown eyes.

"He is unconscious," Aveline explained, trying again to search for the correct key. "If you leave quickly, you can hide before anyone realises you are gone."

"It is in your best interest that you do not help me." He stayed unaffected, so unsettlingly calm. Did he not realise what was happening? Did he not care that he could have died? Or was he trying to put on a brave face like she was?

"Hurry, and I will not have to worry about my reputation being sullied." Aveline bit back a sigh when one of the keys got stuck and she had to jimmy it back out again. Luckily, it didn't snap.

With the same air as one might speak about their preference on a stroll through the park, he said, "Pardon me, but I'd rather you not help."

Aveline locked eyes with him. "You would rather be brought to the King so he can force you to pledge your magic to him?" Then she went back to unlocking the door, certain that they only had a matter of minutes before people's curiosity outweighed their fear enough for them to peek out their windows.

"You, an upper-class lady, would risk your status by setting an illegal wizard free?"

If she were not so determined to finish what she'd started, Aveline might have stormed off. "Stop being so stubborn! Just let me help, and then I shall take my leave of you."

He paused, studying her. Heat crept up her neck, only made worse when he dipped his head and said, "As you wish."

A key finally fit. She tugged on the lock harder than necessary, and the door fell open, forcing her to take a few steps back. The wizard awkwardly manoeuvred his way out, stretching his long legs. He stood at least a head taller than Aveline, more if she'd not been wearing heeled shoes. His colourful clothes were rumpled and his hair dishevelled, but other than that, he seemed unscathed by the whole affair. A cuff dangled from his left wrist, the other side closed around nothing.

"I suppose I should thank you." He gave a half-smile.

"You are welcome," she replied out of habit, her gaze fixated on the cuff. "How did..."

The wizard followed her line of sight. "I guess he didn't put it on tight enough." With a snap of his fingers, it unlocked and fell to the ground. "You should hurry home before you are missed."

"You should find darker clothes so you're less noticeable."

The corner of his mouth twitched in amusement. "What if there are certain people I want to find me easily?"

She had no words. This wizard, who was just captured, survived an explosion, and had the chance to escape, was lingering here to *flirt* with her?

Despite his smile, there was a heaviness to the depths of his eyes, almost as if he pitied her for some reason. Aveline rolled her shoulders back, holding her head high.

"I am Sebastian," he stated, reaching for her hand, and pressed a kiss to the back of it before she thought of pulling away. "If you have need of me, close your eyes, put your hand over your heart, and speak my name."

His kiss tingled, like it had imprinted on her. He smiled sadly, apologetically, but what he was sorry for, she could not comprehend.

"You should return the keys before he wakes," Sebastian suggested, then bowed. "Until next we meet, Aveline."

The moment he released her, he disappeared, leaving behind only footprints of where he stood. She sought for a sign of him tricking her, but found only the aftermath of the explosion. The fires were dying out, nothing but flickers, and the smoke thinned. Aveline scooped up the keys and hurriedly returned them, thankful that the officer had yet to stir.

"Sebastian..." she murmured aloud, making sure her hand was nowhere near her heart. Odd did not begin to describe him, and yet it was the only word she could come up with that fit. She'd always been better with paints anyway, but she would have needed multiple palettes with an array of colours to capture his essence properly. Even if she did, she had no idea how she would replicate his eyes, with all of the intensity they carried.

He knew my name and title, she realised as she knelt down to shake the officer awake. *How did he know my real name?*

CHAPTER 2

AM I NOT MERCIFUL?

"You are unharmed? How?" asked Hanna, as she helped Aveline into a formal gown, more appropriate for the night's celebration. Aveline had thought that, after the magic-users of the neighbouring kingdom of Katin attacked earlier, their engagement celebration would have been cancelled. But King Byron refused, stating that the kingdom would not be intimidated. They would celebrate tonight, and have the wedding tomorrow.

Tomorrow, she could stop pretending to be a princess because the title would be hers, and her family would live in comfort once again. Aveline scanned her reflection in her bedroom mirror, taking inventory of what little improvements she could make: straightening her shoulders, lifting her frown into a demure smile, covering the beauty mark on her neck with cosmetics...

"I do not know," Aveline said, realising Hanna was waiting on her response, glancing up every so often as she worked to make the dress fit Aveline just right. Although the soft orange fabric was not one she would have picked out herself, the handmaiden seemed to have an eye for fashion, and in the few months of Aveline being here, she had learnt to trust Hanna's judgement. The handmaiden was eager to please, and even more eager to share the kingdom's history and customs as much as the latest gossip. The nobles had thought to crush Aveline's chances of becoming their princess by giving her a young, inexperienced handmaiden, but Aveline thought of Hanna as a blessing in disguise. Let them underestimate her. With Hanna's help, Aveline would prove them wrong.

"You are fortunate, Princess Gwendoline." Gently, Hanna twisted and pinned up Aveline's blonde hair. "Magic will destroy a person if it gets the chance. It sounds like you have more luck than the average person."

While Aveline had given Hanna the overall story, she had kept the details about the wizard to herself, only saying that he was a street performer who had escaped. She had thought not to bring him up at all, but word had spread quickly about him. A rogue wizard was not a complication the King wanted to deal with, especially in the middle of a war.

"Hanna," Aveline asked, lowering her voice, "do you know all the names of the wizards in this kingdom?"

"Most of them," Hanna replied with a grin, then matched her quiet tone. "Are you asking about anyone in particular? The street performer, perhaps?" Her eyes glittered with excitement as she fastened a simple golden necklace on Aveline.

Of course Hanna had figured that much out. If Aveline asked his name, would she be endangering him? She had no true intentions about seeking him out, but curiosity niggled at the back of her mind. He'd told her not to help, and then given her a way to call upon him. Odd, strange... compelling. Her hand still tingled, even with the elbow-length gloves on. If she were in any danger, shouldn't she find out?

"You cannot speak a word of this to anyone," Aveline said.

Hanna leant in close. "I'll take it with me to the grave, Your Highness."

I hope so. Aveline took a breath, although it did little to calm her nerves. "Do you know of a wizard named Sebastian?"

Unexpectedly, Hanna frowned, the first time Aveline had seen her do so. "That is not an uncommon name, but... I don't know of any wizards by it. Maybe he gave you a pseudonym?"

Her curiosity unsated, Aveline pursed her lips. She had not put the stranger in jeopardy, but how was she to know if she was in trouble or not? It was not as if she could ask anyone else and risk drawing unwanted attention to herself. Until she found another solution, she had to settle for paying extra close attention to conversations.

"Or he could be a witch," she whispered.

"Is there a difference between a wizard and a witch?"

Hanna nodded quickly. "A wizard is born with the capability to use magic; it's a natural part of them. Witches, on the other hand... They sell their souls to dark, unnatural creatures in exchange for power. Some call it stolen power, but it seems more like a bargain, terrible as it is."

Aveline shuddered. She had been told tales of such dark creatures when she was little, but it was not something often spoken of, except to scare children into behaving. "Let me know if you hear anything."

"Of course, Your Highness!" The frown vanished, replaced by her usual bright demeanour. Hanna finished readying Aveline, all the while chattering about various rumours of the visitors who would be in attendance.

Aveline memorised what she could, on the off chance it could help her make it through the night unscathed.

THICK VIOLET CURTAINS MUFFLED THE SOUNDS OF THE BALLROOM party below the indoor balcony where the elite gathered to dine. If they so wanted, they could peer down on those deemed unworthy of joining the royal family, who would not attend the ball until they were finished with their meal and conversation. Aveline resisted the urge to tap her feet to the beat of the rising music. There would be a special dance for just the Crown Prince and herself—to mark the last night before the two of them would be forever bound, never to part until death wished it so.

While she could not see herself ever wanting to be stuck with someone for eternity because of love, doing it for the sake of her family's well-being seemed like a wise enough decision. A rational one, at least. Running off to marry someone you barely knew because you "loved" them—

Enough, Aveline chastised herself, settling gracefully into the chair Prince Alexei pulled out for her. *No more ruminating over Edith.* She ignored the pinch in her chest and forced herself to smile demurely up at her fiancé. He offered her a brief smile in return before his sights darted to his friend sitting across the table.

Everyone took their places, and servants set down dishes with gilded edges that barely kept the high piles of food contained. Meats, fruits, potatoes—more than enough to go around. If Aveline didn't know better, she would have thought that the wizards were joining them since there was an abundance of food, but they were stationed about the palace, keeping a watchful eye. All except for Ralph, the King's top wizard, who was always by the ruler's side, now sitting at his right hand, the Queen at his left. Unlike the street performer's bright colours, Ralph wore a sleek grey suit that was a slightly fancier version of his normal work attire. Simple thin gold bands graced his fingers, the number of them openly displaying his power, that he could channel large amounts of magic at once. Aveline had counted three or four rings per hand at most on the other magic-users, but Ralph had twelve in total, counting both hands. Each ring was inscribed with a foreign language she wished she could understand, or at least know the name of so she could seek out answers in the library.

She assumed that the rings contained at least small amounts of nickerite to aid in magic casting, giving the wizard more control over his spells. After all, that was why King Byron was happy to wed his heir to Aveline: King Charles agreed to give him first access to their mines, and she doubted gems were what he sought, not when those could be found elsewhere more easily.

No one began eating until the King took the first bite. Aveline took small bites, even though the rich flavours tempted her to indulge. A sliver of guilt pricked her at the thought of her family. *They will have more than enough soon,* she told herself. *Marry the prince tomorrow, and they will never go hungry again.* It was a small sacrifice, really, marrying the Crown Prince everyone desired. With his strong, clean-shaven jaw, his wavy blond locks he kept neatly tied back, and his enchanting light grey eyes, Crown Prince Alexei had the attention of everyone he came into contact with. Aveline often reminded herself that she should feel proud to have secured this match.

"We are lucky Katin did not send more magic-users than they did," one noble commented between bites.

"They were merely testing our might," Alexei said. "They wish to find a weakness in our defences."

"And they shall find none," scoffed King Byron. "We have more magic-users than any kingdom, so it will be their blood spilled long before any innocent's."

Aveline wanted him to clarify if he meant the blood of enemies or magic-users, but she had a feeling she wouldn't like the answer either way.

Ralph lifted his glass. "We will protect you with everything we have, Your Majesties. You are safe with us."

When the others raised their glasses in cheers, Aveline followed suit, but the sherry left a strange taste behind.

"Are you quite well, Princess Gwendoline?" Queen Eugenia inquired, drawing all attention to Aveline. "Is your illness returning?"

"No, I am quite well, Your Majesty." She added a smile she hoped was somewhat satisfactory. To their knowledge, Princess Gwendoline had recovered from a nearly lethal illness, of which the details were not disclosed, since it was improper subject matter. As for her twin sister, Maribelle was on the mend.

King Charles had spent a lot of money and favours to keep their true fates a secret.

"The poor dear is still shaken from this afternoon's events, as we all are." Grand Duchess Katarina dramatically fanned her face as she gave a great sigh. "Before the attack, we were having an awful day, what with my favourite carriage having a broken wheel, and the four of us having to get a ride back to the palace from police officers."

"It was horrid," Princess Lucille agreed, and took another sip of sherry.

The Grand Duchess sighed again. "At least the officers caught that street performer who was enchanting those poor onlookers. Peasants have no protection against illegal magic like that."

Prince Alexei frowned. "I do not recall anyone being taken to the dungeons."

"Because he slipped away during the attack," King Byron clarified. When the Grand Duchess gasped and pressed a cloth napkin to her mouth, he added, "You can put your hysterical heart at ease, dear Aunt, for I have men tracking him this very moment. He shall not remain hidden for long."

I do hope you are wrong, Aveline thought. No one seemed to be under Sebastian's thrall, just charmed by his magic tricks.

"Enough depressing talk," Queen Eugenia said. "Gwendoline, I am sure you will feel much better after your father and brother arrive tomorrow for the wedding. 'Tis a shame they were delayed."

Aveline almost choked on a bite of chicken, but managed to say, "I look forward to seeing them, Your Majesty."

"Of course you do." The King changed the subject to the great hunting event they planned for after the wedding. Aveline ate in silence, her thoughts keeping her company. Her "father" and "brother" were on their way, delayed by weather and, if this afternoon were any indicator, possibly the warfare shutting down major travel ways. As long as neither of them was injured or captured, she could rest easy. The ruse was only important until after tomorrow, as everyone's attention would be diverted to other pressing matters, like the war.

Just a little longer.

Aveline's plate was long empty and her glass had only a few sips left by the time King Byron stood and announced that they would join the party. Everyone coupled up, Prince Alexei taking Aveline's arm. Servants pulled back the thick curtains, letting the music and chatter from downstairs flood the room like a serenade beckoning them to partake.

"I need a moment," Aveline found herself saying, garnering strange looks from the others. "Just to freshen up."

"Nerves seem the more likely explanation," Alexei said in a low tone, but not enough to keep from prying ears. "Come now, you should be used to these kinds of celebrations, being royalty."

Aveline was almost relieved when King Byron cut in with, "I should think not, seeing how impoverished their country has been. It's a miracle they lasted as long as they did."

All but Alexei and his mother chuckled. The Prince reluctantly released Aveline's arm when Queen Eugenia offered her a small smile and said, "Go on, but do hurry."

Hanna hurried forward to lead Aveline to a powder room. When she heard the click of the door shutting behind her, Aveline took a shaky breath and leant against the vanity. She could do this. She knew she could, especially since she was so close to the finish line.

Logic was not enough to calm her thrashing heart.

"Are you sure this is what you want?" Hanna asked quietly, standing close to the door like she was guarding it.

Aveline met Hanna's gaze in the mirror. Her features dainty and soft, Hanna could have fit in with the royals, if only she had been born under different circumstances. Her station kept her beauty from being appreciated—not only physical beauty, but inner beauty as well. Aveline hoped that, if she were to make it through the wedding ceremony tomorrow, she would be able to keep Hanna as her handmaiden. And, secretly, her friend.

"Why wouldn't it be?" Aveline straightened, donning her calm and collected facade once more, and faced the handmaiden. *No more "ifs". You will marry Prince Alexei tomorrow, and you will save your family from complete ruin. Do what Edith could not bring herself to. Do not pass it on to Jeanette.*

Hanna looked at her with sympathy that nearly found a crack in Aveline's mask. "I fear you are settling, Your Highness. You deserve much better."

"Better than marrying the Crown Prince?" What could be better than that? She and her family would have complete security and protection for the rest of her life.

"Better than being an armpiece for the Prince."

She must really trust me if she feels comfortable enough to speak against the Crown Prince like that. "It is not about me and my desires," Aveline said carefully, keeping her tone soft. "This is the right choice to make."

Hanna nodded, which Aveline took as the girl accepting her decision, not that she agreed with it. Truly, it did not matter what the handmaiden thought of the situation. But Aveline found she cared regardless.

"We should return before you are missed." Hanna timidly tucked Aveline's stray hair back into place.

"Of course." She inspected herself one more time before they left the powder room.

King Byron was the first to note Aveline's return. "Very good. Now, time to join the party." He gestured at the herald, who stood at the top of the carpeted stairway.

"Presenting His Majesty King Byron Voland IV and Queen Eugenia Voland."

With the dignity expected out of royalty, the couple descended the stairs, all eyes pinned to them.

"Are you all right?" Alexei whispered, pulling Aveline towards him.

"Perfectly," she said with an ease that almost convinced herself that it was the truth. *I will be.*

The music had grown quieter and changed from an upbeat song to a slower, more intimate one. Once the King and Queen crossed the long room and were seated upon their thrones, the herald continued.

"Presenting Crown Prince Alexei Voland and his bride-to-be, Princess Gwendoline Allard of the western kingdom of Arreth."

Aveline focused on keeping a pleasant expression as she walked with the Crown Prince. It surprised her that they gave her that title, since they no longer deemed her kingdom worthy of being called a kingdom anymore. But the title would officially be hers tomorrow, until King Byron passed away and Alexei took the crown. Then she would be Queen.

Aveline swallowed before her throat could get too tight. One step at a time—that, she could handle. A celebration tonight, a wedding tomorrow... She would only be expected to look pretty, say some vows, and kiss Alexei.

Just breathe.

The rest of the elite were announced, and Alexei brought Aveline to the middle of the vacated floor. The music picked up again in an invitation to dance. Accurate in the steps but lacking in heart, Alexei led and Aveline followed, hoping they did not look as rigid as their movements felt. By some miracle, the song ended with a round of applause.

Aveline wondered if the musicians cut the song short.

Other couples eagerly re-entered the dance floor, but Alexei and Aveline moved off to the side. With a kiss to the back of her hand, he said, "If you wish for another dance, we can end the evening with one."

Please, no. Aveline widened her smile. "What a wonderful idea." Before she could think of topics of conversation he might engage with, Alexei took her arm and positioned them beside his father's throne.

"Seems Lucille will pass the evening away with dancing, as usual," King Byron said, eyes following his daughter. Unlike her brother, she moved with grace and passion, flirting with subtle movements instead of words.

"Her dance card is always full," Queen Eugenia said with a hint of pride.

"It will not be, come next season." Knowing that he had surprised his family, King Byron took a moment—attention never leaving Lucille—before explaining, "I have an offer in progress, similar to the agreement made for our dear Gwendoline."

Aveline fought not to fidget as King Byron's gaze darted to her. His blue irises were so dark that they could almost be considered black. She doubted she could accurately mix the right shade of paint, and certainly would not want to spend time trying to replicate the unnerving colour.

"An agreement is much more preferable to forcing us into a needless war that will only end in their bloodshed." He paused, unblinking. "Am I not merciful, Gwendoline?"

"An agreement is certainly preferable, Your Majesty." She bowed her head.

Her heart thundered as she waited for him to press her for a direct answer to his question. Luckily, his attention drifted back to the sea of swirling silks following the beat of the music. Had Alexei been more like his sister, Aveline would have suggested they rejoin the throng. Once was more than enough.

Still, her toes wiggled in her shoes, drawn by the entrancing notes and the offer to make her forget all of her weighty thoughts, even if only for a short while.

Enough, she chastised herself. *Many would give up everything they have to be where you are now.*

"Pardon us, Father, Mother," Alexei said suddenly. "We will return shortly."

His parents had barely spared them a nod before Alexei whisked Aveline away with no explanation. She assumed they were headed towards his friends, but to her surprise, he brought them outdoors, to the garden. Soft light from the palace scarcely reached the tall rose hedges, and when they turned a corner, Aveline noted they were out of sight from even the palace guards.

Were she not engaged to him, this would have been a much bigger scandal. Did no one care for her reputation?

"Prince Alexei—"

"Just Alexei is fine," he said, releasing her arm. "I know parties can be a little suffocating, and Father's questions can make them even more so. I thought you might want some air."

Aveline took a cleansing breath, relaxing her shoulders a bit. "What about... What will others think of us sneaking off to the gardens alone?"

The corner of his mouth twitched into a small smirk. "That I could not wait one more day to have my way with you, I'd imagine." He nodded towards a split in the garden pathway. "If you go right, there is a small bench where you can sit and collect yourself. I'll wait here for you, although I will suggest you not take too long."

Aveline stared at him. The Crown Prince had gone from being smitten with her to distancing himself in a matter of weeks, but now he was helping her. Her head swam, trying to piece together the conflicting sides he'd shown thus far.

For her sake, she desperately hoped this was the real him, full of understanding and sympathy that he could only show in glimpses to keep his own reputation intact.

"Why do you think I need a moment to collect myself?"

Alexei grimaced. "Because after living with my father for my entire life, I know to take scraps of peace where I can get them."

She had no idea how to respond. So, instead, she took the opportunity, saying, "I will return shortly."

"I'll stand watch," he called after her, and she glanced back at him. Surely, he was not playing some sort of trick on her. It would be too juvenile for a Crown Prince, especially one who seemed so well put together and always knew what to say and do to fit in with the crowd. He was many things, but cruel was not one of them.

Just for a few moments, Aveline told herself. A few moments to breathe, to calm her mind.

Just as Alexei said, there was a lonely bench tucked away in the corner, surrounded by leafy hedges. She sank onto it and closed her eyes, listening to the distant sounds of merriment while she focused on breathing. In and out. In and out. In and—

Something rustled nearby. Aveline snapped her eyes open and waited. A few seconds later, it happened again. "Alexei?" she whispered, afraid of drawing someone else's attention. But it was not him: it was coming from the wrong direction. *It is probably just an animal.*

The rustling happened again, this time closer, but before Aveline could decide what to do, a figure rounded the corner, wearing the same colourful attire he had been in earlier that day.

CHAPTER 3
WHAT ARE YOU DOING HERE?

"Sebastian," Aveline hissed, standing so quickly that she tripped on the hem of her dress. He caught her arm, his touch warm on her bare skin, but she shivered and yanked away. Something akin to hurt flickered across his features, too quickly for her to be certain.

Putting a finger to his lips, Sebastian nodded towards one of the long pathways that would take them farther away from Alexei and the palace. Like he assumed she would follow without question, he disappeared around another corner.

Return to Alexei, Aveline told herself. *Leave Sebastian to his troubles. You owe him nothing.*

Yet she stood there, staring into the dark. What if he needed help? What if one of the guards spotted him? She could convince him to leave before they did. Despite King Byron's words, she doubted he would be merciful if he captured Sebastian; the wizard would have nothing to barter that the King would want.

Her feet made the decision for her, carrying her deeper into the darkness of the gardens. The clouds smothered the moon and stars, refusing to light her way as she followed where Sebastian had gone, but her eyes adjusted enough to spot his smile in the darkness.

"What are you doing here? I did not call for you," Aveline whispered sharply. "You have to leave, now, before they capture you again."

The smile slipped. "I had to come back for you."

"What do you mean? I am in no danger here—" *If the secret stays safe* "—but you are."

"You are in grave danger here," he argued quietly, solemnly. "The Heart Thief is looking for you, and she will soon find you."

"The Heart Thief?"

"A terrible witch with great power," he clarified. "She does not like others to touch what she deems is hers."

A witch, after her? She'd barely interacted with anyone or anything outside of the palace since she'd arrived. "What did I..." Aveline trailed off as she went back through earlier events. The explosion was the only thing out of the ordinary, along with her releasing him—

"I did warn you not to help."

Her stomach knotted. "Do you belong to her?"

Instead of answering, he took a small step closer. She knew she should not let a stranger get this close, especially not a strange *man*, and yet, she felt no fear, not toward him.

"She seeks you now," Sebastian warned. "Leave. Flee as far as you can before she catches up. If you make it to the kingdom's border, she will be unable to follow."

Leave, when she was so close to her goal? That was not an option. Whatever this witch wanted to do to her—which she could only imagine based on her title—Aveline had to risk it. She rolled her shoulders back, projecting more confidence than she felt. "The King's magic-users will protect me."

Sebastian paused. "I hope you are right."

"Gwendoline!" Alexei called, keeping his voice down. "Where are you?"

Aveline peered behind her, even though the Crown Prince was not yet in sight. Leaning forward, Sebastian touched her shoulders. She was prepared for the same warmth, but his right hand felt like... nothing, just a slight pressure. No warmth, no cold, no callouses like his other hand, no sensation to suggest he was wearing a glove. She wanted to look, but his face was beside hers as he breathed in her ear, "If you have need of me, call."

Then the wizard was gone, leaving no trace of his visit.

"Gwendoline." Alexei sighed in relief. "Are you all right? Do you feel better now?"

For longer than she should have, Aveline stared into the darkness. "I am fine," she said sheepishly as she turned towards him. "I thought I saw something. We should return to the party."

She was grateful that he did not ask questions. If their marriage was to be one of tolerance and accepting that each of them would carry secrets, that was something she supposed she could handle.

By the time they left the gardens, Aveline resolved that she would ask Hanna about The Heart Thief. The King's wizards would undoubtedly protect her—if only to keep their kingdom safe—but it would not hurt to know more about this magic-user who was allegedly after her. Sebastian could have been lying, for all she knew. *He* could have been the Heart Thief, trying to lure her away from the palace so he could do what he wanted with her without risking himself. After all, the way he told her to call upon him was to put her hand over her heart.

But he could have taken me away after I set him free, and no one would have known, she mused. Trying to understand what was happening was irksome, like trying to put a puzzle together with too few pieces.

The one thing she was absolutely certain of was that leaving the palace and giving up her marriage to Prince Alexei would mean the ruin of her family. That could not happen.

When Alexei and Aveline returned indoors, arm-in-arm, the guards said nothing, but they did look them up and down, as if searching for incriminating evidence at what the two of them could have been doing in the gardens.

We did nothing of the sort. Aveline kept her head held high, even as her stomach clenched at the thought that they would be doing such things the next night, after the wedding. It would be expected, just as she would be expected to bear heirs.

Aveline redirected her mind to the present, preparing herself for the judgmental glances of attendees noticing their return, but everyone was staring at the stairs, where two men descended.

"Presenting King Charles Allard and Prince Ivan Allard of Arreth!"

One of the knots in her stomach unravelled. They made it safely, no injuries to be seen. At least one of her silent prayers had been answered.

Alexei and Aveline hurried to position themselves near the thrones before the new arrivals made it.

"Charles," King Byron greeted, "good to see you have arrived safely, and just in time for your daughter's wedding."

"Hell itself could not have prevented our attendance," King Charles said. "Might Ivan and I steal away Gwendoline for a few moments? It has been far too long since we've last seen her."

"Of course." King Byron waved them off. "But do bring her back shortly—she has one more dance to end the night."

Alexei released Aveline, and she took King Charles' arm. For how long they had been travelling, she was impressed at how impeccably they were dressed for the evening, fitting in despite the barely noticeable scuff marks on their boots and the way their well-maintained suits were slightly faded.

King Charles waited until they were at the farthest end of the room, away from everyone else, before embracing Aveline. She stiffened for a moment, then made herself relax.

"Everything is coming together beautifully," he whispered, his beard scraping against her cheek. "Have they given you any trouble?"

Prince Ivan positioned himself in Aveline's peripheral, his unreadable gaze locked on her. Once upon a time, she had pined for his attention just like her sisters had, but now it made little difference to her. Even if she still cared for him, it would not matter, not when she was already spoken for.

"Everything is going according to plan," Aveline said, fighting the urge to pull away. How would it look, after all, if she were seen rejecting affection from her 'father'?

"Perfect. I left a note from your mother in your room."

Her eyes widened. It'd been months since she'd seen her true family, all to keep up the illusion that she was the Princess of Arreth. He'd risked that much? Why? *Do not question his kindness—you'll only end up with answers you wished you never knew.* "Thank you, Father."

"You are pretty when you smile." He kissed her cheek, then said to Ivan, "Look after her," before strolling back towards the party.

Alexei peeked over his shoulder, seeking out Aveline. He raised a brow, and when she gave a single nod, he refocused on the dancing.

"Does he treat you well?" Ivan stood with dignity and pride befitting a prince, and for a moment Aveline remembered why she had giggled and swooned with her sisters when they were children. Unlike Alexei, Ivan was an excellent dancer, as far as Aveline had spectated for all those years. No one ever rejected his offer to dance, and not just because it would be considered an insult.

"Well enough," she answered honestly. "I have no complaints."

After a few moments, Ivan reached up, his fingertips trailing her hairline down to her ear.

"You are supposed to be my brother," Aveline warned in a hushed tone. With their blond hair and light eyes, it was only a bit of a stretch to believe that they were related. That was where their similarities ended.

His touch lingered on her jaw; a memory flashed before her eyes, of a stolen kiss and the spoken wish that she did not have to leave. "You had a hair out of place."

"Did I?" Aveline challenged, locking the memory away again once more. "Hanna is normally impeccable when it comes to readying me."

Slowly, Ivan lowered his hand. "Would you like to dance?"

"Somehow, I do not think that would be considered appropriate given the circumstances."

After all of these years, now he took notice of her, when she was someone else's? Suddenly The Heart Thief seemed like much less of a threat than Ivan's sudden interest in her spoiling everything they had worked so hard to achieve.

His reply never came. Instead, his eyes darted over her shoulder and darkened, despite the polite smile at his lips.

"Pardon me," Alexei interrupted, offering his arm to Aveline. "I thought we might have one last dance before the party concludes for the evening."

"Yes, of course." Aveline tried not to look too eager to accept the gesture.

Just one more night. You can make it one more night.

AVELINE LEFT THE PARTY AND RETURNED TO HER BEDCHAMBER AT the earliest opportunity that others would deem socially acceptable. She was, after all, a bride-to-be, and would need her beauty sleep... if her nerves would let her.

She had ignored the comments that the men made about her not getting any rest come tomorrow night. While she was not entirely certain what to expect, Aveline assumed that, given his calm, gentle nature, Alexei would be kind to her.

Better to leave tomorrow's worries for tomorrow. Aveline watched in the mirror as Hanna undid the pins in her hair and brushed out the fine silken strands.

"Hanna, do you know who The Heart Thief is?"

The handmaiden stopped mid-stroke. "That is not a name we utter carelessly," she said, barely loud enough for Aveline to catch. "It is held as even worse than The Magic Collector. Who said it to you? Did someone invoke her name while insulting you? The King would have them publicly flogged for it."

On my behalf, doubtful. "No one insulted me. It was more of a... warning." Aveline shifted in her seat. "Nothing to worry about, I assure you. Even if The H—*she*—were to come here, King Byron has plenty of magic-users to combat her. She would not get far."

"Who warned you? Why were they warning you?"

Aveline shook her head, trying to appear nonchalant. "Please, forget I asked. I was merely curious, but really, I should go to sleep. There is much happening tomorrow."

Silently, Hanna finished brushing out Aveline's hair. As she set the brush down, she said, "Princess, if you are in trouble, please do not discount it. The King would be more than willing to provide protection."

Maintaining a smile, Aveline squeezed Hanna's hand. "If there were something to fear, I would, but there is no reason to concern anyone. Now, time for some rest. I shall see you early in the morning."

Mouth pinched, Hanna dipped into a curtsy and left.

Things will be better in the morning, Aveline thought. *She will be too excited about the wedding to fixate on what I said.*

Distracted, Aveline nearly forgot about the letter from her mother as she strode towards her bed. It waited for her, resting against her pillow. Aveline lifted it to her nose, inhaling the hint of jasmine her mother always rubbed onto the parchment, and then carefully opened it to read the contents.

> *My darling daughter,*
>
> *I wish we could all attend your wedding. I am sure you will be breathtaking, the perfect princess. You have always been sensible, doing what was necessary instead of pursuing your desires, so I hope this will open up a world of possibilities for you, and that you take advantage of them. Your selflessness will never be forgotten, but you must remember to live, too.*
>
> *All my love.*

It was unsigned, for the sake of keeping her secret safe, but Aveline could tell it was her mother's handwriting without the signature; each letter was perfectly looped, written with elegance and care. She had been a stricter teacher than the governess who originally taught them, until they no longer had enough money to keep her employed, and so her mother had taken over their lessons.

Slipping under the covers, Aveline held the letter against her chest and dreamt of her mother's laugh, her smile, and her warm embrace.

CHAPTER 4
NO ONE CAN HELP YOU

Aveline woke early enough to hide the letter before Hanna arrived to ready her for the day. Six other handmaidens helped perfect Aveline's appearance. Even Princess Lucille joined them, bringing her court wizard to put a few illusion spells on Aveline's makeup and dress.

"Nothing major," Lucille ordered the petite wizard. "Brighten her eyes and darken her lashes; oh, and for the dress, give it a little sparkle and make the train look like water flowing over a shallow riverbed."

The wizard wiggled her fingers—five rings on one hand, four on the other—and Aveline stared into the mirror as her appearance shifted ever so slightly. The high collar of lace shimmered, matching the bits of lace throughout the soft fabric. The sleeves reached her wrists, but her hands were left bare. A simple silver tiara was placed carefully on her head; not gold like the rest of the royal family. But she would get there soon. After all, the chances of her becoming Queen someday were quite high.

Princess Lucille made King Charles wait at the door while she did one last meticulous survey of Aveline's appearance from the top of her head to the end of the long train that would take multiple handmaidens to carry.

When she finally allowed him in, King Charles stopped short, jaw slipping open.

"Is she not perfection?" Lucille asked with a smug twist of her lips.

"You are divine, my darling." He took Aveline's hands and kissed her cheek in such a way that she could almost pretend her real father was there with her.

"Thank you, Father." Aveline stiffened when she caught sight of Prince Ivan in the doorway. His gaze roamed over her.

"Come, we must not leave everyone waiting," King Charles insisted, wrapping Aveline's arm around his own. "Especially not your soon-to-be husband."

Prince Ivan turned away sharply, heading down the hallway before anyone else could notice his dark expression. Aveline let King Charles lead her downstairs to the throne room, where the attendees were already waiting. Four wizards stood with guards outside of the double doors, each with a respectable amount of rings. No one could stop her now: she was safe. Everything they had been working towards would finally pay off, and she and her family and kingdom would finally be secure. The thought nestled around her heart, bringing a true smile to her face—the first she'd worn since she'd arrived.

Where they had been cleared out the night before for dancing, pews now filled the room in perfect sections, filled to the brim with guests eagerly turning around to watch her entrance. Soft music accompanied her journey towards the front, where a priest and the wizard Ralph stood side-by-side at the top of the short set of stairs leading up to the thrones the King and Queen sat upon. Prince Alexei waited patiently at the bottom, his soft smile reflecting Aveline's. No, he did not love her, and neither did she love him, but by the way her heart fluttered at his smile, she thought perhaps someday, they might. Not a passionate, all-consuming love like her eldest sister abandoned her family for—that was not in Aveline's future, of that she was certain. It would be a quiet, sensible love, and she could be content with that.

King Charles and Aveline stopped in front of Alexei, who stepped forward and projected clearly, "I, Prince Alexei Voland of Salise, do so swear to you, King Charles Voland of Arreth, that I will always protect and care for your daughter, Princess Gwendoline Allard of Arreth, for as long as I shall live. I shall honour your name and crown, and if we are so blessed, I will give you grandchildren to carry on your legacy."

Aveline's smile slipped briefly. *Focus on now, not tonight. One step at a time.*

"I accept your declaration," King Charles responded in kind, "and gift you my daughter, to protect and care for from this day until your last." Then he tried to pry her fingers from his arm. Gently, he pressed a kiss to her temple, and she released him. *No more mistakes*, she chastised herself. If she were lucky, people would assume that she was just nervous, not trying to fight off an impending panic attack.

"Almost there," Alexei murmured in her ear, and brought her up the stairs. They knelt before the priest and wizard, the servants carefully laying out the train of her gown before taking their places off to the sides of the room.

"Today, we are gathered to bear witness to the bonding of not only Prince Alexei's and Princess Gwendoline's relationship, but also of their souls."

Aveline's gaze flitted to Ralph. He would be the one to finish the ceremony by binding their souls together. Aveline wondered if it would hurt, or if she would feel anything at all. *Please, let me feel nothing. I am not sure I could take it.*

The priest's speech was cut short as the temperature of the room plummeted. The petals of Aveline's bouquet frosted over, and her shallow breaths came out as white wisps. Murmurs rippled through the crowd until there was a sharp tapping on the floor behind Aveline, getting louder with each passing moment.

She glanced up at the priest, hoping to gauge how she should react, but he was unmoving, unblinking... Ralph was the same, staring at whatever was behind her. No one moved, no one spoke. The tapping resounded, her heart thudding in time. Could she stand and flee? That seemed unlikely to be a wise decision, even though she knew she had full control of herself. Or did she?

As indiscreetly as she could, Aveline stretched her index finger, then tucked it back with the others, hidden under the wide bouquet.

A low feminine voice urged, "Come now, you should face me, at the very least. I would like to look upon the woman who thought to challenge me for the heart of The Magic Collector."

The Magic Collector? Aveline's thoughts swirled into a dizzying array of colours that bled together to make a murky brown. A shaky exhale escaped past her trembling lips, the urge to scream caught in her throat. *Maintain your composure. This is a nightmare born of stress, nothing more. You will wake soon.*

The tapping stopped. Shivers trickled down her spine and solidified in the pit of her stomach like a stack of bricks. She should have been safe. Why were none of the wizards attempting to stop the interloper? Why was everyone so still?

Bodiless shadows crept into her peripheral, stalking closer, trailing up the steps.

"No one can help you," the stranger continued, sounding so close that Aveline nearly jumped out of her own skin. "Face me."

The shadows halted just out of reach. Their forms shifted from one thing to the next, resembling beasts and monsters that belonged in myths alone.

She managed to take half a breath, and slowly pulled her arm from Alexei's, which was rigid, like he was made of stone. Then she turned around.

Even though the woman was at the bottom of the stairs, it felt like she was towering over Aveline. She had to be a witch to be able to enchant an entire room at once, and her appearance only solidified Aveline's theory. She floated a few inches above the carpeted rug that ran the length of the room, the skirt of her dress swaying lazily like it was underwater, the bust and sleeves barely hanging onto her thin frame. Her skin was far too pale, as if she had never seen the light of day, a striking contrast to the flame red of her hair and the pitch black of her eyes, no white or colour to be found in them.

But what disturbed Aveline the most: the witch had no shadow of her own.

Bits of frost clung to the attendees' clothes and hair, but Aveline could only see her breath, no one else's. She was in a room full of lifelike statues… and she envied them, because surely whatever the witch had in store for her would be a far worse fate.

The witch's scowl sharpened her angular features. "You," she spat, "are nothing more than a child."

Sebastian's warning rang in her mind, but Aveline stuffed it down. "I believe you have the wrong person," she said, impressed at how well she kept the tremor from her voice, "because I haven't the slightest idea of what you are talking about."

Her mouth curled into a malice-filled grin. "Oh? Is that so?" The shadows rippled in response to her voice, growing even more restless when she pressed, "It was not you, then, who set free The Magic Collector? It was not you who urged him to flee?" A cane in her right hand, she banged it against the floor and grew louder in her speech, nearly yelling: "It was not you for whom he came back, to warn you of my arrival?"

Sebastian, The Magic Collector? He did not fit what the others had said about him. If this witch was, indeed, The Heart Thief, then he had risked himself in hopes of rescuing Aveline.

And she had not listened.

There was no use in lying to the witch. Even if Aveline hadn't helped Sebastian, this witch was determined to believe whatever story she had concocted in her mind.

"I had no idea who he was," Aveline said. "I only thought to keep him free." She stopped herself short of saying "from the King" or anything of the like, in case the others could still hear. It was damning evidence regardless, but she was far more afraid of the witch than anything the King could do to her if she happened to survive this, against all odds.

The Heart Thief floated closer, her cane tapping against the floor, and stopped a few stairs below Aveline. This time the witch spoke in a hushed tone that chilled her to the core. "I do not believe you."

Aveline hated that she could not stop trembling. Hated that her mind reeled too fast to formulate a plan. Hated that this was the end, that she had failed her family.

The shadow creatures inched closer, snapping silent jaws. She flinched. Paying them no mind, the witch placed her bony, ringless hand over Aveline's chest. Cold seeped through the thin lace and wrapped around her heart in a tight grip. Her heartbeat stuttered painfully; Aveline gasped, dropping the bouquet.

The witch tilted her head, eyes of unending darkness focused on the dim light now emanating from Aveline's chest. "Your greatest desire is to be seen and loved..." A malicious grin slashed across her face. "Well then, you have made cursing you very simple."

Aveline prepared herself for the words that would seal her fate for the remainder of her life, however short it would be. Instead, the witch kept grinning. The cold sharpened, the grip turning to icicles that stabbed her heart. Unable to inhale, a cry lodged in her throat. Through blurred vision, she watched as her light pulsed, then travelled down her arm and up the witch's. It nestled behind her sternum, the glow darkening.

"Goodbye, Aveline." With a snap of her fingers, the witch and the shadowy creatures disappeared.

The cold seeped away, leaving Aveline feeling hollow. But she was still here, still alive...

Soft gasps caught her attention. The attendees moved once more, looking around with furrowed brows as though they had fallen asleep and could not remember where they were. Slowly, flickers of recognition lit their eyes but did not completely snuff out the confusion.

"Charles," King Byron's voice boomed impatiently, startling Aveline. "Where is your daughter?"

"I am here," Aveline said faintly. She tried again, raising her voice, but the words barely made it past her lips.

"I..." King Charles shifted in his front-row seat and frowned at Prince Ivan, who had a similar expression.

"I am here!"

They looked right through her, to King Byron.

"Alexei—" She reached for him, but he bent down, snatching the bouquet she'd dropped, and when he stood, her hand went through him.

Trembling far worse than before, Aveline lifted her hand in front of her face. Her pale, *translucent* hand. To shove down her rising panic, she tried to gulp the air, but there were no cleansing breaths to take, not for her. Not like this.

Alexei descended the stairs with intense purpose. "Where is she? Where is..." he trailed off, and stopped at the bottom step.

No one offered up her name. *They do not want to embarrass Prince Alexei further,* she assured herself, watching as his cheeks reddened and the furrow in his brow deepened. *That has to be it.*

"If you will give us a few moments." King Charles bowed before rushing out of the room, Prince Ivan on his heels. Unsure what else to do, Aveline followed soundlessly, her movements slow, like trying to run underwater. The guards opened the double doors for the men, and then shut them again before Aveline made it. She halted, close enough that she would have hit her nose if she were still corporeal. Luckily, no one witnessed her blunder, and she realised that she could not feel the door.

When she tried to push it open, her hand went straight through. *You have to try to speak with them before they do something rash.* Aveline moved past the door, fighting against the disorienting feeling of having nothing to hold her down and nothing to feel.

The men rounded a corner, and Aveline picked up her pace as best she could. With everyone in attendance at the wedding, the halls were empty, and suddenly much bigger than before.

"—do not, what makes you think that I would know?" Prince Ivan snapped as Aveline made it to their hiding spot, a broom closet big enough that the men could stand amongst the servants' tools with barely an inch to spare. For a moment, she worried about brushing against them in close quarters, but neither man startled nor gave any notion of being aware of her presence. They left the door cracked, a scrap of light peeking in.

"She was supposed to be here already!" King Charles fumed, running a gloved hand through his greying hair. "I knew it was foolhardy to trust that strong-willed girl... What was her name?"

With bated breath, Aveline waited for Prince Ivan to tell him. Ivan who had known her since childhood, who had been the object of her girlish fantasies, who had decided the moment she was destined to marry another that he had fallen irrevocably in love with her. He would not forget so easily.

But he stared at his father with a pinched expression, like a schoolboy frustrated that he could not work out the maths equation even after it was explained to him. "Does it matter?"

Aveline balled her hands into fists. She was helping his father save what little was left of their kingdom. How could she *not* matter? "Aveline," she whispered, just to assure herself that at least she remembered her own name, even if they had forgotten it.

"She was our key to salvation!" King Charles grabbed his son's lapels and shook him so forcefully that the prince's normally perfect hair became mussed, strands falling forward into his eyes. "Without this alliance, we are ruined!"

Prince Ivan latched onto his wrists in a failed attempt to make him let go. "All is not lost!"

King Charles stilled. Slowly, he released him. "Yes," he said, a grin spreading across his face. "You will marry Princess Lucille."

Eyes wide, Prince Ivan stormed after King Charles, who was already marching back toward the throne room. "Father, wait!"

This time, Aveline did not follow. What was the point? Whatever this curse was, no one could help her—

She paused, staring down at her palms. There was one person who *might* be able to help her, if she were willing to risk it.

What other choice do I have?

To undo magic, she needed someone with magic. None of the court wizards could see her, but perhaps, she thought with fragile hope, he would at least be able to sense her. He did, after all, give her a way to call him.

All alone in a dark broom closet, Aveline closed her eyes, placed a hand over her heart, and whispered, "Sebastian."

CHAPTER 5
I DO NOT KNOW WHAT I WAS EXPECTING, BUT IT WAS DEFINITELY NOT A BROOM CLOSET.

A few seconds passed. Aveline opened her eyes. She had imagined seeing sparkles, or feeling a chill or a tingling sensation, something to assure her that it had worked, but really, she had no idea what magic felt like, other than the curse.

Her stomach sank. What if it couldn't work because she was no longer a human, but some sort of phantom? The rules of magic were unknown to her, but she assumed it had to have limitations, or else magic-users would be the ones ruling the world with chaos.

What else was there to do? How could she possibly—

The air twisted and writhed, bending colours and shapes until a figure appeared in front of her. He hit his head on the ceiling and grunted, hunching over a bit as he rubbed at the sore spot. With a snap of his ringed fingers, a flame appeared in his hand, bathing the room in a soft blue light.

"I do not know what I was expecting," Sebastian said, "but it was definitely not a broom closet." His amused smile dimmed as he surveyed Aveline. "So, The Heart Thief did find you. How unfortunate."

"You can see me," Aveline blurted, embarrassed at the emotion bubbling up in her tone.

"Of course I can."

"But no one else could."

Sebastian paused, his dark brown eyes searching hers. "I do my best not to overlook anyone."

Aveline hoped she could not blush in this spirit form. "Can you help me? I do not know exactly what the witch cast, but no one else can see me, or even seems to remember my name."

Amusement gone, Sebastian nodded. "There might be something I can do, but not here. I am afraid you'll have to put a little more trust in me."

"Anything," Aveline whispered, and only half regretted it. She didn't know what he would ask of her, but if she could find a way to help her family, where would she draw the line?

His right brow ticked up. "You might not be so hasty to agree once you have heard my idea."

"Well, what is it?"

"It is not an idea to fix your curse as of yet, given we have little to no understanding of the parameters, but to keep you from fading away long enough to find a solution."

"Fading away?"

"Ghosts often fade away when they have no place or person to keep them rooted," Sebastian explained, shifting uncomfortably, careful not to hit his head again.

Ghost. It had not occurred to her that that's what she was. Ghosts were legends, myths, monsters that prowled about in nightmares. They were… "I am… dead?" She would never see her family again, never be able to explain why she failed them. Would they think she ran away like Edith had?

"I do not think so. The Heart Thief would have little to gain from killing you. Or anyone, for that matter. She prefers making others miserable, and it's hard to top it once you've already passed on." He grimaced. "That's… not helping. What I mean to say is that there's hope for you yet, but we should hurry. If I'm not mistaken, you are far from home, and there is no one here you have bonded with enough to keep from fading."

Aveline hated that he was not wrong. She wanted to know how he had figured all of this out, but if she really were fading, she was not going to waste precious time asking questions. "How would we fix that?"

"Well, I would bind you to me," he said, then added hastily, "temporarily. I will be sure to make it so that once you are free of the curse, you will be able to walk away a completely free woman, no strings attached."

Before Aveline jumped on the opportunity, she had to ask, "What is your price?"

Sebastian frowned in confusion. "There is no price."

"You are trying to convince me that you are doing this out of the goodness of your heart, nothing more?"

The wizard sighed. "Aveline, feel free to argue with me all you want, but you are fading, and there's bound to be a servant coming in here sooner or later. I'd much rather discuss this at home."

Home. The word twinged in Aveline's chest. What would a wizard outside of the court call home? If he was The Magic Collector, Lady Beatrice had said something about a castle... reappearing? Aveline had been too busy by that day's events to ponder it.

"Let's be off, then," Aveline agreed, just in time. Footsteps sounded, growing closer to the closet, and as the doorknob turned, Sebastian circled his arms around her and winked them out of sight.

Dizziness, reeling, the feeling of being everywhere and nowhere at once. Then they stopped, suddenly in the grand hall of a poorly lit castle. Aveline was grateful to be a ghost then, or else she would have fallen onto her hands or knees, or, heaven forbid, retched on the carpet. That would have been a terrible way to repay Sebastian for his help.

"Welcome to my home." Sebastian gestured about the giant foyer. From what Aveline could tell, this was only the entrance, and King Byron's throne room could have fit inside of it. The ceilings were far too high for her to tell where they ended, same with the hall. Two wide staircases that started off to the sides of the room converged at the top, but she had a feeling that there were other stairways to get to higher levels.

"We'd better hurry." Sebastian peered at her over his shoulder. "I can give you a tour afterward, if that is what you desire."

Even his bright-coloured clothes appeared dull in the near darkness. The sunlight from outside barely touched the windows, as if it was barred from entering. She would ask him a great many questions when the chance presented itself, but for now, she had to swallow them and hurry after him. Only a handful of the sconces lining the vast hallway had barely a wick left to burn. The carpet muffled Sebastian's quick steps, and yet the castle creaked and groaned of its own volition, not quite matching his pace. Aveline struggled to keep up. The path split off into multiple ways, but the wizard continued his course, much to Aveline's relief; it would have been all too easy to lose him.

They finally entered another room, but it was devoid of light, its purpose obscured until Sebastian conjured fire in his hand once more. He flicked his fingers, and the flame shot upward, lighting a crystal chandelier above them. One by one, the candles burned, casting a myriad of colours onto the floor below. The room was completely empty save a single high-backed golden throne.

"We'll have to make do here," Sebastian said apologetically. "I am sure the palace had a much more glamorous decor, but at least you are already in a wedding gown." He glanced down. "I do hope you'll forgive my attire, but I'd much rather save my magic for more pressing matters."

Aveline stared at him. It took her a few moments to manage, "When you said you would bind me to you... you meant in *marriage?*"

Sebastian grimaced. "It is the only thing powerful enough on such short notice, I'm afraid. Unless you're willing to sign over your soul to me."

She gawked.

"That was supposed to be a joke," he clarified. "Now probably isn't the best time for humour. I apologise, I haven't had much social practise outside of these walls for quite a while."

"Bash!" called a young voice, accompanied by the pitter-patter of small feet. A boy emerged from one of the side rooms, two large hounds keeping pace with him, their heads almost as high as his. "I'm so glad you're home! I have another trick to show..." The sandy brown-haired boy halted mid-step. "Who is she?" he asked excitedly. The hounds' ears pricked, and they sniffed the air.

"Leo, *moy mal'chik*, I'd greatly appreciate it if you'd go find your mother and help her get ready for dinner," Sebastian said with a smile. "You can meet our guest then."

Leo cocked his head, and the hounds followed suit. "But it's not even time for lunch yet."

"Lunch then," Sebastian amended. "For your own safety, I ask that you remain out of this room. We'll come find you shortly, and you can show us your new trick."

With a huff, Leo left, glancing back once or twice before sprinting away. The hounds took off after him.

Sebastian extended his hand to Aveline. "If we are going to do this, it has to be now."

I was going to marry a prince for my family's sake... This wizard has been honest thus far, as much as I am aware... And it is not as if I have another choice.

"We do not have a priest." Hesitantly, she placed her hand atop his, disappointed that she could not feel him.

"We have the essentials. Put your other hand on my shoulder."

With a puzzled frown, Aveline obeyed. *Should we not be holding both hands? Perhaps he needs one free to cast magic.*

His gaze locked onto hers, so intense that she considered looking away but was too afraid to. "Lady Aveline Clément, do you agree to bind yourself to me, Sebastian Blaise, in body and soul?"

Again, Aveline marvelled that he knew her real name and title. There were many things that happened recently that should not have been possible, and that was minor, all things considered. He was about to *bind* them, just as Ralph had been about to bind her to Alexei. Since she was a ghost and could feel nothing, surely it would not hurt her...

I have no choice, not if I want to see my family again. "I agree," Aveline replied, surprised at how much louder her voice sounded.

Sebastian's clothes and shoulder-length hair whipped about him like there was a strong wind. "And I, Sebastian Blaise, agree to bind myself to you, Aveline Clément, in body and soul."

The sudden warmth of his touch surprised her. She briefly glanced down at her semi-solid hand before Sebastian stole her attention back by leaning closer.

"One final thing," he murmured, then pressed a chaste kiss to her lips, so quick that Aveline did not register what was happening until it was already over. Heat crept up her neck as Sebastian pulled back and studied her. After a moment, he let go. The winds died down; Aveline pushed a few strands out of her face. Not entirely corporeal, but much more than before. Goosebumps covered her arms, and Aveline nearly smiled as she shivered at the castle's chill.

"You may slip back and forth between being ghost and human," Sebastian informed her, taking a couple steps backwards. "But that should give you more time to find a way to break the curse. I will help you as much as I am able."

"I... Thank you." At a loss for words, Aveline cleared her throat. She was married to a stranger, a *wizard* at that. What could she possibly say? Then another thought hit her: now that they were wed, would he have certain expectations? As her husband, he could ask things of her, but she hoped he would not press the issue. She did not owe him that.

She did not owe anyone that.

Sebastian's lips parted, and Aveline waited, curious to what else he had to say. "I suppose you have—"

"*There* you are," interrupted a female voice. It came from the same door the boy had left through. Aveline peered over Sebastian's shoulder to see the woman.

But the voice belonged to a ghost.

CHAPTER 6

IT IS A TEMPORARY FIX

A ghost. Aveline stared, willing her mind to process what was floating in front of her. Unlike the tales her cousins would tell to scare her and her siblings, nothing about the woman seemed scary, no fanged teeth or open wounds or glowing eyes. Pale and mostly transparent, it was difficult to make out the woman's features, but she seemed almost normal, having her hair not quite to her shoulders and wearing a simple dress. Aveline wondered if she was kin to Sebastian, perhaps a cousin or sister. From what she could tell, the woman was not old enough to be his aunt or mother—but could ghosts age?

Was this ghost cursed like her, or dead?

"I told Leo to find you," Sebastian said, not fully turning away from Aveline.

"If it was to witness your ceremony, you were a little too impatient to wait for us." The ghost eyed Aveline, lingering on her wedding dress.

"You know binding souls is tricky business enough as it is."

The ghost merely nodded, and was saved from responding by the boy bounding back into the room, the hounds still chasing him. They panted, tongues hanging out the side of their mouths, while the boy was unfazed.

"See," Leo said, pointing, "I told you, this time he saved—"

"My name is Maud," the ghost cut in, floating closer to Aveline. "And this is my son, Leonard."

The boy stuck out his hand. "You can call me Leo. Pleased to meet you!"

Hesitantly, Aveline reached out, but her fingers slipped through his.

"I thought you helped her," Leo pouted, trying to grab her hand as if that would force her to become corporeal.

Sebastian rubbed the back of his neck. "It's a temporary fix, just enough to keep her from fading while we find a way to break her curse."

"The Heart Thief did it to her?"

Aveline found it strange, how casually the boy said the name, when Hanna acted like it was taboo. But since the curse didn't seem to affect Sebastian, she supposed that Leo felt safe with him.

"Who else would have?" Maud asked as if it were obvious, although not unkindly. "No other witch would be so bold as to openly curse someone, not when there are so many court-bound wizards protecting the kingdom. Her insanity and greed know no bounds."

Did she curse you as well? Aveline wanted to ask, but before she could, Sebastian assured her, "You will be safe here. The Heart Thief is many things, but not idiotic. There are too many wards in place for her to make it inside."

"Or anyone else, for that matter," Maud added. "Thankfully, we can be left in relative peace."

The dogs sniffed Aveline as Leo inquired, "What's your name?"

She could not help but smile at his big blue eyes, full of curiosity. "You may call me Aveline." Her voice projected better now, no longer a wheeze, but still barely louder than a whisper.

He grinned. "Are you joining our family? Now that you and Bash are married—"

"Leonard, that is quite enough," Maud chastised. "It was nice to meet you, Aveline. We shall give you and your new husband some privacy. Come along, trouble muffin."

"But I—" Leo started to argue, then stopped himself at his mother's raised brow. "Can I show you my new trick later, Bash?"

"Of course." Sebastian ruffled Leo's hair. The boy reluctantly scurried off after his mother, the dogs obediently following when he whistled. The wizard watched them leave, looking like he was trying to decide if he wanted to say something. Finally, he looked at Aveline. "Are you hungry?"

"Um... Well, I cannot feel much of anything at the moment. I did, during the... ceremony..."

Sebastian cleared his throat. "Well, be sure to let one of us know, and we can show you to the kitchens. Unfortunately, Leo and I are the only humans, so we don't have any servants. Although I will warn you that there are ghosts and ghouls who roam the halls every so often. As long as you leave them alone, they should do the same."

The creaking noises began again. Something sighed faintly, but from which direction, Aveline had no idea. Instinctively, she took a step towards Sebastian.

"Can ghosts harm other ghosts?" She checked the shadows, half-expecting another one to appear.

Sebastian paused before admitting, "They can, but I have banished those that would. This is a sanctuary." Aveline met his gaze again as their shoulders brushed. He added quietly, "At least, I hope you come to see it as such, for as long as you choose to be here."

With only the dim light from the chandelier, the shadows cast harsh lines on Sebastian's face, edging his cheekbones—one of which had a thin scar across it, matching the tiny one on his chin. Hardly noticeable, except that she was so close to him...

He took a small step away. "If you are tired, I can show you to your room."

Her heart thudded painfully, and then she faded back into the nothingness her ghost self had to offer. Like it was instinct, a way to protect herself at the thought of Sebastian expecting more from her. But he'd said *her* room, not *their*...

Sebastian frowned. "Did I say something to offend you?"

Aveline stuttered a few nonsensical syllables, which grew worse when Sebastian's eyes widened.

"I will be taking nothing from you, I assure you," he said hastily. "I am merely offering what hospitality I can in this decrepit place."

That was not an adjective that had come to Aveline's mind to describe the castle, but with how dark it was, there was really no confirming Sebastian's view of it. The darkness could hide all manner of secrets.

"Your room is this way." Sebastian began walking toward a set of stairs, and the creaking continued, as if the castle were protesting their presence. The wizard paid it no heed, waltzing up with ease, albeit with a hint of tension in his shoulders.

Odd, Aveline thought. She would come up with a better word to fit him later, but that seemed to be as close as she could get at the moment.

His hand skimmed atop the handrail as they ascended, unbothered by the cuts and gashes in the wood. She suspected if she tried the same, she'd end up with a splinter or two. Curious, she reached out... and her hand went through the bannister.

"As I said, it is a temporary fix."

Aveline jumped and yanked her hand back. Sebastian watched her with a suppressed smile, and she was suddenly grateful to be more ghost than human, if only because it kept her from being able to blush. What had gotten into her, acting on her curiosities instead of stuffing them down? She would never have given into such impulses at the palace, especially not when someone could bear witness to her foolishness.

They ascended two more flights. "That one leads to the attic," Sebastian said dismissively as they forewent the final stairway. The other stairways had mates, one for each side, but this was all alone, and instead of being made of polished wood with carpeting, it was made of dark metal, and wound its way up as if it were hiding, curling in on itself.

Faint sobs sent pins and needles down Aveline's spine; she jolted as Sebastian grabbed her upper arm.

"Please, do not go up there," he implored her.

Aveline stared at his hand. If she did not see it with her own eyes, she would not know what the floor was beneath her feet, or if there even was a floor, but she could feel the gentle strength of his grasp. Slowly, she looked at him. "What is up there?" *For survival purposes,* she told herself. *That is why I ask. Surely, that is a reasonable explanation.*

A muscle in his jaw twitched. "Another ghost. Her mind is fragile, and she does not recognise friend from foe. So, I ask you to leave her to her sorrows."

The sobs quieted, punctuated by a heavy sigh. Aveline thought of Lottie, her tiny, delicate sister who had grieved her precious cat for months. All Aveline could do was hold Lottie as she sobbed and sobbed and sobbed. She'd told no one of the terrible plotting she'd done in secret, of ways to get back at the visiting duke for letting his hounds loose on the poor cat. Because, of course, there was nothing she could do, not without it being connected back to her family somehow. Instead, Aveline bore the weight of her sister's grief in silence.

"It would be better if you do not try to help," Sebastian said, drawing Aveline back to the present. "There is nothing that can be done for her, not right now." He released her. The intensity of his eyes held her in place, a hundred emotions brimming just beneath. *Whoever she is, she means something to him.* If he had truly gotten rid of the other dangerous ghosts, then there had to be a powerful attachment for him to keep her here, somehow locked in the attic. *He wants to help her.*

Noting that he was still waiting for her response, Aveline said, "I have no intentions of going up there."

His expression eased as he dipped his head in acknowledgment. "Much appreciated." After a moment's hesitation, he offered her his arm. "The castle is not entirely without its merits." Once Aveline tucked her arm into his, Sebastian continued down the hallway, ignoring the louder creaks and groans of the walls and floor. "There is a beautiful library that has been mostly preserved—Meredith makes sure of that—and lovely gardens that have all sorts of flowers. The kitchens have whatever you could need, and I'm not sure what your hobbies are, but plenty can be arranged. Oh, and I, uh…" He stopped suddenly, and Aveline strained to make out his expression in the near darkness. Was he *blushing*?

"What is it?"

Sebastian did not meet her eyes. "If you have need for any… well…" He cleared his throat. "I'll arrange for some feminine products to be supplied in your bedchamber just in case." Not giving her a chance to process or respond, he picked up pace again, only this time Aveline stayed in place, slipping out of his grasp as if she were made of smoke.

Those were the last words she'd expected to come out of his mouth—or any man's, really. Despite being married, even if they were not strangers, that should not have been a topic of discussion, even to insinuate. Here she was concerned about running into the wrong ghost, and he was thinking about her time of the month?

Without turning around, Sebastian said, "That was rather awkward. I'm not quite sure how to bring that up without it *being* awkward." He rubbed the back of his neck, his rings glinting in the dull candlelight. Finally, he faced her with a rueful expression. "I only meant that we have no idea how long it will take to break your curse, and if you keep shifting between ghost and human..." He sighed. "I like to consider all of the factors at play, and I hate being caught unawares."

"I, um... Thank you." What else could she say? No response felt quite right.

"Whatever you need, just ask." He extended his arm again, and she accepted it. If he truly was going to help her break the curse, then it would be better to keep on decent terms. The sooner she could fix this, the sooner she could help her family.

Her heart sank. Without her marriage to Prince Alexei, there were too many variables, too many loose ends...

Sebastian led them a little farther down the hallway until they reached a set of double doors. As he reached for the handle, the doors swung open to reveal a spacious bedroom with a high ceiling. The chandelier's candles sparked aflame, casting a soft glow about the grey and purple tones the room had to offer.

"This is all yours," Sebastian informed her as she took in the luxurious room. "I'll ward it so no one can come in without your permission, not even ghosts."

"Or you?" Aveline wanted to ask, but decided that was far too rude, even if she did not mean it that way. Instead, she took in the vanity with the gilded edges that had some chips and scratches, the bed big enough for three people even with the abundance of pillows, and the sitting chairs with a small table between them, no doubt for tea.

"Is it to your liking?"

Aveline turned back around to face him. "It is most generous," she said, trying to smile despite the knot in her gut. "Where might I find you should I have need of something?"

"Normally in one of the drawing rooms downstairs. If not, Leo and Maud are easy to find, and they know how to retrieve me. But if you are in a great deal of trouble... you know how to summon me."

The few moments that passed between them were silent but weighty; Aveline found herself unable to look away from the wizard standing in the doorway. Based on his rumpled clothes and dishevelled dark hair, Aveline would not have pegged him for being a magic-user at all, at least not like the court-bound ones in the palace. Those were like Ralph, well-dressed in neutral tones and always silent and stony-faced. Sebastian, from what she'd seen of him, was the opposite in many ways. He would have hated being court-bound, of that she was certain.

"We will find a way to break your curse," Sebastian promised softly. "It may take some time, but I will help as much as I can."

Then he left, shutting the doors behind him.

For far too long, Aveline stood there, afraid that if she moved, the glass case housing her emotions would crack, or worse, shatter. They pressed at the sides, seeking a way out. *Not now,* she thought, but what she really meant was *Not ever.* Why spend time crying over what could have been, when she could instead plan to fix what could be?

Carefully, she pressed them down, and took a look around her new room again. Heavy silk curtains covered the windows. Aveline attempted to open them, only to find her hand going straight through. She stared at her wrist as she processed the unease of having no sensation of the curtain, of having not even made them move. In the bedtime stories her mother told, some ghosts were supposed to be able to affect their surroundings, sometimes unlocking doors and moving objects. Sebastian, as well, had made insinuations like that, saying that ghosts could harm. Was she just a terrible ghost?

She resolved that, for as long as she was stuck in this form, she would not allow herself to be so vulnerable. That would not do at all.

And so, she began to practise.

CHAPTER 7
HUNGRY AGAIN, ARE YOU?

It took a few hours before Aveline finally got the curtain to ripple at her touch, but not consistently. With a huff, she decided to be done with it for the night—or was it still afternoon? She had no way of knowing, not when everything was so dark.

Except...

After a bit of contemplation, Aveline took a small step through the curtain, and ended up partway through the wall and window as well. She inhaled sharply, and stared down at the gardens a few stories below. The sun was sinking behind the nearby mountains, whose peaks were barely covered by dark clouds, the light quickly fading. Carefully, she walked backward, like she was on a tightrope. She imagined that would have been a terrible time to accidentally become corporeal; would Sebastian have been able to help her if she had gotten herself stuck in the wall, or worse, if she had fallen into the gardens below?

That would be one way to break the curse, Aveline thought with dark amusement. *Make myself a ghost forevermore.*

She made a quick mental check, only to find that she still had yet to feel tired, hungry, or even thirsty. It made sense, and yet it irked her. *Can I only feel Sebastian?*

There was a scraping sound at the door. Something clinked, then scraped again. It kept to a steady rhythm, growing louder every few beats. *Scrape, clink-clink-clink, scrape, clink-clink-clink.*

Aveline looked around the room, hoping against all sense that she could see something that would assure her that Sebastian's wards were intact.

But, of course, there was nothing. Being a ghost gave her no advantages to seeing magic. But she'd seen the protective barrier the King's wizards had cast during the attack—had that been intentional, to give the people assurance? Aveline would have wagered that it was more likely to allow King Byron to survey everything and give his commands.

Regardless, yet again, she had to trust Sebastian.

The sounds persisted. Aveline waited, listening intently for any other clues that might tell her what it was. It passed her bedchamber with a rumbling groan that shook the walls.

"Hungry again, are you?"

Leonard? Aveline slipped through the door and peeked into the hallway. All she could make out was a hulking mass that took up the width of the hall, head almost scraping the ceiling. With each laboured step, the chain attached to its leg clinked, dragging along a large iron ball behind it.

The creature's low growl had Aveline hastening towards it, especially since Leonard seemed undeterred by its menacing tone. Surely, his mother would not wish for him to be in danger?

"Come along, we'll get you something from the kitchen, but you have to be quiet," he said in not quite a whisper. "Mother said she doesn't want to see you again."

"Leonard!" Aveline hissed.

The child's head poked into the small space between the creature and the wall, and he flashed a grin. "Aveline! Want to join us? We're getting a snack from the kitchen. Only we have to be quiet so Mother doesn't find out."

"Leonard..." Aveline started, unsure what she was going to say to him. If he were one of her siblings, she would know exactly which tactic to use.

"Call me Leo," he insisted, running past the creature to get to her.

While the castle still creaked, it seemed not to do it whenever the child stepped. "My mother only calls me 'Leonard' when I'm in trouble. Come along! We have sweets hidden in the pantry. Bash says to only grab a few at a time so Mother doesn't get suspicious." Leo grabbed for her hand, and frowned when he was unable to. "Well, you can just follow me. I suggest staying in front of Titan in case his ball goes through the floor again."

Leo bounded back the way he came, expecting Aveline to follow of her own accord, which she did. With all of the warnings Sebastian gave her, would the child not be in more danger than she was? Not that she could protect him, but she should at least stay with him.

Aveline got ahead of the creature—Titan—and made sure to keep pace with Leo. She snuck glances over her shoulder, noting the patches of coarse black fur across the ape-like body. Titan had beady eyes and the snout of a lion, and when his mouth hung open, it displayed three rows of razor-sharp teeth to match the claws that dug into the floor with each step.

"You know this creature?" she asked, her tone hushed.

"Titan is a friend." Leo took the steps two at a time and then slid down the bannister when they had passed the broken parts. He landed gracefully at the first landing and turned around to wait for them.

"Yes... But... what exactly is Titan?"

Leo shrugged. "Bash says he's a creature born of strong emotion and wild magic mixed together. He thinks Titan was accidentally created when someone tried to make a deal to become a witch but it went wrong."

Titan clomped down to their landing, and Leo descended once more, this time taking the bannister halfway down before sliding off and using the stairs for the remainder of the way, avoiding the wobblier, dented sections.

"I'm not exactly sure where Mother is," Leo whispered, "so be careful."

Aveline refrained from pointing out that, while they could sneak around, there would be no missing Titan. Even on the bottom level, the creature's steps sent tremors through the castle, setting paintings askew and causing the dangling pieces of the crystal chandeliers to hit each other like a wind chime. Aveline took solace in the fact that, if there were others who would consider harming them, they would think twice when seeing Titan, although she was not completely convinced that he was safe either.

"Almost there!" Leo called after they had traversed down multiple halls and taken one too many turns for Aveline to keep track of. Finally, they arrived at a room with plenty of counter space and ovens and cabinets both above and below. *Timothée would love this*, Aveline could not help thinking wistfully as she imagined her brother preparing meals and treats, happily humming all the while.

The hounds were busy gobbling up food from their bowls, and barely took a moment to glance up at them and wag their tails before returning to their meal.

"Be quick," Leo said to Titan as he retrieved some fruit from the counter and tossed it. "Mother will be done talking with Bash anytime now."

"I thought you said you were unsure of her whereabouts?"

He smiled sheepishly. "I mean, I know where she *should* be, but I can never tell how long their talks are going to last. They'll come looking for me the moment they're done." He threw some bread at Titan, who caught it in his mouth and swallowed it whole. At the creature's insistent growling, Leo said in exasperation, "No more tonight! You have to sneak away while you've still got a chance." The child made a shooing motion, and, with a heavy sigh, Titan turned around and left.

"Where is he going?"

Again, Leo shrugged. "He's not entirely cor... corpor... He doesn't always have a physical body either, like you. He can disappear entirely when he wants to. Bash says there are places we can't see with our eyes, and he thinks that might be where Titan goes when I can't find him."

If Sebastian had that much understanding of the supernatural, at least enough to develop theories, then she surmised that she might not have the worst person helping her break the curse. "Where are your mother and Sebastian now, if they are still talking?"

"I'll show you!" Leo hurried off, sticking to the bottom level. Without Titan's tromping, the groanings of the castle were apparent once more. Somehow, the child wove through the castle's corridors despite the lack of light. Aveline doubted he had ever been afraid of the dark, not if he was raised in it.

He stopped at a door and pressed his ear up to it. "Here," he whispered excitedly. "We'll be able to listen better this way."

Aveline opened her mouth to question the morality of it, but Leo was already tugging off the grate from a vent and slipping inside. He beckoned her, and she obliged, although she thought how silly it was that, as a ghost, she was crawling through a vent. She would not have fit if she were corporeal: the boy barely squeezed in. They only had a short distance to move before Leo settled off to the side and patted next to him. Then he put a finger to his mouth.

"But why a wedding ceremony?" Maud asked. Through the decorative grate, Aveline could make out a small study, the walls lined with books. Sebastian stood in front of a lit fireplace, his back to Maud, the two lounge chairs behind them vacant.

"What other option would you have had me pursue?" Sebastian calmly rested his forearm on the mantle.

"You cannot keep taking in those whom The Heart Thief curses!"

"I will not leave them to an unfair fate. It is because of me they are being cursed."

"Because she is trying to get to you!" Maud moved into his line of sight but maintained a respectful distance. "Do you not see this? Each time you help one of them, it takes away everything you have, piece by piece, and soon there will be nothing left of you."

The flames cast shadows across his features as he turned a weary expression towards the ghost. "I know, Maud."

"Then why do you continue when you know there is no rescue for them?"

"Because I refuse to believe that." He clenched his jaw. "Everyone deserves a chance to be free."

Too many seconds passed in tense silence. Finally, Maud questioned in a careful tone, "Is it because of Lila?"

Sebastian broke eye contact, instead staring into the flames.

She gave him a few moments more to answer, then said, "You've mentioned before that the marriage binding might be strong enough to keep them here, but you said you didn't want to try it, that it was far too risky. What changed?"

"I... There is something about her... I couldn't let her fade."

"Then when are you going to consummate the marriage?"

Leo's brow furrowed; Aveline hoped he didn't ask her what that meant.

"Interesting that you assume we haven't." The jest fell flat, his mouth twitching towards a smile but not quite making it.

"I know you better than that. I would bet anything that you brought her to her room and gave her time to process all of this."

Sebastian sighed. "You are lucky you are correct, or else I could have come up with some fun missions to send you on."

"Sebastian, stop deflecting. When are you going to complete the binding?"

His throat bobbed. "I'm not."

Maud uncrossed her arms; her mouth fell open. "You risked this much and will not complete it?"

"I did what was necessary."

"And what if this is as well?"

"Then I suppose we will find out."

"Why will you not at least *talk* to her about the possibility? You are, after all, married now. It's not as if you'd be stealing her virtue."

"What are they talking about?" Leo whispered so quietly that Aveline almost missed it. She pretended she did anyway.

"We are *strangers*. Why does this matter to you so?" He straightened, meeting her gaze again.

"You said you wanted to keep her here, so it seems odd that this is where you are choosing to redraw the line." Maud pressed her lips together. "Besides, you know that if you do not, chances are it will take more of your energy to keep her here."

Sebastian rubbed the back of his neck. "Thankfully, there are other ways to connect with someone."

"True," she conceded, lightening a little. "But she could fall in love with you. You are lovable, you know." That brought a small, surprised smile to his face, and Maud quickly tacked on, "Not by me, of course. You're too irritating to sweep me off my feet. Plus... I'd need actual feet." She kicked at the hem of her dress. "Just... don't close yourself off from the possibility."

"I wouldn't want to permanently tie someone else to this place if I can help it."

"You've tied her to *you*, not to this place."

"You know that is one and the same."

Crossing her arms, she threw him a look. "Because you choose it."

"No, because I choose you. All of you."

Maud's expression softened. "You know that, even if you find a way to help me, Leo and I would stay with you, right?"

Aveline squirmed, considering telling Leo that they needed to leave, but she feared they would be found out. How would she explain this? She failed to tug on Leo's sleeve, but still got his attention. He shook his head emphatically and returned to peeking through the grate slats.

Sebastian took a deep breath, and exhaled slowly through his nose. "That is your choice to make."

They stood there in silence, as if challenging each other to make another argument. If not for Maud's earlier statements, Aveline might have wondered if they'd had a romantic relationship in the past.

Sebastian broke the tension by looking back at the window and saying, "We should put Leo to bed."

The referenced child stiffened, then waved Aveline back towards the hallway, as if he couldn't move right through her. She acquiesced, and just as Leo was about to scurry away, the door opened.

"Well, hello there, *moy mal'chik*." Brows raised slightly, Sebastian looked at Leo, then at Aveline. He showed no sign of being upset, but that did nothing to alleviate the guilt that tugged tight in her gut.

"Leonard!" Maud put her hands on her hips.

"Aveline asked where you were!" Leo scrambled to reply. "I was helping her—"

"And spying, no doubt." Maud sighed. "Come now, off to bed."

"But I—"

"Bed."

Begrudgingly, Leo put his fingers in his mouth and let out a shrill whistle. Seconds later, the hounds came running. "Night, Bash. Oh! Can I show you my new trick tomorrow?"

"Of course." Sebastian leant down so the boy could give him a hug.

"Good night, Aveline." Leo stepped toward her, then thought better of it. "You can see the new trick too."

"I look forward to it," Aveline said with a smile. Because, to her wonder, that was the truth. There seemed to be many secrets in the castle, and somehow a human child held some of them.

CHAPTER 8

GHOSTS, MONSTERS, AND A LITTLE BOY WITH A WILD IMAGINATION...

Aveline expected Sebastian to berate her or, at the very least, demand to know what she'd overheard. Instead, he watched as Maud, Leo, and the hounds disappeared around the corner, and then he nonchalantly asked her, "What can I help you with?"

Surprised by his calm demeanour, Aveline stammered, "I, well, he, um..."

The way Sebastian kept his gaze on her did not help matters. There was a kindness to his eyes she found herself wholly unprepared for, one she certainly did not deserve.

"We did overhear," she confessed.

His smile was half grimace, half amusement. "I have no doubt."

"All of it," she supplied, even though he hadn't asked. "Well, I assume it was."

"Then I think it's safe for me to assume that you have plenty of questions." He pivoted and waved for her to follow. "This study will do. It's the safest of the lot, away from most."

"Most what?" Aveline stepped inside, looking around it now that she did not have to peer through the grate bars. It was small but cosy, a perfect hideaway for those wanting a few moments to themselves. The night sky prevented her from seeing the landscape outside of the window, but she imagined that this would be a wonderful room to set up her paints if she ever got the chance.

That is not what you are here for. This is not your home.

"Ghosts, monsters, and a little boy with a wild imagination and a penchant for getting into things he isn't supposed to." Sebastian settled into an armchair, stretching his long legs and crossing his ankles on the footrest. He sunk into the chair with horrible posture, the most relaxed Aveline had seen him.

It took a moment or two for her to remember what she'd asked.

"I hope you'll forgive me, but it's been a rather long day, so I'd appreciate sitting. Care to join me?" He propped his elbow on the arm of the chair. The firelight glinted in his rings, all varying metals and colourful jewels. Every finger had at least two, some three or four. The rings were what Aveline imagined one might find in a pirate's treasure chest, not the uniform iron bands with colourless stones the court-bound wizards wore. She wanted to count how many he had in total, to see if any had traces of nickerite, but Sebastian had his right arm cradled against his torso, his hand out of sight.

"I'm afraid I cannot," Aveline replied solemnly. "It seems that, in this form, I sink through almost everything."

Sebastian reached out. "I think I can help with that."

Hesitant, Aveline accepted his offer, and was relieved when his warm hand held hers. He encouraged her to take a seat, and did not let go until she did. Then he resumed his lounging, exhaling contentedly.

"I know there is a lot to explain," he said, "but I am honestly at a loss for where to start. Perhaps I should let you ask your questions, and we can go from there."

"All right." Aveline sat up straight, pulling her gaze away from his profile. The way the shadows cast themselves upon his visage had her itching to pick up a paintbrush. "What is that term you call Leo?"

"Term?"

"In another language."

"Oh! It means 'my boy'."

"Is he your son?"

Sebastian shook his head. "I suppose it must seem that way. No, he is not, and neither was Maud ever my lover, if that is what you are wondering. But we are a family in every other way that counts. I have raised him since the day he was born eight years ago, so I suppose I am, in a way, his father." His attention returned to the fireplace. "I will admit, I expected your first questions to connect more to your predicament."

"I do have plenty of those, but Leo fascinates me. I wasn't expecting a child in a place like this." Hurriedly, she amended, "Not that this is a bad place, I just—"

"It is fine." Sebastian waved it off. "This is not where I would have wanted him to grow up, if I could have helped it. Circumstances did not give us a choice."

Aveline weighed her options. He was being understanding so far, but one wrong question might shut him up. Asking things that only pertained directly to her seemed to be safest, as much as her curiosity would nettle her for it.

"The witch..." She trailed off before regathering her courage. "The witch said that she was cursing me because I helped you. And you had warned me against it yourself. Why was it wrong?"

"It was not." Sebastian paused for so long that Aveline assumed he was not going to be more forthcoming, but then he said, "You are not the only one who is cursed."

"She cursed you?"

"Not directly." He snapped his fingers, and a tea set appeared on the table between them. "Would you like some?"

"I..." Helping her into a chair was one thing. Drinking tea? She imagined it would end up staining the cushions.

"My apologies," he said. "How careless of me."

"No, not at all. Have a cup. I am content." When he did not reach for it, she insisted until he did.

Sebastian sipped as he stared ahead, not looking at anything in particular. "The Heart Thief collects what you would expect, given her name: hearts, the essence of who someone is. I thwarted her once in regards to someone I hold dear, and she has not forgiven me for it. For one magic-user to bring another under their control, or to even curse them, is no small feat, so while she is powerful, she is no match for me." He took another sip. "She could not curse me directly, so she cursed what she knew I could not bear to undo."

Aveline remained quiet, waiting to see if he would divulge more.

"I am forever drawn to the city, and whenever someone helps me avoid death or capture or servitude, they are marked, and The Heart Thief goes after them." The teacup clinked against the saucer as he set it down. "It is my punishment for getting in the way of what she deemed was rightfully hers."

"That is... horrible." Aveline couldn't help studying him, the words casting him in a new light. "You help me because you feel responsible."

His dark eyes drifted to hers. "I help because I *am* responsible. And I cannot bear to witness anyone's suffering, not if I can do something about it."

Aveline suddenly wished she could grab one of the teacups, if only to hide her face. "So... you knew she was coming after me, and that's why you gave me a way to call upon you."

"Yes."

"I am clearly not the first person you have saved."

His mouth pinched into a thin line. "I have saved no one, despite my best efforts. But I have hope for your situation."

Aveline frowned. "Why?"

His eyes danced between hers. "I have not bound someone to me like this before."

"Why not?" she pressed, equally curious and nervous to know the answer.

"Binding souls is extremely powerful and invasive. You and I are strangers, but, while it was necessary to keep you here, tying us together will be hard to reverse when the time comes."

Aveline never heard marriage spoken of in such terms. It was a lifetime commitment born out of duty or adoration, not a temporary way to minimise the effects of a curse. But these were special circumstances...

"If we truly are strangers," said Aveline, "then how did you know my name that first day? And how do you know that I am not, in fact, a princess?"

He shifted in his chair, but to his credit, did not look away. "The day you released me was not the first time we met. I have been keeping an eye out for you for a rather long time."

She froze. "What?" Her racing mind kept being interrupted by the noises of the castle, now much more adamant, demanding their attention. She glanced up, expecting to see splitting beams, but Sebastian remained unfazed.

"I know how strange that sounds. For me, the first time we met was years ago, but for you, it has not yet happened."

"...If you are attempting to explain, you are doing a terrible job at it."

"Fair enough." He huffed a laugh. "Well... what if I were to tell you that this castle does not like to stay in one place for very long?"

Lady Beatrice's gossip rushed back to her, of the castle disappearing and having reappeared recently. "Where does it go?"

"Different places, different times." He finished his tea and gently returned it to the tray. Within a few seconds, the entire tea set vanished. "That is a story for another time. Just know that, when the castle shakes like it's in the middle of an earthquake, it's taking us somewhere else. No need to be alarmed, but make sure you find me."

She felt that was every reason to be alarmed, but decided against arguing about it. *What kind of circumstances is Leo growing up in?* "The castle took you to... where I was? When was this?"

"I was a young boy then, perhaps Leo's age. We barely exchanged a few sentences before you disappeared, but I knew I would see you again."

Aveline leant towards him. "What did I say?"

He gave her a lopsided smile. "Well, you will find that out sometime soon, I'd imagine."

Did he not remember? She found that unlikely. First wizards and witches, then ghosts and ghouls, and now a castle that travelled through space and time... A dull headache formed between her brows.

"I think that is enough for one night," Sebastian stated, taking his time getting out of the chair. "I can answer more questions tomorrow, and maybe show you around the castle more so you can get your bearings."

Aveline followed suit, noting that he was waiting for her to answer before he would take his leave. The way he looked at her, as if she were not just a stranger...

But apparently I am not. Besides, we technically are husband and wife—at least for now. It hadn't escaped her notice that Sebastian had left the vows open-ended.

"I..." She cleared her throat and started again. "I thought you would have wanted to know everything I heard. Or, at least, confirm what I did hear."

His smile waned. "I do, but I figured my curiosity would be sated during your array of questions, so there was no point in getting ahead of the conversation. You have been through a lot, and I owe you that much courtesy, at least. There are things I would like to clarify, but let us retire for the evening. You have enough to process as it is, and I fear that, if I stay up any longer, I may fall asleep in the middle of my sentence."

Sebastian walked her back to her room, and they parted ways, leaving Aveline with the rest of the night to mull things over.

After all, she found, ghosts did not sleep.

CHAPTER 9

CAN I SHOW YOU A TRICK?

By the time the sun peeked over the mountains, Aveline had managed to make the curtains ripple with a decent amount of consistency. She had also tried to lift the pen on the desk, to no avail. Still, at least she had spent her waking hours making a little progress, even if her mind was too muddled to think straight. Just when she thought she had made peace with a fragment of what Sebastian had told her, another crop of questions sprung up.

But really, all that mattered was finding a way to break her curse so that she could try to salvage what she could for her family. There was no time to sate her curiosity. Their well-being had hinged on her marrying Prince Alexei—where did that leave them now? Edith had already fled, and now she, too, was missing…

A knock at the door snapped her out of her thoughts. "Yes?"

"It's Sebastian. I thought I might check on you to see how you are faring."

"I am fine," Aveline said. "You may enter." Unable to help herself, she wondered how long it would be until his generosity and hospitality ran out, or if his guilt ran deep enough that it would continue endlessly. She didn't plan on staying long enough to find out.

Sebastian remained in the doorway as he looked her over. "It seems as though you are more present than before. I can make out your form a little more clearly." He nodded in approval. "Did you happen to find a way to sleep?"

She scowled at the untouched bed. "I haven't been so fortunate. I did, however, manage to move the curtain."

"That is good progress! You are in less danger of fading away then."

"Marginally, I suppose. When I say 'move the curtain' I really mean 'make it ripple'. I have yet to get it to open."

After a moment's pause, Sebastian drew close to her. "We should fix that. The view is quite lovely."

She accepted his hand, the warmth overpowering the chill of the rings that graced his long fingers, which wrapped around hers. He brought her to the window, where the thick curtains remained shut, repressing any light from entering the room.

"Go on," Sebastian encouraged, gently squeezing her hand.

Aveline hesitated. It was a silly thing, to be afraid to touch the curtain, but she had spent hours failing, alone in her frustration. Perhaps with Sebastian holding her hand, she could do it.

Heart racing, Aveline let out a small sigh of relief as the fabric brushed against her fingertips. She parted the curtains. Their small part of the room lit up; Aveline squinted at the morning sun, and when her vision adjusted, she gasped. The black and grey tones of the castle made the bright flowers stand out all the more, a myriad of colours she itched to paint. The gardens stretched almost as far as the gate, with a plethora of various paths one could take so that a stroll through them could always feel new.

"How lovely," Aveline breathed.

"If you would like," he offered with a smile, "we can walk and talk. I did promise you more answers, after all."

They stood close to one another, still holding hands. *Should I let go?* Being this familiar with a stranger should have made her uncomfortable, and yet she found herself oddly at ease, despite the intensity of his gaze setting her stomach aflutter. *You only want to hold his hand because feeling something is better than feeling nothing,* she rationalised, pulling away. He did not try to stop her.

"That would be nice," Aveline said.

"Well then, let's be off." For a moment, he looked like he was going to offer her his arm again, but seemed to think better of it. Aveline floated alongside him, and was confused when he skirted around her back to position himself on her right. He said nothing of it, and she did not ask why, because if she had a limited number of questions, she wouldn't waste one on something so inconsequential. Perhaps he came from another country, where women were meant to walk on the men's left side. She snuck a glance at his profile. While his features did not quite indicate that he was from this land, he had enough similarities that he could have been a native. But then why was he an outcast? Was he isolated by choice? He said he would have chosen another upbringing for Leonard—*Leo*—but that didn't mean he wouldn't choose this for himself.

That wasn't right either, given the conversation Aveline overheard. He acted like a person who was resigned to his fate, making the best of things. Something she could understand all too well.

Silence heavy between them, the castle creaked louder. Were they going to travel in time soon? While Aveline would have hated the tremors under her feet, she also wished she could have used them to gauge how serious it was. How could one prepare to travel through *time*?

A painting on the wall shifted. *It could be worse,* Aveline told herself. But then the sobs added to the noise, and she scrambled to find something to discuss, anything if it meant drowning it out before she decided to help the poor soul. "I—"

"You should let me know if you do regain your appetite," Sebastian said, speaking louder. "It may hit you suddenly, and while Leo would be more than happy to cook for you, I'd warn against letting him do so. The child is brilliant and clever in many things, but the culinary arts are not his destiny, alas." The corner of his mouth quirked upward, then fell flat again. "Maud is an excellent cook, but I'm afraid she hasn't had the same luck as you when it comes to being able to manipulate the physical world."

The crying grew quieter, then stopped altogether. Aveline resisted the urge to look back, imagining a terrifying, deranged phantom behind them, like in one of the stories her cousins used to tell to scare her and her sisters. "Stop! We don't need to know what was behind that door!" Jeanette and Lottie would cry as they clung to each other, but Aveline and Edith always wanted to know what happened next.

You never need to open the door. You don't have to know how every story ends. Sebastian told her that the ghost was contained upstairs, and she had to trust that either he was right, or that if she escaped, he would take care of the situation.

"I'd hardly call it luck." Aveline kept pace with him down the stairs, trying not to think about how much it would hurt if she suddenly became corporeal and lost her footing. "I can barely do anything without your help."

"For now."

She caught him peering at her, but he quickly looked away again, his expression unreadable. At the bottom level, Sebastian stopped and frowned at the ceiling. Aveline followed his line of sight but saw only shadows. The light from the chandelier barely reached the floor and somehow did not touch the ceiling at all.

"What is it?" Aveline started to say, only to be interrupted by Leo bursting into the room with his ever-present animal companions.

"Bash!" He skidded to a halt and almost knocked into Sebastian, but the man stepped backward.

Any concern in Sebastian's expression was gone by the time he smiled down at Leo. "Good morning. You're up rather early. Are you working on something?"

"I am! Remember, I—Oh, Aveline, good morning! Are you hungry yet? I made some eggs and bacon." He wiped his mouth on the back of his sleeve, ridding himself of most of the crumbs. There were bits of white powder on his arms and shirt—flour? She couldn't imagine why he'd think he'd need flour for eggs and bacon.

"Good morning," Aveline returned the greeting. "Unfortunately, no, I have yet to regain an appetite, but thank you for being so courteous as to consider my well-being."

Leo cocked his head to the side and scrunched his nose. "Do you always speak like that?"

"I am afraid I do not understand your question," Aveline said at the same time Sebastian warned him gently, "That is not a polite question to ask."

"Are you a noblewoman? Mother says that people from the higher classes talk fancy. Like princesses and ladies and du... duc..."

"Duchesses," Sebastian supplied. "Leo, Aveline is speaking like any person would with people they have yet to get acquainted with."

"But we're family now."

Grimacing, Sebastian rubbed the back of his neck.

Aveline bent down so that they were eye to eye. "What Sebastian means is that we know very little about one another, but that is easily remedied. I recall you saying you had a new trick to show us?"

The child beamed. "Sure do!"

With another quick glance upward, Sebastian suggested, "How about we take this outdoors? Solas and Luna need a walk."

"We get to go outside?"

"As long as you follow the rules—"

"I won't get close to the gates, I promise. Race you!" Leo sprinted away, the dogs dutifully keeping up with him.

Aveline furrowed her brow as she cast a questioning look Sebastian's way. "Are there creatures outside I should be aware of?"

"Unlikely but not impossible," he said, strolling in the same direction as Leo. "The gates are the borders of the castle's magic; everything within them is transported through space and time. The thought of leaving Leo alone or him ending up stranded elsewhere, where we have very limited means of finding him... It's just easier to have him remain indoors unless I'm with him."

"Is the castle about to move?" Again, she looked, hoping to notice the signs so she could watch for them later.

"Sometime soon. Normally, I'd say we have another month or two, but as of late, the castle seems to be increasingly erratic. But don't worry—you will travel with us. It's an annoyance, but for the most part, quite safe if you remain indoors."

Aveline pursed her lips. At least the man was still being open, even if it was clear he was keeping a few secrets. "I assume 'Solas' and 'Luna' are the hounds."

"Yes, I am aware they have no need of exercise with how much he has them running around, but being outside for a bit will do us all some good."

"Come on, Bash, Aveline!" Leo disappeared around a corner, his hurried steps echoing down the hallway.

"That is an interesting nickname he has for you," Aveline commented.

Walking a little more quickly than before, Sebastian smiled. "Yes, I do rather like it. Leo had the most difficult time saying my name. I told him to call me 'Bast' like others have, but he refuses to call me anything else other than 'Bash'. The child is nearly as stubborn as his mother." He kept his voice light, but the words were laced with a hint of sadness.

Aveline checked behind them, half-expecting the ghostly woman to appear. But there was no sign of anyone, not that it would be easy to anticipate a ghost's arrival. It also unsettled Aveline to think that the constant noises the castle made could mask some of the ones monsters did. If Leo let Titan in, who knew what else could lurk freely about?

"Maud will probably seek us out soon. She might have wanted a short break from Leo and his antics."

"Of course," Aveline said, assuming a more relaxed demeanour. "My mother often sent us on impossible errands to give her a few hours' break." Her chest tightened. How careless could she be, revealing information about her past, even if it seemed minor? It was the little things that people could realise didn't add up to the role she was trying to play.

But she was no longer in the palace, no longer trying to marry Prince Alexei by pretending it was a decent match between a Prince and Princess of neighbouring countries. She was with Sebastian, her for-now husband, a kind stranger who felt responsible for her well-being. And he was already aware that she was not a princess, just a duke's daughter.

Sebastian broke the quiet by asking, "How many siblings do you have?" They turned a corner, and he picked up pace again, craning his neck to spot Leo through the windows. The boy teased the hounds with a ball, his infectious laughter loud enough to hear even with the door shut.

"Six." She grinned at the way Leo tried to hold the ball out of reach, but the hounds easily tackled him and gave slobbery kisses as the boy wiggled and burst into a fit of giggles. "There are seven of us in total: four girls, three boys."

"Where do you fall into that lineup? Based on how you interact with Leo, I assume you're one of the older children. You have a maternal nature about you."

From what Aveline could tell, he was genuine in his curiosity. She tried not to preen at the compliment. "I am the second oldest," she confirmed, and intended to stop there, but it was a relief to not put on an act. For far too long, Aveline had not been herself, but a fabricated version. No one had wanted to know about *her*, they had wanted her to be the perfect princess, even though they made sure she was aware she would never actually meet their approval. Leaning into that relief, she added, "Father loves us girls, but he wanted a son, and so Mother obliged him."

"Somehow you ended up with three brothers? He wanted more sons after having four daughters and a son already?" Sebastian stopped, also clearly entertained by Leo, and wiped at his brow.

"The twins were unplanned, a welcome surprise." Aveline turned her face up toward the sun, wishing she, too, could bask in the heat. If she were corporeal, she would have risked sunburns and sweat so she could walk barefoot through the gardens.

"What about you?" she asked, suddenly remembering her manners. Besides, she did find herself curious about his past. If he had other family members, where were they? Was he keeping them away in hopes of them remaining safe?

If she hadn't been paying attention, Aveline might have missed the way his eyes dimmed and his smile grew tense.

"I had a small family, only one half-sister," he said. "I loved her more than anyone in the world."

The barking and Leo's laughter became distant. "I am sorry," she said. "I cannot imagine how it feels to lose a loved one. The very idea of it terrifies me."

"I hope it is a long time coming for you."

Leo bounded over to them, clothing covered in dirt and ruddy cheeks glistening with sweat. "May I show you my new trick now? Please?" He tugged on Sebastian's sleeve.

"You have our undivided attention, *moy mal'chik*." Sebastian affectionately ruffled the boy's hair.

Beaming, Leo retrieved from his trouser pocket a discoloured white handkerchief with frayed lace edges. Carefully avoiding the tear in the corner, Leo unfolded the handkerchief and lay it out flat on his palm. "Mother told me a little about weddings last night. She said there's usually a big party and flowers and cake and a ring bearer." He closed his fist, tapped it a few times, then slowly unfolded the handkerchief to reveal a golden ring. Tiny diamonds decorated the sides of the band leading up to where a scarlet jewel rested at the top, cut into the shape of a rose.

"Oh my," Aveline blurted, then covered her mouth. She hadn't expected such skill from a child, and certainly not something so extravagant. Her mother's wedding ring, which Aveline had admired many times over the years, paled in comparison, the craftsmanship exquisite.

"Where did you get that?"

Leo answered Sebastian hastily, "I know you said to stop exploring, but I already knew where this was, and Mother said there are supposed to be rings and I thought this would be perfect for Aveline. It's as pretty as she is, isn't it?"

It took most of Aveline's courage to look at Sebastian. The furrow in his brow softened when he met her gaze. "Almost," he said finally. She could not blush as a ghost, but somehow felt the echo of her heartbeat.

Sebastian refocused on Leo. "But you know you are not allowed to swipe my keys. There are too many dangerous things you could accidentally unleash."

"You can blame me for this one," Maud interrupted, appearing beside her son. Aveline studied her, wondering if she, too, could so easily disappear and reappear if she put her mind to it. "He wouldn't go to sleep, so I told him he could get the ring for you if he promised to go to bed directly after. Then he begged for us to have a celebration."

"A celebration?" Aveline found her voice after mentally chastising herself that it was preposterous, being so unsettled about conversing with a ghost when she, in fact, was technically one as well.

"That you joined the family!" Leo hopped in place, clutching the ring tightly. The dogs joined in, barking and howling and jumping.

With a pained expression, Sebastian opened his mouth, then snapped it shut again when Maud raised her brow.

"How thoughtful of you," Aveline said to Leo, shoving down the thought that, if everything went according to plan, she was going to break his little heart by leaving. Perhaps she could visit to soften the blow.

Leo offered the ring to Sebastian, not-quite-whispering, "You're supposed to give this to her."

"Oh, Leo, I am not sure—" Aveline started, but stopped when Sebastian reached for it.

"May I?"

Swallowing her argument, Aveline nodded and held out her left hand. The coolness of the metal was barely noticeable in comparison to the gentle touch of his fingers as he slipped the ring on. Aveline ignored the pinch of disappointment when it didn't fit properly, too fixated on the fact that it was *staying on* and she could feel the weight of it. Brows furrowed, Sebastian leant a little closer, his dark locks nearly brushing against her forehead. There was a thin scar above his brow, no longer than a fingernail, and another starting just outside of the inner corner of his eye and ending before the bridge of his nose.

Aveline tore her attention back to his hands, which were fiddling with the ring. His left bore scars as well, some more obvious than others, while his right was seemingly unscathed. No marks, no freckles, and the rings were much more simplistic than the ones on his left hand, none bearing jewels. *Odd,* she thought again. But really, she didn't know how magic worked—for all she knew, the scars were a toll for using it.

The band of the ring shrunk to fit her finger, and the gems shifted to accommodate the new layout. "There," Sebastian said approvingly as he released her, "that should be better."

The ruby rose glowed in the sunlight. Her sister Jeanette would have been jealous to see such a treasure. She would have begged their father, who would have caved and bought one for her back when they had the finances to spare. In truth, he would have bought all of his daughters one, and made sure to get an even more luxurious one for their mother.

Guilt weighed down her hand. They had barely enough to eat, and here she was receiving a trinket that could feed and clothe them for the next year.

The ring fell through her finger and made a small imprint in the dirt at her feet.

"Progress." Sebastian picked it up and tucked it into his waistcoat pocket. "I'll keep it for the time being."

Leo's disappointment was quickly dispelled by Maud saying, "There is something in the kitchens to help celebrate."

"Yes!" He hopped and waved his arms. "I made cake!"

The boy tore back inside, and Maud offered an apologetic grimace. "I gave him directions, but... well, you'll see for yourselves."

"I'm sure it'll be quite the mess to clean." Sebastian shook his head. "But it's the thought that counts, right?"

CHAPTER 10

YOU NEVER QUITE GET USED TO IT

Flour coated the countertop, raw egg dripped onto the floor—it was a wonder Leo kept as clean as he had, given the current state of the kitchen. The hounds left a trail of pawprints as they followed Leo to the oven.

"I'll get it." Sebastian hurried to retrieve the cake.

"How does it look?" Leo stood on tiptoes, craning his neck to get a glimpse of his creation on the counter.

"Well..." Sebastian tried to pry it out with a spatula. "It is definitely done baking."

Aveline flinched as Maud appeared at her side, watching Sebastian and Leo attempt to salvage the cake.

"I gave him what advice I could," she said with a pinched expression. "There is only so much I could do."

"Like Sebastian said, it's the thought that counts," Aveline replied graciously. "To learn, he has to try."

Maud huffed and looked down at her transparent hands. Her features were a little clearer than before, allowing Aveline to spot a few freckles and the faint lines on her palms.

"You never get used to being a ghost," whispered Maud, so quietly that Aveline strained to hear over the ruckus of Leo begging Sebastian to let him have a go at removing the cake from the pan. "There are too many times that I forget, and when I try to pick up a fork or push Leo's hair out of his face..." She swallowed hard and crossed her arms. "You never get used to it."

Sebastian waved his hand and the burnt cake vanished, materialising on a plate a split second later. Leo whooped and hollered, hurrying to the pantry in search of frosting and prattling on about what berries they could get to put on top.

"I'm sorry." Aveline had no comforting words—there was nothing to make the situation better.

"All we can do is keep trying, right?" Being a ghost had not quite drained her of all colour—Aveline wondered if, when she was a human, Maud had the same blue eyes as her son. There was just a hint of it left, like she was clinging to what little she could manage.

"Right." The urge to ask how she became a ghost welled up, but Aveline stuffed it back down. Would it be rude, asking someone how they died? Or were cursed? There was no social protocol for how to proceed in such situations.

Sebastian and Leo returned, the child's shoulders slumped. "No ingredients for frosting," he lamented. "But it should be good as is. Can I cut it?"

"You can help hold the plate steady for me." Sebastian had to half-saw his way through the cake to get it to split.

"Aveline, that piece is for you." Leo set it on the counter near her.

"Oh, Leo, I'm not sure I can..." At his crestfallen expression, Aveline amended, "But I will try." She reached for the fork, willing it to stay in her hand, then sighed when she failed.

Sebastian intervened. "Not to worry, you can make her another later." He made a show of taking a bite, and stifled a cough. "Thank you for your thoughtfulness, Leo."

"How is it?" He eagerly scooped some into his mouth; his face soured. "Not very good."

"I can help you make another later."

"Granted that you stop feeding creatures that are currently outside of this room." Maud raised a brow at Leo, who ducked his head.

"How about we give Aveline a tour of the castle?" Sebastian suggested.

"Excellent idea!" The boy rushed out, the hounds trailing him.

"You should have had him clean first," Maud scolded.

"He was put out enough as it was with the cake not turning out right." He snapped his fingers and the cake vanished, along with all evidence of the baking disaster.

"Be honest, how horrible was it?"

"Well... I suspect he used salt instead of sugar, and I'm not sure how old those eggs were."

Maud chuckled and shook her head. "Come on. We'd better catch up to him before he finds something else to experiment on."

"He's more likely to come running back to us, given he has a new audience to show all of his tricks to."

"Our apologies in advance," Maud said to Aveline, patting her arm. To Aveline's surprise, she could feel the touch—not quite solid, but there nevertheless, like a breeze brushing against her skin. Was it because they were both ghosts that Maud could touch her? Sebastian had warned her that ghosts could hurt other ghosts, but Aveline hadn't considered civilised, acceptable actions like this one.

"Hurry!" Leo's voice echoed through the trembling halls.

"We're coming, no need to rush us, my delicious disaster." Maud glanced about warily, and somehow kept the trepidation out of her tone. Yet again, Aveline found herself grateful that she could not feel the tremors underfoot, or else she feared she wouldn't find the courage to move. How was one supposed to live in anticipation of being transported through space and time at a moment's notice?

Just as Sebastian had predicted, Leo returned, walking backward alongside them as he asked, "Do you think Meredith is in a good enough mood today for a visit to the library?"

"Only one way to find out, I suppose." Sebastian paused. "Would you like to scout ahead for us? Be careful to keep out of sight in case she's in a strop."

"I'm on it!" Leo saluted dramatically and took off again. How the hounds had as much energy as the boy, Aveline had no idea, but was satisfied that they got more exercise than they needed.

As they ambled down the hall, Sebastian pointed out certain rooms and explained what they were. "A good number of these are locked on the first floor, unfortunately. I am trying to keep certain things locked away so Leo does not try to play with them, but perhaps after what we witnessed today, I should figure out a more secure system." He fidgeted with his shirt collar, giving a glimpse at the chain dangling around his neck. Whatever hung from it was safely covered by his shirt and waistcoat. The chain reminded her of the ones her father had attached to his pocket watches, only thinner. *If I asked, would he tell me what it was carrying?*

"I'm not sure if you'd have better luck coming up with a new system or training the child to actually heed our warnings. He's too clever for his own good. I would say that he'll be the death of me someday, but seeing as that's already happened..." Maud had a hint of a smile, but Aveline felt too awkward to chuckle.

Dead, not cursed... "At least the hounds seem to keep good watch over him," Aveline said. "So, is Meredith a ghost as well?"

"A troublesome one." Maud snorted. "She keeps to herself mostly, but if you mess with the books, she exacts revenge in the form of throwing things like quills and sometimes chairs, if she is angered enough. We had to keep Leo away for a few years after he tore out a page when he was a toddler. Thankfully, they have an understanding now."

Sebastian said, "There is no need to worry about Meredith bringing harm to anyone. I have not seen her leave the library in... well, I cannot remember when the last time was."

A shriek pierced the air. Leo scrambled around the corner, nearly knocking into Sebastian, who helped him regain his balance. "No library visit today, Bash! Meredith saw me and screamed for me to get out. I think she's reorganising again."

"Another time, then." Sebastian squeezed the boy's shoulder and changed direction.

THE MAGIC COLLECTOR

The "tour" of the castle ended up being mostly walking down hallways while Sebastian recounted which rooms were locked; the unlocked ones were guest bedrooms, the library (which they peeked in briefly then scurried off before Meredith caught sight of them), spare rooms for various recreational uses, and a music room with a grand piano as the main focus. Layers of dust covered the violin, cello, and flute cases in the corner, but not the piano, worn as it was. It was by no means new, and the bench cushion was flattened from use, but Aveline could tell that it was well-loved. Her sister Jeanette would have flounced into the room and started playing without permission, hoping to inspire such wonder in those listening that they would forgive her boldness.

"Are you all right?" Leo asked Aveline, looking up at her with his big blue eyes.

"Quite, thank you." She turned away, hoping to squelch the emotion rising in her chest.

"I think it's time for lunch," Sebastian announced. "Leo, would you make some food while I show Aveline the rest? We'll meet you in the dining room shortly."

Leo's face scrunched in confusion. Maud stepped in, saying, "I have a new recipe we could try. You're sure to love it."

As soon as the two of them were out of earshot, Sebastian said, "If you do not wish to talk about it, I will not pry, but know that if you do wish to, I am here to listen."

Aveline could not bring herself to look at him, so she focused on the fleur-de-lis patterning on the carpet. What good would come from telling him her troubles? She would cry and perhaps have a little relief for the moment, but then what?

Still, what bad could come from it? Revealing her secrets meant nothing now. It was not like marrying Prince Alexei was an option any longer, not when he certainly was already marrying someone else. King Charles seemed to be trying to replace her the moment she disappeared, and even if he did not succeed, what excuse would King Byron accept if she did come back?

"My family," Aveline barely managed to say, throat tight. Instead of prodding her on, Sebastian remained silent. Half of her wanted to

93

thank him for understanding, and the other half wanted to demand why he was being so patient. Had he not already proven himself trustworthy with all of the help he'd given?

"My family," she repeated, trying again. "I worry for them. I was supposed to save all of us—the entire kingdom—from financial ruin by marrying Prince Alexei." Once she started talking, she couldn't bring herself to stop, as if she had opened the floodgates. "King Charles lost his daughters recently, and King Byron already has his eye on a suitor for his daughter, so offering Prince Ivan wasn't an option. Having kept their passing a secret, King Charles approached my father about creating the ruse that I was one of the princesses, and that by marrying me to Prince Alexei, we could unite our kingdoms and solidify our stance in the war. We would have protection and provision, and King Byron would get access to our nickerite mines, whatever is left of them, to outfit his magic-users with rings for the war." Aveline shook her head. "I messed it all up by getting cursed."

Sebastian took a small step towards her. "You did nothing wrong. If it is your family's financial well-being you are concerned about, I can help."

Aveline searched his face and only found genuine kindness. "How?"

"I'd offer to take you to visit them, but even if they were nearby, I'd be afraid to leave the castle given how close we are to transporting. However, I can send some money to support them for the time being. You could also send a letter if you'd like."

Money. He was offering to send them money... It shouldn't have surprised her that he had wealth, not when he lived in a castle. But it wasn't as if he had subjects paying taxes to him. Did he create money with magic somehow...?

Does it matter, as long as he is helping your family?

"I... Yes, that would be wonderful. Thank you." She sniffed, realising that tears were rolling down her cheeks. Strands of hair that had fallen out of the pins tickled the back of her neck; fatigue ached in her bones; her stomach growled.

She only remembered that she should be mortified when she noticed Sebastian smiling at her.

"Come along," he said, offering his arm. "We will get everything together after a bit of lunch."

Aveline wiped at her cheeks and grinned. She could wiggle her toes in the stiff, tight heels and rub the fabric of Sebastian's sleeve between her fingers. She would be able to eat—

"Wait... You said not to eat anything Leo makes."

Sebastian chuckled. "No need to worry: I will change the taste and texture with magic so that it's edible."

CHAPTER 11

WHAT EXACTLY DID SHE SAY TO YOU?

By the time they made it to the dining room, Aveline was no longer corporeal enough to eat, so she stood with Maud, watching Sebastian and Leo sit side-by-side at the head of the long table as they partook in the green soup the boy made. Sebastian wiggled his fingers and the soup shifted to a lighter colour and did not look as thick. The hounds suddenly took interest, getting as close as they dared so they could sniff.

"Lie down," Sebastian ordered, and, tails drooping, the hounds obeyed, curling up next to one another in a nearby corner.

"Delicious!" Leo crowed after taking a large spoonful. "Thank you for the recipe, Mum."

"You are welcome, darling."

"Do you like it, Bash?"

"It's good." Sebastian ate with his left hand, to Aveline's surprise. At least that made things easy, avoiding him bumping elbows with Leo. The child passed the utensil back and forth between his hands, like he was making a game out of eating.

"What are we going to do for the rest of today?" Leo inquired between bites. "I have more tricks I can show Aveline, or OH! Bash, why don't you play piano—"

"Aveline and I have some important business to attend to first," Sebastian calmly interrupted. "Perhaps we can play a game together afterward."

Leo waved his spoon, flicking bits of soup about. "Brilliant! We can play hide-and-go-seek!"

"As long as you do not stray to the areas that are off-limits." Maud raised a brow at him.

"It's not *my* fault if you keep adding places to the off-limits list."

"It's for your safety." Sebastian wiped a spot of soup from his cheek, then magicked the rest of the mess clean.

"Sebastian..." Maud turned her judgmental look from her son to the wizard. With a sigh, he undid the spell, returning the mess as it was. Nodding approvingly, she ordered, "Leo, clean everything, including the dishes and mess you made, and then we'll find something fun to do."

"But, Mum—"

Sebastian and Aveline excused themselves, fleeing to his study. The noonday sunlight lit the room in warm tones and glinted off one of his dangling earrings as he ran a hand through his hair. The small teardrop gems were barely noticeable, and when his dark, shoulder-length hair fell back into place, they were obscured once more. Sebastian pulled out the chair at his desk, which was full of haphazard stacks of papers that were clearly in some sort of order that probably only he knew.

"We could try having you pen the letter yourself, if you'd like." He gestured towards the chair, then moved the stacks to give her room. "Although I'd probably have to hold your hand for that to work."

A letter to her family—no doubt her mother especially was waiting for one. Since no one seemed to remember who she was, did King Charles send word to her family? Then a more horrible thought clenched around her heart: What if her family had forgotten her as well?

"Perhaps we should forgo the letter this time."

Sebastian threw her a puzzled look. "Are you certain?"

No. "Yes. I have no idea what I'd say to them," she admitted. "I myself am still processing all of this—how would I explain it in a letter? I'd only worry them." *They would probably question my sanity and hurry to find me.* She couldn't let them see her like this. Not that they could see her, just because Sebastian and Leo could.

"We can try visiting them when the castle brings us back." Sebastian put away the quill and ink bottle.

"When will that be?"

"That is hard to estimate as well. It could take days, weeks, even months, and when we return, we could return to the moment we left, or a few weeks or months from then. I can spend magic energy trying to redirect it, but there's never a guarantee we'll end up where we want."

Despite feeling a little selfish, Aveline couldn't help saying, "I assume it would take too much magic to stop it entirely."

Expression grim, he nodded. "It nearly killed me when I tried."

How can he say something like that so calmly? She examined his features as if they would give her a clue to how much this man had endured. There were hints of weariness in the line of his shoulders, in the set of his jaw, in the depths of his eyes.

Sebastian cleared his throat and came around the desk. "If you would like, now would be as good a time as any to try to decrypt the curse The Heart Thief put on you."

"Decrypt it?"

He stopped a couple of steps away from her. "Understanding how she cursed you will help solve how to undo it. What exactly did she say to you?"

Aveline broke eye contact, looking down at her clasped hands. Even as a ghost, she could make out the lace of her sleeves, the wedding gown she had been wearing since yesterday. Her spine prickled as she recalled the event. "She told me that my greatest desire is to be seen and loved, which made it very easy for her to curse me."

She waited for him to judge her. How silly it all sounded—those desires fit her eldest sister Edith better, since she abandoned their family to wed a man she had fallen in love with. Aveline would have guessed that her greatest desire was to keep her family safe and provided for. It was a good thing that the witch had not seen that—it was better that she alone was cursed.

"To be seen and loved..." Sebastian rubbed his jaw. "When you called for me, you said no one else could see you."

"They couldn't see me, and couldn't remember my name. They remembered I existed, but not who I am." She locked away panicked thoughts before they could shove their way to the forefront of her mind. Her family would never forget her, no matter how powerful the curse. She was one of seven children, but they were all loved equally. She would never be forgotten. Never.

He frowned. "I can see the edges of the curse, but they're very faint lines, impossible to read at the moment."

"You can see magic?" She stared hard at herself, to no avail. Still translucent and pale, no different than before.

"It depends on the type of magic and how powerful it is. Simple charms and spells are easiest to spot since they shimmer and sparkle with bright colours. Curses are usually noticeable; they look like lines of smoke. Illusions are typically the hardest to see, but if I stare at one long enough, I can tell that something is off, like the hues don't quite match." After a pause, he added, "Normally only magic-users can see magic, but there are some normal humans who have the Sight."

Unfortunately, I am not one of them. "You said something about reading it. Are there words in this... smoke around me?"

"In a sense." His eyes flitted about her as if he were tracking a fly. "Not quite words like we would write, but symbols that radiate their meaning to those who gaze upon them." He leant a little closer, making his dark locks fall forward, covering parts of his brow. "I'll let you know if they reveal themselves to me. I am curious to try revealing spells, but I fear the repercussions of what they might do to you."

Aveline considered taking a step back. They weren't touching, and yet warmth radiated from him, which was very welcome amongst the vast nothingness her ghostly presence could appreciate.

"No need to look so worried," he told her as he straightened. "All puzzles have solutions; we will figure this out. Perhaps I should start by asking this question: When do you truly feel seen for who you are?"

Aveline furrowed her brow. She'd never considered such a thing, had no idea where to start. When had it ever mattered who she was?

Any interest people had in her was because of her title and the fact that she could bear children. Outside of that...

"I... I don't know..." she whispered, wishing she could sit on one of the chairs instead of sinking through it. *He must think poorly of me, that I have no honest answer to give.* She could have lied, could have made something up, but what good would that have done her? Breaking this tentative trust between them so she could protect her bruised pride seemed foolish.

Who am I? The thought nettled her, burrowing deep into her mind like it intended to take up permanent residence. All of the answers rang hollow: a daughter, a sister, a lady, a woman... a wife... *For now.*

Aveline didn't meet his gaze, fearing the tears stinging her eyes would fall unbidden. *Why is it that I feel neither hunger nor thirst and yet I am still shackled with emotions?*

Tone soft, Sebastian asked, "What of your hobbies? What brings you joy?"

"Well... it sounds silly, but... I like to paint."

"I do not find that silly at all. Actually, I have an idea. Care to join me?"

"I do." Aveline accepted his arm. "Where are we going?"

After being in the sunlit study, the hall was darker than before. Sebastian walked with renewed vigour, a man on a mission. "I'd prefer to show you rather than tell you, if you'll spare a bit of patience." He threw her a lopsided smile that made her stumble. She quickly recovered as he tightened his grip on her. "I apologise," he said, "I tend to go too quickly when I'm excited."

A giggle escaped her. He was acting like a schoolboy Leo's age, and she found it *charming*.

Enough, she chastised herself. Once she broke the curse, they would part ways, never to see one another again.

Aveline exhaled in relief when she realised that they were only going to the second floor, avoiding the weeping ghost in the attic. How did the others ignore her?

Sebastian brought them to a bare room with a large window overlooking the garden. She caught sight of Leo bounding through the bushes with the dogs, Maud following behind and shaking her head.

"Should we help her?" Aveline craned her neck to see where they had gone, but the ivy-covered pillar obscured her line of sight. "Leo seems like a handful."

"What eight-year-old boy isn't?" Sebastian chuckled and let go of Aveline. She turned back to face him just in time to see palettes, paints, brushes, and a canvas materialise out of thin air, gently landing on the floor in an organised fashion. "These were my sister's paints," he explained, "meant for a child. Our mother used to make them and put them into jars for safekeeping. I'll get you better ones when we return to the city."

Aveline bent down to inspect them. "No, this is lovely, thank you. I..." She looked up at him, expression pinched in thought.

"What is it? Is something wrong?"

"No," she said quickly, "not at all. I suppose I feel a little silly, because I thought you somehow used magic to make things."

He knelt beside her. "It's a common misconception. I cannot create anything that does not already exist..." He opened a jar and held it up for her to see. "...but I can manipulate it." The blue paint shifted to red, then green, then back to blue. "Magic has many limitations, just like anything else." There was a twinge of melancholy to his tone as he set the jar down. Before Aveline could decide whether or not to pry, Sebastian handed her a paintbrush. "Shall we?"

Tentatively, she reached for it, but stopped short when Sebastian said, "Oh, where is my head?" He wiggled his pinkie and ring fingers, and fabric suddenly joined the rest of the supplies. "You should probably wear a smock over your dress just in case. It'd be a travesty to dirty such a beautiful gown."

While it was beautiful, Aveline hoped she'd be able to change into something else soon. She did not fancy looking like a haunted bride.

"One moment." Sebastian ran his fingers along the side of the smock; it grew from a child's size to an adult one. "That should fit a little better."

"If you don't mind me asking, do you have to use your hands to cast magic?"

"No, but it does make it easier." He fussed with the supplies and then handed her the smock. "Care to give painting a try? It might help you find your sense of self, or at least help you relax enough to think of something else."

"Something else?"

He shrugged. "I find that when I'm stuck, sometimes the best solutions come to me when I stop focusing on the problem."

Deciding that she had nothing to lose, Aveline reached for the smock. At first, her fingers started to go through the fabric, but when they brushed against his, they tingled, and the fabric settled into her hand.

"That's a good start." He let go; it fell to the floor in a heap. She sighed, and he proposed, "I can hold your hand for the time being, if you are comfortable with that."

What other option do we have? "Very well."

Awkwardly, she held his hand while fumbling with the buttons of the smock.

"Here, I can—"

"No magic," Aveline snapped, then softened her tone. "What I mean is, I would like to do this myself as much as possible."

Sebastian did not say a word or even make a face when she had to undo a mismatched button so she could redo it properly. Then he stooped down with her as she chose her paints, carefully pouring them onto the palette.

"I do believe we have reached a snag in our plan," Aveline said with another sigh. "You will have to hold the palette for me."

"Or..." A small circular table appeared where he was looking. "You could rest it on that."

"Have you reached your limit on helping me?" she teased.

Sebastian smirked. "I thought you wanted to do as much of this by yourself as you can."

Aveline found herself smiling back. Very aware of his callouses against her palm, heat crept into her cheeks. She broke eye contact, readied her paintbrush... then stared and stared and stared at the canvas. What should she paint? It had been years since she'd last done it, when her family had money and she could create fantastical dreamscapes for her siblings to enjoy as Edith wove tales of love, adventure, and magic. They were always inspired by her sister's words, not by Aveline.

Gently, Sebastian squeezed her hand. "You can do it."

Do not let him pity you any more than he already does.

Something moved outside the window. Aveline expected to see Leo or Maud, but it was a bird flying over the beautiful gardens, full of colourful flowers—

With renewed determination, Aveline brought her paintbrush to the canvas. One small test stroke, then a more confident one, and another. Soon the colours took the forms of flowers and leaves and thorns. Aveline imagined Edith telling their siblings a story about an enchanted garden that few returned from because they could not be parted from such beauty. Perhaps there was a magical creature that resided in the centre, or a well that was a doorway to another world...

Ignoring the hunger gnawing at her stomach, Aveline started on the tiny details, leaning forward and placing one hand on the side of the canvas. As she began dotting the inside of one of the flowers, she stopped, gaze drawn to her hand, then to Sebastian, who stood a couple feet away, happily watching her work.

"Did I... let go of your hand?"

He nodded.

She held the paintbrush, paint drying on her fingers... and she was so ravenous that she'd consider eating something Leo cooked. All without Sebastian anchoring her to the physical world. "When?" Her voice cracked, her throat too dry.

Sebastian checked his pocket watch. "I'd guess about ten minutes ago." He inspected her work from over her shoulder. "I think this was a good thing to try. You are very talented."

Her, talented? Aveline took a step back; the paintbrush slipped from her grasp and clattered on the floor, the smock following suit. "It is nothing, just flowers." *Childish,* she silently added as the hunger faded. *He is just being polite.*

Sebastian stilled. Distantly, Aveline felt a pinch of guilt for rejecting his compliment—after all, it was rude, not gracious as a young noblewoman should be. After so many years of acting exactly as she was supposed to, why was she finding it so easy to let that mask slip in front of him? *It must be the binding. It's tricking me into thinking we care for each other, when in reality we are still strangers.*

"I apologise if I have made you uncomfortable," Sebastian said finally.

Aveline wound her hands together. "It is I who should be apologising. Thank you for the compliment. I only meant that it has been a number of years since last I painted, so the skill is lacking."

Instead of replying, he studied her a little longer, then her painting, expression ponderous.

Say something, she almost blurted. *Why do you always take your time to speak?*

"I think it's beautiful," he said. "It's like a glimpse into your soul."

As Sebastian turned back to her, Aveline found herself caught between wanting to search for vulnerable truths in the depths of his eyes, and wanting to hide before he could find them in hers.

Without warning, the entire castle shuddered.

CHAPTER 12

I HATE THIS PART

Sebastian stumbled but managed to stay on his feet, even as the canvas fell and the paints splattered the floor. The door slammed open, then swung back and forth; the windows rattled like they were going to shatter.

But it was the shrill screams that pierced Aveline's chest, making her feel like she still had a pulse and it was going to beat its way out of her.

"The castle is moving," Sebastian informed her, confirming her guess. "You'll be safe; just stay close to me."

He sprinted down the hallway on wobbly legs as the floor pitched this way and that. Aveline hurried to keep up, trying to ignore the incessant screams. How was the sound reaching them from the attic—unless it was coming from another ghost or creature?

The castle's violent rumblings inspired Aveline to imagine bits of the ceiling crumbling, the stairs collapsing, the chandelier chains snapping and the crystal fracturing into sharp pieces on the floor. She and Maud were safe from damage, but what about Sebastian and Leo?

Where *was* Leo?

Holding onto the bannister, Sebastian raced down the stairs, taking two or three at a time. Leo skidded to a halt in the foyer, wide eyes seeking out Sebastian. Maud hovered nearby, hand on her son's shoulder. The boy put his hand over hers, but it just went through it.

"Bash! Aveline!"

The four of them grouped together in the middle of the spacious room, the hounds keeping close, tails tucked under.

"Keep near me, and you will be safe," Sebastian repeated, hand already moving, eyes trained on the ceiling. The chandelier swung back and forth above them, making Aveline want to question Sebastian's placement choice. The wails continued, punctuated by tremors that shuddered through the castle. Solas pressed his head into Leo's chest, and the boy hugged his neck.

"I hate this part," Leo said to Aveline, "but it doesn't last long."

Despite the windows still being intact, gusts of wind yanked at Sebastian's and Leo's hair and clothes. A chill cut through Aveline, then spread, slowly creeping over her.

This is not the definition of 'safe'. Yet she remained in place, schooling her features in case Leo peeked up at her. They had done this before, so she could do it too. She could trust Sebastian and his invisible magic, wherever he was redirecting them to. Sweat beaded at his brow; his hand began to tremble.

I assume it would take too much magic to stop it entirely.

It nearly killed me when I tried.

The wind thrashed, fury unbridled. The screams grew louder. Leo clapped his hands over his ears, burying his face in the hound's fur. Sebastian's skin paled significantly, sweat dripping down to dampen his shirt collar. The chain around his neck slipped out from its hiding spot, the key at the end of it flailing about, close to his face. He was too concentrated to notice, staring unblinkingly upward as if he could see something past the ceiling.

Leo whimpered. Maud drew closer, hand at Leo's back. "It will be over soon, my love." She reached towards Sebastian, touching his shoulder. He flinched, and with one final tremor, everything went silent and still and completely dark. No screams, no creaks, no groans, no breaths. None of them moved or spoke until Leo slowly lifted his head.

"That was the worst one yet," he said hoarsely.

"We made it just fine." A flicker of hurt crossed Maud's face as Sebastian pulled away and produced a small orb of light in his hand, dim against the weighty darkness. "Sebastian..."

"I told you there is no need to risk yourself like that." He swayed but righted himself, wiping at his brow with a silk handkerchief from his waistcoat pocket. Like Leo's, his tousled, knotted hair made him look wild, not to mention the mussed clothes that had some minor tears and a missing button. An ornate key rested against his chest, which he carefully tucked back under his shirt.

"And I told you that you are not the only one who can help," Maud snapped.

"Please don't fight..." Leo cut in.

"Don't worry, my sweet: it's not a fight yet, and if it comes to one, Sebastian knows it is not one he can win."

The wizard grunted in response before turning to Aveline. "Are you all right? I know how unsettling that can be."

Fearing her flurry of emotions would bleed into her tone, Aveline settled for nodding.

Sebastian parroted the nod. "Very good. Well then, if you three will stay here, I'll scout the area for potential dangers."

"Absolutely not," interjected Maud. "You're about to collapse—you need rest."

"I'll rest after a quick look around, I promise."

"I don't believe our definition of 'quick' is the same."

"Still, it has to be done." He took a few stilted steps backward. "Now you know why I 'risked' helping."

Leo tugged on Sebastian's sleeve. "Bash, will you please take Luna and Solas with you, at least?"

With a resigned look, Sebastian agreed, "I'll take Luna with me, but you keep Solas with you and, more importantly, *stay here*. Come, girl."

Movements tense, the hound heeled, keeping alongside Sebastian as he made his way toward the front of the castle. Just when his light no longer reached them, Leo retrieved a small cylindrical item from his pocket. At his touch, it glowed a soft blue.

"What is that?" asked Aveline, finding her voice. She winced at the unease, but Leo did not seem to notice as he answered, "A light stick. Sebastian enchanted it for me in case these kinds of things happen. Which they do. A lot."

The front doors closing echoed throughout the castle. *I should have offered to go with him,* Aveline thought. Not that she had any way to help... unless Maud could teach her what she did. Sebastian probably would have refused her, but offering would have been the right thing to do, regardless.

"We should find something to do while we wait," Maud proposed. "Something *indoors*."

"Not the library," Leo said. "Meredith's certainly all out of sorts reorganising the books that went everywhere."

"We can read one of the books in your room."

He shook his head. "We've read those hundreds of times."

Aveline said, "Sebastian set up a painting room for me today. We could paint." *Or, rather, Leo can paint while we watch.*

"Splendid idea!" Leo gestured towards Solas, who followed alongside the boy. "Which room is it?"

It took a little bit for Aveline to remember exactly where, but they eventually found the paint-spattered room.

"Oh..." She grimaced. "I suppose I hadn't thought about it being a mess." At least there were no broken windows or toppled furniture.

"It doesn't bother me." Leo lifted the canvas. "Did you paint this? It's pretty!"

Parts had been smudged, but overall it was in better shape than she had expected. "Thank you."

"Is there another canvas?"

"Not that I know of, but you're welcome to add on to what I did."

"Are you sure?" Maud asked as Leo whooped excitedly, holding a paintbrush in one hand and his light stick in the other.

"It was nothing really, just an experiment." The statement rang hollow, even to her. Sebastian's words drifted back, gently tugging at her: *I think it's beautiful. It's like a glimpse into your soul.*

While Leo painted, Solas walked through the paint and curled up beside the boy's feet, resting his head on his foot. Leo reached down to pat his head, then resumed painting. In the silence, Aveline realised that there were only little sounds, like the castle was resting until it regained enough strength for another tantrum. If these episodes were getting worse and unpredictable, what did that mean? Was it an omen of something to come? And what was causing the castle to be able to travel in time to begin with?

Too many questions flooded her mind, and they all led back to Sebastian. She wished there was at least a grandfather clock for her to see how long he'd been gone. He'd been far too pale and unstable before he left...

"He'll be fine," Maud assured Aveline, bringing her out of her spiralling thoughts. "It's just a precaution. More often than not, we end up in an older version of the same place."

How many times have you endured this? She asked instead, "What happens when you end up elsewhere?"

"Sebastian deals with the creatures and tries to get us back to our time as soon as possible. It's not the safest system, but we don't have much of a choice." She added in a whisper, "If this imp would stay here with the hounds and keep out of trouble, I'd help Sebastian."

Leo was too engrossed in his art to hear his mother, since Aveline was sure he would have said something otherwise.

"How did you help Sebastian?"

The fear she'd crossed a line dissipated when Maud answered, "If I'm being honest, I only have a theory to offer you. When I died, Sebastian tied my soul to the castle so I would remain here as a ghost. Because of that, I believe I can lend some of my energy toward swaying the castle a bit. It's not much, but if that's all I can offer in help, I'm more than happy to give it—even if he's ridiculously stubborn about accepting it."

"If that is the case, then... perhaps he is terrified of losing you if you spend too much energy."

Maud looked at Aveline. "I know that is the reason, but he does not get to make my choices for me. What if he spends too much magic and pays for it with his life? What good will that do for any of us?"

If Aveline were corporeal, she would have sat down as she reeled from the revelation. She was bonded to Sebastian—if he died, what would happen to her? She would fade until she ceased to exist, probably within days, weeks if she were lucky.

In silence, the women watched and waited, listening to Leo tell stories about the creatures he was painting. They were all dark with sharp angles and sharper teeth, but none of their stories were brutal or violent. It was unclear whether these were creatures he knew or ones he made up—one of them could have been Titan, but the child glossed over it, focusing on the others. Aveline's attention waned, drawn away by imagining what Sebastian would find. From what she could see out the windows, it seemed to be as pitch black outside as inside. What creatures could be out there? Surely, since Sebastian had been dealing with this for a long time, he was prepared...

"I'm sorry!" Leo sputtered. "I didn't mean to!"

Aveline looked at the paint-smeared flower. "No harm done. Please, keep painting." The boy paused for only half a second before he continued again. It truly did not bother her—what did was the incessant itch to pick up a paintbrush and join him, but she decided against it. Without Sebastian, it would be futile to try.

Hours later, Sebastian returned, covered in dirt and scratches, shoulders slumped and smile weary. From a respectful distance, Aveline examined him, trying to assess if there was anything serious he was trying to hide for their sakes. He leant against the doorframe as he said, "We're somewhere new, but we should be safe. I added extra wards around the castle. Hopefully, we can go home in the next few days."

Luna rushed into the room and licked Solas's face, waking him from his nap. There was no blood on her, just dirt, but she carried a nervous energy that made Aveline curious.

"Wonderful," Maud said. "Now, time for you to rest. Aveline and I can look after Leo."

Instead of arguing, Sebastian merely nodded. "If you have need of me, wake me."

CHAPTER 13

HE WON'T TELL ME, BUT I THINK MOTHER KNOWS

Two days passed without seeing Sebastian. Aveline forewent returning to her room, choosing instead to stay with Maud and Leo. The child had a large bedroom full of various toys and gadgets like wooden soldiers, a slingshot, and spinning tops, some of which he'd made himself. When Maud and Aveline wished him goodnight, Leo crawled into bed and tucked himself in, the dogs curling up on either side of him. Aveline caught the hint of sorrow in Maud's eyes as she ran a hand over her son's hair, as if she could stroke it.

How did you die? Aveline refrained from asking. If she were unwilling to let Maud pry into her life, she had to give her the same courtesy of not prying into hers.

The three of them spent their days indoors. Leo made his own food (with his mother's instructions), fed the hounds, played with toys, and painted. Leo's light stick kept glowing, giving them enough light to get around the castle safely. Aveline was relieved that Maud and Leo did not suggest that she leave them alone—the thought of going near the attic terrified her even more than the eerie quiet that blanketed the castle. She imagined going upstairs alone, and the screams starting again...

Aveline had never known such thick, unending darkness. Where had they gone, that the sun could not reach this place?

By afternoon of the third day (from what Aveline could tell), Maud left Leo with her so that she could check on Sebastian. The boy's smile was gone, but he kept painting, albeit with less gusto.

"Bash should wake soon," Leo said. "This is normally how long he sleeps. He has to get his magic back so we can go home." He put down the paintbrush and used his fingers instead, making large sweeping motions across the canvas. There was no white left, just a mosaic of colour. "He just spent too much magic energy fighting off monsters and trying to get a magic artefact."

Aveline frowned. "How do you know that?"

"That's what he always does when he's not visiting Lila."

The name was said simply, but it prickled down her spine. She waited for him to elaborate, and when he didn't, she inquired, "Who is Lila?"

"His sister. Sometimes he gets to see her when we go back in time."

Poor Sebastian. Was it harder to see a deceased loved one? Did he speak with her? Did he tell her about the future? None of those were questions for Leo, so she asked instead, "Why does he want magic artefacts?" It seemed to be the safer option, and the boy did not mind answering her.

"He won't tell me, but I think Mother knows. She says it's no one's business but his own, but I can tell she doesn't like him collecting them."

I suppose that is how he got his name, Aveline mused. *The Magic Collector.* Was he trying to find a way to break The Heart Thief's curse, that way he would stop being drawn to the city? That was the most likely reason she could come up with. If he could avoid drawing anyone else into the situation, then that would stop adding to his list of people he was trying to help.

Each time you help one of them, it takes away everything you have, piece by piece, and soon there will be nothing left of you, Maud had told Sebastian. It was his very nature to help everyone he could, all in the name of responsibility. Would he give his dying breath for someone if he thought it would make a difference? Would he do it for her?

Aveline decided that was not something she wanted to dwell on.

ON THE FOURTH DAY, MUSIC GENTLY PARTED THE SILENCE. THE piano notes were stilted but gentle, stirring a quiet longing within Aveline, somehow conveying the emotions she had been keeping at bay.

Without a word, Maud nodded at the door and took a step closer to her sleeping son, who was sprawled across his bed, Solas and Luna snuggling him. The light stick on the nightstand glowed enough for Aveline to see Maud mouth the word "go".

She stepped through the doorway, leaving behind the last shred of light. *You would think being a ghost would either help you see in the darkness or make you less afraid of what could be lurking in it...* If she had known, she would have been able to assuage Jeanette's fears of ghosts and get her to fall asleep more easily when she was a young girl.

But at that time, Aveline had thought they existed only in scary stories.

Funny, what lies we tell, believing they are truth. Aveline waited one moment, then another, and told herself the lie that would convince her to venture into the darkness to find Sebastian: *There is nothing that can hurt you.*

Over the creaking of the castle, the music called to her. She let it lead, reminding herself that she was incorporeal, so there was no risk of tripping or falling down the stairs. That did little to comfort her.

At least she was not making noise with footsteps or breaths. Creatures would not hear her as long as she did not speak. But if she listened too hard, Aveline could hear the faint sound of crying, and so she focused on the music before she could lose her nerve. It was too late to turn back now—how would she find her way to Leo's room?

There was no other option than to find Sebastian. *Don't stop playing,* she silently pleaded.

By the time the music grew louder, Aveline reached the end of the hallway, where a soft light peeked from under the doorway of one of the rooms. She gravitated towards it like a moth to flame, and slipped inside.

Sebastian sat in the candlelit room, hunched, fingers drifting over the keys. His left hand never faltered, but his right tripped over itself, the notes mixing in a cacophony of sweet and awkward.

"I hope I did not worry you," he said, looking up at Aveline long enough for her to spot the bruise-like circles under his eyes, the sallowness of his skin, and the unruliness of the black hair that framed his face and fell into his eyes. "I know how terrifying it can be to travel through space and time."

Aveline opened her mouth to say she was not worried, but then closed it. It felt wrong to speak lies, at least to Sebastian. "How are you feeling?"

His eyes trained on his right hand, slowly experimenting with pressing one key at a time. "Exhausted."

Perhaps there was no room for lies between them, Aveline thought, then wondered if there would come a time when there would be no room for secrets either. *There won't be, because we will break the curse soon, and I will return to my family.*

"But everything will be righted." He grimaced as the last note clunked. "I'll make one more trip outside, and then we'll hopefully return home soon."

Odd, that he thought of a place and time as his home, not the castle itself. She supposed she could not blame him, not when home had the connotation of safety and at least some level of consistency.

"Would you care to join me?" he asked with a hopeful expression.

"I am afraid I would not be much of a partner," she confessed. "I know very little, and much prefer listening to playing."

Sebastian slid to one side of the bench and patted the other. "I don't mind teaching, if you're interested."

Aveline could hear Jeanette telling her to move away from the bench so she could show her what it is *supposed* to sound like, all but shoving her in the process. Yet Aveline stepped forward anyway, craving the feel of something, anything, beneath her fingertips, something she could touch and move and feel like she was still real.

Sebastian helped her sit beside him and placed her fingers over specific keys. "Like this." He gently pressed them down, repeating the order a few times. The sounds tripped over one another as Aveline tried to mimic Sebastian, plunking away on the keys instead of coaxing the music out.

She sighed; he offered her a smile. "It takes practise."

"How much practise to sound as professional as you do?"

"I do not sound remotely close to professional." To emphasise his point, he tried the same notes with his right hand, which fumbled. "You already sound better than that."

Sebastian looked at her with an expression of self-deprecation, which faded the longer Aveline studied him. *Should I ask? Would that be rude? He seems hard to offend, but either way, I would loathe unintentionally crossing that line—*

He shifted his hold on her, his thumb rubbing the back of her hand. "Are you all right?"

A few lies sprang up but could not make it past her lips. "I am as well as can be expected in this kind of situation, I suppose. I'll admit that I have many more questions than answers, but I do not wish to be burdensome."

"I think we all are burdened with questions, but you are far from burdensome." Heat spread across her cheeks, but he either did not notice or decided not to comment. "Feel free to ask anything you like."

"Anything?"

She expected him to look away, but he did not. "Anything. I will not promise that I'll answer all of it, but what I am able to, I will."

"I can accept that." Deciding that questions about his right hand might be a bit too much to start off with, she opted to ask, "Where did we end up?"

"I'm not entirely sure. We seem to be in a cave that is home to some rather unpleasant creatures."

Instinctively, Aveline brushed some hair out of his face, revealing a superficial cut across his cheekbone. "Are you hurt? I saw some scratches and I..."

In the dim light, his irises appeared almost black, making them impossible to read.

You are invading his personal space. Just because you can touch him doesn't mean you should. "I apologise." She let her hand fall away. "I'm not sure what came over me just now."

The corner of his mouth ticked upward. "Caring about someone's well-being is an odd thing to apologise for," he teased. "No, I'm not hurt, just a few scratches and bruises that are already nearly gone. My exhaustion is solely from magic use."

Now that he was no longer holding her hand, Aveline wanted to reach out but decided against it. She needed to learn to be self-sufficient. He was fatigued enough without spending more energy to help her.

Maud's words to Sebastian reverberated in Aveline's mind, and she silently promised, *I will not be the one who undoes you, Sebastian Blaise.*

Sebastian leant toward Aveline, the strands she'd pushed out of his face falling back down to cover his brow and parts of his eyes. "You must be thinking hard about which question should be your next."

Was that her heart beating in her chest? Her palms sweating? A small part of her considered fleeing to the safety of being a ghost, distant from emotions, but she had no idea exactly how to switch back, and her curiosity pinned her to the spot, encouraging her to not miss whatever this moment was going to offer her.

The bond is making me feel this way. That was the only explanation. Aveline swallowed. "Leo said you sometimes bring back magic artefacts."

His amusement dimmed. "That was not a question, but yes, I do."

"I'll not ask you why, since that is your business and I'm sure you want to keep that to yourself, but I thought I might offer to help you retrieve them."

The extended pause had Aveline itching to find something else to say, some way to fix it so he'd continue talking to her, but then he asked, "Why would you want to help?"

"Because you have done everything you can to help me. I thought I could return the favour."

Sebastian considered her statement with an expression Aveline realised with great irritation that she could not decipher. She instead caught fragments of emotions: sadness, concern... hope?

"It would be very dangerous," he said, and Aveline waited for him to add something about her not being able to help. Because what could she do, as a ghost who could not affect the physical world?

"Still..." Aveline pressed, "if there is a way I can help, I would like to. Is it not dangerous to you as well?"

"...Yes."

"Is there a way I could help?"

Sebastian furrowed his brow. The candlelight flickered, casting shadows that danced across his features. "There might be... something..." He sighed and explained, "Do you remember how I told you that I can see magic? That is what helps me find the artefacts."

"All right. How would I help then? I do not have the ability." *As much as I am starting to wish I did.*

"No, but I have a magic artefact that can fix that, which I might be able to temporarily enchant so that you can hold onto it in your current state."

"I thought binding takes a lot of energy."

He nodded, running a hand through his hair. "It does, but not as much when it's an inanimate object. That would keep you mostly out of danger, and you could help me spot the artefacts so we could leave more quickly."

"Mostly out of danger?" Aveline tilted her head. "Are there other ghosts?"

"There is always a chance that there are other ghosts. The wards I've placed are only around the castle, so outside of that, any sort of ghost or spirit is free to act as they please." He pressed his lips together. "This is a bad idea. If—"

Aveline grabbed Sebastian's hand without a thought. He went rigid, stare pinned on her. "Let me help you," she said gently. Based on what she'd seen of him, she figured that a genuine request would go along better than a demand. His shoulders relaxed.

"Perhaps we can plan something."

CHAPTER 14

GHOSTS AND GHOULS AND SPIRITS, I'D IMAGINE

"How did you manage to convince Sebastian to let you go with him?" Maud asked Aveline. "I've only managed that once or twice because he couldn't stop me, before Leo was born, before..."

"Before what, Mum?" Leo bounced from one foot to the other, waving his light stick around. The hounds barked and hopped about his room, almost knocking him over.

"Do be careful," Maud warned, then asked again, "So, how did you do it?"

"I... I am unsure," Aveline said. "I merely requested that I wanted to help him, and when he said that it would be dangerous, I pointed out that it is dangerous for him as well."

Maud crossed her arms. "That's a point I've made plenty of times!"

"Yes," Leo said, "but Bash really likes her."

Am I blushing? There was a hint of heat to her cheeks, so real that she had to look down at her hands to check if she was still a ghost. Which, oddly enough, she was.

With a sigh, Maud shook her head. "Well, I am glad he is taking someone with him. The man really needs to learn how to accept help. And ask for it, but one step at a time."

"I'll admit, that is easier said than done," Aveline said.

Maud's expression softened, her gaze unfocused. "I cannot argue that."

Sebastian announced his arrival by knocking on the half-open door.

"Bash!" Leo cried gleefully. Tails wagging, the hounds looked about to see why their game had ended. Luna had a hold on one end of Leo's light stick, which the boy attempted to retrieve.

"Why on earth are you knocking on an open door?" Maud teased. "You can clearly see us standing here—you're not interrupting anything."

Sebastian cleared his throat. "I... It's not my room...?"

"But it's open! And besides, it's *your* castle!"

"Not mine." His tone was edged but not quite sharp. When Maud did not reply, Sebastian turned to Aveline. "Are you ready?" he asked, but she heard his unspoken meaning: *Are you sure?*

Leo finally tugged the light stick free, unbothered by the slobber dripping from it. "I want to go on an adventure!" He rushed to Sebastian but stopped short of barrelling into him. The wizard patted the boy's shoulder as the hounds barked like they, too, were asking to join whatever fun their favourite human wanted.

"Not this time. I need you to protect your mum and the castle." He smoothed Leo's hair, but it fell right back into his eyes.

"That's what you say every time!"

Sebastian knelt so that they were at eye level. Even though it was obvious they weren't related, their movements and expressions were kin, slightly modified mirrors of one another. "Do you know why I ask you, *moy mal'chik?*"

Leo shook his head.

"I ask you because I can trust you. I trust that you're more than capable of looking after the castle while I'm away, and I trust that you'll do whatever is necessary should something happen."

"I don't have magic like you though. I don't think I could fight the monsters."

"It's often easier to solve problems without magic. Besides, I prefer solutions that don't involve fighting."

With a quick peek at his mother, Leo not-so-quietly whispered to Sebastian, "I think if something did happen, Mum would tell me what to do."

Sebastian leant closer and mock whispered back, "She would, and I'd advise you to listen. More often than not, she's right. But don't tell her I said that."

"I am glad to know you have *some* sense." Maud smiled smugly.

"Well, if I had all of the sense, there'd be no room left for fun. Which reminds me—Leo, may I borrow your light stick for a moment?"

Leo handed it over; the wizard made a face at the slobber. A split second later, he handed it back, and the boy marvelled at how much brighter it glowed.

"That should keep until we return. If you have need of us, bang it on the floor three times."

"Thank you!" Leo hugged him, then got a running start so he could leap onto the bed with Solas and Luna. His giggles rose as they licked at his face.

"We shouldn't have need of it." Maud then said to Aveline, "Make sure he returns safely."

"I'll do my best."

"Good. Go on then. Hurry off so you can hurry back."

Aveline followed Sebastian out of the room. He wore different clothes than before, simple trousers and a button-up shirt with rolled-up sleeves. He forewent his normal bright colours, instead opting for shades of black. Catching her staring, he asked, "Are you certain you want to come? I'll not hold it against you if you wish to remain here."

The darkness swallowed up what little light the candles lining the hall had to offer, and yet Aveline could still see the depths of Sebastian's eyes.

"I am coming with you," she said. "I was just noticing that you look much more prepared for this than I am..." She gestured to her wedding gown. Normal women wore theirs for one day, afterwards tucking it away for safekeeping, whereas she had been stuck in hers for a week straight. *Am I just the luckiest woman in the world?*

"I'm not sure if this helps, but I think this is one of those times that being a ghost will be to your advantage."

"That is true." She could keep out of danger and look out for Sebastian all at once, maybe even help find the magic artefacts he was looking for, if she were lucky. They would return to their time regardless, but she was adamant that she was going to do this before then, if only because it would pay back Sebastian in some small way.

"From what I can tell, there might be more than one artefact here." He slowed his long, quick strides so that Aveline could keep pace. The castle groaned as though it protested them leaving, but it was still muffled and quiet, like someone grumbling from under the covers that they just wanted a few more minutes of sleep. "We obviously want to grab what we can, but not at the risk of sacrificing our safety."

You mean mine, Aveline did not dare speak aloud, in case Sebastian changed his mind about letting her come along.

As they passed the library, they heard Meredith griping to herself.

"It takes her a while to return everything to its normal places," Sebastian explained when Aveline tried to peek into the open doorway. "It doesn't help that she changes her mind on how to organise them about three or four times before she is through. Then the process tends to repeat itself again, because by that time, the castle is ready to move."

His fingers grazed the edge of her hand, sending sparks up it. Aveline jolted, pulling her hand to her chest. "It must be a large library," she said.

"It is." He stepped away from her. "It's easiest just to leave Meredith to it, but I can find a time to show you the library another day, if you'd like."

"I'd appreciate that."

With a nod, Sebastian continued their course towards the back of the castle. Aveline hurried to catch up. *The bond made a connection between the two of us, so of course I will feel it. It does not mean anything, so quit being a silly little girl,* she chastised herself, as if she could begin to understand how the magic and its effects worked.

Despite that, Aveline wished that she could talk about all of this to her family, her sisters and mother especially. They would help her sort out her thoughts and feelings and encourage her that she would find a way to break the curse and return home.

One step at a time.

The further down the corridor they walked, the darker it became. Sebastian conjured an orb of light that hovered by his shoulder, illuminating their path. It bobbed slightly but overall remained in place, and it was small enough that it made Aveline think of the faerie stories Edith would tell about pixies and will-o'-the-wisps, the ones that, depending on the story, would either guide travellers to their goals or lead them into mischief. Aveline hoped they were not real, because she had enough trouble as it was with magic and ghosts being real.

She could only imagine how Edith would have romanticised this situation: Aveline the cursed ghost, being swept off her feet by the handsome, mysterious wizard known as The Magic Collector as they went on an epic adventure together. Because if Edith were telling the story, of course she would have the main characters fall in love. It was a rule with her, and to break it was sacrilege.

Edith would have loved to switch places with me, if she were not already married. At the pinch in her chest, she hoped that, wherever Edith was, she was safe and happy, and that Aveline would get to see her sister again.

At the back door, Sebastian stopped and turned toward Aveline. She waited for him to ask her yet again if she was sure, or to try to convince her to stay, but instead he said, "There are a few things I need to give you before we step outside."

"Oh?" She drew closer as he fished a ring out of his pocket. Not the same one as before—no, this was plain, ordinary silver.

"Sound and light of any kind will draw attention, so this is to help us find one another in case we get lost," he explained, slipping the ring onto her index finger. When he released her, it stayed in place, humming with power.

"How?" Aveline studied the band, the etchings nothing but squiggles to her, yet something in her gut told her they held meaning.

"Think of me, and it will lead you to wherever I am," he said simply, as if it were child's play to him, nothing out of the ordinary. *Just how powerful are you?* If King Byron had captured Sebastian and forced him to do his bidding, he might have already conquered half of the world.

Sebastian donned the ring's twin before he retrieved another item from his pocket: a pair of thin-rimmed glasses that reminded Aveline of the ones her father used for reading. She wouldn't have assumed they were anything special had Sebastian not said anything. "Put these on. They'll help you see magic."

It took a moment for Aveline's eyes to adjust to the glasses, and even after, there was something off about Sebastian, his form a tad hazy. She blinked, and it cleared.

"It may take some getting used to," Sebastian said apologetically, "but we don't have much time. Look for something that shimmers or sparkles—it'll most likely be an enchanted object. If you see something that has lines of smoke on it, it's cursed, so do not touch it. Even in your state, it might still latch onto you." Before Aveline could ask how, Sebastian continued in a rush, "There might also be some illusions, which are harder to spot. You'll probably have to stare directly at it for a few seconds before you notice there's something off. If you find any of these, call for me like you did in the broom closet, and I'll find you." He tapped his chest and gave a small smile Aveline had a hard time returning.

You cast an illusion on yourself? ...Unless someone else cast it on you. What is it hiding?

"Are you ready?"

Focusing on what was important, Aveline replied, "Yes. If I find anything, I'll call for you. If I get lost, I'll use the ring to find you."

Sebastian dipped his head in approval. "Those enchantments should last until we return, but if you feel them start to wane, try to return here as soon as possible. As long as you are inside of the castle gates, you'll be safe."

"Safe from what, exactly? Did you see something last time?"

"I saw a few creatures, nothing to be nervous about. Although there is a decent possibility of ghosts and ghouls and spirits, I'd imagine. Magic has a tendency to draw all sorts of supernatural beings."

That only drew up more questions, like what the difference was between those things, but Aveline tucked them away for later. They had a limited amount of time to reach their goal, and she would not squander it.

"I am ready," she declared.

Sebastian hesitated, eyes dancing between hers. "Be safe."

"You as well." It felt like another bargain was struck between them, and by the way he was looking at her, Aveline wondered if maybe she was no longer a stranger to him, that since their alleged meeting when he was a child, she had meant something to him.

What could I have possibly said that stuck with you so?

Sebastian waited so long that Aveline expected him to say something more. He raised his hand, the matching ring gleaming in the light of the orb, and with a wiggle of his fingers, it went out, leaving them in utter darkness.

CHAPTER 15
STAY WITH ME

The creak of the door told Aveline where to step, although she could just as easily have walked through the wall to get outside. She'd thought they had gotten used to the pitch black this area had to offer, but quickly realised that she had never known heavy darkness such as this. How was she supposed to see anything?

What was worse was the utter lack of sound. The moment she crossed the threshold, the castle's noises ceased. She listened for Sebastian's footsteps, his breaths, but there was nothing, making her draw the conclusion that he had enchanted himself for safety. She itched to call out to him, to reach for his hand, but refrained. No matter how afraid she became, Aveline resolved not to call upon him unless it was absolutely necessary.

The sooner we find the artefacts, the sooner we can return to the castle.

Aveline moved forward, assuring herself that the darkness could not obscure magic. The glasses would work. She had no reason not to trust Sebastian.

If Edith were telling this story, she would say how the main character braved the dark—Aveline felt anything but brave. It took everything in her to put one foot in front of the other. Even though being a ghost gave her some protection, there was no guarantee she would come out of this unscathed. But then she thought of Sebastian returning to the castle with cuts and scrapes, looking worn down, and that invigorated her determination.

Water dripped, the echo carrying from her right. Aveline paused. If she were someone trying to hide a magic artefact, would she use water as a marker for her trail so she could easily return to it? Not a great idea, but at least it was something to help her navigate without vision. Part of her wished she could feel, so she could scrape her feet across the floor to ground herself, or run her hand along a wall... if she found one.

Sparkles caught her attention. If the cave were lit up, she might have missed them, but in the complete black, they were like a signal flare, calling to her. Aveline frowned, trying to understand why they looked so far down. As the dripping continued, this time louder, it hit her: the artefact was underwater, in some sort of pool. But how deep? Would she be able to hold her breath long enough to get it?

You are a ghost. *Do you have to breathe?*

Something sniffed and let out a low, rumbling growl. Was it a creature like Titan, or something else entirely? Her mind ran wild with ideas that she quickly stamped down. Whether or not it sensed her, she had to obtain the artefact for Sebastian. If she fled now, she might have trouble finding it again. Certainly, this was not the only water source in the caves.

But calling Sebastian with the creature nearby was foolish at best. She'd have to wait for it to pass first, which meant hiding until then...

Despite knowing she did not make noise, Aveline carefully inched towards the artefact. *This would be a terrible time to become corporeal,* she thought, and then almost immediately took it back when she realised she was hovering over where she wanted to be. Indignantly, she stared down at the sparkles, willing herself to sink. She imagined freezing water soaking her skin, weighing down her dress like it was trying to claim her as its own. Slowly, she descended, and tried to ignore the breaths and snorts of the nearby creature.

Aveline made it to the bottom just as the creature began to lap at the water. To distract herself, she studied the sparkles, trying to make out what the artefact could be based on the shape of them. She reached for it, only partially disappointed that she couldn't touch it.

Probably not the best idea anyway—I'm not sure I'd be able to see a curse in this darkness.

If she were human, she would have drowned by the time the creature finished drinking. It eventually ambled away, its steps resounding. Aveline waited a little while longer, listening intently, before she put a hand over her heart and whispered, "Sebastian."

Something roared, drawing closer with thundering steps. Aveline shrank down. Had it somehow heard her? Was it the same creature as before, or a different one? How many were there? Was there a way to warn Sebastian to wait?

Aveline heard the slap of water a split second before pain sparked across her chest. Impulsively, she gasped, inhaling water. Cold, wet, heavy, lungs burning, body trembling, choking—

Light flared. The creature roared; the cave shuddered as something hit the wall. Frantic, Aveline mustered all of her strength to launch herself to the surface, gasping and hacking up stagnant water that coated her mouth and sickened her stomach. Her hands scrabbled for purchase on the side of the pool, her vision clearing enough to see a four-legged scaly monster lunging at Sebastian. His gaze flicked to her and then he dodged, the orb of light following his every move. The monster's paw struck the wall instead, sending broken bits raining down to the cave floor.

"Run!" Sebastian ordered—pleaded—as bolts of electricity jumped from his fingers to strike the monster. It shuddered, and after a few more menacing steps, it collapsed at his feet, sending a quake throughout the cave. Sebastian swore. "We have to leave. Now."

"Not without the—"

Howls screamed through the air. A pack of mangy wolves descended upon Sebastian, snarling and snapping. He whirled around to defend. Aveline sucked in a breath and dove back down. If nothing else, they had to get at least one of the magic artefacts, or else risking their lives would have been for nothing—and now she was human. She could retrieve it herself.

But as she sank, it dawned on her that she had also lost the glasses.

The dim light above moved constantly, throwing shadows every which way, none of the beams strong enough to reach the bottom.

Cold seeped into her bones, slowing her movements and stealing her strength, yet she persisted, hands wildly sweeping back and forth, scraping her palms as she sought out the items. The water muffled the snarls and yelps, but her heart raced all the same, her lungs seizing.

For Sebastian for Sebastian for Sebastian—

She knocked against something. Aveline scrabbled at the area again, snatching the glasses and fumbling to put them back on. By the time she had them hooked over her ears, she caught sight of sparkles off to her left.

"Aveline!"

Lungs screaming for air, she grasped the artefact, a small albeit heavy box that required two hands to carry. She kicked off the bottom, silently cursing the gown with all of its lace and tulle and long train that threatened to keep her hostage in the pool—

Sebastian caught her wrist and yanked her the rest of the way out, making her drop the artefact. "Your life is not worth risking for me—for anything."

"This is why we came here!" she spat back in between coughs, her violent shivers undermining her sharp tone. She snatched up the box once more, holding it against her chest with numb fingers.

A roar cut off whatever Sebastian was going to say. He pulled her against him, pinning the box between them. The air rippled, contorting the colours and shadows. She buried her face in his shoulder.

Sharp hot pain sank into her ankle. She gasped and her legs gave way, but Sebastian tightened his grip. Stumbling, they landed, Aveline catching sight of bushes and flowers as her head fell back and her body went limp.

"Aveline? Aveline!" Sebastian scanned her hastily. She tried to open her mouth, tried to say that the burning sensation was climbing up her leg, but could manage nothing. He swore. Something zapped and popped. Gently, he lowered her to the ground. Aveline stared at the bushes, a tear rolling over the bridge of her nose and hitting the dirt. Could she even blink? Breathe?

"I have to check your ankle," he said, sliding up the skirt of her gown. Then he yanked something out of her leg, bringing a split second of relief. Or was it that her heartbeat was slowing, so the pain was no longer affecting her as it should?

Sebastian swore again, face coming into view. "Stay with me, Aveline."

I am trying.

He lifted her into his arms, all but sprinting towards the castle. The back door slammed open before they even reached it, Sebastian not breaking stride as he barrelled down the hall, calling for Maud. Aveline jostled with each step, but all she could focus on was the beat of his heart railing against her ear.

I don't want to go. I want to stay, to live.

"Maud!" Sebastian's footfalls echoed, making far more noise than the castle. Aveline could not even hear the cries of the attic ghost, just the pounding of Sebastian's heart: *Stay-with-me stay-with-me stay-with-me don't-go don't-go don't-go.*

Wizards do have hearts, she thought, distantly aware of Sebastian laying her on a bed. She sunk into the mattress, her head propped up by a pillow.

"What happened?" Maud asked, not quite in Aveline's peripheral.

"Snake bite." Sebastian exposed the wound. "Demon snake. The venom has magic properties that will eat away at her soul before it kills her."

"She's dying?!" Leo exclaimed.

"Get my medical bag and a bowl of water, now!" Maud demanded, stepping into Aveline's hazy line of sight. Leo's frantic steps tramped down the hall. "I've given you time, Sebastian. Do what you have to before he returns."

Instead of answering her, Sebastian brushed Aveline's stray hairs out of her face. "Stay with me," he implored in a murmur, pressing a quick kiss to her forehead.

Black encroached upon the edges of her vision, then swallowed it whole, dragging her under.

I want to.

CHAPTER 16

TO HELP SOMEONE

A veline slowly returned to the waking world like a lazy tide bringing her back to shore. She was in pain, she was tired, she was hungry—

Her eyes snapped open, taking in the shadow-filled bedroom. *Not a ghost...* She wiggled her fingers in front of her face. Her smile dimmed when she noticed her other hand clasped in Sebastian's. In a chair pulled up to the side of the bed, Sebastian was hunched forward, head resting on the mattress, dark hair spilled across the silk sheets. His lips were parted slightly, soft breaths barely audible.

It hit her then, the urge to run her fingers through his hair, to push it out of his face so she could study it without the unreadable mask.

Sebastian woke suddenly, his grip tightening as he composed himself. "I am glad to see you awake." His voice was raw and scratchy, not from too much sleep but a lack of it. He cleared his throat, which did little to help. "How are you feeling?"

Slowly, Aveline pushed herself up into a seated position, taking in every sensation: the fabric against her legs, the shifting of the mattress underneath her, the ache of her muscles. Her ankle throbbed and her chest stung—both had been bandaged, and she no longer wore the wedding gown, but a lightweight, soft nightgown.

Heat kissed her cheeks as she realised who must have changed her into it. *Do not be a silly girl. This would only be a scandal if you two weren't married.* Besides, she noted, Sebastian's gaze remained on her face, his expression too full of concern for there to be room for anything else.

"Overwhelmed," she said, "but not in a terrible way. I'm getting reacquainted with feeling anything at all after being a ghost."

A furrow formed between his brows. "I can only imagine. Leo was fretting over you, so I sent him to make soup. It should be here shortly."

Memories of the night before—or was it longer than that?—came back to her, of the three of them trying to save her before she slipped into unconsciousness. "How long have I been asleep?"

"A day and a half."

"What happened, exactly?"

Sebastian sighed, his thumb idly stroking the back of her hand. "From what I can tell, a ghoul scratched you, forcing you to become corporeal. I'd already dealt with it, but a demon snake latched onto you as we were teleporting back to the castle."

So many creatures I don't know. "What is a ghoul?"

"It's a creature that's not quite spirit, but not quite flesh either. They are created when someone tries to barter their soul for magic, but things don't quite go as planned, and the spirit that offered to turn them into a witch instead takes too much, leaving them a husk that is no longer human."

Titan. Maud had hinted that she knew Leo was feeding something, but did she and Sebastian know the details? "That sounds horrible."

"It is." After a beat, he added, "Leo wants magic like I have, but even if he succeeded, being a witch is not something to desire. The hole in their soul drives them to fill it with items, people, power, and they are driven mad because there is nothing that can patch it. They no longer have empathy, only the need to claim and consume everything they can in a futile attempt to right themselves."

Aveline rested against the headboard as she watched Sebastian, taking in the subtle twitches in his jaw and the way his thumb's circular motions changed direction every so often. Methodical, purposeful. A way to contain his emotions while he answered her questions? Did he know someone who became a witch? Did he know The Heart Thief prior?

"I think Leo only wants magic because he wants to be like you," Aveline said gently.

The tension in Sebastian's face melted. "That's true. But he does not understand what a burden it is. If I'd had a choice in all of this... Well, it does not matter."

He had been born with magic, and saw it as a curse of its own. "It can be a gift. You help people with it."

That snuffed out the flicker of a smile he had. "I have tried to, but have done nothing yet. If I didn't have magic, we wouldn't be in this situation in the first place." Sebastian squeezed her hand and let go, lounging back in his chair. Panic shot through Aveline, waiting to fade back into a ghost. It would dull her pain and hunger, but she would have gladly suffered through it just to *feel*. Seconds passed, and she remained just as solid.

"Ghouls can affect both the spirit and the flesh," Sebastian told her. "It forced you to become corporeal when it wounded you, and the demon snake even more so. You'll be stuck in the physical world for at least a day or two while your body heals."

Aveline touched the bandage under her collarbone. "Where is the box? Did we at least get that here?"

"The box and the glasses are safe in the artefact room."

They had retrieved an artefact, and she was human for the time being? There could have been worse outcomes. "What about the other one?"

Leo bounded into the room with a silver tray, soup sloshing over the side of the bowl. "You're awake!"

"I am." Her stomach growled as he placed the tray on her lap. Sebastian fidgeted like he was trying to decide whether or not to help, and by Maud's pinched expression as she walked through the doorway, she was probably wishing that she could.

"Mum says good soup will help you regain strength," Leo explained, hopping onto the foot of the bed and crossing his legs. The hounds curled up beside him, their eyes trained on Aveline's food.

The strange burnt orange colour of the soup gave Aveline pause. She lifted the spoon, fully aware of Leo's undivided attention on her—

As her spoon touched the surface, the hue shifted closer to yellow, and the thickness watered down, looking less like sludge. Aveline cast a quick glance at Sebastian and took a bite. Warm, flavourful, soothing... She smiled and ate more.

"There's bread too," Leo pointed out. "I like to dip it in the soup."

Aveline ignored the creaking of the castle, which sounded louder than it had previously. She tore a piece of the soft bread and offered it to Leo. "Would you like some?"

"Just a piece." Leo snatched it, broke tiny bits off for the hounds, and popped the rest in his mouth. Maud frowned, but the boy either didn't notice or didn't care.

When Aveline offered it to Sebastian next, he shook his head. "Like Leo said, you need to regain your strength."

"After not eating for the past week or two, my stomach isn't quite ready to handle all of this at once," Aveline insisted. As much as she would have loved to devour it, her stomach twisted like it was trying to remember what to do with food.

Hesitantly, Sebastian accepted it. "Thank you," he said, and then to Leo, "and thank you as well. It was thoughtful of you to make lunch."

"Family helps each other." Leo grinned and clapped. "Oh! Now that Aveline is human again, she can wear the ring!"

Aveline coughed; Sebastian's throat bobbed.

"We should clean the kitchen," Maud interrupted. "Come along, little imp."

"Mum!"

"Now, before it sets and gets harder to clean."

The child sighed, taking his time getting off the bed. "By 'we' I know you mean 'me'."

Maud ran a hand over his head like she was ruffling his hair. "You are such a bright boy."

With one last longing look at what remained of Aveline's food, the hounds exited after Leo.

"You don't have to wear it," Sebastian said, leaning back in his chair. "Leo doesn't understand how complicated this situation is."

"I think none of us quite understand it," Aveline replied carefully. His eyes danced about her face, and she wondered what he found. He was giving her an out—would she take it? It would make Leo happy, but what would that mean to Sebastian?

You are overthinking things. Any affection you might have for one another is from the binding, naught else. Still, her heart squeezed as she said, "I would like to wear it, if it is all right with you."

Sebastian studied her. She waited for him to ask why, her mind fumbling for an answer. She could tell him that it was because she wanted to have something tangible to hold on to, but that would seem to make the ring have little value—and this surely was a family heirloom he offered her, not something to be taken lightly.

Sebastian retrieved the ring. Aveline tried to still her trembling hand as she lifted it. His gentle touch sent shivers through her as he slipped the ring into place. This time, when he slowly let go, it remained in place, fitting perfectly. Aveline admired it in the candlelight. For now, she could have it, and then she would return it to Sebastian before she left. For now, she could belong to their little family, even if it could not last forever.

"It is beautiful," Aveline breathed, mentally kicking herself for not having an adjective to better suit it.

"Every wife should have a ring... Even with our unusual circumstances."

She met his gaze, almost certain he could see the blush in her cheeks despite the dim lighting. But, to her amusement, she could have sworn his were tinged pink as well. Unsure how to respond, she showed off her other hand. "Well, you did give me this one, and it matches yours."

With a chuckle, Sebastian shook his head, mirroring the way she held her hand. "These are plain, merely meant to help us find each other. The enchantment will wear off soon."

Hopefully, not too soon. Aveline broke eye contact. Surely, the thought was only because she wanted to help him find the other artefact, to repay him for his many kindnesses.

"I'll enchant them again, if need be," he said.

"Will there be a need? Will you wait for me before you venture to find the other artefact?"

The lengthy pause set Aveline on edge. "Do you want me to wait for you?" he asked. "I would've thought your injuries would've deterred you from returning."

Lifting her chin, she looked him in the eye again. "I have a feeling you've sustained worse injuries than this and yet continue."

"You are correct."

It was Aveline's turn to pause, inwardly debating how far she could press for information. "If I may be so bold, why do you collect these artefacts? What do you use them for?"

"To help someone."

That much she could have guessed. But who? Certainly, it was not for her sake, since Leo made it sound like Sebastian had been collecting for a long time. Was it for Maud? Or to find a way out of The Heart Thief's curses once and for all?

Then it hit her: Could it possibly have to do with whoever the ghost was upstairs in the attic?

Is that going to be my fate? Was Sebastian going to have to lock her up in a room of the castle, or would she eventually fade to nothing when he could no longer use his energy to keep her here?

Would she never see her family again?

I'm trying, I promise I'm trying, but I might fail you, and you'll never know what happened to me, and I'll never know what happened to you...

"Aveline?" Sebastian sat on the edge of the bed so he could tuck her blonde strands behind her ear. "Did I say something upsetting?"

Her breath caught in her throat. She had the sudden urge to laugh, as if her body was desperately trying to find a way to release the panic clawing up her chest. How had she handled such emotions before? *Store them away, deep down. Do not give into the emotions. Push them until—*

Her vision blurred. Aveline opened her mouth, unsure whether she was trying to speak or breathe, but only a strangled wheeze slipped out. She shuddered, inhaling, but it felt like if she breathed too deeply, she might shatter. Or perhaps she already had, and the pieces were about to give way.

The mattress shifted. Sebastian pulled her to his side, cradling her. She froze.

"It's all right," he murmured, pressing a kiss to her brow. "You can let it out."

Tears flowed freely then. She buried her face in his shoulder, crumbling under the weight of it all. Aveline had let down her family by becoming cursed, had done no better for them than Edith had by running off to marry a man she hardly knew in the name of love. They had both failed to provide for their family, had both left them stranded. Even if Aveline managed to break her curse, what could she do to help? Prince Alexei was surely already married off to someone else, or at least engaged. The best she could hope for was to find a duke or a lord with enough standing to save her family from financial ruin. Nothing was going to plan. Nothing at all.

To her, the worst part was that a fraction of her was glad that it happened. She was selfish, happy to avoid marrying a man she knew she could never love and would never love her, and happy to have met Sebastian and Maud and Leo, despite knowing that she could only fit in their world for a short amount of time.

Aveline sobbed and Sebastian held her, sometimes murmuring soothing things and sometimes saying nothing at all. Not once did he pull away or tell her to stop or demand an explanation from her.

When all of the tears had been wrung from her, Aveline leant heavily against him, not caring that she was truly selfish for clinging to this small comfort. They sat together in the silence that stretched on, and she pondered how much longer it could last.

Sebastian rested his temple on the top of her head, his hand stroking up and down her arm. She closed her eyes, listening to his heartbeat. If she were not careful, it would lull her back to sleep.

"I'm sorry," she whispered. *In this regard, it is easier to be a ghost, to be able to slip through the clutches of emotion before they can capture you.*

"I'm not."

Surprised, Aveline shifted slightly, tilting her head up to peer at his face, which was only a few inches away from hers. He had stubble at his jawline, a bruise across his cheek, and... oh, his eyes. They were a rich brown, with hints of honey hues towards the centres. Aveline swept aside the dark locks obscuring them, hoping to get a better view, and noted the bright red patch of blistered skin.

"What happened? Were you burnt by something?" She sat upright, getting a closer look at it.

Sebastian grimaced. "Sometimes artefacts have small curses that can trigger if they aren't carefully disengaged first. This is nothing; it should go away on its own in a few days' time. I was just tired and worried, so I got a little careless."

"The box did this to you?" *That is why he hasn't used magic to heal it. Or maybe he thought it wasn't worth it?* If he could have used magic to heal hers, she reasoned, he probably would have, but she could also see him not bothering to help himself, calling it a waste of energy.

"As I said, it's nothing to fret over. I've had much worse." He touched his forehead to hers.

"Somehow, that does not assuage my worries," Aveline replied, meaning to come across as teasing, but her voice sounded strained. How was it that he seemed to feel at ease with her, while she was tightly coiled?

"I think you and I might be alike," Sebastian said quietly, eyelids fluttering closed.

"How?"

"We worry about far too much. A common side effect of overthinking." Slowly, he pulled away, just enough to press a kiss between her brows. "You should sleep, Aveline. I'll be here."

Sleep was the farthest thing from her mind, despite her body suddenly feeling heavy. She bit back a complaint as he untangled himself from her and returned to his chair.

"You won't go on another adventure without me?" she asked as she sank back against the pillows.

"I'd rather stay here with you." Sebastian's smile was the last thing she saw before she fell asleep, thinking, *That does not answer my question...*

CHAPTER 17

I DIDN'T KNOW YOU WERE A BARBER

By the end of the next day, Aveline had had quite enough sleep, and there was only so much she could think about before her mind went in circles, trying to figure out everything from what she could have possibly said to Sebastian when he first met her to what illusions he had cast on himself to who the ghost was in the attic. The questions spiralled her into fitful dreams of teeth and cold and blood and screams, of never-ending darkness she could not escape no matter how far she ran.

"I'm here," Sebastian said, dabbing at her face with a cloth. *Hold me*, she tried to plead, but sleep pulled her under again before she could.

When Aveline finally had the strength to open her eyes, there was nothing but a dark, empty room to greet her. Sebastian had left a few lit candles on the nightstand and dresser, wax pooling in their stands. Her heart pinched, seeing that he was nowhere to be found.

Everything ached. Her hair and nightgown stuck to her sweat-soaked skin, sheets tangled about her legs. Resolved that she couldn't be in bed any longer, she freed herself. The first contact of her bare feet on the cold wood floor shot goosebumps across her skin, reminding her that she was still, in fact, human. But for how long until the curse began to take its toll once more?

I have wasted enough time. She would find Sebastian and the others, but first, she needed to change.

Using a candlestick to light her way, Aveline limped to the armoire, her bandaged ankle barely holding her up. The armoire opened after a few tugs, revealing an assortment of dresses in many fabrics and colours. There was no dust, nor holes eaten through by moths, each kept in pristine condition. She took one that she judged to be about her size, a simple gown of pastel blue with long sleeves and a bit of lace at the wrists and hem. There were others she wanted to try, but they were much too fancy to be comfortable or practical. How would the others react if she were to flounce towards them in a floor-length ball gown with intricate beading and a full skirt? Besides, after being away from the sun for so long, she was bound to be too pale for such a rich colour, not that she hadn't already been pale to begin with.

Aveline set the candlestick atop the desk and was fumbling with the stays at her back when Sebastian stepped inside. They froze, staring at one another.

"I apologise," he said, whirling away. "I should've knocked. I thought you were sleeping and didn't wish to wake you."

"No apologies necessary." Aveline cleared her throat.

"Although, if I may, before you dress, I'd like to change your bandages. You picked something with a high collar, and that will make it rather difficult to tend to the wound, unless you want to do it yourself."

Aveline shook her head, then mentally kicked herself—he couldn't see her with his back turned. "You may check them. I'm afraid I have little healer knowledge other than tending to scrapes and bruises my siblings often acquired."

Hesitantly, Sebastian sat in his chair and gestured toward the bed. He waited until Aveline had sat on the edge before he said, "I'll need your arm out of that sleeve."

Her face became flushed. Any other place, any other time, with anyone else, that would have been scandalous. The whole situation would have been, especially with her in just a nightgown. *He is my husband,* she reminded herself, but the word felt different to her than it had previously. In her mind, it had meant someone she belonged to, who would own her and make all of the decisions.

Sebastian didn't make her do anything. He didn't talk to her like she owed him or that her feelings or opinions didn't matter. He was there for her, helping her.

Hands trembling, Aveline slid the sleeve off of her shoulder. The chill of the room no longer affected her, not as Sebastian unwound the bandage with care, his left hand moving more fluidly than his right. *Did he injure it?* Aveline recalled Leo's comment about getting hurt, and Sebastian's statement that he had been wounded far worse. Whatever had happened, she was almost certain that it had to do with magic.

"How are you feeling?" Sebastian drew Aveline out of her ponderings with the question. "Your fever finally broke early this morning, so I think the venom has lost its effect on you."

"I don't feel wonderful, but I'm far more concerned about lounging in bed for one more day and risking going stir crazy."

"Well, I think we can find something outside of this room for you to do without straining yourself." Sebastian smiled up at her, then applied a salve that cooled her skin and left a tingling sensation. As he rebandaged her, she wondered how he could see with his hair obscuring his vision as much as it did.

"If you want," she offered, "I can trim your hair for you. At least so it's out of your eyes. Leo looks like he needs one as well."

Sebastian carefully tied off the bandage.

"Unless you want to use magic," Aveline continued. "But I used to do it for my father and brothers." *After a trip to the barber became a luxury we could no longer afford.* She had no idea how much time had passed for her family, but she hoped that Sebastian's money had reached them safely. After everything he'd done for her, a haircut seemed a poor repayment, but at least it was something. Aveline did not quite count the artefact retrieval, considering how messy that turned out, what with him having to save her.

Surely, he would decline. He could use magic to easily alter his appearance, right? But the dark circles under his eyes told her that all of the magic he'd used recently was taking a toll on him. If she could ease his burden a little, she was more than happy to.

"Are you certain you can stand on your ankle for that long?" He eased the sleeve back up onto her shoulder.

"If it's necessary, we'll find a way to do it sitting down."

The corner of his mouth quirked upward. "Very well. Only if you're up for it."

"Sit still," Maud reprimanded Leo for the fifth time in the past few minutes.

"I promise I will not cut you," Aveline told him, hoping that would soothe his nerves.

"I'm not nervous, it just tickles when the hair hits my neck." Leo fidgeted in the dining room chair they had pulled into the kitchen, deciding it would be easier to clean up the hardwood floor than the rug. Sebastian had pointed out he could clean it with magic, but did not argue when both Maud and Aveline immediately rejected the idea. Maud had nodded at her approvingly, making Aveline feel like she had received a badge of honour.

"Almost done." She combed his hair, smoothing out tangles as gently as possible. She ignored Sebastian's gaze on her, knowing he watched as he leant against the wall. He was probably curious to see how it was turning out, but every time he was near, she got the impression that he was focused on her.

Quit being so self-centred.

"I didn't know you were a barber," Leo said. "I've only read about them in books."

Aveline chuckled. "I'm not. I only learnt so I could do it for my family. My sister Edith was especially grateful for the skill when she gave herself a terrible haircut, which is what you will end up with if you don't sit still."

Leo pressed his lips together and sat on his hands. His knees bounced a bit, but not enough to agitate Aveline. Maud, on the other hand, raised a warning brow at her son.

"All done." Aveline swept the cut hairs from his shoulders as he bounded to his feet.

"I'm so much lighter!" he shouted, eliciting laughter from the adults. "I wanna see what I look like." He dashed away in search of a mirror, and Maud and the hounds went with him.

"You did well." Sebastian pushed off the wall to settle into the chair. "I'm terrible at keeping up with mundane things. Maud has to constantly remind me. Leo deserves someone who is more attentive to his needs. I didn't even consider that he needed a haircut. Or that I did, for that matter."

"From what I've seen, you take good care of him." Aveline ran her fingers through his thick black locks, repeating the same procedure of undoing knots as she had with Leo, although there were far fewer.

Sebastian sighed. "I try, but I tend to get sidetracked. He needs a better father figure, if I'm being honest."

Aveline paused, fighting the urge to check his expression. From what she could tell, he wasn't trying to gain pity, but rather let loose a burden weighing on his chest. She almost smiled at his trust in her. "Well, if *I'm* being honest, things like haircuts are minor details."

"What do you mean?"

"I mean that they're easily forgivable, easily remedied. Leo knows you love him; it's obvious in the way you encourage him, the way you play with him, the way you make sure he is safe and fed. He's one of the happiest children I've ever seen." Sebastian remained quiet, so Aveline continued, "You are just one person doing the best you can."

He still gave no response.

"How would you like me to style your hair?"

"Not too short," he answered, "but whatever you think is best."

Aveline pondered a few options as she ruffled his hair, relishing the soft strands between her fingers.

"I would like to hear about your family," Sebastian said after Aveline started snipping, beginning with a trim before making her final decision on what to do. "From what you've said, it sounds like you're close with them."

Aveline ignored the twinge in her chest. She would see them again, no matter what. For months, she had to pretend that they did not exist, that she did not miss them, but now... Talking about them was like letting her heart breathe after being suffocated for so long. "I am. What would you like to know about them?"

"Anything you're willing to share. Why did Edith cut her hair in the first place? Were you able to salvage it?"

"Barely." Aveline shook her head. "Edith is just... Edith. She is a true romantic, a wild soul. Sometimes I wonder if she is one of those faeries she used to tell us stories about." Bits of hair fell to the floor, Sebastian's black mixing with Leo's honey brown. "She dreams bigger than most, and when an idea latches onto her, there's no talking her out of it. She'd read a story about a woman cutting her hair and decided it sounded like a brilliant idea, that it'd make her stand out from everyone else. And she was right, but she had no idea how to style it, and so it was all sorts of lengths by the time she'd come to me for help. She's always doing things on a whim. It shouldn't have surprised me that she left the way she did, marrying a man she barely knew all for the sake of love."

The silence stretched on for far longer than was comfortable.

"She left... Was she originally supposed to marry the Prince?"

You are far too perceptive. "Yes."

"I imagine that felt like a betrayal to you. Are you still upset at her for it?"

Aveline stilled. Nothing about the question compelled her to answer, and yet she wanted to. "Yes, but only a little. I mean, after she chose that man over us, I was furious, but I didn't have time to stew over it because our family needed the finances. Needs," she corrected. "Although your funds will help as soon as they receive them. Thank you again."

"It was my pleasure." His sincerity pricked her conscience. Sebastian *liked* to help people even though he also felt responsible—Aveline helped people *because* she felt responsible. Because her sister did not step up, she had to. She resented the fact that there was no other choice, that the weight of it all was placed on her shoulders.

Sebastian looked for opportunities to help, like they brought him joy.

"I used to follow Edith everywhere so much that she called me

THE MAGIC COLLECTOR

her little shadow... so it still stings," Aveline admitted, slowly measuring and cutting his hair, "the fact that Edith left without warning. But I do love her, and I do not wish her any unhappiness." She circled to face him, bending down so she could cut the bangs. With each snip, she became more aware of his dark eyes fixated on her.

"Besides," she said, noting that her voice was coming out strained, "I... I cannot be upset about the turn of events, especially not when they led me here."

"Do you mean cursed and stuck in an enchanted castle?"

Aveline set down the scissors so she could smooth his hair and inspect her work. It no longer hid his face, displaying the sharp cheekbones and strong jawline.

And those eyes. They drew her in, enticing her to come closer. She did, despite her protesting ankle, letting her hand trail down the side of his face. He leant into the touch; Aveline's heartbeat stuttered.

"I mean that I am glad to have met Maud... and Leo..." Aveline cleared her throat, as if that would bring her voice back. Breathily, she added, "And you."

His gaze dipped to her mouth, then refocused on her eyes. "Selfishly, I am glad for that too," he whispered.

Distantly, Aveline thought that the idea of him being selfish was ridiculous, but she was too captivated by him to linger on it. One more heartbeat, then two, and she leant forward, sliding her hands down to his shoulders—

Sebastian recoiled, staggering backward, barely catching himself on the edge of the table. The chair fell sideways onto the floor with a resounding *thunk*. They stared at one another, unmoving.

How could I be so stupid?

Aveline took a step back. Her eyes stung; she blinked, but that only made things worse. "I-I'm sorry. I don't know what came over me. I just..."

"Is everything all right?" Maud called, followed by the patter of small feet and Leo yelling, "What happened?"

"Everything is fine," Sebastian called back, wincing as his voice faltered at the end.

153

They burst into the room a split second later. Aveline turned away, stooping to pick up the scissors.

"I just knocked over the chair," said Sebastian.

"Klutz, as always." Maud clucked her tongue. "But Aveline did a fine job. You look grand. I knew there was a gentleman somewhere under that bird's nest."

"Mum's right, you look grand, Bash! You did a great job, Aveline!"

Aveline swiped at the traitorous tears brimming over her lashes. She should stay and clean, but risking them seeing her so distraught was not something she could handle. "Thank you. Pardon me, I need a moment. I'll be back to clean this up."

"Aveline." Sebastian caught her arm, but she yanked out of his grip, briskly walking away.

"What did you do?" Maud asked pointedly, but Aveline didn't stay to hear the answer.

Foolish, foolish girl, Aveline thought over and over as she journeyed through the halls and up the stairway. On the fourth step up, she halted, white-knuckling the railing. If she strained her ears, she could pick up the soft sobs of the attic ghost. No, it was too much for her heavy heart to bear, and she was not yet ready to return to her room anyway. So, she turned heel, hurrying back down, and did not stop until she reached her painting room. There was no lock, and Sebastian had not put up wards to protect it, but as she sat against the wall, looking at the painting she and Leo had done together, she was certain it was the better choice.

Hugging her knees to her chest, Aveline bowed her head and sobbed.

CHAPTER 18

I'M THE IDIOT

Aveline didn't know how she was going to face them. Sebastian had probably explained what happened, and now they either judged or pitied her, and she was unsure which was worse. He might have been her husband in title, but what were they to each other, really?

What did she want him to be to her?

That didn't matter, not when he clearly did not care about her the way she thought he did. Besides, when did she start caring, and why? It was all too easy to blame it on the binding, but if he wasn't feeling it, then...

She pressed the heels of her palms against her eyes, willing the headache to go away.

Three soft raps on the door temporarily drew her out of her misery. "Aveline," Sebastian said softly. "May I enter?"

She considered keeping silent, but she couldn't be rude to him, and she had to face him sooner or later. Better to do so when they were alone and (hopefully) out of earshot. "Yes."

Sebastian settled beside her, stretching out his long legs and crossing them at the ankles. "I suppose I—"

"I am s—"

They exchanged an unsure glance.

"Go ahead," he urged.

"No, I cut you off, you go first."

"I insist. I am the one who hurt you, so you should have a chance to let me have it before I say anything."

Brow furrowed, Aveline looked down at her clasped hands. "I shouldn't have tried to, um... What I mean to say is that I apologise for trying to..." How was one little word so difficult to say? She blushed.

"You have nothing to apologise for."

Aveline huffed a mirthless laugh. "Of course I do. I nearly..."

"Kissed me?" Sebastian finished for her.

"Well... yes." She was turning into Edith: heartsick over a man she hardly knew. That wouldn't do in the slightest, only serving to break her heart when things didn't work out. Besides, she needed to return to her family and try to secure a good match. There was to be no happy ending between them—Aveline would not take more from Sebastian than necessary, and asking him to stay married to her so she could send his money to her family was distasteful. He had enough responsibilities as it was.

Sitting up straight, Aveline forced herself to make eye contact with him. "Sebastian, I apologise for trying to kiss you."

The corner of his mouth twitched, not quite turning into a smile. "Are you sorry because you would have regretted kissing me or because you think I did not want you to?"

Is he teasing *me?* "I think it's rather obvious you didn't want it."

Sebastian ran a hand through his hair. When it settled, it no longer obscured his features. "I suppose it looked that way... I bungled this splendidly."

"What do you mean?" Aveline refrained from trying to read into his responses. She would let him explain instead of jumping to conclusions again. Being mortified once was quite enough for the day.

Shoulders slumping, Sebastian sighed. "I am rather terrible at... this." He gestured between them. "Being vulnerable with people, I mean. There are so many who come in and out of our lives that it makes me nervous to create connections that break once the person succumbs to their curse or..." Trailing off, he broke eye contact.

"Or?"

Another heavy sigh. "There is no 'or', unfortunately. I have yet to truly help someone, but I imagine they would leave if they had their curse broken. There is no reason to stay."

I could stay, Aveline thought, entertaining that lie longer than she should have. As much as she was coming to like the three of them, could she see herself abandoning her family to stay here, constantly enduring the whims of the castle and the monsters that found their way in?

Or were locked in the attic?

"So, I came here to apologise. I'm the idiot."

Aveline blinked. "You are?"

"I am. I... I'd like to get to know you better, Aveline, for however long we have until we break your curse."

If this was the best they could do with what was available to them, then why would she turn it down? "I'd like that too," she agreed with a small smile, which he returned, making her heart skip a beat. "You seem certain we'll find a way to break my curse. How is this different from the others?"

Sebastian studied her, pausing as if to weigh his words carefully. "It just... feels different. I always have hope for the best, but there is something about you that I... I have complete faith that you will find a way."

His sincerity hummed in her soul, a note that soothed her. He might not have been right, but at least he believed what he was saying to be true. He believed in her. Not what she had to offer or what he could use her for, but *her*, as a person.

"You are far more than you realise, Aveline." Hesitantly, Sebastian reached out, running his thumb across her cheekbone. "I promise, you will find a way." Even after he let his hand fall away, the warmth lingered.

They sat in comfortable silence until Aveline asked, "When are we going to retrieve the other magic artefact?"

He raised a brow. "I thought we already discussed waiting. You need to heal."

The castle creaked, the floor wobbling beneath them before

settling. It was even eerier, being human in this castle. Leo grew up in this, but Aveline still marvelled at how he remained unnerved for the most part. Sebastian gave her hand an assuring squeeze.

"We might not have time," she protested.

"We can wait a bit longer."

"You said yourself that the castle is unstable and unpredictable. For all we know, it could move tomorrow. Or in the middle of the night while we sleep. Not that we'd be able to sleep through that..."

His expression shifted, the muscles in his jaw flexing. "It's much more dangerous to go back out there with you being human. I won't stop you from going, but neither will I hide the fact that I fear for your safety." His grip on her hand tightened, as if he could protect her just by holding on.

For having confessed that he was terrible at opening up to people, Sebastian had his heart on display, just for her.

Aveline threaded her fingers between his. "I worry about yours as well. You are always tired, and when you came back with bruises and cuts, I... I do not want to drain you any more than I already have. I want to be of use. I might be risking myself to do it, but you've already risked far more than any of us." She implored, "Let me help you. Please."

Pink dusted his cheeks, drawing another smile out of Aveline.

"All right," he relented. "If we are still here tomorrow morning, then you and I will talk about braving the cavern once more."

"Very well."

Sebastian smiled back at her. "In the meantime, I thought I might show you the library, if you're still interested. Meredith seems to have calmed down and is open to meeting you... as long as you refrain from touching the books without her consent."

Aveline raised her free hand in oath. "I promise to be on my best behaviour."

"That remains to be seen," he teased, and stood, drawing her up with him. "Come along, before she changes her mind."

Dim light poured out of the library doorway, provided by a plethora of candles carefully covered by glass encasings that kept them from dripping wax onto anything. Despite the door being halfway open when they arrived, Sebastian knocked. "*Babushka*, we are here. May we enter?"

Unsure what the term meant, she raised a questioning brow at Sebastian.

"If you must, but be quick about it." The voice sounded much closer than Aveline anticipated. When Sebastian opened the door fully, they could see Meredith floating over an ornately carved desk that was full of stacks of papers of various sizes. Short-statured with a full figure, the woman looked as though she might be too short to sit at the desk, unless she found an abnormally tall chair. Luckily, she was a ghost and could hover as she pleased.

I need to learn that trick when I turn back into a ghost.

As they approached, Meredith did not bother to look up at them, her transparent fingers running over a letter. "I cannot for the life of me, boy, understand why your father lacked organisational skills *and* had a penchant for harbouring the most useless scraps. I thought he was supposed to be a well-respected member of society."

Sebastian went rigid. "He was not my father."

Meredith peered up at him from over the rim of her petite-framed spectacles. She removed them and straightened, casting a cursory glance over Aveline before returning her attention to Sebastian. "His marriage to your mother says otherwise, no matter how much you loathe that fact."

Aveline considered reaching for his hand to comfort him, but decided that might not be the best timing. Instead, she curtsied. "I am Aveline..." She stopped short. Being technically married, it would be odd to use her own last name, but she wasn't sure how Sebastian would take to her using his surname. So, she ended with, "It is a pleasure to meet you, Meredith."

"Is it? Here I thought I was a crotchety old woman who drives everyone away so I can spend time alone with my books. I'll have to try harder."

"*Babushka*," Sebastian said in a warning tone, "Aveline is a friend. Please treat her as such."

A knowing expression crossed the woman's wizened face. "As you wish, Lord Sebastian." The honorific came out like a jab. He winced but quickly recovered, schooling his features.

"Come now, follow me and do not wander," Meredith insisted. "I'll know if you even breathe on one of the books." She moved fast, skirts rippling like she were actually walking instead of floating. Her white hair was pinned up in a tight, neat bun, not a hair out of place, and the dress she wore reminded Aveline of what her grandmother used to wear.

Aveline did as she was told, keeping a few paces behind Meredith and avoiding touching the books, even though she longed to read just one. Sebastian sidled up alongside her, knuckles brushing the back of her hand in a silent question as Meredith droned on about her organisation strategies and why they did not work and why *this one* would.

In answer, Aveline slipped her hand into his and was rewarded with a flicker of a smile.

They crossed rows upon rows upon rows of bookshelves that each had ladders, and as they made it into the centre of the library, Aveline got a better view, noting that every wall was also lined with shelves that were full to the brim, and reached the ceilings. All except for the far wall, where a large stained-glass window depicted a single red rose surrounded by a thicket of thorns. She imagined what it might look like when the sunlight came through it, and decided she was going to try to come again if she got the chance.

Edith would live in this room if she could. Her sister would pour over the pages, insisting that all of the siblings gather by the window to hear her read the stories aloud, using dramatic voices that often had them in stitches. Timothée would bake mouthwatering treats that would be consumed within minutes. Jeanette would insist on braiding Aveline's hair and then Lottie's, unbothered that they were painting and sewing. The twins would poke and prod each other during the parts that didn't have their full attention, which is where Edith's comical voices seemed to be more present, drawing them back into the story.

"Over here is the fiction section," Meredith said, gesturing. "My daughter had more of a whimsical mind than I, which I came to terms with since it got her reading. She influenced Lila, gifting her books and trinkets as if she were her mother instead of her aunt. It might have irritated me, but I did appreciate getting to see Lila, even if she couldn't see me."

"Meredith is Lila's grandmother, but she passed before Lila was born," Sebastian whispered to Aveline.

"I am your grandmother as well, as you like to call me." Meredith pivoted to face him. "Marriage is just as strong as blood, child. I liked my son little more than you did, but we are family."

"It is not you I have an issue with being related to." He spoke calmly, despite the jaw twitch. "It was my mother he wanted, not me."

Surprisingly, Meredith was quiet for a few moments, her gaze turning soft. "He wanted Lila as well, I think, but not as much as he wanted a boy of his own. He did not realise that he already had a perfectly good heir, if he'd only have let you take on the family name." Without waiting for his response, she turned back around and proceeded to talk about the tomes they had managed to salvage from the ruins of an ancient city. Aveline soaked it all in, the history Meredith shared, the ambiance the candlelight offered, the comforting ache of being reminded of her siblings. How she wished she could show them this place, to see their faces light up with excitement and joy.

But when she peeked at Sebastian, his expression remained stoic, borderline tense, his gaze lost in faraway thoughts. He obviously loved his sister—and his mother, from what she could tell—but what of the rest of his family? She couldn't imagine hating her father, even if she were not related to him. Edith was from their mother's previous marriage, and their father doted on her just as much as he did the rest of the children. To him, Edith was his child, blood-related or not.

Who could not want Sebastian?

"I think I have shown you quite enough for today," Meredith concluded, leading them back towards the door.

"Thank you very much. I have never seen such a beautiful collection." Aveline's heart sank, but lifted again as the ghostly woman replied, "Perhaps you could visit again for the rest of the tour."

"I would be delighted."

Stone-faced as ever, Meredith nodded. "Go on now. Get your bride something to eat, boy. Her stomach is making all sorts of pitiful sounds."

Cheeks burning, Aveline bit the inside of her cheek.

"Thank you, *Babushka*." Sebastian dipped his head in farewell. "I'll bring her by again tomorrow or the day after."

"Not tomorrow. I just had a clever idea of rearranging the classics by depth of tragedy, so that should take me most of the day." She gestured them away as if they were birds perching too close to her picnic.

As they left the library, Aveline noticed Sebastian relax the further away they got. She stored her questions for later, instead keeping hold of his hand.

CHAPTER 19
WHERE IS YOURS?

Leo, Maud, and the hounds found Sebastian and Aveline shortly after their trip to the library. They'd barely reached the main hall when Leo skidded to a halt in front of them. Glancing down at their interlocked hands, the boy beamed.

"There you are, Aveline. I'm glad Bash found you, and you seem to be in better spirits. I know, since you're out of bed, let's play a game! I'll hide first, but I'll let Bash and Mum help you since you don't know the castle as well as we do."

"How magnanimous of you," Aveline said, trying to keep up with the quickly-strung-together sentences. *The twins would adore playing with Leo.* She could easily imagine them being the best of friends and getting themselves into a lot of trouble in a short amount of time.

"But stay downstairs," Maud ordered, much to Aveline's relief.

"All right. But you can't use magic to find me." He crossed his arms and looked pointedly at Sebastian, who promised, "I'll refrain." Aveline doubted he would have anyway, given how many more important things he needed to conserve his magic for.

Appeased, Leo said, "Close your eyes and count to fifty!"

Aveline did, listening to the patter of his feet and the dogs' paws as they scampered after him. They grew more distant until there was nothing left but the creaking of the castle, which was just loud enough to give her pause. What if they really didn't have tomorrow to find the other magic artefact? What if it was the one Sebastian had been seeking over the years, however long it had been?

"Here we come!" Sebastian yelled, then waited, as if he thought Leo might respond.

"I think he listened this time," Maud mused. "His normal spots are the vents and cupboards. Once he managed to squeeze underneath one of the sofas, and another time he climbed onto the roof from one of the balconies. Took us hours to find him."

"That would have terrified me." Aveline ambled down the hall alongside Maud and Sebastian.

"At first, we were happy to have a little reprieve from his shenanigans, so we took our time. But we got more nervous the longer it took to find him, and after the roof incident... Don't look so worried, Aveline. He slipped, but Sebastian got him down safely, just a few scrapes on him. We learnt we had to be specific with rules. This boy lives to find loopholes."

"And trouble," Sebastian tacked on. With each candle they passed, the flames flickered to life, lighting their way. "He would keep every ghost, spirit, and ghoul if we let him."

"It's bad enough that you haven't banished Titan."

Aveline almost tripped at the mention of the creature. *Of course* they had known all about his visits.

Sebastian raised a brow at Maud. "He needs at least a few friends outside of us."

"But a ghoul?" She wrinkled her nose.

"I admit, a ghoul is not the best option, but Titan has been docile. Everyone deserves a chance."

The conversation ceased abruptly. The trio searched the rooms one at a time, checking every place the child could possibly manoeuvre himself into. Aveline tried not to stare, but she found her gaze drifting toward Maud, awestruck at the way she moved through objects and walls and doors with ease. She knew she must look the same as a ghost, but it was different to watch someone else disappear and reappear without warning.

How long has this been her reality? Aveline lingered, letting her fingertips run along the edge of the cabinet and across the drapes. She even welcomed the slight throb in her ankle, anything to remind her that, for the moment, she was grounded in reality.

"He's not here either," Maud said. "Do you suppose he went to the kitchen? He might have wanted a snack to hold him over until dinner."

Following her hunch, they ventured into the kitchen. Just before they reached the doorway, a dog whimpered and Leo hissed, "Quiet, they'll hear you." Aveline smothered a laugh with the back of her hand and was about to let Sebastian and Maud take the lead, but he tugged on her wrist, inclining his head in the direction of the noise.

Aveline tiptoed towards the pantry and eased open the door. Solas and Luna stood at the far end, sights trained on the top shelf, where Leo sat, curled up so his head didn't hit the ceiling. He munched on biscuits, crumbs spilling onto his clothes. "Rats, you found me."

"It was a clever hiding spot." She tried not to wince as he clambered down, foregoing the ladder. "It might have taken us longer had Solas and Luna not given you away."

"That's true." He jumped the last few feet, landing gracefully. "Fair's fair. Your turn to hide, and we'll find you." The hounds nosed at his arms, and he caved, sharing his snack.

"My turn to hide?" She knew how to play the game, but the idea of hiding by herself, where something could be lurking... Sebastian had put wards around the castle, so she was safe as long as she didn't snoop through his magic artefacts, wherever he was storing them. The last thing she needed was another curse cast on her.

"Yes, you found me, so you get to hide. We'll find you." Leo held the biscuits out of reach with one hand, covered his eyes with the other, and began to count. As Aveline pivoted and made her way back through the kitchen, she passed Sebastian and Maud, who joined the boy.

Where should I hide? Thankfully, the candles were still lit down the hall, so she opted to keep to the illuminated, previously ventured path. Ideas for hiding spots flipped through her mind, but she dismissed all of them. Wouldn't it be easy for them if she were to use a place they'd already searched when trying to find Leo? If she was going to play the game, she was going to do it properly.

But that meant stepping into the darkness. Aveline hesitated at the edge of the light, where it turned to grey before succumbing to pure black. If she took a candle with her, they would easily see it... unless she took a few turns and possibly got herself lost in the process.

Leo's counting reached thirty.

Where is your sense of adventure? Edith would have asked with a wink. As if she could feel her sister pulling her along, Aveline snatched a candle from a sconce and slipped around the corner. Just like in the foyer, there were darker squares on the walls in between the doorways, and just about as many rooms, all of them shut. Instead of investigating, Aveline fled further, trying not to jump at every noise the castle made. She took another turn, then another, too nervous to pick a spot when their footsteps and voices echoed.

Her competitive spirit urged her on, reasoning that, if nothing else, she at least would be hidden from them for a little while with how far she'd gone. She didn't recall it being so large when Sebastian had given her a tour, but he had probably kept it brief, not wanting to bore her with an endless amount of rooms to inspect. Even with a map, she imagined it would be easy to get lost with everything looking the same.

Until it suddenly didn't. There were fewer doors, and the rug stopped partway down the hall, as if guests were not expected to venture this far. Or anyone, for that matter. There was no artwork, and no faded sections to indicate that there had ever been any, but there were also no windows for sunlight to affect the wallpaper. The hallway narrowed, and Aveline halted, finding herself at a dead end. At the furthest reaches of her vision was a door with a simple handle, nothing ornate like the others.

I should turn around. But she kept staring at it. What could have been kept off to itself like this? Was this the room Sebastian used to store the magic artefacts? She had imagined something more hidden, perhaps in the basement, sealed with plenty of locks and spells.

From what Aveline could hear, the others were far enough away that she could go back the way she came and still have time to find a decent hiding place. Instead, she took a step forward, then another, then another, her mind tumbling over itself trying to imagine what could be in this secluded room. If Sebastian did not want her in it, it would be locked, or at least warded—

The cold metal knob turned without resistance. Cautiously, she stepped inside and shut the door behind her.

Her candlelight cast a multitude of shadows across dust-covered frames. The painted faces stared at her, none of which carried a hint of joy. All had dark hair, with similar round faces and petite noses.

Leaning forward to get a closer look, Aveline hissed as wax dripped onto her hand, making her drop the candle onto a rug. She snatched it back up, stomping on the spark trying to burst into flame. It sputtered out into a thin line of smoke that dissipated within a few seconds, but her hammering heart continued. She doubted Sebastian would care that there was a tiny burnt spot on a dusty old rug in a storage room, but she decided to tell him as soon as they found her.

Taking extra care, Aveline knelt down to better assess the paintings. One was of a portly woman with a plethora of gaudy jewellery. None of her rings matched, one mirroring Sebastian's, a square-cut emerald on a silver band. But other than their dark hair, the woman and Sebastian shared no similarities. *Reginald Alexander Blaise* read the painting of a man with cold, sharp grey eyes and a frown that would have made the Grand Duchess proud. His facial hair was neatly trimmed, contained to his jawline. Was this Sebastian's father? His attire looked contemporary enough for her assumption to make sense. *He was not my father*, Sebastian had said, as close to anger as Aveline had ever seen him. She hadn't known he could express anger like that, not with the understanding and kindness he showered on all of them.

But she knew better—she knew how it was to keep the intense emotions locked away, suffocating them until they briefly came up for air, and then shove them back down again. Only... here, she had felt like she could breathe, relax, examine her anger and sadness and guilt and worry piece by piece. They were not vicious monsters trying to consume her from the inside out, but rather injured animals that needed tending to.

The likeness of Reginald Alexander Blaise bore into her, judging that no one who looked upon him was good enough. If the painting were any indication of how he was in real life, Aveline could see why Sebastian did not like him. Quite possibly hated him. Meredith and Sebastian had spoken as if this man was long dead, and there seemed to be no grief there.

How lonely it must be, to know there would be no one to mourn for your passing. Maybe that was why his ghost did not linger in the castle.

Aveline moved on, inspecting each one as she sought out what she truly desired to see. If every family member had been painted—by the sheer number of them, it seemed likely—then there was bound to be one of a young Sebastian. Her mind conjured ideas of what he would look like, with big brown eyes and messy dark hair... or maybe it was lighter when he was a boy? But she was certain he would not have the same cold expression. There was too much light and life in Sebastian to be hidden.

Shifting some out of the way, Aveline moved toward a dust sheet covering a pile. She crouched down, lifted it, then stopped.

The familiar brown eyes belonged to someone else, a little girl. She bore great resemblance to her family, but there was undeniable relation to Sebastian as well, her frame petite and the set of her mouth soft and kind, like she could burst into a grin at any moment. The same hint of a smile Sebastian had flashed at Aveline too many times to count.

Lila Vivienne Blaise read the inscription at the bottom. Keeping the candle a safe distance away, Aveline traced the side of the girl's face. How had she died? And when?

"Aveline?"

She jolted, jumping to her feet and stumbling backwards. Sebastian caught her wrist, and she sucked in a breath as the candle slipped from her grasp again. Before it could hit the floor, the flame expired, leaving them in utter blackness. A split second later, tiny lights like stars filled the room.

"I didn't expect you to be in here," he said, looking around with a pained expression.

"I was trying to find somewhere good to hide, so I kept going further down the hall and then I saw this door and I... Well, I suppose I forgot we were playing." She picked up the candle and offered him a sheepish smile. "The artist is impressive, very realistic. I have not yet found one of you, though."

As his gaze drifted to Lila's painting, Sebastian's grip on Aveline loosened.

"She was so pretty," Aveline said. "You two look a lot alike."

"Are you calling me pretty?" He joked half-heartedly; his voice was far too raw for her to joke back.

"Where is yours?" She debated offering him a hug. Was it too soon after their almost kiss? Would he take it wrong? He had held her before, but would he let her hold him?

Sebastian lowered the dust sheet again, like he was tucking his sister into bed for the night. Then he turned away, silently urging her out of the room. "I never got one done."

"Never?" There were multiple of some people, while Sebastian had nothing to honour his memory?

He paused at the door, the lines of his back and shoulders tense. "Lila's father didn't much care for me. There was no reason to pay homage to a bastard sired by his wife's previous lover, a commoner with no name or title to speak of."

The little lights dimmed, but Aveline could still make out Sebastian's silhouette. She stepped towards him. "I'm sorry," she whispered. "I didn't mean to cause you distress."

"You didn't," he said. "Leo is still looking for you. I can leave and pretend I didn't find you, if you'd like."

She could feel his desperation to leave this room, as much as his desire for her to come with him. She revelled in the fact that he took comfort from being near her as much as she did him.

"Or we could end the game now and start on dinner," Aveline suggested. "I can help this time, that way you won't have to spend magic to make it edible."

He exhaled in a half chuckle, half sigh of relief. "That is a splendid idea."

CHAPTER 20
AT LEAST WE GO TOGETHER

After a decently cooked dinner, Aveline forced herself to part ways with Sebastian and return to her own room. They needed rest, and she doubted she'd be able to if he were near.

At this point, as she stared up at the ceiling, she wondered if she'd be able to sleep at all. The bed was comfortable and her body sunk into it, but her mind raced through a forest of thoughts, taking one trail then another, and another. They went in circles, her irritation quickly rising.

Scrape, clink-clink-clink, scrape, clink-clink-clink.

Aveline threw off the blankets and put on a robe, hurrying towards the door before she could fasten it properly. Her ankle smarted as she half-limped down the hall after Titan and Leo.

"Hush! Mother will hear you," the boy chastised. Then, spotting her, he called out, "Aveline! Come to join us?"

Titan halted to look over its shoulder as Aveline hurried to Leo's side. He took her hand, and she smiled despite the pang in her heart. *He's never been able to do this with his mother...*

"I think there are some biscuits left," he said. "Titan would love those."

"You mean that you, Solas, and Luna didn't gobble them all in one sitting?" Aveline teased, earning a lopsided grin from him.

"I could if I wanted to."

"I believe you."

They stopped speaking until they were past the attic stairwell. In the near darkness, the sobs carried an even heavier weight, crushing Aveline's chest until she found it hard to draw breath.

"I wish we could get her to stop crying," Leo said glumly. "I don't like her being so unhappy all the time."

"Who is she?" Aveline dared to ask.

"I don't know. Bash says she doesn't mean to hurt anyone, but she's too dangerous to be let out." He shook his head. "I'd go mad, being locked up in one room for so long."

"Anyone would," she murmured in agreement. Was the attic ghost the same as Aveline, someone cursed by The Heart Thief? Was there a bond between her and Sebastian too? She reminded herself that Sebastian had said he'd never married before, but that didn't assuage her worries. Clearly, the attic ghost meant something to him if he were keeping her here.

Sebastian does not belong to me, not truly. Aveline thumbed at the wedding ring. *He does not belong to me, but if I had a choice, I would belong to him.*

She stopped in her tracks. Was she actually falling for him? It didn't matter—she couldn't allow herself to think that way. There were too many obstacles between them, too many curses and secrets and responsibilities for this to last. Not to mention he'd rejected her kiss.

Maybe I am just as reckless as Edith.

Tremors rumbled underfoot with each step Titan took. Leo was unaffected, tightening his grip on Aveline as she tried not to stumble.

"You'll get used to it," he tried to assure her.

Sebastian stood outside of the kitchen, leaning against the frame, mouth quirked in amusement. Realising he'd been caught, Leo squeezed Aveline's hand. "Bash! I was just... he was hungry and I..."

Chuckling, Sebastian straightened. "Come on, feed him quickly so he can go on his way and you can get back to bed." He ruffled Leo's hair, and the child rushed into the pantry. The hounds skirted around Titan as the creature hunched down to fit through the doorway.

"You don't seem frightened of Titan," Sebastian remarked, watching Leo toss the ghoul biscuits and crackers. Solas and Luna whined until they, too, got some.

"He terrified me the first time I saw him," Aveline said. "I'm still wary, if I'm being honest."

"As am I. But he seems civil for the moment, and I hate to make too quick a judgement on anyone."

Her focus drifted to the wizard. How many people had made judgements without knowing anything about him, or never even having met him? Outside of this castle, he was known solely as The Magic Collector, someone mysterious and to be feared. Would others change their opinion of him if they met him, or would they refuse to give up on their preconceived notions?

Warmth sparked low in her gut as he caught her staring at him. The beginnings of a smile formed. "What is it?"

Aveline shook her head, not knowing how to convey her thoughts. "Judgemental is not a word I would use to describe you."

The air between them became heavy. She waited, itching to know what he would say in response, to see a glimpse into his thought process.

"I am curious to know what words you would use to describe me."

She paused. Odd had been the first one to come to mind after their initial encounter, but so had entrancing and intriguing and curious. Now...

"Are we having a party in the kitchen?" Maud interrupted. She moved past Sebastian and Aveline, catching sight of Titan trying to stick his head into the pantry. "Leonard, what are you doing out of bed at this time of night?"

"It is technically morning!" Leo called back, manoeuvring his way under Titan's bulky forearm. "Very very early morning, according to the grandfather clock in my bedroom."

Maud crossed her arms, eyes narrowing. "How does that help your argument?"

"Well..." He ran his hands through his tousled hair, the shorter strands sticking up at random angles. "I did go to sleep when I was supposed to, I just woke up extra early."

Aveline bit the inside of her cheek to keep from laughing. His response was something she would have expected from her brothers, or her sister Jeanette, who was notorious for finding loopholes when they suited her.

If Jeanette had been the one cursed instead of Aveline, she would have already found a way around the curse, if not broken it.

Maud did not share in Aveline's amusement. "Back to bed," she snapped. "Go on."

Leo opened his mouth as if to argue further, then thought better of it and scurried off with the hounds. Titan tried to follow as well, but Maud scowled. "You've had your fill. Leave, and let the child sleep."

The creature's deep rumbling noise made the glass of water on the counter vibrate, but he turned and walked towards the wall, vanishing through it.

"I'll make sure he's in bed," Sebastian offered, but Maud shook her head and sighed.

"I'll do it. Thank you for making sure he was safe. Good night. Or, as my little monster pointed out, morning." She snorted and left.

Aveline and Sebastian made eye contact, each expecting the other to speak. She waited for the anxiety to creep up on her, but it was nowhere to be found—she did not fear what he was thinking, only curious to know what it was. Thus far, Sebastian had proven himself to be trustworthy, looking for ways to help her instead of using her like some of the other men in her life. His pauses were not used to plot against her, but rather to consider his words carefully, or so she suspected.

If I could just see into your mind for a moment, she thought wistfully, knowing that even a glimpse would not be enough to satisfy her.

"I would say we should return to bed," Sebastian started, "but I'm afraid sleep has eluded me thus far tonight, so I'm sure lying in the dark with nothing but my thoughts would be entirely unhelpful."

Aveline tilted her head to the side, trying to read his expression: tired, solemn, yet there was a hint of contentment amidst the turmoil. "What thoughts plague you?"

"Far too many, I wouldn't know where to start." He took a deep breath, exhaling slowly as he sank back against the doorframe. "Is it safe to assume that you couldn't sleep either?"

Aveline nodded, trying not to let her gaze dip down to his unbuttoned collar, where the chain of his necklace peeked out, the one that held a special key that only added to her plethora of questions. "I can never escape my thoughts."

He did not pry like she hoped he would, giving her the excuse to do the same. "It's a bit too early for breakfast... We could have tea."

Neither of them moved to make it.

"Or..."

"Or?" he pressed.

"Would you be willing to go after the artefact now? If you need rest first, I understand—"

"I'm fine. As I said, sleep is far from me anyway." He looked her over. "Although if we're to go now, might I suggest you change into a shirt, trousers, and boots? They'd be easier for you to move in than a dress, I think. You can borrow some of mine."

It was Aveline's turn to take in his tall, slender form. There was a decent amount of height difference between them, and she had curves. "Are you certain they'd fit?" She prayed she'd refrain from blushing.

"We'll make alterations as necessary." Standing straight, he offered his hand, which she accepted, happy to let him lead her, and even happier still that he wasn't refusing to let her join him. "I should probably also re-enchant our rings and fetch the glasses for you."

"And I should probably tie up my hair."

"If I'd have waited any longer for a haircut, I could have tied up my hair too."

She teasingly nudged him in the side with her elbow. "It was already long enough to tie half of it back."

"Then it's a good thing you helped me when you did." He brought her up the stairs, taking the first door past the attic stairwell. The ghost's moans were muffled, like she lacked the energy to give into her sorrows.

"Who knows how much longer I'd have looked ridiculous," he said.

"You never looked ridiculous."

He smiled back at her, and walked into his room. It took a moment to sink in that it was his bedroom, this fairly empty place with barely any furniture, just a bed, a full-length mirror, and an armoire. No artwork, no desk, no nightstand, nothing to indicate that anyone spent time here. She could have just as easily believed that he slept somewhere else.

On the untouched bed, Sebastian laid out a button-down shirt, trousers, socks, and boots for her. Then he excused himself, saying that he was going to retrieve the glasses while she changed.

The door clicked shut. Aveline set about untying her dress, gritting her teeth at the sounds of the ghost in the attic. Why did he choose this room, near her? Was it to ease the guilt of her suffering, or to make her feel like she wasn't alone? Did she even know he spent his nights here—did she even know him?

With nowhere else to put it, she neatly placed her dress on the bed and slipped into Sebastian's clothes. She had tried on her father's things once when Edith got them all to perform a play for their extended family one holiday, deciding that Aveline would be best suited as Prince Charming because she was old enough to remember a lot of lines but young enough that she didn't yet have her womanly figure. She'd felt like she was swimming in her father's clothes then, and while this was not nearly as dramatic, Sebastian's were ill-fitting, too much fabric in some places and barely enough in others. The shirttails almost reached her knees, and tucking them into the pants only helped marginally. The socks were easy to put on, but the boots were going to fall off unless she planned on shuffling across the cave. She'd hoped to avoid Sebastian spending magic to tailor the clothes, but it couldn't be helped.

Aveline was securing her blonde hair up in a bun with a ribbon when Sebastian knocked. "Come in."

"I found the—" Sebastian halted, hand still on the doorknob, barely suppressing a grin.

To her frustration, she blushed. "I know, none of it fits right," she said as though in apology. "I hate to make you use more magic, but I fear I'd be useless like this."

He set the glasses down. "Easily remedied." As his fingertips trailed down her shoulders, the clothes shifted to fit her. "Better?"

Aveline twisted to get a better view of herself in the mirror. With the way the clothing formed around her frame, there was no mistaking her as a man, except perhaps if someone saw her at a great distance... and she wore a hat to hide her hair. She'd thought it would feel constricting, but there was something freeing about not carrying weighty petticoats and skirts.

Focus. Aveline leant forward to examine her hair, and tucked a few strands back into place. Satisfied it would hold for the time being, she glanced up to find Sebastian looking at her. A muscle in his jaw twitched, his stance was rigid, he did not seem to be breathing—although neither was she. She couldn't.

They locked eyes in the mirror. The intensity his bore sent a jolt of excitement through her, but she dared not move. She had read things wrong last time, had sent him recoiling...

His cheeks reddening, Sebastian took a step backward and cleared his throat. "We, uh, we'd best hurry. That is, if we don't want... Leo to sneak out of bed and find us before we've had the chance to..."

Aveline schooled her features and faced him. "I think I am better prepared now," she stated, proud of how even her voice sounded. Surely if she showed nervousness, it would only serve to make him worse.

Sebastian handed her the glasses. "I have to warn you again that this will be even more dangerous," he said, barely audible. He rolled up her sleeves, and then pressed her enchanted ring between his thumb and forefinger. Aveline did her best to remain still, breaths small and short, hitching with each brush of skin.

"I want you to call for me even if you're uncertain of the level of risk." Sebastian twisted the ring, and it grew warm, humming like it was happy to be re-enchanted. She wondered if Sebastian had intended for her to feel it this time.

"I will." Even after he let go of her hand, the ring had a faint pulse of its own, and it thrummed through her veins. *Is that Sebastian's heart-beat I feel?* After all, it was supposed to connect the two of them, drawing them back together. She hadn't felt anything from it before... *Is it because I'm a human now, and I was a ghost when he gave it to me?*

Gently, he raised her chin so that she'd meet his serious gaze. "No artefact is worth your life."

With an almost smile, Aveline responded, "Or yours."

Brow furrowed, Sebastian stepped backwards. The distance was only a footstep, but it felt far greater. She struggled to come up with something to say, to smooth over whatever just put a wedge between them, but Sebastian's expression softened, and he said, "With both of us worrying about each other, this is probably the best course of action. If we are to brave the dark, at least we go together."

Aveline took his extended hand, holding the glasses tightly in the other. She itched to put them on, to see if he still wore the illusion and try to figure out what it was, but refrained; Sebastian was slowly opening up to her, and she would not risk losing this tentative trust between them by forcing him to share parts of himself he was not yet ready to.

Together, they traversed the poorly lit hall, creeping further into shadow until they reached the back door. Sebastian paused. She could barely make out his silhouette, and she was grateful for the black hiding her face from him. She could only imagine what he read in her expressions.

"Are you ready?" he asked.

"Yes," she said. "At least we go together."

The door creaked, and Sebastian pulled her through before it clicked shut behind them.

CHAPTER 21
NOT WITHOUT YOU!

The darkness suffocated her. Being human left her terrified, knowing there were creatures out there she couldn't see that could hear and smell her, and she was entirely at their mercy. *I should have thought of that sooner,* Aveline lamented. *I should have asked Sebastian to at least cover my scent for me.* She shook the thought away. He was spending enough magic as it was. They'd retrieve the magic artefact and come out of the cavern unscathed. They had to.

Despite her trembling fingers, Aveline managed to put on the glasses. Nothing illuminated or sparkled or shimmered; she stifled a sigh. It would have been far too easy.

To her surprise, Sebastian kept hold of her hand, leading them outside of the castle gates. Soft dirt that sunk under her boots quickly turned to immovable stone. Aveline winced, waiting for her footfalls to resound, but they didn't. Had Sebastian enchanted them to be soundless? Knowing him, it was likely.

The moment they crossed into the cavern, the temperature plummeted. The air was earthy and stale and cold, chills snaking along her skin, making her want to roll down her sleeves. It made sense that ghouls, demons, and evil spirits resided in a place where it was a struggle to draw breath.

They sneaked further, Aveline listening intently to the dripping water, trying to catch any sounds of potential danger. Sensing them before they sensed her and Sebastian would give them that much more of a chance of survival.

The further in they traversed, the harder it became to still her chattering teeth. Aveline suspected that, if she could see at all, there would be clouds of white at their lips. Somehow, Sebastian remained warm... or maybe she had gone so cold that he felt that way in comparison. *Whoever he is doing this for, he must love them a great deal.*

The dripping continued, echoing. She jumped as her shoulder scraped against the rough wall. Sebastian stopped, and she squeezed his hand to assure him that she was fine. Unable to stop trembling, she let her fingers brush against the uneven wall as they continued, giving herself something else to focus on other than the monsters her mind was conjuring. The abrasive stone with its grooves and bumps wore at her numb fingertips.

Abruptly, the wall vanished. She swallowed. Slow, steady breaths rumbled through the open space and reverberated back.

Sebastian halted, as tense as she was. Aveline scanned the room, hoping he hadn't sensed the magic artefact here. Her stomach clenched as she caught sight of faint sparkles deeper in the darkness. Was this creature guarding it? Was it going to be feasible to get the magic artefact without alerting it?

Something pressed against her mind, warm and light and gentle. She went rigid, warring between her curiosity and fear. An image flickered in her head, of a young girl with dark hair and big brown eyes running beside her in a field of tall wildflowers. The girl grinned, holding up their intertwined fingers... fingers that belonged to a young boy.

"*Stay here,*" Sebastian's voice entered her thoughts. "*Let me investigate first.*"

Before she could try to figure out how to respond, he pulled away from her tight grasp, and the vision disappeared. Soundlessly, her heart pounded against her ribcage as if trying to beat its way out of her chest. Aveline stared at the shimmers, trying to decide if she should listen or go after him. *Surely,* she reasoned, *if he were in need of help, I* would've heard something more from the creature by now. She fidgeted, picking at her nails, and considered taking a few steps back so she could touch the wall again. But he'd told her to stay *here*...

Aveline flinched as Sebastian touched her elbow. He entered her mind again, bringing with him a vision of a broad hand coming down on Aveline's head, shoving her to the floor. She caught sight of herself in a mirror on the other side of the room: a young man with dark hair, a bruise blooming along his cheekbone—

"A ghoul is guarding the artefact," he explained. *"We'll have to wake it one way or another. It will sense any magic I use."*

The vision shifted, this time to a beautiful woman with long black hair, mouth pinched, grey eyes lined with tears—

"Don't go by yourself," Aveline thought, hoping it would reach him. She felt silly doing so, but didn't dare speak aloud for fear of waking the beast.

"I was merely preparing you," he replied, to her relief. *"The moment I use magic to pry the object away, we have to run. It will wake and chase us."*

The woman appeared in her mind again, kneeling, reaching towards Aveline with bony fingers, her weighty grief making her face and body all hard lines and sharp angles. *"Moy mal'chik..."*

"I understand." The quicker she assured him, the quicker he'd get out of her head and the visions would leave her. *"Let's hurry."*

The woman disappeared. Blue smoke-like symbols formed in the black, glittering as if in anticipation. They were foreign, something she'd never seen, and yet she somehow knew that they meant *pull, object, forcefully, quickly, quietly*. Once completed, a satisfied hum reverberated in her mind and a gust of wind rushed by.

The creature shrieked.

In a cloud of vibrant colours, the symbols exploded. Aveline stifled a yelp as the image in her head shifted to another woman, this one with ash brown hair, thin frame, and a swollen belly. Chin held high, the woman's piercing blue eyes targeted her.

Maud...

Racing footsteps pounded towards them, claws scraping the ground, breaths releasing as manic growls. Sebastian yanked on Aveline's hand—

"This is not charity," Maud declared with a stern look. *"If we are going to stay with you—"*

A mighty paw struck. Ripped from Sebastian's grasp, Aveline tumbled and slid, scrabbling for purchase, anything to make the spinning stop. Her shoulder collided with stone; she hit the ground. Tiny dots of white danced in her vision as she forced her lungs to take in a breath.

The ghoul's roar shook the cavern. Its stomping sent showers of dirt atop Aveline, making her cough. From its frantic movements and desperate roars, she assumed Sebastian had its attention... or it was seeking them out.

She blinked rapidly, trying to clear her vision, only to realise that the impact had knocked the glasses off... and her mind was no longer connected to Sebastian's. She wanted to call out to him, to see if he was hurt, but she latched onto hope as the ring pulsed. He was alive— they could deal with injuries once they escaped.

If they could.

Aveline swept her hands across the floor, knowing the odds of finding the glasses were slim at best. She got nothing but scrapes for her efforts.

Another roar, followed by a yip in the distance. There was no time to worry about the glasses or the artefact; either they escaped now or died by stubborn stupidity. Grateful not to be tangled in skirts, Aveline pushed to her feet. Tremors from the beast's crazed stomping nearly forced her back to the floor. A few shaky steps, then Aveline halted. There had to be something she could do, anything to help. He'd told her to flee to the castle, but she refused to leave him to fend for himself.

Aveline had to call out to him, safety be damned. Besides, every creature was already aware of the scuffle, so her yelling wouldn't change that. She opened her mouth in a soundless shout. She tried again... nothing. And again. Aveline coughed, inhaled, even screamed.

Nothing. He'd not only enchanted their steps, but every noise that they could make.

Sebastian, I want to help you, but I don't know how. Aveline swallowed the lump in her throat as panic coiled in her belly. Being robbed of sight and speech had left her virtually useless, no better than when she was a ghost. *Sebastian!* she shouted in her mind, ignoring the fact that she could not hear him, could not see the visions, could only feel the ring.

The ring.

Think of me, and it will draw you to where I am. What other choice did she have? She could put her hand over her heart, but she couldn't speak his name to bring him to her, to get him out of danger if for only a few seconds. Aveline tried anyway. The creature's rampage continued, and she felt no different. She had to use the ring, to risk danger to find him.

So Aveline gripped the ring, and thought of his kindness and sincerity, of his generosity of spirit, of the way one look from him lit her soul aflame. *Take me to him.*

She expected a tug or an image, but instead she just knew to turn to her right and run, to not worry about tripping or the snarls and pounding of approaching creatures—

Then she saw through his eyes. Saw the wicked fangs latch onto his arm and yank him down, dragging him across the ground as he screamed and fought back. So much thrashing, so much blood. Aveline sprinted to him—

"Run! Now!" Sebastian commanded.

"Not without you!"

Darkness fell again. Aveline stumbled but persisted. She knew she was close, that she was about to find him. Nothing would stop her.

Barks and snarls filled the cave, punctuated by a deafening roar. Something caught her sleeve, but she wrenched away, hearing the tear of fabric before the cold air found her exposed skin.

Pain exploded up her arm, teeth puncturing flesh and ripping and twisting—Sebastian was hurt, she could feel every agonising bit of it, he needed her help—

Aveline collided with something taller than she, and they tumbled backwards. Air whistled above her head. A creature slammed against the wall, raining bits of stone atop her. An arm wrapped around her waist, and that familiar dizziness found her just before the claws did.

Then she was lying on a wooden floor in the middle of the hallway by the back door of the castle. Head swimming, she squinted, trying to make out what she could with the faint light coming from further down. Tangled together, Sebastian held her tightly, face buried in her hair. His frantic heartbeat echoed hers. She pressed closer.

"Sebastian," she breathed, relief flooding her as she realised the enchantments had either worn off or broken. They had made it, they had found each other...

Aveline attempted to jerk away, but he held fast. "Sebastian. Sebastian, let go. We have to tend to your arm."

"I'm fine. Just give me a moment," he said, voice strained.

"Sebastian, you're hurt! We have to tend to it!"

This time he released her. She scrambled to her knees and helped him into a sitting position. If only she had a light so she could see properly. She was no healer, but if she got Maud, maybe she could tell her what to do.

As she reached for his arm, Sebastian shrank away and lifted a hand, a pale blue flame appearing in his palm. Dirt smudges and scratches were all she could find, both of his arms uninjured.

"I'm fine, I assure you. I was just terrified that you'd been hurt when we were separated." He examined the tear in her sleeve.

"But you were hurt." Aveline stared at him through welling eyes. "I saw it. Something attacked you and got your arm and there was so much blood and—"

Extinguishing the flame, Sebastian pulled her into a hug. She rested her forehead against his shoulder.

"You were hurt." Her voice gave way to tears. For years, she had hidden her emotions, and somehow this man drew them out of her without trying.

"I am sorry," he said. She melted against him as he rubbed her back. "I should have warned you about the effects of mind magic. Come, let's clean up, and I'll explain it to you over some breakfast."

Deprived of speech, she merely nodded. Sebastian wiped her cheeks. "I promise you'll feel better after you're cleaned up and have some food and tea in your stomach."

"I'm sure," she agreed weakly. "I'm sorry we didn't get your artefact. We could try again later, if you'd like."

"No need." From his pocket, he retrieved a bronze cylindrical item a little longer than the width of his palm.

"That is the artefact? How did you get it away from the ghoul? Why did it want it?"

Sebastian uncrossed his long legs and stood, pulling her up with him. "I'll explain. But first, breakfast."

CHAPTER 22
I WOULD LIKE TO PAINT YOU

Aveline washed and changed quickly, eager to be away from those dirty, torn reminders of what they'd endured. She chose a cream-coloured dress with short sleeves and a simple ivory sash that ran under her breasts and tied in the back. Something light and airy, in hopes of pulling her out of the mood the darkness had put her in. It reminded her of her youngest sister Lottie, who tended to wear softer tones and carried with her unwavering peace and contentment wherever she went.

Leaving her hair down to dry, Aveline hurried to Sebastian's study, where they'd agreed to meet. The door was cracked, but she knocked anyway.

"Come in." Sebastian was bent over the scattered papers on his desk, but as she entered, he walked to her, gesturing at the trolley of pastries and tea parked between the two lounge chairs in front of a warm, cosy fireplace. "I hope this is a satisfactory breakfast. I'm not accustomed to eating at..." He glanced at the grandfather clock. "...four in the morning. No wonder it's so quiet: Leo is fast asleep."

Aveline wouldn't have called it *quiet*, not with all of the rumblings and the cries. They grew louder each day, just enough to take notice, to build her anticipation that they would return to their proper place anytime now. But Aveline kept this to herself, and sunk into one of the chairs. Sebastian took the other, not quite easing into comfortability.

"It is quite satisfactory," she assured him, secretly debating if it would be rude to scoot her chair closer to the fire. She supposed it was close enough, that the warmth would soon replace the bone-aching cold.

Sebastian poured a cup and offered it to her. "Have as much as you like."

There was a variety of pastries, some glistening with brown sugar, others oozing with honey, all warm and soft, melting in her mouth. A bit of jam dripped onto Sebastian's chin. Aveline hid her amusement by taking a large, unladylike bite that would have sent the Grand Duchess into hysterics. The pastries were gone within minutes, and Aveline was on her second cup of tea before either of them spoke.

"I imagine mind magic took you by surprise," Sebastian started, carefully choosing his words. "I scarcely use it—haven't in years—so I'd quite forgotten how disorienting it is."

She sipped her tea and frowned. Strange, how it'd been hot just a moment ago... Her belly warmed, and she disregarded it, returning to the subject at hand. "What is it I saw? Were those your... memories?"

"Yes. To mind-speak, you have to connect your mind to the other person's, which means they get access to your memories, and vice versa."

"You... You saw my memories as well?"

He shifted in his seat. "A few of them. Nothing I think you'd find embarrassing, if that is your worry. The first was of you baking in the kitchen with one of your brothers, from what I could tell."

"Timothée," she whispered.

"The treats looked mouth-watering. In another, I caught a glimpse of you fixing your sister's hair... Edith, if I recall correctly?"

"Yes." To wash down the rising emotion, Aveline took a long pull of her tea, which had turned lukewarm and nearly tasteless.

"I also saw twin boys. They were causing mischief, and only stopped to ask you why everyone was so upset. You told them that it was nothing for them to worry about, that the adults would sort it out." His gaze remained on her. "If I may ask, was that about the money trouble?"

She sighed. "Yes. Father had just told us at Mother's insistence, and the twins happened to see how upset we were at the news. That was when Edith started to tell a lot more stories, hoping to bring happy distractions where she could."

He reached out, and she accepted his hand. "You'll see them soon, and I'll help you put everything right if I can."

"After everything you've done for me already? At this rate, I will be forever in your debt."

"I haven't helped much yet, but I have hope that we will break your curse soon." He looked at their hands, and his smile disappeared. "I can explain my memories you saw, if you'd like. I have to admit curiosity about them. And a touch of nervousness."

Aveline tightened her grip. "I saw... you running with a little girl in a field of wildflowers. I assume that was Lila."

Throat bobbing, he dipped his head in confirmation. His thumb traced circles on her knuckles.

"I also saw a woman with dark hair. She was so sad, it made my chest feel like it was going to break in half."

"My mother," Sebastian whispered hoarsely. "Julianne."

"Another memory was of Maud," she said, hoping to lift his spirits before bringing up his wounded arm. That couldn't be helped, since he knew she saw that, but perhaps she could forgo the last one—she did not want to think about someone hitting Sebastian. "She was standing at the entrance of the castle, rain-soaked and pregnant."

Sebastian huffed a laugh. "I'd met Maud on one of my trips to the city. She was passing through, hoping to find work and somewhere to stay. Everyone treated her like an outcast, either ignoring her or telling her she should have found a husband before carrying a child. At first, when I offered her a room, she turned me down because I told her I didn't expect anything in return. She changed her mind and insisted I let her help clean the castle and cook meals as payment."

"That sounds like her."

"What else did you see? Other than the attack, I mean?" At Aveline's hesitation, he said, "I saw five of yours, which means you must have seen five of mine. It'd give me a little peace to at least have the chance to explain them to you." His dark eyes lifted to meet hers again, as if he had gathered enough courage to face what was coming.

She cleared her throat. "There was... a man. I think he was your stepfather. He was... hitting you."

Sebastian released a deep exhale. "That happened a few times. He hated that I am illegitimate, hated how my mother loved me as much as Lila, hated that I have magic... There was a time when I wondered if he would have grown to love me had I been normal, but I find that difficult to believe. He wanted a son of his own, a 'pureblood' without magic. The closest he ever got was Lila, and he did not treat her half as well as he should have."

There were no words. Nothing to say to make any of it better. So Aveline squeezed his hand and said, "I am sorry."

He squeezed back. "The man is gone, and I refuse to let him haunt me in death like he did in life. As for the memory with my arm... It happened not long after Maud moved into the castle. We teleported, and the monsters had found a weakness in the wards. I protected her, but my arm was badly injured. She nursed me back to health."

Aveline waited, feeling there was something unsaid, disliking the way he rushed through the words. "Does it still hurt?"

"Sometimes it feels like it does."

She wanted to pry further, to know what it was he was carefully manoeuvring around. Was it scarred and deformed? Was that why he wore an illusion? Did it not move as fluidly anymore, and that was why he tended to use his left hand most of the time?

The weightiness in his eyes stifled the urge to pester him with questions. She would not force him to be more vulnerable with her than he was ready to be.

"I am sorry they were unhappy memories," Sebastian said. "I never want to burden you."

Aveline made sure he was looking at her before she stated, "You are never a burden to me."

He smiled. "I did see a much happier memory of yours. Of you painting a scenescape."

"Which one?"

"It looked like a night sky with two stars. It was beautiful."

Aveline inhaled slowly. She could still hear her sister speaking, could still feel the paint on her fingertips as Aveline brought it to life as she saw it in her mind. "That was the Tale of the Lonely Stars," she told him, turning her gaze to the flames. "It might have been one that Edith made up, because I could never find it in any of our books."

"What was it about?" He'd stopped tracing circles on her knuckles, and she almost asked him to do it again. At least he hadn't let go.

"As the title suggests, there was a lonely star. It did not shine as brightly as the rest, and so it felt left out, unseen." As she recounted the tale, Edith's voice danced through Aveline's mind and tugged on her heart. "One day, it decided to travel across the sky in search of a spot it could brighten, if only a little, and that is when it found its match, a dim star that hovered over a tiny island.

"The dim star's light flickered and waned, and yet it persisted, determined to give what it could to the small village on the island. The lonely star saw this and joined the dim star, and together they brightened the night sky, reminding the island that they, too, were not overlooked or forgotten.

"Tale has it that, from the island, only one star can be seen on most nights, but once or twice a year, you can see the second star."

Sebastian stayed silent. Aveline didn't have the courage to look at him, afraid the tears would slip if she did. "Strange, how a bittersweet story somehow managed to lift our spirits. I think she wanted us to remember that, if we have each other, then that is all that truly matters." Bitterness welled within her, but she instantly squelched it. Edith had her reasons for leaving, and no matter what, Aveline loved her. The feeling lingered regardless, leaving her in unease. *I will get to speak with her again, and I will hear what she has to say about it.*

"The painting and the story match well," he said. "You are both talented."

"Thank you." She cleared her throat. "If... If it is all right, I would like to paint you. All three of you, really, and perhaps Meredith as well, if she would consent to it." While it was not a lie, she truly longed to paint him, to see how many colours it took to replicate those eyes, to play around with techniques to get the stubble at his jaw just right. Would she be able to capture a scrap of his essence?

Sebastian's brow furrowed. "You want to paint us?"

"Only if you are comfortable with it," Aveline stressed. "Looking at the paintings in the storage room gave me the idea. I think it is a horrible injustice that the inhabitants do not have their likenesses on the walls."

He did not reply until she made eye contact. "I think that is a wonderful idea."

"...However?"

"However, I do have a favour to ask of you." Sebastian shifted in his seat so that he faced Aveline a little better, not once letting go of her hand.

"Yes?" she pressed, hoping not to sound too eager.

"If the others agree, I would appreciate it if you painted me last."

Aveline heard the unsaid *Do not ask me why* as if he had whispered it in her ear. She pondered over the possible explanations, most of which had to do with his arm. Would he show it to her? Were there scars left behind he was self-conscious about?

Do not make him uncomfortable by asking questions. He will explain when he is ready.

"As you wish," she consented, then tightly pressed her lips together before the questions could spill out anyway. They stared at one another.

What are you thinking? Aveline wondered. *Can you feel this pull between us, whatever it is? I pray that it is not the bond, because I could not bear it if this longing is a lie, and yet I pray that it is, so that it will be easier to leave when the curse is broken.* She shoved the thought of that away, too heavy of a burden to carry. They had here and now, whatever this was, and it would have to be enough.

Sebastian let go of her hand. "We should see if Leo is awake. Knowing him, he probably never went back to sleep, and I'm sure Maud would appreciate a break from his antics."

Aveline quelled her disappointment, and stood to set the teacup and saucer on the trolley when they slipped through her fingers, shattering on the floor. The rings followed suit, clinking as they hit the wood.

No heartbeat, no breaths, no warmth, no cold...

Aveline was a ghost once more, as transparent as ever. The dress had thankfully gone incorporeal with her. Amidst her disappointment and frustration, she was grateful not to be stuck in the wedding gown again.

Gradually, she raised her sights back up to Sebastian.

"It is all right," he assured her. "We knew you were bound to turn back into a ghost, so don't lose hope. This just means that you've healed from your wounds."

Hope was a hollow-sounding word to her, a mockery. Aveline had grown too comfortable with being human again, and this was a cold bucket of water dumped on her head, reminding her that she was no closer to being free of the curse.

"I'm sorry about the teacup and saucer."

"No apologies necessary." Sebastian's fingers wiggled; the shattered pieces lifted into the air and seamlessly fit themselves back together before landing on the trolley. Then he stooped down to retrieve the rings, slipping them into his vest pocket. "I'll keep these safe for you, for the time being."

"Thank you." Half of her wanted to ask him to bind them to her, but the other half won out with the logic that it would be silly and unfair to ask him to spend magic on something frivolous. She'd find a way to become human again, of that she was certain. Then she could wear them again until...

Sebastian took a step closer, just out of reach. "Aveline...?"

She looked up at him. "What was the final memory you saw?"

"...What?"

"You spoke of four memories, all to do with my family. What was the fifth one you saw?"

A few moments passed before he answered, "You were at a ball with your sisters and friends, wishing that Prince Ivan would take notice of you and ask you to dance."

Of course, out of all the memories he could have seen... She would have blushed if she were human. Why did he hide it? Did he not want to dwell on it, or did he want to save her from feeling exposed?

"I'm sorry you didn't get the chance to be with the one you care for."

"I'm not." Sebastian's lips parted in question, but she pressed on before he could speak: "I fancied him as a child, just as all the girls our age did. He stopped meaning anything to me a long time ago. I do not love him, and never have."

The fire went out, mere smouldering embers. She could only make out his silhouette, but she knew his gaze was locked on her.

"What of Prince Alexei? I know it was a betrothal of convenience, but I... I should not be asking these things, but I suppose I hate the idea of having pulled you away from someone you... love."

The final word was barely audible; Aveline's breath hitched, a spark zipping down her spine. Was she still a ghost, or had she returned to being a human? She could no longer feel the cold of the room or the ache of her sore muscles, but Sebastian's voice thrummed in her veins like she still had a pulse.

"I never knew him long enough to love him, although I doubt that I would have even if there had been time," Aveline said, finding that the darkness provided some level of safety to be vulnerable. "Did I... Did our arrangement pull you away from someone?" She steeled herself for the answer. Was that why he rejected her kiss? He had said that he didn't get close to people anymore, but was there someone he had left behind? Or was the ghost in the attic a past lover he was trying so hard to resurrect?

"No," he stated huskily. Seconds passed, but he did not say more. Aveline was at a loss for words. There was something there, something unsaid ...

Sebastian drew closer. Aveline tilted her head back to look up at the shadowy shape of him. A tingling sensation danced across her skin—

"Bash! Aveline! Where are you? It's time for breakfast!"

Sebastian released a shuddering sigh that skated across her cheekbone. He reached past her and opened the door, letting in candlelight from the hallway. "Shall we?"

Out of instinct, Aveline reached for his hand, but Sebastian had already started walking toward the dining room, his hurried pace stilted. She thought to call after him, to ask if she had said something wrong, then decided against it. From the quick glimpse at his face, she had noted the storm in his dark eyes...

...and it terrified her.

CHAPTER 23
THAT MIGHT HAVE BOUGHT YOU TWENTY MINUTES

Sebastian was already seated at the dining table with Leo by the time Aveline arrived. He did not quite meet her gaze, eyes flicking upward then back down again at the bowl of porridge. Aveline halted, trying to decide if it'd be better to give him space, but for what reason, she had no idea. Had he wanted her to be in love with someone else? Had he somehow heard her thoughts and been scared off?

"Why are you a ghost again?" Leo asked. "I thought you were getting better." His shoulders slumped. "Bash, what's wrong? What can we do to help her?"

"She healed from her wounds. We'll find a way to break the curse, no need to worry." He absent-mindedly stirred the lumpy, odd-coloured porridge but did not partake in eating, did not bother to fix it.

Maud's sympathetic expression pinched as she shifted her attention to Sebastian. Then, in a gentle tone, she said to her son, "My lion cub, we forgot sugar and milk. Would you be a dear and fetch them?"

Leo's frown deepened, but at his mother's raised brow, he scurried off to the kitchen. The hounds remained, sniffing at the edge of the table.

"What happened between the two of you?" Maud demanded.

"Nothing happened," Sebastian answered.

"Rubbish. You're sulking, and Aveline hasn't moved from the doorway. Something happened. Whatever it is, you need to fix it."

He pushed his chair back and stood. "We had an eventful morning. I just need some rest. If you'll excuse me."

"We do not. Sebastian, sit back down!"

He exited through a different door, not once looking back. Aveline stared at the carpet, fully aware that Maud had refocused on her.

"Well?"

Aveline suddenly wished for hunger gnawing at her belly, for exhaustion to weigh on her, anything to distract from the ache in her chest. "We did have an eventful morning, retrieving another artefact, and we chatted and then... I don't know."

Leo returned with a jar and a pitcher, droplets of milk slipping down the side, and scanned the room. "Where'd Bash go?"

"He is tired and wanted to rest," Maud said, gesturing for Leo to sit and eat.

With a huff, the boy flopped back into his seat. "I know it's going to be time to go again soon." He propped his elbow on the table so his chin could rest on his hand. "Castle's getting restless again, and so is that ghost. She was crying so hard last night, I couldn't sleep."

"It will be pleasant to be in the light again." Maud glanced at the windows like she expected the sun to come out of hiding. "This much darkness is suffocating."

He picked up his light stick and waved it around half-heartedly. "This was fun at first, but now it's bloody tiresome to—"

"Watch your language," his mother chastised with a frown. Aveline stifled the surprised laughter bubbling up her throat.

"It's not *that* bad of a word."

"It's bad enough. I cannot believe Meredith hadn't hidden that book in a better spot, or locked it up entirely, knowing you'd be visiting."

"You know I'm good at finding things, Mum. Picking locks too. Meredith didn't stand a chance."

She sighed. "Yes, I am well aware, my gremlin. Luckily, Sebastian found a way to hide it so you couldn't get it."

"Only because I don't have magic," Leo grumbled, tilting his spoon so the porridge plopped back into the bowl. Aveline imagined that, if Sebastian were there, he would have either dissuaded the boy or changed topics, so she opted for the latter.

"If I may interrupt," Aveline said, finally entering the room, "I had an idea of sorts I was hoping you would agree to."

Both perked up immediately, giving her their full attention.

"With what?" Leo asked. A glob of porridge fell to the floor, where Solas and Luna licked it up, then stared at their master.

"Well, as you know, painting is a hobby of mine, and it seems to help me become more connected to the tangible world. If you'd be willing, I'd like to paint portraits of you."

"Us?" Maud tilted her head as Leo shouted, "Fantastic idea! Oh, and I could do one of you, Aveline. Come on, let's go!" He shot out of the room, ignoring his mother yelling for him to deal with the dishes first.

Sighing, Maud said to Aveline, "Are you sure you want to paint him? I'd be shocked if you can get him to sit still for more than ten minutes."

"Maybe I'll paint him as he's painting me."

"That might have bought you twenty minutes."

They shared an amused smile, but Maud's waned. "I am glad to help, but is that the only reason you want to paint us? The garden flowers or landscape might be more interesting."

The two of them walked side by side. Maud's description of the suffocating darkness rushed back to Aveline as they crossed the foyer and headed towards her painting room. The dim sconces that barely lit the hallway were preferable in comparison to the unending pitch of the cavern, but Aveline still craved the light of the sun. When they returned, she resolved to stay outdoors for one whole day, even if she couldn't enjoy the warmth and the breeze. Leo would certainly need it, and Aveline hoped it would restore Sebastian and draw him out of whatever mood he was in.

"Those are interesting, but I'd like to paint the three of you, and possibly Meredith, too, if she'd allow it. This place needs some life, and sometimes art can give that certain spark."

Maud nodded, gaze distant. "You're right. I asked Sebastian once about why, in a place as grand as this, there's no artwork on the walls. He said he removed unwanted reminders, and I haven't had the heart to pry since. Although I did get a little more information out of Meredith, who said the castle had been full of portraits of the Blaise family, extending back dozens of generations. But then she prattled on for hours about the family history, and I finally had to excuse myself, telling her I was fighting a bout of morning sickness." She glanced sideways at Aveline. "I was pregnant with Leo at the time. I'm not sure how much of my story Sebastian has told you."

"Not much. I know you arrived here pregnant with Leo, and that you turned down his offer to stay here at first."

Maud gave a half smile. "Well, considering Leo was conceived out of wedlock and I was disowned by my family, I didn't have a lot of options, but I also wasn't about to trust just anyone... Although Sebastian does have a certain quality about him, something that makes you inherently trust him. I thought at first that it was an act, but he's a very genuine person, which makes him a terrible liar—not that he does that often. He'd rather deflect than speak an untruth."

So I have noticed. His illusion gnawed at her. She nearly caved and asked Maud about it, but stopped herself. Sebastian didn't give details about Maud, so Aveline didn't think Maud would so easily give up details about him. This wasn't high society where gossip and secrets were currency and weapons to be stored until the perfect moment to bring about someone's downfall.

"That soft heart of his has gotten him hurt too many times to count," Maud said, voice quiet and tender, "and yet I cannot fault him for it. I love him like a brother, and if he lost that soft heart, everything he is would cease to exist." Outside of the painting room, she paused and looked over her shoulder at Aveline. "From what I've seen, your heart is a mirror of his. Whatever happened between the two of you, I can almost guarantee it wasn't your fault. He is battling some inner demons, just as you are, and if you give him time, he might share the burden."

Aveline floundered for a reply. What made Maud think that she was anything special? Had he opened up to others in the past? He'd said he struggled to, so what was so different about this time? The marriage bond? "He told me that he does not open up easily."

"No, but I have seen more of his light since your arrival than I have ever seen. You ignited something in him, Aveline. You cannot convince me that you are nothing special."

Aveline glanced down the way they came, the way that would take her to his room, if she were so inclined to seek him out. Or would he be in his study? Or playing the piano?

"You can go to him, if you want."

"No, I... We were going to do portraits."

Maud smiled. "Go to him. Portraits can wait, but you might regret it if you take too long to speak what is on your heart."

She hesitated. He'd wanted a moment alone, but when there was last something between them, Sebastian had given her a little bit of time before seeking her out, hadn't he? The worst he could do was tell her to go. Nothing major, really... except that imagining it made her want to give up on the idea entirely.

"I'll tell Leo that you'll join us shortly." Maud vanished through the door, leaving Aveline alone in the poorly lit hallway.

Do I regret more the things I've spoken or left unspoken?

She was halfway toward the main staircase before she'd realised it. Wishing she could knock instead of intruding, Aveline first called out to him in front of his study. Since there was neither an answer nor a hint of light under the door, she pressed on despite the loud laments coming from up the stairs. *I'll check the piano room first, and only venture up to his room as a last option.*

Relief welled within her as soft notes reached her ears. Aveline hurried, then made herself stop in front of the door. The music was slow, sad, reminiscent. "Sebastian?"

The sudden silence was unbearable. She started to consider leaving when he said, "You may enter."

She stepped through the door, still finding it unsettling how there was nothing to feel, nothing to bar her. But that was quickly forgotten when she caught sight of Sebastian hunched over the piano, shoulders slumped, expression weary. A thousand tiny lights filled the room, twinkling like stars.

"I don't mean to disturb you if you don't want company," Aveline said, "but I wanted you to know that, if you do want to talk, I'd be happy to listen. I'm not sure what is weighing on you, but if it's something I did, I—"

"It was nothing you did." Sebastian patted the bench beside him.

"I can't—"

He offered his hand, and she reluctantly settled down next to him. As if he could sense her fear of becoming incorporeal again, he tucked her hand into the crook of his elbow and moved closer so they were flush against each other. The intimacy of the action made her blush.

She felt the muscles in his arm move as he began to play once more, coaxing the bittersweet melody out of the instrument with just one hand. "Your sister's story of the stars inspired this song," he said. "I find there is something fascinating about being lonely together." The song slowed to a stop, the final key ringing out until there was nothing more to give. Only then did he lift his hand away and reach for her free one.

"I hope you can forgive me. I just needed a moment to..." Sebastian stared downcast at the keys. The lights flickered out one by one until there were only two remaining, so close that they seemed to be reaching for one another.

Aveline rested her head against his shoulder. "You do not have to explain." *As much as I want you to.*

Her heart swelled as he copied her, resting his head on hers. "I want to," he whispered, voice raw. "There is so much I want to tell you, but I'm... I'm so afraid, Aveline."

What could terrify a man who braved what he did, who fought demons and spirits and ghouls, travelled through time and space, and watched those he tried to help succumb to their curses? She wanted to ask, but instead, she promised, "I will be here to listen when you are ready."

Aveline sat with him in the darkness, hoping that there would be enough time left for her to fulfil that promise.

CHAPTER 24
THAT IS NOT A QUESTION FOR ANYONE ELSE TO ANSWER

Leaving Sebastian to rest, Aveline returned to find Leo contentedly painting what looked like the hounds.

"Sebastian brought some paints and canvases," Maud explained, gesturing to where they were stacked neatly against the wall. "He said he'd retrieve more next time he was in the city."

Neither of them discussed the fact that it'd probably be soon, given how the castle and the attic ghost were acting. Leo sighed at the splotches that the minor quakes forced him to make. "It's ruined."

"Not necessarily." Aveline moved beside him to better inspect his work. "You could make those into muddy paw prints."

He beamed. "Thanks, Aveline!"

Leaving him to continue his painting, she approached the supplies. *It will not hurt to try,* she told herself.

...But it might hurt to fail, the doubts whispered. She had done it before, but was it because Sebastian had helped?

It was unfair of her to keep relying on him. She reached for the paintbrush, imagining the feel of it, the weight, the way she could roll it between her fingers while she decided what to paint next or what colour would suit the portrait best.

Her fingers went straight through it.

She fought the urge to huff. After a week or two of being corporeal, how could she be so separated from the tangible again?

"Mum, look, I put a biscuit in Solas's mouth!"

"I see that, dear. Are you going to paint yourself as well?"

"Ooh, I could be doing a magic trick!"

They're not paying attention to you. Try again. Smooth wooden handle, fine bristles she could thumb through... It didn't even budge. *When do you truly feel seen for who you are?* Sebastian had asked, as if it were that simple.

I am Aveline Clément, daughter of Duke Raphael and Duchess Colette Clément, sister to Edith, Jeanette, Lottie, Timothée, Amos, and Alan. They see me and love me.

But they were far away, ignorant of her current situation and whereabouts, and she was no closer to grabbing that paintbrush.

"Have patience with yourself."

Aveline whirled around, finding Maud behind her. Leo slowed his painting, curiously watching them. "It has been nearly two weeks," Aveline protested. "I thought... I thought it'd at least be easier. I'd managed to nudge the curtains before, but now it's as if I do not exist."

"I understand."

She winced. Of course Maud would know. This had been her nature for years, never having any sign of hope that things could change for her. "I apologise, that was insensitive of me—"

Maud shook her head. "I understand what you mean. We do exist, but it can be taxing, feeling as though you are doomed to watch the world continue on without being able to affect it. To no longer belong."

The paintbrush clattered as Leo dropped it on the table, and it rolled off onto the floor. His paint-covered fingers reached for Maud but went straight through. "Mother, you belong with me and Bash and Solas and Luna and Meredith. So do you, Aveline. You both do."

With a sad smile, Maud hovered her hand over her son's head like she was trying to smooth his hair. "You are right, my little genius. I'm glad to have you to remind us of that."

Aveline's heart ached as she witnessed mother and son exchange looks of adoration. Could she live with seeing her family but never being able to hug them, to brush her sisters' hair, to playfully elbow her brothers, to kiss her mother's cheek?

"Thank you, Leo," Aveline said. "I, too, am grateful for the reminder."

He grinned from ear to ear. "You're welcome! I'm done painting now. Wanna play hide-and-go-seek with me?"

"You need to wash up first," Maud interjected.

"Aw, Mum!"

"I'll take no arguments. You cannot tell me your natural skin colour is green."

"Your mother is right," Aveline stated, garnering a scowl from the boy. "You wash up. I have something I need to do first, and then I'll come find you so we can play."

Maud might not have been able to touch the tangible world as a ghost, but Leo had reminded her that there was someone else who could.

MEREDITH'S GRUMBLING COULD BE HEARD JUST OUTSIDE OF THE library, but Aveline did not let that deter her. "Meredith, it is Aveline. May I speak with you?"

A tense hush fell. "Fine. You may come in, but do not touch anything."

If I could, I wouldn't be asking for this discussion.

Neat stacks of books filled the room, leaving the bookcases mostly bare. Meredith floated above the ground, scowling at them. The silence stretched out, to the point where Aveline weighed the pros and cons of clearing her throat to remind the woman of her presence.

"What brings you to the library?" Meredith questioned, not bothering to look at her as she sorted through titles, mumbling authors' pedigrees and how well they upheld their family names. "If you were hoping to get a more in-depth tour, I'm afraid you'll have to wait another day or two."

"Actually, I was hoping to ask for your help."

The murmuring ceased. The woman pivoted, locking in sharp eye contact with Aveline. "When did you leave the living to join the dead?"

I have no idea why I'm holding to societal politeness when she is so very matter of fact. "I'm not dead. The Heart Thief cursed me to become a ghost." She recounted the tale as briefly as possible, explaining why she'd been human when Meredith met her. *She likes histories and details. Perhaps that will get her interested enough to humour me.*

While Aveline spoke, Meredith scrutinised her from head to toe. Then she harrumphed. "I told the boy to rid the world of that witch, but he does not listen to me. Instead, he takes in those unfortunate souls like he can do something to ease their suffering—in reality, he only prolongs it."

Aveline took a moment to process the information. She'd known there were others, but she hadn't stopped to consider that their curses varied. Of course they would, since everyone was different; The Heart Thief had stated what was most desirable to Aveline, so surely she had done that with the others. How many had Sebastian tried to save?

"Will you help me?" Aveline hoped that matching Meredith's more direct approach would convince the ghost librarian.

"I fail to see where I can be of service to you. I *am* dead, and have not been human for more than a decade."

"I want to be able to touch the physical as you do."

"Of course you do. Have you not asked Sebastian for help? Certainly, the boy has enough magic to solve all of the world's problems. At least, he seems to think it can, but it got us into this mess to begin with."

Refraining from sighing, Aveline replied, "Sebastian has taken on many things, and I do not wish to be more of a burden."

They stared one another down. There was no true reason to be nervous: For once, she had no secrets to hide, no agenda to disguise. She had told the complete truth, and Meredith would either believe her or not, help her or not. If this ended poorly, it wouldn't be for a lack of trying.

"Why must you become human again? Is the marriage bond not enough?"

"It has kept me here thus far, and I don't think I am fading, but I would like to be completely human again, not relying on Sebastian. It's taxing for him, and—"

"I am not talking about Sebastian. I am talking about *you*. What is so important to you? You act as though time is of the essence."

Aveline swallowed. "I wish to see my family again. They are in major financial trouble, and I was supposed to save them... would have saved them, had I not been cursed."

Meredith *tsked*. "If that were all, you would have had Sebastian send money. We have no shortage of it."

"I cannot ask that of him."

"Why not? It is the duty of the husband to take care of the family, especially his wife's family."

"It is not a *real* marriage..." Aveline stopped short, losing what she was about to say as those words sunk into her soul. Not real... The emotions felt real, but that could be a trick, nothing more. They had spent time together, begun to be vulnerable with one another, so it made sense that affection had blossomed between her and Sebastian. But love?

"It is not real?" Meredith snapped a book shut. "Come now, you were being so honest with me. I have little tolerance for liars."

"As I told you," Aveline said, finding her voice again, shaky as it was, "the marriage was a decision made out of necessity, to keep me from fading. I cannot ask something of him like that, not when we agreed that this was temporary. My family needs me, and I would hate to see one of my sisters be forced into marrying someone to save the family name and treasury."

"Yet you would willingly offer yourself?"

"Yes." She had, and would do it again if given the chance.

With a ponderous nod, Meredith placed the book on a shelf. "Tell me about your family."

Aveline hesitated. The other ghost was not stalling; this was some sort of test of worthiness. "My parents are Duke Raphael Clément and Duchess Colette Clément," she started, recalling how Meredith had given all sorts of details about the Blaise family last time. The woman seemed to like family history, especially random facts. "Mother was married prior, and gave birth to my older sister Edith. When her first husband died in a war, she was given to my father."

"Do your parents love one another?"

"They do now. Mother said they didn't always." Truthfully, she couldn't recall a time that they didn't seem to be the perfect match. There was always more than enough love; even when they were upset with one another, they couldn't bear to be apart long. Father claimed he always loved her, even when she seemed to not know he existed.

Methodically, Meredith organised the books, levitating to reach the higher shelves when necessary. "How many siblings do you have?"

"Six. Three sisters and three brothers." Aveline listened to the ticking of the clock as she waited for Meredith to continue drilling her for answers. There was nothing in the woman's face or stance to judge whether she was passing this unproclaimed test or not. "I miss them terribly," she added.

"How far would you go for them? What lines would you not cross?"

Aveline stilled. What did Meredith want to hear? She had demanded the truth, much as Aveline disliked not being able to give a clear answer. "I... I haven't a clue. But I do know that if they are provided for and safe, there are many sacrifices I can learn to live with."

Another long stare had Aveline feeling like the old ghost woman could somehow weigh her soul to ascertain her worthiness.

"Please. I do not know how I would repay you, but I will find a way—"

Meredith batted at the air like she was swatting away a fly. "Pish posh. I'm not asking for payment, girl. I just want to know that my efforts will not be in vain."

"So... you will help me?"

"Yes. Family is everything, child." Abruptly, Meredith stalked down the aisle, leaving Aveline to hurry after her. "You said The Heart Thief cursed you based on your desire to be seen and loved?"

"Yes."

They made it to the other side of the library before Meredith took a sharp left and floated upward to better see the titles of books. She retrieved one and returned to the ground, thumbing through the pages. "Hmmmm... Not quite what I was seeking. I'll need to remember where I sorted the spell-crafting texts, and perhaps the magic histories. I do know, from what Sebastian has told me, that understanding what the spell—or in your case, curse—is made up of helps with undoing it." She cradled the book against her chest, brow furrowing.

"Sebastian asked me when I feel like I am seen, but that hasn't gotten me far. I can't seem to touch anything unless he aids me." To demonstrate, she reached out to the bookshelf, unsurprised that her fingers went through the wood.

"What did you tell him?" Curiosity lit her features, sparking a feeling of kinship between them. *Is this how Aveline would be, if she were unafraid to voice her wonderings?*

"My family sees me for who I am: a duke's daughter, a sister, a—"

Meredith cut her off, declaring, "Who you are should have nothing to do with other people, at least at the core of it. You are your own person."

I am my own person. The idea tumbled into her, making her take a step back. She was her own person, an individual just like everyone else. But were the threads of her existence so tied up in others that there was nothing left for herself?

"Family is important," Meredith continued. "Friends are important. But you must know who you are for all of those relationships to flourish."

"Then... how do I find myself?"

"That is not a question for anyone else to answer."

CHAPTER 25

THE ONLY PERSON STOPPING YOU IS YOURSELF

Hours slipped by. Aveline accepted Meredith's every critique and suggestion, repeatedly attempting to grab the book off the shelf. No matter how many times she tried, how she pictured picking it up, it was to no avail.

"You're doing it all wrong," she sighed.

"I am doing as you explained!" Aveline replied sharply. "I'm not sure what else to do."

"What I do is different—I am not cursed, I am dead."

"As is Maud, yet she cannot touch the physical world like you do. There must be something different, perhaps something you've never considered, just know innately."

The creaks and groans of the castle filled the silence as Meredith pondered. Aveline's eagerness to learn was quickly being replaced by exasperation that she was worse off than before, now unable to even make something ripple or budge. But giving up was not an option —ever.

"What I do may be of little help to you. I will things to happen, and they do. You, on the other hand, your curse is not about willpower, but emotion, and knowing who you are."

"This is not a revelation to me." Aveline waved her hands as she ranted, "I am quite tired of mulling this over inside and out. Who am I? When do I feel truly seen? When does anyone, really? For most, our roles are predetermined, and there is little we can do but accept them. I knew what mine was, and I was about to fulfil it before that witch came along and changed my entire life. I was known, and seen, and..."

"You did not feel loved," Meredith finished for her. "Not for who you are, but for what you could do for them. You fit into their plans, could bring them something they wanted; therefore, you had value. And now..."

Slowly, Aveline sunk to the floor, sitting amongst stacks of books. "Now, I feel useless." If only she could cry, release this weight on her soul. For once, she didn't want to slip further into being a ghost and leave these feelings behind: She wanted to wallow in them. To understand them, to let them breathe and move. Maybe then she could find a way to deal with them, something better than trying to suffocate them, which only resulted in suffocating herself.

Meredith set a book atop one of the stacks, and then knelt near Aveline. She gently took her hand, and Aveline was surprised to find that she could feel her. It was not the warmth or solidity of flesh, but a comfort nonetheless.

"Your value does not come from someone else, or from what you can do or offer." Her eyes pinned on Aveline, vaguely reminding her of Sebastian's, not necessarily in colour or shape, but in the sincerity they bore. "I pride myself in being an excellent judge of character, and from what I see in you, I can tell that you are priceless. I guarantee that you deserve so much more than whatever fate you thought was unfairly taken away from you."

So close to Hanna's words: *"I fear you are settling, Your Highness. You deserve much better."* It felt wrong to think so highly of herself, and yet Aveline wanted to hold fast to that idea, which reminded her so much of something Edith would believe. In Edith's perception, there were no limits that could stop her; she lived life to the fullest, enjoying each moment and forging new paths when necessary.

But that took you away from us. I am not brave like you, Edith. I fear I am ordinary, all too willing to do whatever makes everyone else happy.

"You are the only one holding yourself back." Meredith patted her hand.

An unsettling truth that conflicted with everything she'd known and believed. There were societal rules, expectations, limitations— how could she be the only one holding herself back?

The castle rumbled and shifted, pitching the books. Some flew through Aveline, scattering.

Swearing, Meredith hurried to her feet. "Moving again! Could you not have given me another day to finish organising?!"

"We should find Sebastian," Aveline suggested, noting the papers that had been on Meredith's desk were now strewn across the floor. *Perhaps it's good that I'm still a ghost.*

"Go, child, if you must! I will stay with my books." Meredith gathered as many as she could into her arms, lamenting where their pages had been bent or torn.

Aveline fled towards the foyer. She held fast to the reminder that they were returning to their time as the tremors continued and the screams almost made her turn back. They were agony, grief, a terrible loss of something one could never recover from. She sped past, relief trickling in at the sight of Maud, Leo, and the hounds huddled together in the centre.

"Where is Sebastian?"

"Bash went to find you!" Leo shouted over the roaring winds, shrieks, and rumblings.

"Which way did he go?"

A beam emitted a resounding crack but kept in place.

"To your room, I believe." Maud stared up warily.

"We might need to move before that beam splits." Aveline looked at the stairs, hating the idea of going anywhere near the attic ghost's hysteria.

"This is where Sebastian has to cast the spell." She moved closer to her son. The hounds whimpered, tails tucking under them, and Leo stroked their heads in comfort, despite his furrowed brow. "It will be the safest place once he's here," she added. For ghosts like Meredith and Maud and Aveline, there was little to fear from the transportation —in theory—but for Leo and the hounds, it was another story entirely.

Maud would not be separated from her son, and Aveline was not about to leave them either.

Knowing Sebastian, he wouldn't return until he found her. Even if Aveline were to hurry, it might have been too late by the time she found him and brought him back to the foyer. She reached for the ring, remembering at the last moment that she was still a ghost and that the rings were in his vest pocket.

Stepping close to the others, Aveline placed a hand over her heart and whispered his name. *Come here, please. Hurry.*

The air in front of them warped. In the next instant, Sebastian appeared, eyes wide. The tension in his shoulders melted a little as his attention locked onto Aveline. Then he refocused on the ceiling.

"The beams are about to split!" she warned.

"They'll hold," he said. "Stay close."

The tempest of wind raged and railed against the walls, but Sebastian's expression was a mask of calm concentration. Aveline wished she had the enchanted glasses so she could see what he was doing, to witness the invisible war clashing about them while he tried to redirect the castle. Instead, she studied his face, ashen and dripping in sweat, his extended hand, the way it trembled, his body, swaying but somehow remaining upright. How much magic was too much to spend? How much rest had he truly gotten in the time she'd known him?

Maud clasped his shoulder; Sebastian's lips pinched into a thin line, but he didn't pull away. He shook more. Praying it would help, even if minutely, she grabbed his other shoulder. Sebastian jolted and inhaled sharply.

"Let me help you." The winds stole the words from her mouth and carried them away. *I know you were wounded on this arm, I'm sorry.* She moved closer, shifting her hand to his chest, over his pounding heart. *Take my strength, let me help you. Please, Sebastian.*

He trembled at her touch, eyelids shuttering halfway closed before opening wide. Something thrummed between them, as if trying to fuse them together. Aveline pressed harder. *Take what you need, Sebastian. I'm here for you. Let me help you like you've helped me.*

Abruptly, the howling winds tore at her skin and clothes and hair.

The pulse between them increased, urging her to him with desperation. Aveline embraced Sebastian, rested her head just below his collarbone, and squeezed her eyes shut as if to block out the tempest threatening to collapse the castle atop them.

"You can do it, Sebastian," she said, knowing the words could not reach him. "Don't give up."

One last shudder, then everything fell silent and still, save for some dust and wood splinters that sprinkled down from the ceiling. Listening to his racing pulse and heavy breathing, Aveline reluctantly began to release him, but Sebastian wrapped his arms around her.

"I need a hug too," Leo interrupted, joining them in a group hug. "Aveline, you're human again! I can touch you!" He grinned up at her, blue eyes bright.

"I... I am..." *I can see.* Aveline scanned the room, taking in the soft light coming through the windows. The candles had been snuffed out and scattered in pieces across the floor, along with a few bits of the chandelier that had broken off. "For the moment."

Sebastian took a step back and ran a hand through his hair. His skin was not quite as ashen as before, but the dark circles under his eyes remained. At least he stood steadily now. He watched her, waiting. After a few seconds, Leo's arm passed through Aveline once more. She sighed. "I'm glad we're all unharmed."

"That is definitely something to be grateful for," Maud agreed, staring up at the beam that barely held together. "We might want to fix that before the next transportation."

"Don't want that coming down on us." Leo shook his head. "That'd hurt."

Sebastian followed her line of sight. "I'll see to it soon, after some rest."

Maud seemed as visibly relieved as Aveline that he wasn't jumping at the chance to spend what little strength he had left.

"I can check the area for you," Aveline offered.

"No need. We're back to where we were before, I just need to figure out *when*. You and I can visit the city tomorrow, see if we can catch some details that might help."

"That sounds like a good plan."

"Go on," Maud urged with a shooing motion. "Get some rest. We'll stay here and keep out of trouble."

Sebastian excused himself, slipping away to his room, and Aveline joined Maud and Leo outdoors. Watching the boy play with the hounds in the gardens, Aveline smiled. For now, she could not feel the warmth of the sun or touch the flower petals or press the dirt under her feet, but she could see it all.

For now, that was enough.

CHAPTER 26
YOU HATE TO LIE, DON'T YOU?

Early the next morning, Sebastian found Aveline walking down the hallway. "Off to the kitchens for breakfast?" he asked, his tone much lighter than the previous day. Sconces had been relit for the long, windowless hallway, but overall the castle carried lighter shadows, more charcoal grey than pitch black. Other than the muffled crying, Aveline enjoyed the atmosphere. For however long it'd last, she intended to bask in it.

"Soon. I was actually on my way to visit Meredith and see how she and her books fared."

Sebastian raised a brow. "You're really brave if you're willing to visit her while she is in a frenzied state of fixing the mess the transport made."

"We are on better terms as of yesterday, I think. I asked Meredith for help affecting the physical world, and she agreed."

She worried his pause meant he was offended, but there was nothing but genuine curiosity when he inquired, "Has it helped?"

"It was only one lesson. The castle transporting interrupted us."

"Ah, that makes sense."

They walked side by side, not quite touching. Aveline considered reaching for his hand but lost her nerve at the last moment.

"Unless you were set on Leo's cooking," Sebastian said, "I'd like to show you a bakery on the outskirts of the city. It's a small shop that doesn't get the attention it deserves, not for how delectable their food is. And we could get what information we need. There's a lot of gossip all throughout the city, but I'd rather remain as far away from the palace itself as possible, if that is all right with you."

"That's probably wise. Will anyone be able to see me?"

"I cannot say for certain, but my guess would be no. When I rescued you from the castle, you said the others couldn't, if I remember correctly."

Rescued. He'd *rescued* her, like a character in a story book, a tale of Edith's. Never before had the image of a hero brought such a smile to her face.

"What is it?"

If she told him, he'd probably brush off the statement. "You're right. I was just thinking how grateful I am that you could see me and help."

His expression grew solemn. "If you held onto my arm, you could go into the city as yourself, but I'd advise against it unless you're willing to risk word of your sudden reappearance getting back to the King."

"If they'd even remember me. They couldn't recall my name after it happened, even though they were talking about me."

"So, they did not truly forget you. There is one positive, if you choose to see it that way."

Aveline mulled it over as they headed downstairs, barely hearing the whimpers from the attic ghost. "We should go now, before Leo wants to join us. I'll remain a ghost, but I do want a taste of those baked goods you mentioned."

Sebastian smiled. "I'll make sure we find a spot where you can turn human and enjoy them while they're still warm. If we hurry, we should get them fresh out of the oven."

Instead of causing a stir by risking someone spotting them walking away from the castle, Sebastian opted to teleport them just inside of the city gates, avoiding the guards posted outside.

"What if others can see me?" She noticed early risers in the distance, readying their shops for a busy day's work. "Leo sees me."

"Leo has the Sight. Maud did too, when she was still..." Aveline waited for him to say "alive", but he finished with, "human."

"That is lucky."

A breeze ruffled Sebastian's hair; he adjusted his jacket. Unlike the brightly coloured shirt she'd first seen him in, he'd chosen discreet attire this time, easily playing the part of a lower lord with enough money to spare but not enough to make him noteworthy. He'd forgone a hat, but his buttoned jacket and gloves would protect him from the autumn chill. Or at least, that was what Aveline guessed, seeing the others in layered clothing, scarves and gloves and hats aplenty. A thin layer of frost covered the ground, but the morning sun that was slowly rising from behind the mountains would melt it within the hour.

"Definitely lucky," Sebastian whispered in agreement, as they neared the stalls and storefronts that were beginning to draw the curtains and flip the window signs to say "open" in flourished script. "If he'd not been able to see and hear his mother, I would've had to figure something else out."

Finding yet another thing to drain your magic. She kept the thought to herself and scanned the city. The Grand Duchess had kept them to the inner portion, closer to the castle, but this area she had seen once, when she'd first arrived to meet Prince Alexei and start their wedding preparations. After being in the higher-class areas for so long, she noted how worn and simple things were here, not gaudily decorated. While she took no issue with any of the stores, these had a homier feel to them, and the shopkeepers' friendly demeanours only added to it. They greeted Sebastian as he passed them, who returned the greetings in kind. Part of Aveline wished she could be human so she could peruse the colourful woven blankets and shawls, the trinkets carved from wood or made with twisted metal, the books and jewellery and artwork—she could have spent hours.

She followed Sebastian into the bakery, admiring its cosy arrangement of seating at small tables, and the plethora of carved animals on various shelves.

A flush-faced woman hurried through a small door from the back and wiped her flour-covered hands on her apron. "Well, good mornin' to you, Aleksander. Been a bit of time since we've seen the likes of you."

Relieved the woman hadn't noticed her, Aveline raised a brow at Sebastian, who ignored her. "Good morning, Anne Marie. I'm afraid I've been a tad busy, but I'm glad to see you and Francis whenever I get a chance."

"Flattery to get some extra rolls?" she teased with a wink. "Aye, that'll work still. Where's your boy?"

"At home this morning, still sleeping. I thought I'd surprise him with some treats."

She wiped her greying hairs from her sweat-slick forehead. "I'll tell Francis to make one of the dog-shaped sweetbreads for him, if you're keen to wait a few extra minutes."

"He'll appreciate that, thank you."

Anne Marie disappeared into the back, the door swinging shut behind her.

"She thinks Leo is your son," Aveline said, keeping her voice low just in case.

Sebastian walked towards one of the corners, pretending to inspect a painted scenescape. "I hate keeping him cooped up in the castle," he murmured, finger trailing down the side of the frame. "Every once in a while, I'll bring him with me into the city, when I can't feel the tug of The Heart Thief's curse."

"She thinks you leave him at home alone? Or do you mention Maud?"

"I avoid mentioning Maud—brings up too many assumptions of my being married and wonderings of why she's always absent." He shrugged. "I tell them his mother is dead, which is true, and that he has a caretaker who looks after him while I'm away, which is also true. Technically speaking." Sebastian shifted slightly to avoid accidentally touching her and making her corporeal. She appreciated that he had kept her within his peripheral since they stepped into the bakery, even if he didn't look directly at her.

"Technically speaking," Aveline repeated. "You hate to lie, don't you?"

"Unless I am mistaken, you do as well." He smirked half-heartedly. "Lies are constricting, painting you into something you are not instead of celebrating what you are. Half-truths... while not pleasant, are much more preferable than creating a falsehood you have to ensure stays intact."

Aveline traced the edges of his profile with her gaze. *Surely, he is too good to be true,* she thought. *There has to be something about him I have not seen, something that would show me why falling in love with him would be a terrible idea.* Unfortunately, nothing came to mind.

"Why did she call you Aleksander? Is that not a lie?"

Sebastian ambled to a shelf with various carved woodland creatures, each the size of his palm. He wore gloves, but she noticed that there were no bumps at the base of his fingers to indicate rings underneath—surely an illusion. "Not a lie. She asked for my name, and it is one of mine. Mother had always loved the name Sebastian, and she gave me my father's name as a secondary one."

"So, your name is Sebastian Aleksander?"

He nodded, picking up a carving of a fawn, its legs tucked under as it slept peacefully. "My father was from the country of Olster. He escaped here in hopes of a better life for himself." The pause carried on for longer than it should have. Aveline attempted to read the emotion in his eyes, but it vanished as Sebastian replaced the carving. "Instead, he sired a bastard and died of pneumonia shortly after."

Cautiously, Aveline moved closer. Hugging him was out of the question, but she wanted him to know that she was here for him. His gaze flicked back and forth, never quite focusing on her.

The door swung open again, but this time it was a young girl on the verge of adolescence. "Aleksander!" she greeted, eyelashes fluttering. "So wonderful to see you. How are you?"

Sebastian put on a smile, walking towards the counter, never giving Aveline his back. "I am quite well, Winny, thank you for asking. How is your schooling?"

Winny's expression soured, and she fussed with a speck of dust on her sleeve too small to see. "Awful, really. I'm not sure why I bother, not when I know I won't use it."

"No? Why not?"

"Because I'm set to take over the bakery when Da and Ma pass or are too old to work. That is..." She leant on the counter. "...unless a lord decides to make me his lady."

Aveline rolled her eyes. It was no surprise that the girl found Sebastian attractive, but to be so blatant about it...

You tried to kiss him, she reminded herself.

"I think you have many possible futures ahead of you," Sebastian said kindly, but took half a step back. "I do wonder, has there been any news of late? I'm afraid I got caught up in my work and haven't been as sociable as I should be."

"Hmmmm..." Winny pursed her lips, brow furrowing. "Well, I suppose the biggest news has been Prince Alexei's marriage, set to happen next month." She glanced at the windows, then propped her elbows on the countertop. "If you ask me, it's crazy how everything with his last intended fell apart and was quickly covered up. Some say she vanished in the middle of the ceremony without a warning. One minute, she was there, and the next..." She snapped her fingers. "Poof! Gone. No one's seen or heard of her since. Everyone's been calling her the Runaway Bride."

As much as the title stung, it didn't escape Aveline's notice that Winny didn't speak her name. Odd, to be known about but not known in truth, to be a mystery to all but a few. She wondered if Sebastian ever felt that way, if it ever bothered him.

"That is strange, but politics wait for no one," Sebastian replied. "Have they announced who the next bride-to-be is?"

"Aye, it's the last one's sister, Princess Maribelle, I think her name is. They say she's recovered from her illness, same as her twin, and is eager to marry Prince Alexei."

Time stopped for Aveline. Lottie was too young, so it had to be Jeanette... But how? Yes, she was old enough to marry, but... to have to? *It should be me, it should never have fallen to her, how could I—*

Winny prattled on, "I'd have thought they'd be worried she'd disappear too, but they're taking extra precautions this time around, being *very* stingy on the guest list, and extra guards. No chance now of getting a peek, I'd wager." She sighed. "I bet her gown will be gorgeous, with a long train and jewels and—"

"Here we are!" Anne Marie returned with a sheet of steaming baked goods, plopping them on the countertop. Winny straightened and moved aside, flirtatious demeanour nowhere to be found. "Child, you're up rather early."

Her cheeks turned red. "I am not, Mother!"

Anne Marie snorted. "Aleksander, I appreciate your patience. Will this be all for you? We have some pies in the oven if you're keen to come back in an hour after they've cooled."

Jeanette... Aveline wanted to beg Sebastian to leave, almost left by herself, but she feared getting lost. She needed space, somewhere to process, another source to confirm the news.

She could be in the city, Aveline realised. *And so could my family.* If she could figure out where, convince Sebastian to take her to them... then what? Explain that she was cursed and may never see them again? They would not take the goodbye, would not let her go so easily.

"That is a kind offer, but not today." Sebastian paid and took the box of pastries. "I'm afraid I must be off."

Despite him being two steps ahead of her, a pressure at Aveline's back urged her out of the bakery. It did not stop until they had rounded the corner, obscured by a precarious stack of boxes, and led her to stand against the wall. The rough stone pulled at the thin fabric of her dress. A cool breeze cut through Aveline; she opened her mouth, as if that would alleviate the distress crushing her chest.

Sebastian stood in front of her, his body caging hers, obscuring her from any possible onlookers. "Breathe," he whispered, and gently smoothed back the stray hairs that had slipped out of her bun.

She sucked in a shuddering breath, letting it out in a half-sob. "I—I —It's my f—f—f—ault."

"What is?"

Her insides twisted. "Jeanette." She sniffled. "She's marrying Prince Alexei because I didn't. I abandoned them—"

Sebastian tilted her face up towards his. "None of this is your fault.

You did not choose to be cursed." After a beat, he continued, "We do not know the whole story, just a rumour. If you'd like, I can return you to the castle while I find confirmation."

Inhale, exhale. Inhale, exhale. The panic eased enough for Aveline to register everything around her. She had somehow turned corporeal without Sebastian's help.

Are my emotions the key?

"You're shivering." He shrugged off his jacket so he could put it on her. "It should warm up shortly, but hopefully this'll do in the meantime."

Aveline might have thanked him, she wasn't sure. Her mind tumbled over itself, trying to sift through this possible revelation amongst the onslaught of escaped emotions.

"Aveline," he murmured, drawing her attention back. "What would you like to do?"

"Stay." She pulled the jacket tighter around her, relishing the warmth he'd left. "I have to find out what is happening to them, if that is true."

"Very well. Eat first," Sebastian urged her, handing over a pastry. "I find good food often soothes the soul."

The first bite melted in her mouth, cinnamon and sugar dancing on her tongue. The second was just as good, and before she knew it, the pastry was gone. He'd been right—she was much better equipped now, having replaced her panic with determination.

"I'm glad you enjoyed it." Sebastian grinned, half of one still in his hand. "Would you like another?"

Aveline shook her head. "Finish yours, then we have work to do. We're going to sneak into the higher-class part of the city."

CHAPTER 27
WHAT FUN IS LIFE WITHOUT A LITTLE FRIVOLITY?

Sebastian prepared enchantments to disguise Aveline, but she slipped back to her ghost self, which made things easier. He altered his own appearance instead, lightening his hair to a medium brown and giving himself a short beard. Together, they walked up the street, through the crowds, as Aveline told Sebastian of the places they might spot one of the royal family, such as Grand Duchess Katarina—and, if they were lucky, Jeanette. Not such a farfetched thing to hope for, since the Grand Duchess loved to visit the shops, bringing Princess Lucille and a few others in tow. Aveline had been on far too many of those day trips, but she imagined Jeanette would love them. In truth, she was much better suited to the excessive, gaudy lifestyle.

But did she actually want it?

While there was no gate to bar the lower classes from visiting the pricier shops, there were guards posted along the road, sword on one hip and a firearm on the other. The rifles in their hands looked much newer than the ones she'd seen a few weeks ago. *They're afraid of another attack,* she thought. What guns and swords could do against magic, she had no idea, but it was better to be safe than sorry.

Sebastian paused near one of the shops and bent down to get a closer look at some flowers. They were in the very place she'd first seen him, moments before he had been arrested.

"Sebastian?" she whispered, keeping close. "Is something the matter?"

"There is a court wizard posted among the guards," he breathed almost inaudibly, making it appear to the passersby that he was muttering incoherently to himself. "The attack must have caused them to increase security."

She'd noticed the guards, but with a second look, she spotted the court-bound wizard. He hid in the shadow of one of the shops on the other side of the street, lounging against the building with his arms crossed, his sharp eyes roaming back and forth. Aveline might have seen him once or twice in the castle, but had no idea what his name and rank were.

"Three rings on one hand, all bronze," Sebastian said. "Just powerful enough to not be the lowest rank, but not high enough to warrant silver or gold rings."

Sebastian was far more powerful. "Will he sense your magic?"

"Probably, unless I cast an obscuring spell over it. Really, it all depends on how clever the lad is."

At second peek, the wizard appeared to be a boy, not quite an adult. Dread knotted her stomach; her brothers were safe from being drafted into the war because of their age, and yet this wizard, who couldn't have been older than her fifteen-year-old brother Timothée, was expected to serve the Crown, even lay his life down if necessary. By Sebastian's tight expression, he liked it no more than she did. What would the King have sent him to do by now, if he'd been forced into servitude? She imagined it would have been far worse than guarding the shops.

"How do you want to approach this?" If she wasn't so desperate to find out if her sister was really engaged to Prince Alexei, she would have recommended they return to the castle to come up with a better strategy. Unfortunately, there was little time to waste. If she had to, she could go on alone...

No. They would stick together.

With a furrowed brow, Sebastian said, "It'd be best if I use only a little magic, simple things that don't give off much energy for him to sense." His features slowly shifted back to himself. In the bustle, no one paid attention to him. "Follow me."

Aveline was grateful to be invisible; if she were human, the guards might have been suspicious of her nervous energy. As Sebastian approached, they stepped forwards.

"Pardon us, sir, but we must ensure you carry no weapons on you."

"I commend you for your diligence," he said calmly. The guard inspecting him grunted in response, dutifully checking every pocket.

A chill prickled at Aveline, as if she were corporeal. She stiffened, glancing down to make sure she was still a ghost. Her relief was short-lived: as she looked up again, she caught sight of moving shadows in the alleyway across the street. Formless darkness, it swayed back and forth like a snake, never getting close to the sunlight. There were no eyes, and yet Aveline knew it was staring at them.

The Heart Thief is here. Sebastian hadn't mentioned being drawn to the city now—would she curse yet another person, while Aveline was still struggling to free herself?

"Public safety is not something the King wishes to be lax about." The wizard strode to Sebastian, eyeing him like a cat would its potential prey. "Underestimate your enemies, and they will make a fool out of you." He missed brushing against Aveline by a hair's breadth as he circled about with unhurried, intentional steps. She had to force herself to not move, not speak. The witch was keeping a low profile for the time being—once Sebastian dealt with the wizard and guards, then they could focus on the next problem.

Please do not sense any magic. If Sebastian was arrested again, she'd have to find a way to release him, to keep anyone else from helping him and being entangled in the mess. Beat the witch at her own malicious game.

Sebastian remained a vision of nonchalance. "No one likes to be made a fool."

The guard stepped back. "He carries no weapons on him, Sir."

"Is that so?" The wizard forced him out of the way. "I need to see your hands."

Without argument, Sebastian acquiesced. For all Aveline knew, he still wore his rings. Her sights trained on the shadows. Had they been there that day, watching as he had been arrested and she'd helped him escape? In the chaos of the attack, it was possible she'd overlooked them.

"What is your name?" The wizard squeezed various points of Sebastian's hand and fingers.

"Aleksander."

Frowning, he squinted at him. "No surname?"

To everyone's surprise, Sebastian chuckled wryly. "I suppose I do, but being a bastard, I do not feel it is rightfully mine, much as some insist otherwise."

Would half-truths really be enough protection?

"Married?"

Sebastian had one ring, a simple one. "I am, as of a few weeks ago."

Had it been a few weeks? Aveline tried to do a quick calculation, but the time travel made it difficult for her to keep up.

The wizard snatched Sebastian's other hand; Aveline winced, but Sebastian did not react. The more poking and prodding he did, the more the wizard's frown deepened.

"Is something the matter?"

He dropped Sebastian's hand like it was searing his skin. "Your surname," he snapped.

"Beauchamp."

Beauchamp? Is that a lie, or a twisting of the truth? His mother's maiden name?

While the guards whispered amongst each other in puzzlement, the wizard glared at Sebastian. "That is not a name any of us recognise."

"I apologise," he said, "but that is the only surname you would possibly know. The other one I could claim is Dmitriev, but that's much more common to hear in other countries."

"Foreigner..." He clicked his tongue, and took half a step back. "What business do you have here?"

"There are some items that are a little more difficult to acquire elsewhere. My wife loves to paint, and I heard there is a shop here that sells beautiful colours."

He is speaking of me. Amidst her jittery nerves, Aveline started to smile.

"Paints?" the wizard scoffed. "You come into the city for something so frivolous as *paints*?"

"I do, Sir. What fun is life without a little frivolity?"

The guards said nothing, just watched as the wizard opened and closed his mouth a few times, then snorted. "Off with you. If you dawdle too long, I'll be sure to check you again."

"Very well." Sebastian bowed his head and left, ignoring the man's scowl. Aveline slipped past and caught up to him. The chill had lessened but not completely gone.

When they were out of earshot, she said, "The Heart Thief is here."

"I know."

"You know? What are we going to do?"

"Nothing. She is merely observing for now. I assume she's curious that you've yet to succumb to your curse. None have made it this long." His expression hardened and shoulders slumped, as if he carried all of their fates upon his soul. With how many years he'd endured this, she could only imagine how many there had been.

"I'll let you know if I start to feel it," Sebastian said.

"And I'll find a way to rescue you if something does happen."

He offered her a fragile smile that bruised her heart.

"I'm glad that turned out all right. That was close."

"A bit," he agreed. "It was rather amusing that he could tell *something* was off but had no proof. If I could train him, he'd be formidable within a few months to be sure, with his keen senses."

Far fewer people in this area of the city, the shoppers moved at a more leisurely pace while their attendants waited on them hand and foot. It was more crowded than Aveline had expected for this early in the morning—the sun had risen, no longer touching the mountain peaks. "There might be a social event this evening," she deduced, noting the majority were visiting dress shops. "Something announced without much warning." Was the King making things up as he went along, or was he keeping secrets until the last moment to avoid surprise attacks at his important events?

"I was thinking the same thing." Sebastian surveyed the street, which was now cobblestone instead of dirt, so that the upper class could keep their garments and shoes clean. "Do you think they would bring your sister here? Do they not have a modiste in the palace?"

"They do, but I'm banking on the assumption that she'll be toiling away on a wedding gown. If the wedding is supposed to be soon, there's no time for any party dresses, and King Byron will not settle for simple attire. There is an image to uphold."

Sebastian sneaked a quick peek at her; she waited for him to comment on how her tone suddenly shifted, but he must have decided against it. "Is there more than one dress shop?"

"The one they'd most likely visit is Frills & Quills, closer to the palace." *Please, please, please be here.*

"Then we should head that way. But first, I have one stop to make." Before Aveline could put together the words to ask, Sebastian had already crossed the street, headed towards an art shop.

"That is very kind of you, but unnecessary," she said, narrowly refraining from catching his arm.

Sebastian halted with an amused smile. "Aveline?"

"Yes?"

"If I bought you the paints, would you use them?"

She blinked. "Yes, I would. Well, as much as I am able."

"Then I shall get them."

"But—"

"Are you advising me on how to spend my money?" His smile widened; her heart fluttered.

"Well, no, of course not, I just meant—"

"I *want* to do this. Unless you would not like them."

She found herself so very glad he was not looking directly at her, because she had no strength left to disguise the overwhelming gratitude. It was silly that something as simple as receiving paints as a gift felt so vulnerable, and yet it meant everything in the world to her.

It would be easy to fall in love with you, Sebastian.

Lightning struck her veins and set her pulse to racing. "Thank you," Aveline managed, and watched as he entered the shop and spoke with the owner. She had to rein in her thoughts and emotions before they carried her too far.

"Now now, that gown was perfectly acceptable," argued a voice that immediately set Aveline on edge. Out of the corner of her eye, she saw Grand Duchess Katarina Lestat exiting one of the shops, hurrying after a woman wearing red.

Jeanette.

It had been close to seven months since she'd seen her sister, and yet there was at least two years' worth of difference in her figure and face alone, much more womanly than the girl on the cusp of adolescence that Aveline recalled. Despite that, there was no mistaking who she was, the way she carried herself with such confidence and entitlement. It was as if she were born to play this role, of a princess who would one day become a queen.

As Jeanette's face turned her way, Aveline's breath caught; she had always favoured their mother in appearance, but now it was almost like looking at a young version of her.

"It was perfectly *simple*," Aveline's sister declared, as she cast a frown over her shoulder. "Not even close to befitting a princess." Without awaiting a response, Jeanette entered the carriage. The Grand Duchess, Princess Lucille, Lady Beatrice, and a few handmaidens followed behind—Hanna at the end.

I hope you are not too demanding of her, Jeanette, Aveline thought, then whirled around at the sound of the tiny bells announcing Sebastian's exit.

"That is them," she said in a rush, pointing at the ancient carriage making its way up the street. Motorcars pulled to the side to allow them to pass first, then continued on their way.

Sebastian crossed to the other side of the road, making sure to keep enough distance so as not to be obvious that he was tailing them. "It is your sister, then?"

"Jeanette," she confirmed.

"Are you thinking of a way to speak with her?"

Aveline hadn't gotten that far. She had acted on instinct, eager to be near one of her family members even if she couldn't be seen. But what if they could manage a private audience? "Could we somehow get a note to her?"

"Whatever you like. What do you want it to say?"

A hundred scraps of sentences jumbled in her mind, a hundred ways to explain her disappearance and a hundred questions to ask...

The carriage stopped beside Frills & Quills, just as Aveline had predicted. It was the fanciest dress shop in the city, carrying everything from special garments to elegant stationary. The sign out front read "Everything a noble lady needs for social events, from planning to attending", and Aveline knew it to be true, having been in that shop a few times while under the care of the royal family.

The footman hurried to help the women exit safely. It made sense that the Grand Duchess would heckle Jeanette as much as the old woman had Aveline, treating her as less than. But where Aveline had been complacent, in Jeanette, the Grand Duchess had met her match. Her sister didn't cower or even flinch at the sniping remarks as she strode inside.

"That I wish to meet with her," Aveline said, standing with him in the alley between the buildings. "Pick a time and a place, and so that she is certain this isn't a trick, do not use my name, sign it as 'Addy the Lion Tamer'."

Sebastian quirked an eyebrow but did as he was told, pulling a bound book of sketch paper and a pen out of the bag he'd gotten from the art shop. She couldn't see what else was in there, but it looked to be more than just a paint set. He wrote with his left hand, penmanship barely qualifying as legible, and folded the note. "Under what pretence would she accept a note from a stranger?"

Jeanette had never seen Sebastian before, and while she was unafraid of meeting new people, she took no issue with setting boundaries, for her own safety and others'. Not to mention that the Grand Duchess would certainly take offence to a strange man approaching the Princess.

The personal guards tailed the group of women into the shop. They had to think of something fast—but preferably without it ending in Sebastian's imprisonment.

"Let me follow them inside first," Aveline suggested. "Perhaps I'll think of something."

Sebastian reached for her, but stopped short, letting his hand fall back at his side. "Be careful. Although highly unlikely, there may be someone who has the Sight."

"The wizard did not see me."

"No," he conceded, "but I believe that had more to do with his drive to find something off about me. He either saw you and thought you were human, or did not notice you at all." He offered her a small smile. "I know you'll be careful. I just... I'll wait here in case you need me. I think I've drawn enough attention for now."

"It'll only be a moment," Aveline assured him before slipping through the wall. The shop was filled with dresses for all occasions, an array of colours, fabrics, and decorations to explore. A green one caught Aveline's eye, a full-length ball gown with hints of black trim. She admired it for only a moment, then refocused on the task at hand: her sister, who sifted through the stock while the energetic shop owner prattled on about her suggestions for such a prestigious event. Princess Lucille and Lady Beatrice parroted whatever opinions the Grand Duchess gave, most of them negative and entirely unhelpful. Jeanette ignored it all, stating what she liked about the pieces.

Aveline drew closer, aching to hug her sister. Would she feel anything at all, if Aveline focused on the emotion?

She stilled as Jeanette turned her way. Was it possible that she had the Sight? Out of all of the children, Aveline would have guessed Edith, perhaps Lottie, but it would be fortuitous if Jeanette did. She watched for her eyes to light up with recognition, for Jeanette to drop everything and rush towards Aveline and ask her a flood of questions. Hope sparked within her, believing that they were actually making eye contact, but it was snuffed out a moment later when Jeanette walked a different direction, intent on better inspecting the gowns that were hidden in the back.

How was she supposed to get the note to her sister? With that many people trailing Jeanette everywhere she went, it would be nigh on impossible to have Sebastian get it to her... unless they risked using magic, and there was no guarantee that Jeanette would accept it.

"What do you think of this one, Hanna?" Jeanette ran the sleeve between her fingers.

"She asks a handmaiden's opinion but rejects ours," huffed the Grand Duchess. "I doubt she wishes to be royalty; she prefers her place among the swine."

"Very odd," Princess Lucille agreed loudly, snapping her fan open.

Gaze locked on Hanna, Jeanette pressed, "Well?"

The handmaiden peeked back at the others, cheeks reddening. "The colour would suit you well, Your Highness, but I do not believe the cut would flatter you, and the fabric would be too heavy for you to enjoy the evening."

Aveline stared. Hanna had been outspoken with her, but when they were not around others who certainly would take issue with a servant being so bold.

"Brazen fool," the Grand Duchess hissed between her teeth.

"A perfect response, Hanna." Jeanette grinned. "You are right, as always." She set off to find others, unaffected by the glares the others shot at her.

Hanna's expression brightened slightly, and she started to look behind her at the other women but seemed to think better of it. Then she stopped, lips parting, widening eyes pinned... on Aveline.

CHAPTER 28

I COULD NEVER HATE YOU

Had she been corporeal, Aveline would have tripped and knocked over racks on her way out of the shop, but as a ghost, she moved through them until she reached outside, instincts driving her to run.

"What is it?" Sebastian strode towards her. He'd spoken a little too loudly, and a passerby muttered something dismissive as she continued on. Her companion switched sides with her, glowering at Sebastian.

"I think Hanna saw me."

"Who?"

"My handmaiden when I was living in the palace. Now Jeanette's, from what I gather. But she seemed shocked to see me, so I think..." Aveline peered at the closed shop door. "I wonder... Perhaps she would—"

The bell chimed as Hanna exited, urgently searching the crowds. It did not take her long; the moment they saw one another, the handmaiden froze in place, staring at her, then at Sebastian. She paled.

"It is I," Aveline assured her. "Your mind is not playing tricks on you."

Neither of them moved. A breeze toyed with the stray hairs that had fallen loose from Hanna's braid.

"Do you have a moment to talk?" Aveline prepared herself for rejection. After all, Hanna was supposed to be with Jeanette, staying by her side at all times.

"If we are quick about it," she answered in a hushed tone, reluctantly drawing closer. Her attention kept cutting back and forth between Aveline and Sebastian.

"I'll give you two a moment alone," Sebastian offered. "Might I suggest you stand near the alleyway?" With that, he turned heel and walked back to a watch shop. She didn't know if he'd be able to hear them—she assumed he wouldn't waste magic, but something told her he was more interested in assuring her safety than conserving energy. Hanna accepted his suggestion, peeking at him out of the corner of her eye as she positioned herself in front of the outdoor display advertising exotic items.

"You're a ghost," she whispered almost inaudibly. "What happened? Who is he? Are you in trouble? I know you mentioned something the night before your disappearance—I should have called for help, or—"

"Hanna, you did nothing wrong. The Heart Thief cursed me on the day of the wedding. The man I'm with is Sebastian. He is helping me find a way to break the curse so I'll be human again."

The woman's shoulders relaxed the tiniest bit. "You're not dead." She exhaled in relief. "Sebastian... isn't that the name you gave me, the... *wizard*... you were asking about?"

Keen memory. I'm lucky she never used it against me. "It is."

Aveline didn't realise her blunder until Hanna murmured, "A rogue wizard."

"A *kind* wizard." She didn't think Hanna would call for the guards to arrest him, but it was better to be certain. "A helpful one. He's not a danger."

Hanna's eyes roamed over the display, every once in a while flicking to Sebastian. "I would not be so certain. What do you know about him?"

How much was too much to tell? "I thought you had a short amount of time to talk."

"I told your sister that my stomach was upsetting me and I needed fresh air. That should buy me a little time."

Aveline supposed their saving grace was that there were far fewer people perusing the high-class, expensive shops, trickles of people passing them instead of streams. Far less of a risk of someone seeing her or overhearing them. "He is a friend. I promise you, he is helping me. I can give you more details another time, but first, I need you to give a note to my sister. It's a difficult thing to ask, but I'd like to have a secret meeting with her... and you, if you would like."

A small smile tugged at her lips. "I would."

Aveline returned the smile. "I'm sure I will get more answers later, but for the time being, can you tell me how Je... Maribelle... is faring?"

Hanna bit her lip. "I know that her real name is Jeanette. And that yours is Aveline, not Gwendoline."

A strange mix of anxiety and relief twisted around each other and weighed on her chest. "She told you?"

"Only me. We've become friends, much like you and I were. She said she'd need a friend in the palace if she was going to survive. And she wanted my help figuring out where you'd gone."

Quite the risk, but Aveline couldn't fault Jeanette for it. She, too, would have confided in Hanna eventually.

"She is faring much better than most expected, I think." Hanna checked the door, but it was just another customer. "I don't think the Grand Duchess and Princess Lucille know what to do with her. She refuses to let them belittle her, and the fact that she doesn't care about their approval irks them to no end."

"That sounds like my sister. Hanna, I know you said you might have time, but they'll come looking for you shortly and I'd rather not draw suspicion. Sebastian has the note for you."

"I will take it to her," she promised. "But, Aveline? Please be careful. Magic always comes at a cost, and it will make you pay, whether he expects anything from you or not." She left Aveline pondering the warning as she approached Sebastian and took the note. They exchanged a few words too quiet for her to hear, and then Hanna strolled back towards the dress shop.

Hanna is not wrong about magic taking a price, she thought, surveying the shadows between the alleyways. None moved, to her relief. *I will gladly pay what I can so Sebastian doesn't shoulder all of it.*

Aveline waited, hoping for another glimpse of her sister. She could have gone back inside, but decided it was probably for the best to leave things alone for the time being. She could be patient.

Sebastian's footsteps tapped on the sidewalk as he came up behind her. "Are you all right?"

She wanted to lean back into his warmth, to have him hold her so she could have something to steady her against the torrent of emotions. Instead, she nodded.

THEIR JOURNEY BACK TO THE CASTLE WAS UNEVENTFUL—OTHER than the wizard still on duty being agitated at seeing that Sebastian had bought exactly what he'd said. Sebastian teleported them just inside of the gates, in the part of the garden where roses thrived the most. When he started to let go, Aveline held fast to his hand.

"Thank you." She didn't quite have it in her to look at him directly, not if she wanted to risk being reduced to sobs once more. Her knees trembled, ready to buckle under her.

"You're welcome." Sebastian set the items down and drew closer. "Do you wish to talk about anything?"

Aveline focused on his shirt, at the slight indent where the key lay hidden. "No. Yes. I don't know."

"As I said, none of this is your fault." He pressed a lingering kiss to her brow; she closed her eyes, allowing him to flood her senses. The morning had warmed the air considerably, yet a shiver ran along her spine. "But I understand feeling the guilt anyway," he added, resting his forehead against hers. "There are far too many things I hold myself accountable for that I ought not."

Her ever-present curiosity wanted to press for answers. She resisted. "May I make a confession? I fear you might judge me, but I don't want to hold onto it."

"I will not judge you. I think we are our own harshest critics—you may feel differently about it once it is spoken aloud."

Aveline inhaled, welcoming the scents of earth, lemon balm, and candle smoke, ones she'd come to associate with him. They were subtle, turning sharp when he casted spells, making her think they could be the lingering smells of magic. "I am worried about my sister's welfare more," she began, "and this is childish, but I hate being referred to as the 'Runaway Bride'. It shouldn't matter to me, but it feels like everyone believes that I abandoned them, that I am..." *Just like Edith.* She shuddered. Sebastian grabbed her before she could fall, cradling her against his chest.

No tears came, just a heaviness that desired to pin her to the earth until the vines grew over her body and made her a part of the garden. Sebastian rubbed her back; she listened to the steady rhythm of his heartbeat.

"I'm in Edith's position," she said, slowly processing. "Our family had come to believe that she'd abandoned us for a lover, and here others are believing that of me. My own family might be thinking the same."

In lieu of a response, he held her tighter.

"And what if she had? Left us for a man, I mean. We'd been miserable for so many years, and Edith did everything she could to lift our spirits. If I think about it, it was entirely unfair, how we relied on her for hope. She must have been so tired... How can I be angry with my sister for wanting to be happy? She would want the same for me. For all of us."

Whether her ramblings made sense or not, Aveline did feel a little lighter, albeit sadder for her sister. What would she have done in Edith's position? Seeking comfort seemed like much less of an offence than she'd taken it prior.

"All this time, I said I was happy to help my family, but I resented Edith leaving. I hated her for so long." There it was, the darkest part of her heart splayed open. He was going to reject her, and she would not blame him for it—

"I can understand you're hurt," Sebastian said softly. "I would have been, too, in your shoes. But, if Edith did leave your family to follow her heart, I also cannot fault her for that. People do insane things for love, things that would normally be out of character for them."

Like me, wanting to stay here with you. "Does... does that change your opinion of me?"

"Not at all."

"Even though I admitted to hating my sister?"

"I don't think you ever truly hated her, and it sounds like you certainly don't anymore." He paused. "If you did hate her for that, then you must truly hate me."

Aveline pulled back just enough to look up at him. "What do you mean?"

"You are in this predicament because I did something foolish for someone I love."

She tensed. He'd said there was no one she was keeping him from, but that didn't mean he hadn't once loved someone. And he spoke in the present tense...

"My sister," he clarified. "In trying to save Lila from The Heart Thief, I antagonised the witch to curse anyone who helps me."

Aveline placed a trembling hand over his heart. "I could never hate you, Sebastian."

When his dark eyes locked on hers, she went perfectly still, unable to draw breath for fear of breaking the fragility of the moment. Storms brewed in them, stirred by anguish and fear.

You can tell me, she silently pleaded. *You can trust me.* But just because she bared her soul to him did not mean he had to reciprocate, and she would not force him.

He covered her hand with his. The illusion had been lifted, his rings once more on display. He wore the band that matched the one he'd given her, even though it was nothing noteworthy, simple compared to the rest; she doubted it had much magic value other than when he enchanted it.

"For that, I am grateful," he whispered. The sunlight lit the tones of his irises, giving the dark brown colour hues of burnt caramel. She studied them, trying to commit them to memory for when she got the chance to paint him... after the others.

"I could never hate you either," Sebastian continued. "In fact, I have come to treasure our... friendship."

The word snagged Aveline's heart. Was he going to say something else? She had no idea what term she would use for them; friendship felt the closest, yet did not quite encapsulate it. Maybe it did for him.

She could not love him. She *did not* love him. They had shared vulnerable truths that bound them even tighter together, but it was not love. Aveline just needed a moment to clear her mind after the torrent of emotions of the day.

Sebastian's brow furrowed, his lips parting. Aveline tacked on a smile. "I treasure it as well." She pulled away and ignored the skip in her pulse when he was reluctant to release her. Stooping to pick up the box of pastries, she said, "I do hope these are still warm, for Leo's sake."

He observed her. She readied herself for a question, a comment, something that would easily tear down her facade, but Sebastian said, "Not to worry, I can fix them if they're not."

"I might have to snatch another one if there's enough. You are right: the bakery is excellent, just as good as Timothée's treats. He would love working there." She cut herself off before she could continue babbling and draw more suspicion.

"From what you've told me of him, I agree." Sebastian grabbed the bag of art supplies and joined her up the stairs leading to the castle.

It was then Aveline realised she had never seen it. The dark stonework was overall simple, but the iron knights guarding the entrance drew her attention. The cracks in the armour exposed their hollow insides. Even so, they carried a menacing demeanour, in defensive stances like they could come alive at any moment to protect the castle.

The double doors were wide and tall enough for a giant to enter; Aveline thought back to the memory of Maud knocking on them, and wondered how afraid she'd been to seek help from another social pariah.

"I suppose you've never walked through the front door," Sebastian mused, looking up at the spires that pierced the charcoal clouds. "Not exactly a welcoming aesthetic."

The box began to slip from her grasp when he took hold of her arm, forcing her back into corporeal form.

Her breath hitched. "Not necessarily." To calm herself, she admired the ornate etchings in the archway, depictions of thorny vines with blossoming roses. "I think it is hauntingly beautiful." Keenly aware she had his full attention, Aveline could not bring herself to give him the same. "I'm sure Leo is hungry." She stepped towards the door, desperate for a little space between them.

Sebastian paused before saying, "Then we should bring these to him before he ransacks the kitchen and upsets Maud."

CHAPTER 29

STIFLING YOUR EMOTIONS ONLY STIFLES WHO YOU ARE

The pastries had to be reheated, but Leo gobbled them up quickly, leaving the wolf-shaped one for last. He made it frolic across the table until Maud raised a brow at him, and then he split it with the hounds. "I wish you would've taken me with you," he said, mouth full.

"Next time, perhaps." Sebastian excused himself without explanation. To Aveline's relief, Maud did not ask questions, but she gave an assessing look that Aveline ignored.

Aveline hated waiting. She and Sebastian were supposed to go to a tavern just outside of the city, in hopes that her sister would meet them there... but the meeting had been set for the next night. How was she supposed to fill her time until then?

Her first idea was to visit Meredith, but she decided against it, thinking it was still probably too soon in the organisation process to interrupt her. Opting to try her hand at painting again, Aveline went upstairs, and Leo tagged along, telling her all about his latest invention.

"It detects magic!" He proudly showed her what looked to be a normal metal rod. "It hums when you're near something." He tried to offer it to her, then awkwardly lowered it when he realised that Aveline was a ghost again.

"I can try it later," she said. "Sebastian got us some new paints—would you care to join me?"

"Yes!" Leo sprinted to the painting room. The hounds barked and almost knocked him over as they ran beside him.

"Are you sure you want him messing up your new paints?" Maud made a face.

"They will get just as messy when I use them," Aveline tried to assure her.

"I'm not convinced."

She shrugged. "I like seeing what others create. Besides, I do not mind sharing. It's not as if he's not using them for what they're intended for."

"Spoken like a true older sister."

"I've found if you don't let children join what you're doing, chances are they'll get into worse trouble."

Maud chuckled and picked up her pace to match Aveline's. Their footsteps made no sound—they more so floated above the floor than walked—but Aveline found comfort in her presence. If Maud could spend however many years in this state, Aveline could manage a little while longer until they found a way to break her curse. It was not so hopeless after all; she had accidentally shifted back to a human earlier that morning. Now to figure out what possibly could have caused such a reaction...

"Whoa!" Leo hollered, flashing them a grin as they entered the room. He knelt in front of the shopping bag, pulling out item after item.

"Leo!" snapped Maud. "Those are for Aveline. It is rude to open her gift."

"Honestly, I do not mind." Aveline sank to her knees beside the young boy. She had been right about Sebastian buying more than just paints for her: expensive paint brushes with polished handles, palettes, small canvases, and even a smock embroidered with tiny daisies.

You are too good of a friend to me, Sebastian. She wondered what she could give him as thanks; a note would be too difficult without his help, but so would a painting. She could just tell him, but that didn't seem like enough. Why was he being so kind to her, when he didn't expect anything in return? Hanna's warning flashed in her mind, but Aveline rejected it. *Sebastian is a genuinely kind person.*

"You should try it on," Leo urged, handing her the smock. Hesitantly, Aveline reached for it. For a moment, she held the fabric between her fingers, and then it fluttered to the ground.

I thought I had it. She tried again, with the same result.

"Progress!" he cheered. "You'll be human again in no time! Permanently, that is. Then we can play more games and go on walks and OH! You can help me with my inventions. Usually Bash does, but he's been tired a lot lately."

"So I've noticed," Aveline said neutrally. Maud raised a brow in her direction.

"Bash doesn't mind spending magic to help you." He sorted the paints. "We all like having you as a part of our family."

Her eyes stung. "I like all of you too. Very much."

"Are you crying? Did I upset you?"

Confused, she reached up, then smiled in wonder at the solid hand, at the tear rolling down her finger. "No, I am not upset in the slightest."

"Then why are you crying?" Leo scooted closer. "Oh! You're human again. That's grand! You should be happy."

"She is, little one," Maud chimed in, hand hovering near his back like she was rubbing it. "You were right: progress is being made."

Aveline looked up at them, then to the window behind them, where a sliver of sunlight peeked between the lace curtains. "We should go outside," she said, all but jumping to her feet.

Leo and the hounds were out the door before she was. She ran after them, grinning with an exhilaration she hadn't felt since she was a little girl, racing her siblings through the fields behind their house. Their pounding feet and Leo's excited shouts resounded as they sprinted through the castle, not slowing down until they reached the garden.

Warmth enveloped her; a gentle breeze played with her loose bun.

Aveline undid the ribbon, letting her hair tumble down her back. While Leo zigzagged between the bushes so the hounds would chase him, Aveline kicked off her shoes and wiggled her toes in the grass. She closed her eyes and breathed deeply, tilting her face up towards the sun. Too long she had been in the dark, as a ghost, or held down by her emotions. Too long she had suppressed herself, chained to the worries of the future. For now, she sighed contentedly, letting herself just *be*. She listened to the chirping of the birds, to Leo's laughter—

Footsteps sounded behind her. She turned around to see Sebastian. He'd changed into a blue shirt, the sleeves rolled up. "It is a beautiful day," he said in greeting. "I'm glad you can enjoy it."

Aveline tucked some hair behind her ear. If he thought she was being childish, he didn't give any indication, yet her cheeks burned. "I thought you were resting."

"Hard to rest with Leo's hollering." Sebastian removed his shoes to place them next to hers. "Besides, it'd be a waste to not enjoy the sun after all the darkness we've endured."

Out of the corner of her eye, she saw Maud appear through the wall and walk into the gardens, no doubt in search of her child.

"I wanted to thank you for the paints... and the, um, brushes, and the canvas... the smock too!" Aveline blurted before she'd fully decided to say something. "You are very kind."

His smile brightened her mood more than it should have. "You are very welcome. You're making progress with becoming corporeal, so I'm sure you'll get lots of use out of them." The wind tousled his hair; she resisted the urge to smooth it back.

"I will," she agreed. "I'm not quite sure how I've managed to become human again by myself twice in one day, but I have hope we'll figure it out soon enough." Aveline tore her gaze away, focusing on the long stretch of bushes and flowers ahead of them. "It seems to be tied to my emotions. All this time, I've pushed them down, ignored them, so I could do what was best for everyone else. I think... I've stifled them for so long, being what everyone else wanted me to be, that I lost myself in the process."

"Stifling your emotions stifles who you are. It is all right to feel, even if... even if sometimes the emotion might be overwhelming." His knuckles brushed against hers, a silent offer she answered by slipping her hand into his.

He must be talking about his fear. Aveline revelled in the fact that he had reached for her for comfort, that she could be there for him even if she had no idea what for.

CHAPTER 30

IF IT MEANS ANYTHING TO YOU, I PROMISE I HAVE NOT TAKEN ADVANTAGE OF YOUR SISTER

Sebastian made all the preparations for the meeting. Unable to keep corporeal, Aveline opted to go with him to the tavern as a ghost, but as soon as the owner escorted him to a private room and shut the door, Aveline clasped his hand between both of hers.

"It will go well," he murmured, leading her to sit on the couch beside him. "I'm sure your sister is just as anxious to speak with you."

Aveline chewed the inside of her cheek. "I hope she managed to sneak out."

"If she's anything like you, I'm certain she did." Sebastian gestured to the left, at a door she hadn't noticed. "There's an adjoining room if you'd be more comfortable talking with them alone. Just say the word."

"Thank you." She couldn't bring herself to sit still. Sebastian pressed his knee against hers, and she almost sank against him. How had she ever managed to smother her nerves before?

"The owner seemed to know you," she commented, hoping to give her mind at least a small distraction. While nothing noteworthy, the establishment was cosy, with plenty of seating room and small paintings of landscapes and animals.

"He does," Sebastian confirmed.

"As Aleksander?"

"Yes. I don't often meet with people, but there are still some matters of estate I have to keep up with, and that means business meetings. I'd rather they not visit the castle and get roped into everything by accident."

"Understandable... but, who do they think you are? I assume they know they are dealing with someone who lives in the Blaise castle."

He grimaced. "I may have led them to believe I was a long-lost son."

As Aveline started to ask more, there was a knock at the door. They stood, and reluctantly stepped away from one another.

"Enter."

At Sebastian's permission, the patron let two women inside, wearing heavy cloaks that covered everything but the lower parts of their faces. The moment the door clicked shut, Jeanette and Hanna lowered their hoods.

"Aveline." Jeanette closed the distance between them in three quick strides, pulling her into a desperate embrace. Aveline squeezed her eyes shut too late to stop the tears from flowing but didn't care. Her sister had come, that was all that mattered.

"Let me look at you." Her own eyes glistening, Jeanette never quite let go, gripping her sister's arms so tightly it nearly hurt. Aveline smiled —until she saw the furrow in Jeanette's brow. "We didn't know where you went or what happened to you. We've been so worried! I've been looking for evidence everywhere in the castle, ready to accuse someone of foul play—"

"I am well," Aveline interjected, knowing she would continue rambling otherwise. Their time limited, it was imperative to get Jeanette back to the castle before someone went searching for her. "As well as I can be. Please, sit, and I'll explain everything." She started to move towards Sebastian, but Jeanette held fast, dragging her to the other couch.

"No, you don't. I've not seen you in ages, and I have no intentions of being without you." She raised her chin at Sebastian. "Besides, I have no idea who this man is. Not that I am one to care much about a scandal, but I want to know what you are doing alone with a stranger, Avie."

Aveline sank down beside Jeanette. Hanna awkwardly sat on the opposite edge of the other couch, keeping as far away from Sebastian as possible. "This is..." She hesitated, unsure which name to give.

"Sebastian," he filled in for her. "If it means anything to you, I promise I have not taken advantage of your sister."

Jeanette raised a brow. "So you say."

"He hasn't," Aveline insisted, face flushing. "He is helping me break a curse."

Her sister stared at her with wide, unblinking eyes. Hanna made a sign over her chest in a manner that Aveline assumed was meant to ward off evil.

"A witch named The Heart Thief cursed me to become a ghost," she continued before either could interrupt. "Sebastian is helping me find a way to break it so I can permanently stay human."

"A ghost? But I can feel you right now."

"I'm slowly learning to break it. It is not an easy thing to undo, but I have been practising, and I think I should have it soon."

Jeanette snapped her attention to Sebastian. "How are you helping her with it?" she demanded.

"Magic." He calmly lifted his hand to show off the rings. "To keep her from fading away, I bound her to myself."

"You *bound* her?"

"With my permission," Aveline pointed out.

"Like she was some kind of spirit that you could control?"

"She would have faded away otherwise." Sebastian's tone remained even despite Jeanette's rising volume. His fingers twitched. "I've sound-proofed the room, but I do advise we try to be quiet regardless."

Jeanette exhaled loudly through her nose. "You *bound* my *sister—*"

"I *helped* your sister," he corrected with more patience than Aveline could have mustered. "I do not control her any more than she controls me. Our souls are bound to each other so that she does not fade away. I gave her my word that as soon as the curse is broken, I will undo it."

Silence filled the room, tense as a rope ready to snap.

"He is not asking for anything in return," Aveline said quietly. "He is my friend, Jeanette."

Her sister did not look at her, just kept boring into Sebastian, who maintained eye contact with a neutral expression.

"Sebastian, will you give us a moment, please?"

His dark eyes swiped to her. He nodded, manoeuvring his way past Hanna and into the other room.

"Would you like me to leave as well?" asked the handmaiden.

"No, please stay. I want you both to hear this."

"Hear what?" Jeanette shook her head, her ash blonde curls swaying. "I apologise for snapping, but this is a lot to take in, Avie. You were missing, and now you're telling me that you've been a ghost, and you're bound to a rogue wizard?"

"It isn't as if I had a choice. No one else could see me, much less help."

Jeanette opened her mouth as if she were going to say something, then sighed again. "To find out that ghosts are real, not myths... and you are one sometimes, not because you're dead, but because you're cursed..."

"I'm still unused to it myself."

Tears lined her eyes. "You are not dead?"

"I promise you, I am not dead. You can feel me now, you said so yourself."

"Yes, but... I do not understand the rules of magic and supernatural things. We didn't have to deal with them back home, and it has left me feeling wholly unprepared for life here. For all I know, Sebastian enchanted you so that you could appear alive."

"Is there some way I could convince you?"

After a moment of thought, Jeanette said, "No. If we try, we'll waste what little time we have."

Aveline patted her hand. "I know it's overwhelming, but I appreciate that you're willing to hear my side of the story."

"I never believed King Byron's," she scoffed. "I know you. You would not run away with anyone, especially a stranger with magic."

She resisted a grimace. *Perhaps not the old me...*

"Aveline..." Hanna cut in timidly.

"Yes?"

She bit her bottom lip. "That man... Sebastian... Where does he live?"

Her trepidation set Aveline's nerves on edge. "What does it matter?"

Hanna swallowed. "Does he live in the disappearing castle?" At Aveline's silence, she wrung her hands. "Aveline," she whispered, leaning forward, "he's The Magic Collector."

"I know."

"Clearly, you don't. If you did, you would have never trusted him."

"Hanna, whatever you've heard—"

"What do you mean?" Jeanette's grip on Aveline's hand was iron.

She peeked at the door, then said in a hushed tone, "The Magic Collector is known for stealing magic items of all kinds, and he kills whoever is in his way. He slaughtered the family that lived there—"

"The family that lived there was his," Aveline cut in. "He did not slaughter them."

"Did he tell you that?" Jeanette inquired.

Aveline rifled through their conversations. *I am so afraid, Aveline,* he had said. Of what, she had no idea, but killing his family did not match up with the person she'd come to know. He would never do that. Could never. Unless... it was an accident, a magical one, perhaps.

Who is the ghost he keeps in the attic?

"No, but he's starting to open up about his family and life. I can assure you, if you knew him, you'd agree that he is incapable of killing anyone."

Pinching her lips together, the handmaiden folded her hands in her lap.

"What if he has put a spell on you, and you don't even know it?" Jeanette suggested. "Avie, he could be messing with your memories."

"He is not like that. Jeanette, he's the one who sent money to our family, not because I asked him to, but because he saw how distraught I was that we were in financial trouble." She winced, glancing at Hanna. She'd forgotten that was a secret, that everyone else thought they were daughters of King Charles.

"Hanna put the clues together herself when I first arrived."

Jeanette batted away the concern with a wave of her hand. "She won't say a word. But, Avie, what if he's trying to earn your trust?"

"He already has it. Sebastian has been nothing but kind to me, Jeanette."

She paused, studying her with intense grey-blue eyes. "You're in love with him." Said so matter-of-factly, it hit Aveline like she'd been punched in the chest. She inhaled sharply, but her lungs refused to take in air.

"That's neither here nor there," she said, hoping Sebastian couldn't hear her. "Even if I were, as soon as the curse is broken, we are parting ways as nothing more than friends."

Jeanette snorted. "I find that as likely as him not touching you in all this time alone."

Aveline decided against bringing up Leo and Maud's presence in the castle. "Well, he hasn't touched me, and he isn't interested."

"No one would believe that if word got out about this."

"Since when do you care so much when it comes to what others think?"

"I don't, but I do care that you find a good match after all of this is settled."

Aveline squirmed and tried to cover it up by shifting in her seat. Her marriage to Sebastian was a farce, born out of necessity, yet she recoiled at the idea of being with anyone else. If their family was taken care of, then she could choose to not marry at all; she imagined herself becoming a spinster, spending her days painting in a small house in the countryside. She could be content with that.

"Avie," Jeanette asked, "I know you are not in love with him, but I hope you are not put out with me for taking your place in marrying Prince Alexei?"

"Not at all. The marriage was for duty, and I only regret that I have unintentionally forced you into this position for the good of our family."

"You have nothing to regret, dear sister," she assured her. "I look forward to marrying him and one day wearing the crown. Royal life suits me, does it not?"

Aveline found herself smiling. "It does. You will be a great Princess and a wonderful Queen."

"Thank you, I do hope so... You know, since our family will be well taken care of, you will be free to marry whoever you wish."

She let her gaze drop to their clasped hands. "I suppose I am free to make a number of choices. I don't think I've had this many possibilities open to me before."

"Aveline..." Jeanette waited until she was looking at her before saying, "You have always been the most sensible of all of us, so perhaps I should trust your judgement, but... Please, promise me you'll make some selfish decisions too? Ones that will make you happy, not just others?"

Her heart twinged. She still had time, still had to break the curse. Then Aveline would be truly free, in every sense of the word.

So why didn't that fill her with excitement?

"Whatever you decide, you know I am always on your side." Jeanette tucked a stray strand back behind her ear; Aveline frowned at the echo of a touch, almost no warmth as her sister's finger brushed against her skin.

"Our family will be in town soon," Jeanette informed her, not noticing that Aveline's hand had slipped through hers, and clapped in excitement. "They'll be ecstatic to see you. Oh, and we must get you a new gown for the wedding."

"Nette..."

She halted. "What?"

"Are you certain it is a good idea for me to come to your wedding, given the rumours already circulating about my disappearance? I doubt King Charles would be grateful for his family to be made to look foolish."

"Leave it to me, I'll figure something out. You are my sister, and I want you there to share in my special day."

"I would like that too." Aveline leant forward as Jeanette tried to kiss her cheek, but her sister nearly fell, catching herself on the edge of the couch. Mouth agape, she stood and glanced about frantically. "Aveline?"

"Yes?"

"Where did she go?" Jeanette looked to Hanna, who replied, "She is still next to you, but as a ghost."

Gently, Aveline brushed a lock of Jeanette's hair back. To her surprise, it moved, then slipped through her fingers. Her sister whipped around, eyes roaming. Tentatively, she reached out. Aveline touched her hand; Jeanette tensed at the contact. It was strange, seeing her confident sister so unsettled.

"Can you hear me?" Jeanette whispered.

"Yes." Aveline latched onto the joy at seeing her sister, hoping that following that thread would bring her back to being human.

"She can hear you, but you can't hear her," Hanna explained.

"Why not?"

"Very few people can see ghosts and magic."

Without looking away from where Aveline stood, Jeanette stated, "You really are full of surprises, Hanna." She gasped as warmth sparked between their palms, then immediately died out.

So close... She could have made another attempt, but she wanted to be considerate of her sister's time. "Sebastian, come join us, if you please."

He returned, quickly assessing the situation, and touched Aveline's elbow. Jeanette startled at Aveline's reappearance.

"You use magic to bring her back?"

"Of a sort," answered Sebastian.

"Rather strong magic, to keep her tethered here." Hanna positioned herself beside Jeanette, who pointed out, "He did say he bound her."

"We are bound to each other," Aveline corrected defensively.

She witnessed the moment her sister snapped the last piece of the puzzle into place. "Your souls are bound... you are *married?*"

"Temporarily."

"She was far from home and had neither family nor friends to keep her tethered to this world," Sebastian explained. "I offered her a temporary solution."

While Jeanette did nothing to hide her shock, Hanna merely frowned, as if she'd suspected something of the like.

"You are married... you haven't touched her... and this is a *temporary* solution?" Jeanette raised her brows at them.

"It had to be a powerful connection."

"He did nothing without my permission," Aveline emphasised yet again. "There is nothing to fear, Jeanette, I promise you."

With a huffed laugh and an unconvinced grin, Jeanette shook her head. "I do not fear, my sweet sister; I just think both of you are fooling yourselves."

Aveline started to ask her to clarify, but Jeanette stepped forward to hug her. "I will set up a meeting with our family as soon as they arrive," she promised. "Just please, do consider attending my wedding. It would mean the world to me to have you there."

How could they possibly pull it off without causing a stir? In spite of her doubt, Aveline said, "I will consider it."

Their lingering embrace came to a reluctant end. Jeanette kissed Aveline's cheek. "I will send word when our family arrives. Where should I send it?"

Sebastian retrieved a token the size of a thimble out of his pocket. "Pin this to the letter and it will find its way to us."

After a moment of hesitation, Jeanette dipped her head in thanks. Then she and Hanna replaced their hoods and left. For a short while, Aveline stared at the door. What was to become of her, after all of this? The prospect of so many options constricted her chest like a snake.

"Are you all right?" His voice drew her back to the present.

"I am grateful to have been able to talk with her. Did you hear our conversation?"

"No. You asked for privacy."

The tension in her shoulders melted. At least he hadn't heard her sister's claims.

"Is something bothering you?"

I can talk with you about many things, but not this. "Do you know the rumours people speak about you?"

He shrugged. "I do, but they don't matter—people will always think whatever they want to."

Aveline wished she could adopt his mindset. It would make many things so much easier. "My sister wants me to attend her wedding."

"I heard."

"I do not want to bring drama to her special day."

"Understandable. However, given that it's a royal wedding with many attendants, I'd be willing to bet that, whether you attend or not, there will be drama. Upper class life tends to be a breeding ground for it."

They exchanged an amused smirk.

"I suppose you're right. If I went, would you come with me?" *What a selfish thing to ask,* she reprimanded herself immediately. What was she thinking, wanting to bring a rogue wizard to the castle, where he'd be in the most danger possible?

"If that is what you desire."

Her soul hummed; she forced herself to look away. "We should return home."

It didn't occur to her until Sebastian was teleporting them that she had not called it *the castle.*

She had called it *home.*

CHAPTER 31
WHILE IT WAS A TRAGEDY...

"Look, Aveline!" Leo tugged her towards his canvas, almost making her drop the paintbrush. "It's you!" he announced proudly, gesturing at the mess of colours and shapes that vaguely resembled a human figure. He'd made her hair bright yellow and her eyes green instead of blue, yet Aveline beamed.

"I'm honoured," she said. "Who are you going to paint next?"

"I think Mum," he answered with barely a thought. "I might have enough room to paint everyone together!"

"That is a splendid idea." Maud smiled, hand hovering just above his head like she wanted to smooth his hair. "How is yours coming along, Aveline? Need me to get my lion cub to sit still for a while longer?"

"I have the basics done, so I don't think that's entirely necessary. Or possible."

"I can sit still if I want to," Leo interjected, already slapping a new blob of paint onto the canvas. Neither woman corrected him.

Sebastian ambled into the room, looking a little more rested. Guilt pricked at her as she wondered if the bond between them was what drained him so—Hanna had commented how powerful the magic had to be to keep her here. At least she was starting to improve, having spent the last few days doing nothing but practising being corporeal for as long as possible. There was still a blue splatter on the floor where the paintbrush had fallen during one of her attempts, which Maud told her to leave as a reminder that progress was not without failures.

Meredith seemed to be of the same mind, only with higher expectations. Aveline had been elated when she'd accidentally knocked a book from the shelf, but Meredith grumbled when Aveline could not pick it back up. She'd given her a task: to bring an object for their next meeting, not something from the library. Aveline had thought to bring her a painting, but even holding the paintbrush for too long proved difficult.

"Bash! Look, I painted Aveline, and now I'm painting Mum. You'll be next."

"Excellent job, *moy mal'chik*." When he ruffled the boy's hair, Aveline caught Maud's brief pinched expression.

"What are you working on, Aveline?" Sebastian moved towards her, his hand settling on her back. She straightened instinctively. "Definitely looks like Leo. I can already see the mischievous glint in his eyes."

"Can you really?" Leo rushed to them; Sebastian caught him by the shoulder before he could knock over the easel. "Wow, you're really good, Aveline. But you forgot my freckles." He tapped his cheekbone.

"I won't forget them," she said. "I have a lot of details to add before I'll be through with yours."

"Are you painting Mum or Bash next?"

"Your mother first. I might also paint Meredith, as long as she is agreeable."

"Good luck with that. She's always in a horrible mood." Shaking his head, the boy returned to his painting.

"Perhaps she'd be in better spirits if you weren't in the habit of nabbing her books and hiding them," Maud said with a hint of amusement.

"I thought it was a fun game! I wanted to know how long it would've taken her to figure it out, but she caught me before I could find a good hiding spot."

"Speaking of Meredith," Sebastian said to Aveline, "she asked if you are ready for another lesson, and wanted to remind you that you have a task to accomplish."

"A task?" Leo peeked at them from behind his canvas. "What kind of task? Like a quest, or like chores?"

"I have to bring her something that's not from the library, something I carry myself to show I'm getting better at remaining corporeal," Aveline explained. "I haven't decided on what to bring."

"Something light would be easiest," Maud suggested, "and maybe something that is somewhat close to the library."

"I can give you one of the buttons that popped off my shirt." Leo rummaged through his pocket. His mother sighed.

"Thank you, but I think it'd be best if I bring her something she knows took at least a little effort to bring to her."

"You could bring her a flower," Sebastian said, chiming in. "It'd be easy to see it was freshly picked."

Aveline thought of the stained-glass window in the library, with its depiction of a rose. "That is an excellent idea."

"I want to come too!" Leo was already halfway down the hallway before the adults had left the room.

"I suppose we could all make a trip out of it." She chuckled. "He never tires, does he?"

"Every once in a while," Maud replied. "If he had his way, he'd go until his body collapsed, and then go again as soon as he woke."

Sebastian reached for Aveline's hand, and out of habit, she almost took it. At the last moment, she jerked away, and hated the way he winced.

"I'm sorry," she said quietly, resisting the desire to hug him until she made that look go away. Maud floated faster to get ahead of them. "I just... I want to do this for myself. I want to show that I'm improving."

"Of course." He cleared his throat, pink tingeing his cheeks. "I should've thought of that."

"No, not at all, we've grown accustomed to a certain level of familiarity around each other, you and I, and it doesn't bother me in the least, so there's no reason to apologise, and I hope that it doesn't discourage you from doing so in the fu—" Aveline halted her rambling, and wished she could melt into the floor.

He offered a smile that did not reach his eyes. "You are improving a great deal."

They walked the rest of the way in silence, the distance between them feeling much more than an arm's length.

HOLDING TIGHTLY TO THE ROSE, AVELINE KNOCKED ON THE LIBRARY door. Leo had helped her pick it out, and Sebastian had cut it at Maud's insistence that Leo not handle the pruning shears. When giving it to Aveline, Sebastian had taken care to avoid accidentally touching her; she had pretended not to notice.

"Enter," ordered Meredith.

For a few seconds, Aveline stared at the door. If she shifted back into a ghost, she could go through it with ease but she'd drop the rose and incur judgement. Her hold on her corporeal form felt tenuous at best, but there was no other way around it: she'd have to focus hard enough to push open the door, walk inside, and hand over the flower. If Aveline rushed, Meredith would make her try again. She had to at least appear in control.

"You can do it." Sebastian stood close enough that his long legs could have crossed the distance between them in a few short strides.

"I think you have more faith in me than I do," she admitted, even as courage began to bloom in her chest. It was a simple thing she was doing, she just had to have faith. One step at a time.

"I could say the same." This time his smile was genuine, albeit laced with sadness. "Don't be afraid to fail, Aveline. It doesn't mean it's the end. You can always try again."

"Are you talking to me, or yourself?"

"I said to enter!" Meredith called.

The corner of his mouth ticked upward. "Both. You'd better go to her before she loses her temper."

Aveline risked another moment to study him, to take in the way he stood, completely facing her; the way he looked at her, with a myriad of emotions she wanted to decipher; the way he smiled, like he was barely holding back a thousand unsaid things between them.

"Aveline!"

She broke eye contact and, with a deep breath, pushed open the door. At first, there was no resistance, and she feared her hand would go straight through. So she took a moment to gather herself and tried again, this time sweeping through the entryway with her head held high.

Hovering to reach, Meredith shelved a few bulky tomes. She followed Aveline's every movement, finally looking at the rose she extended with both hands. At the ghost's frown, Aveline dropped one hand to her side and rolled the stem between her fingertips, making the crimson petals flair and twirl. *Look!* she wanted to shout with excitement. *You wanted proof of my progress, and here it is. Please, accept it...* Already the bends and grooves of the stem were far less noticeable, and the natural chill of the castle was fading.

Adjusting her spectacles, Meredith lowered herself to the floor but made no move to accept the token. "What took you so long to enter?"

Aveline thought to mention Sebastian but changed her mind, in case Meredith assumed she had cheated by using his help. "I was summoning my resolve."

One thin brow arched. "You had to summon the resolve to walk through the door?"

Sensing that her grip was slipping, Aveline adjusted slightly, enough to prick her thumb on a thorn. "I had to summon the resolve to not discount myself before I even tried. As a dear friend pointed out to me, failing does not mean it is the end. I can always try again."

Meredith's expression softened. "You are learning not to stand in your own way."

Aveline pressed harder until the thorn bit through her flesh, drawing a bead of blood. She was here, alive, human, a person who could feel and hope and dream and overcome.

"Why a rose?"

Red dripped down the stem. "You wanted something to challenge me, so I thought to bring you something I'd have to go outside to retrieve. Besides," she said, peering up at the stained-glass window, "something tells me they have meaning for your family." The pain dulled; before she could react, the rose fell through her fingers and hit the floor, scattering a few petals. Suppressing an aggravated sigh, Aveline stooped to pick it up again, willing her translucent hand to turn corporeal enough to touch it once more. *She is going to make me try again...*

As she made contact with the rose, its brilliant colours dimmed, its outline wispy. She blinked, slowly raising it. Not quite as translucent as she was, she could make out the general dark shapes of whatever was behind it. The petals on the floor remained as they had been, but when she plucked one up, it changed as well.

"Fascinating." Meredith drew closer. "Place it on the desk."

Carefully, she obeyed, fully expecting it to fall through. Instead, the moment she let go, the rose returned to its natural state, resting on the wooden surface. "What did I do?"

"I am not entirely certain," Meredith admitted, trying it for herself. It remained tangible. "It is definitely something for us to figure out. But I will say, you are right—roses are a symbol of the Blaise family. And you did well."

Aveline inwardly preened at the praise. Not only had she made strides, but she had done something remarkable and new—ignoring that she wanted to be rid of this ghostly curse, it stirred her curiosity that she had, somehow, made a rose temporarily incorporeal.

"Try again."

They spent time on both Aveline turning physical as well as her making objects intangible. She found the bigger the item, the harder it was. There were a few smaller books she managed to make shift, and, at Meredith's request, brought them with her through the wall. On one attempt, the book got stuck in the wall, which she quickly remedied and apologised for, relieved it hadn't done any damage.

"Are you certain this is a curse?" Meredith asked. "I can see how you could use this to your advantage."

"I hadn't thought of it." Aveline thumbed through the pages of the physical book, then successfully shifted both herself and the book to ghostly versions of themselves. "I haven't the slightest idea what I'd use it for. It's not as if I'm seeking a life of thievery."

Meredith almost smiled. "The option is there if you change your mind. I think that is enough for one day. You can meet me here tomorrow, and this time bring me a cake from the kitchen."

Imagining how excited Leo would be when she asked for his help, Aveline liked the idea, but was not ready to be dismissed. "Actually, if you do not mind, I have a few questions for you about your family."

Her brow arched again. "What would you like to know?"

"There are... rumours... about what happened to certain members of your family."

"I assume they are rumours you do not feel comfortable asking my grandson about?" Meredith began putting the books back on the shelves, and Aveline joined her, hoping she wouldn't accidentally drop one again.

"I do not believe them, but I'm afraid that if I ask him, it will pain him to answer. It would wound me if he thought I doubted his character."

Her nerves frayed more and more as the silence extended, until Meredith requested, "Tell me the rumours."

Aveline paused. *I would hate to hear horrible rumours about my family...* But it was already too late to change her mind. "They claim that Sebastian killed his family, but I cannot believe that, not after knowing him. Something must have happened..."

"They know him by name?"

"No, they call him 'The Magic Collector', saying he steals magic artefacts."

Meredith huffed a laugh. "That much is true. But if it eases your heart, no, Sebastian did not kill them, although it was a tragic accident in which he unintentionally played his part."

A wave of dizziness hit her, as though the floor had pitched under her feet. "What? What happened?"

With a sympathetic look, Meredith shook her head. "That is a tale for Sebastian to tell." Before Aveline could press for more information, she said dismissively, "Good night, Aveline. I will see you tomorrow afternoon."

CHAPTER 32

YOU DID WHAT YOU HAD TO, FOR HIS SAFETY

He is not a killer. Too tired from shifting between forms, Aveline found herself stuck as a ghost, pacing her room as she contemplated what she'd been told. Was that what Sebastian was so afraid of? Did he blame himself for whatever happened? But there must have been more than one thing he was afraid of: he also shied away from showing her his arm, and he'd told her that happened when Maud was pregnant with Leo, sometime after the tragedy of his family.

As if vocalising the sorrowful thoughts, the attic ghost's sobs carried down the hall; the walls trembled.

"Erratic," Aveline murmured ponderously. They'd travelled not too long ago, so they should have had more time. If they left again and Aveline missed Jeanette's wedding because they did not make it back...

The cries continued, making the windows rattle. Aveline stepped away from them, even though they were covered by the thick curtains. *That will not become my fate,* she resolved. But had the poor unfortunate soul had a choice in the matter, whoever the attic ghost was?

Scrape, clink-clink-clink.

Where Titan was, Leo was certain to be soon, and that meant going to the kitchens. Even if she could not eat anything, a break from her own mind seemed like it would do her some good, so she stepped into the hall. The candles flickered and the walls shook with each step the ghoul took. His shadow stretched so far that it touched the darkness beyond, where, slowly, candlelight went out in sets of two, like it was creeping along behind him.

"Titan!" Leo bounded towards the ghoul, his ever-present hounds with him. But where Leo skipped from one foot to the other with excitement, chattering about what treats he could filch from the pantry, Solas and Luna shrank back, ears flattened, teeth bared. Titan halted under the attic, staring down at them. Instinct taking over, Aveline rushed forward—

A soul-stabbing shriek split the air; Titan jerked like he'd been hit with lightning, then unleashed a roar. Leo tumbled backward, eyes wide, mouth agape. The ghoul towered over him, raising his monstrous paw overhead. The hounds snarled and snapped and lunged, keeping themselves between their boy and the beast.

"Titan!" He scrambled to his feet. "It's me, your friend Leo! We're not going to hurt you, we're getting snacks."

The paw swung down as Aveline reached Titan and shoved his back, willing herself to turn corporeal for just a moment—

A thousand tiny needles stabbed her mind at once, followed by flashes of images: a man in dark clothes standing over her bed, a weeping woman fallen onto the floor, a music box with a spinning ballerina—

Sorrow took hold of Aveline's throat and dragged her down into its depths. She gaped, desperate to suck in breath enough to fight back.

Sebastian! She made to reach for her heart, but Titan struck her, sending her flying backwards. She collided with the floor with bone-rattling pain that knocked the remaining air from her lungs. The black crept into her vision, ready to overtake her.

One of the hounds yelped; something thudded.

A snap.

A child's scream.

Tasting copper, Aveline gasped and choked as she rolled onto her stomach. She blinked, her vision returning in a haze of colours.

"Leonard!" Aveline could barely make out the shape of Maud as she rushed to her son, slumped against the bannister. Titan moved just enough to reveal Sebastian standing in front of him, hand raised ominously.

"Stop!" Leo pleaded. "Don't! He doesn't mean it!"

"Stay back!" Sebastian ordered. Aveline pushed herself onto her feet and swayed, stumbling her way towards them.

"Bash, DON'T!"

At first, nothing happened. But the air seemed to go still, and Aveline froze in place, leaning heavily on the doorframe. Then bits of Titan's hair began to move, floating away until Aveline realised they were not bits of hair—it was bits of the ghoul himself, like Sebastian had fractured him into thousands of pieces no bigger than marbles. The farther away they floated, the darker and smaller they became until they disappeared entirely. As the last ones vanished, there was a final sigh, and an ear-splitting shriek from the attic.

Then utter silence.

Sebastian fell to his hands and knees. Aveline hurried towards him, a little more sure-footed, but he had already crawled to Leo and inspected his arm, which was bent at an odd angle.

"Don't touch me!" Leo sobbed, shrinking as far into the corner as he could.

Sebastian flinched. "Leo, we have to—"

"You killed him!"

Solas whimpered from where he lay. Tail tucked between her hind legs, Luna licked his face.

"I said don't touch me!"

Sebastian sat back on his heels, expression stricken.

"Leonard," Maud interjected, "he needs to—"

"NO!"

"You're hurt—"

"Leave me alone!"

Maud shot Sebastian an intense look. With a broken sigh, the wizard wiggled his fingers and the boy's head slumped, eyes slipping shut.

"He hates me," Sebastian whispered hoarsely.

"He doesn't hate you," Maud snapped as if that was the most

absurd statement she'd ever heard in her life. "He just needs to calm down. And he *has* to have medical attention. Now."

He ran an unsteady hand through his hair. "I don't have enough magic, Maud. I can't fix all of it right now."

It was then, when Aveline took another step forward to peer over Sebastian's shoulder, that she saw the swelling and discolouration on the boy's legs, the blood trickling down the side of his face.

"I can help set his arm," Aveline offered, still struggling to draw breath, "if Maud gives me instructions."

Maud gave her a grateful nod and said to Sebastian, "Ease what you can, we'll handle the rest."

He placed his hand on Leo's knee. The boy did not react, deep in magic-induced unconsciousness. The swelling went down, and the dark bruises changed to yellowish tones. A bead of sweat rolled down Sebastian's temple by the time he scooped Leo into his arms. "Fetch what you need. I'll meet you in his room."

AVELINE AND MAUD MADE IT BACK TO LEO'S ROOM TO SEE Sebastian in a chair in the far corner, staring at the child. He perked up slightly but remained sitting as Aveline laid out the supplies on the nightstand.

"Sebastian, he did not mean anything he said," Maud insisted. "You can sit closer."

No response.

"You did what you had to, for his safety."

Still nothing.

Aveline studied the child neatly tucked in bed, with his flushed cheeks, dishevelled hair, and furrowed brow. For some reason, he looked smaller than normal, especially with the hounds curled up next to him. Solas took shallow breaths; Aveline wondered if Sebastian had helped him onto the bed.

With deceptive calm, Maud gave Aveline instructions, and she followed as best she could. She imagined the emotional turmoil Maud was warring with, seeing her son in such a state and being unable to do anything but instruct.

"This part is tricky," she warned, "but important. We have to reset the bone before we can bind it."

Silently, Sebastian rose from his seat and crossed the room. He reached past Aveline to place his hand on Leo's shoulder. "I can keep him asleep for the time being. He won't feel any pain."

Aveline resolved to be somewhat quick, so as not to drain too much of Sebastian's magic reserves. She didn't want to know what would happen if he ran out.

Her chest tightened and her stomach flipped as she held Leo's arm. She bit down on the inside of her cheek and listened carefully to Maud, trying not to focus on the way she could bend his arm. When she felt the bump of bone on bone, she tensed and bit harder, willing herself to keep it together for a few more moments despite the bile rising up her throat. Sebastian hurriedly placed the splint underneath. The moment the bandage was secured, Aveline cast her gaze to the ceiling and inhaled slowly.

"Well done," Maud murmured. Aveline did not reply.

Sebastian rubbed her back. "After I replenish some magic, I'll mend the bone. He won't be in pain for long."

"I know he won't," Maud said. "But maybe a little pain will help him understand the seriousness of the situation."

Lowering her sights to Leo, Aveline gently brushed a few damp hairs away from his forehead. It reminded her of when her brothers were little and bedbound by illness—she had found a way to be strong then, and she could be strong now, if not for her own sake, then for his. It wouldn't do to have him wake in distress only to have it magnified by her worry. They were already sure to have to aid him through his anger and grief at losing his friend.

"He will forgive you, Sebastian, I promise," Maud declared with such conviction that neither of them could argue. Aveline believed it regardless, but Sebastian...

"I hope you are right." His hand fell away from Aveline's back, leaving a sudden chill in that spot.

"I usually am." Her joke fell flat, her tone too worn with worry and fatigue—something they all shared. Aveline contemplated finding a chair to place next to his bed so she could sink into it, rest her eyes for a bit. There were far too many emotions for her to slip into being a ghost at the moment, and she had no desire to flee them, not when the others were burdened with them as well.

"Aveline," Maud asked, "would you do us a favour and make lunch? It would do all three of you some good."

"I can make it," Sebastian offered, heading towards the door.

"You sit. You won't replenish anything without rest."

He halted; the two of them stared one another down, a silent battle of wills.

"No need to worry, I will make it." Aveline forced her stiff, aching limbs to cooperate. As she passed Sebastian, he grabbed her hand. "It is quite all right, I assure you." She gave him a small smile despite knowing it would convince no one. "Please, rest."

But he did not let her go. "You are hurt."

"Just bumps and bruises, nothing serious." Aveline took a step back, not entirely upset that he still held on. "Rest," she implored him. "I'll return shortly."

Aveline could feel his eyes on her even after she shut the door and leant against it. Had they been alone with him looking at her like that, she wouldn't have had the strength to leave. She would have melted into him until the stress eventually ebbed away.

He thinks you need him—he does not have much left to give. Do not be greedy.

She ambled towards the kitchen, holding tightly to the unbroken parts of the bannister. It was so unfair that she couldn't be there for him the way he was for her. She longed to give him the same comfort and safety, to make him smile and laugh and feel like there was another layer to life, a new spectrum of colours to enjoy.

Congratulations, Edith, I have the potential to turn into a lovesick romantic like you always hoped I would.

CHAPTER 33

NOT AS SELFLESS AS YOU MIGHT THINK

No one came to check on Aveline, despite how long it took to make the soup. When she brought the bowls on a trolley, she found the door cracked open, and quietly entered in case Sebastian had fallen asleep. She was right: he lounged in the chair, long legs extended outward and crossed at the ankles, a knitted blanket covering him, but the moment she took a second step into the room, he jolted up, eyes seeking her instantly. The blanket slipped, and he jerked it back into place.

"I didn't mean to wake you," she whispered, rolling the cart to him.

"I wasn't completely asleep. I'm too worried to rest properly, if I'm being honest." Moving his legs to make room, he scrubbed at his face. "Unfortunately, the sooner I regain strength, the sooner I can help him. A bit of a conundrum, you see."

Aveline glanced in Leo's direction; he remained unnervingly still. She had to look away. "Eating might help." It was pleasantly surprising how calm and collected she sounded. A far cry from how she felt inside. Not quite a month had passed, and yet worry ate away at her over their wellbeing just as much as it would for her family.

The thought of leaving them after the curse was broken soured her stomach. There would be no reason for her to stay—but maybe she could visit?

"This was kind of you. Thank you."

Carrying her chair over, she sat across from him while they used the trolley as a makeshift table. He adjusted the blanket again so that only his left arm was exposed and could manoeuvre with ease.

Was he so exhausted that his illusion had failed? *You do not have to hide it from me,* she thought. *No matter how scarred, it will not matter to me.* It was whole enough that he wore rings on that hand as well, and he seemed to perform certain functions with it, albeit clumsily.

"You are welcome." She forced her attention away from his arm. Fixating would only succeed in making him feel uncomfortable. "Where is Maud?"

Sebastian paused, the spoon halfway to his mouth. "I am not entirely sure. She said she needed a moment alone."

Aveline could only imagine how difficult it was. She did not blame Maud for wanting a moment alone.

They ate in silence, other than the small clinking of their spoons against the bowls and Luna whimpering in her sleep.

"How long will it take him to heal?"

"Without my magic, maybe a couple of months. With it, a couple of days, depending on how quickly I replenish it." His soup was already gone, as well as a few pieces of bread he'd used to soak up the last of the broth at the bottom of the bowl. He sat back, gaze trained on Leo.

"Do not blame yourself," Aveline said gently, setting her spoon down. Her hunger seemed to have vanished, her soup untouched.

"Can you read me so easily?"

"As well as you can read me, I imagine."

She could practically see the wheels turning in his head. The longer he studied her, the more she wanted to fidget.

Abruptly, she strode to the fireplace. "It's a little chilly in here," she commented, willing her voice not to waver.

"I can—"

"Nonsense. You rest, I can handle lighting a fire." If she were lucky, he'd mistake any rosiness in her cheeks as warmth from the flames.

"I am not sure you are right," he said hesitantly. "About how easily we read one another, that is."

"What do you mean?"

"I mean that you read me like a book, while I feel like I'm trying to translate a tome with you."

She cast him a questioning look over her shoulder as she lit the fire. "That could be misconstrued as rude. Are you saying that I am complicated and boring? Long-winded?"

His brows shot up. "Not at all! I apologise for any insult. I only meant that... the more I get to know you, the more I find I want to know because you see the world in a different, more fascinating way than I do."

Slowly, she stood, staring at the ornate mantle that hosted only a few baubles: a pearl brooch, a weathered book whose title was illegible, and a figurine of a dancer that was chipped in a few places but not in terrible condition. If she stared, she did not have to face him and risk him seeing something in her before she had time to process it for herself.

"I like getting to know you, Aveline."

The sentence did not stand on its own—she could hear that there was a follow up that he had yet to voice. Pressing her lips together, she waited, feeling like she was trying to balance on a tightrope without a net to break her fall. One slip, and her feelings would shatter beyond repair. Or was he reaching out to her, helping her to the other side?

If sparing my feelings is what is giving you pause, I beg of you to end this before my thoughts spiral further out of control, dragging my heart along with them.

"Aveline," Sebastian whispered, his breath tickling her ear.

Shivers rippled down her back even as her face flushed. When had he crossed the room? She closed her eyes, fighting the urge to lean back into him, to feel his arms around her...

"I know..." He cleared his throat. "I know things between us have been... confusing, and that I'm the source of it. Please, do not think that you have done anything wrong."

"But I feel as though I have," she admitted, struggling to keep her voice even. She barely heard the crackle of the fire, or even herself, over the pounding of her heart. "Ever since I tried to... to kiss you, it's as if we've been awkwardly dancing around each other, one moment at ease and the next walking on hot coals. Sebastian, I—"

He gripped her shoulder. She was tempted to turn around, to see if passion drew out hints of other colours in his irises. "It was not you," he insisted. "There is—there is something I must tell you—"

Leo moaned. In three quick strides, Aveline was at his bedside, cradling his cheek as his eyes fluttered halfway open.

"Hurts... Everything hurts."

"I know, sweetheart, I'm sorry." Hands trembling, Aveline tilted his head to help him sip a glass of what looked like weak tea. Maud had told her which herbs to pluck from the garden, herbs for pain and healing to crush and mix into the water. She sensed Sebastian was behind her, watching, and wondered if he was purposefully keeping out of Leo's sight.

The child coughed and Aveline used a handkerchief to wipe what dribbled out the side of his mouth. "Aveline," he rasped, eyelids almost closed, "Titan. Hurts..."

"Shhhhhh..." She pressed a gentle kiss to his forehead. "Sleep. You will be better soon, I promise. Everything will be all right." Out of the corner of her eye, she saw Sebastian retreat to his chair. Ignoring the ache in her chest, she began to hum as she stroked Leo's hair. Within minutes, his breathing slowed, but the furrow in his brow remained.

"You are good with him," Sebastian said.

"Thank you." She squelched the desire to press him to resume. The moment had fled, and if they were going to have a monumental discussion, it would be better done alone. "As are you."

His throat bobbed. "It does not feel that way. I indulge him too often—the boy needs a father."

"He has you, Sebastian. I've seen the way you are with him, heard how he gushes that you're part of his family. To him, you are his father." Settling back into her seat, she softened her tone. "No parent is perfect. You've been there for the fun times just as much as the difficult ones. You not only take care of him, but you encourage and inspire him."

"...I know you and Maud say I'm doing what I can, but it's not safe here, and as much as I'd like to be able to protect them and provide a safe environment, I can't."

There was no argument for that. While nowhere was truly safe, this was the most dangerous place she'd been—yet despite that, she felt protected. There were other ghosts, ghouls, and monsters, but here, Aveline could be herself. She did not have to pretend, did not have to filter out the bad so she could be accepted.

"I know they cannot leave because of Maud... But even if Maud could leave, I would hate to see them go. I always wanted to be a father, but... Maybe I'm not ready, not with all of this baggage. I don't want to pass that on to him." He paused. "I feel selfish, keeping them here."

"You are one of the most selfless people I know, Sebastian."

He finally made eye contact with her. "Not as selfless as you might think," he whispered, and said nothing else.

CHAPTER 34

I NEVER EVEN GOT TO HOLD HIM

Aveline didn't intend to fall asleep in the chair. Leo easily roused her with his groans and whimpers as he slept restlessly, and she tended to him each time, giving him soup or drink, and humming tunes she'd thought were long forgotten, from times when her siblings were still young.

The third time she woke, Sebastian was gone. She pulled her chair close to the bed so she could hold Leo's hand as she stared at the empty seat in the corner. She should continue to be patient, and yet it pained her to know that a portion of his suffering was for her sake, all because he feared telling her.

I am afraid too, she thought. *I am afraid that you will sacrifice yourself because you are terrified of making me uncomfortable, of frightening me. I am afraid of losing you, Sebastian, and while I want the curse broken… I am afraid that leaving this place would mean never seeing you again.*

Aveline kissed Leo's hand. Her exhaustion alone should have yanked her back into being a ghost, yet here she was. It might have been her bruises and aching ribs that kept her human, but it felt like there was more to it than that—determination.

Together, they would get through this. They were battered, but they were not broken.

"Aveline?"

She jolted at Maud's voice; the ghost's hand pulled away from her shoulder. Aveline straightened, crinkling her nose as her stiff neck and back protested about having slept in the awkward position, hunched over Leo's bed while still halfway sitting in her armchair.

"Didn't mean to give you a fright." Maud took a few steps back, casting her gaze upon her son. "Thank you for staying with him."

"Of course." As if she could have left his side, knowing how exhausted Sebastian was and how distraught Maud was? "I admit, I expected he'd be awake by now."

"That medicine is meant to dull pain and make him sleep. I'd give some to Sebastian if I..." she trailed off, lips pressing together in a thin line.

"Sebastian disappeared partway through the night. I'm hoping he got rest."

"I hope so too."

The ticking of the grandfather clock filled the empty air. Aveline peered at the fireplace to find that there was nothing left but ash. As if suddenly realising the room was cold, she shivered, and a shawl slipped off one shoulder. With a frown, she lifted it—not a shawl, but Sebastian's blanket. A smile tugged at her mouth, unbidden.

"I have to confess something to you."

Aveline's attention snapped to Maud. Despite being incorporeal, there were hints of wrinkles at the corners of her eyes, and the set of her jaw was sharp and serious.

"But I do not think you will like it... I think you will look down on me for it, but what does that matter?" Hushed words, all edged. "I must speak my truth before it continues to eat away at me."

Releasing Leo's hand, Aveline wrapped the blanket tighter around her. "Please, feel free to speak plainly, Maud. I count you as a friend."

Gaze never wavering from her son, Maud had a flicker of a smile that might have been easily missed. The hint of blue in her eyes was reminiscent of Leo's, but the longer Aveline studied her translucent, pale form, the more she found the bits Leo got from her: the dainty shape of her nose, the splash of freckles across her cheekbones—there was even enough of a hue to her hair that Aveline suspected that it was only a few shades darker than her son's, and that his would eventually match.

"I like you, Aveline," she began, almost inaudibly, like she was speaking to herself. "But I am also horribly jealous of you."

Jealous, of her? Why? Was it because Aveline could slip back and forth, shedding her ghostly form?

Continuing in a strained rush, Maud said, "Leo loves you, and I do not fault him for it. But I… he holds your hand, he leans into your touch when you brush his hair away from his face, he lights up when he gets to hug you." She pressed the back of her hand to her mouth. "You are becoming a mother to him."

Aveline leant back in her seat, putting a little distance between her and the child who still slept, frowning and twitching as though he were trying to fight his way awake. "I can see where you'd feel that way," she said, treading lightly, "but Leo has known me for only a short while. I am nowhere near a mother to him, Maud. There is a bond between the two of you that could not be replicated. He may insist we are family, but you are his mother. No one could ever take your place."

Maud was as still as a gravestone, all but the transparent skirts slowly swaying about her feet. "Unfortunately, that does not ease the ache in my heart." Aveline scrambled to find something to say, a way to console her, but Maud added in a faltering voice, "I feel like a failure as a mother. I cannot hold him when he cries, or rock him to sleep, or kiss his forehead, or brush his hair away from his face…"

"It is not your fault things ended up this way." Aveline stood but kept her distance. She might have braved hugging Sebastian in a situation like this, but would Maud accept it? Would it even be possible, when Aveline was in her human state?

"Yet I feel guilty all the same. A child needs affection from his mother."

"You have been with him his entire life. That counts for a great deal more than you think."

Maud sniffled. "I died in childbirth," she sobbed, ghostly tears slipping down her cheeks and disappearing as they hit the floor. "I never even got to hold him."

Without another thought, Aveline embraced Maud. To her relief, the woman's forehead rested against her shoulder, muffling her cries. Aveline's sleeve became damp as Maud clung to her. *This is what grief sounds like.* The ghost in the attic came to mind, the screams and wails. There were many sounds of grief, many reasons to grieve—and many ways to grieve. When was the last time Maud had been held, or even touched another person?

Whatever the reason was that Aveline could hug her, she was thankful, even if this was the only way she could make things a little bit better.

LATER THAT DAY, AVELINE BROUGHT HER PAINTING SUPPLIES TO Leo's room.

"Are you certain you want to paint *me*?" Maud asked for the third time.

"I do." Aveline smiled. *If there is a chance I can make you feel alive and human again, I'll take it.*

Unlike when she was painting Leo, Maud was the prime subject, keeping still and patient as Aveline brought her to life on the canvas. "You are allowed to move a little."

"That's one good thing about being a ghost," Maud replied with a half-hearted smirk, "your body never aches." Since her confession, there was more solidity to her form, and a small spark to her eyes Aveline hoped to capture.

"You and Leo have identical expressions at times."

"Unfortunately, we are far too identical in ways I wish we weren't."

Aveline peeked at her with a raised brow. "Such as?"

She laughed. "Well, for one thing, he gets into just as much trouble as I did as a child. I was forever snooping and causing my parents stress. We went through multiple governesses because they all gave up trying to raise me as a proper lady. One thought I was really a changeling, swapped at birth by the Fae, who took the real, human version of me to live in the Wild Lands."

"That sounds like a tale my sister Edith would spin."

When Maud didn't reply at first, Aveline was content to continue her painting in silence, but then she said, "Sebastian told me that your sister is to be wed to the Crown Prince. I hope that doesn't upset you."

"Not at all," Aveline assured her. "It did at first, but Jeanette looks forward to marrying Alexei and becoming a princess. Royal life does not suit me nearly as well as it does her, so if she is happy, I am happy."

"Then you are unencumbered. What will you do then, once your curse is broken?"

She paused mid-stroke. "I don't know... I suppose I'm free to do as I wish, not having to worry about our family's security." There would be too many things changing for her to feel comfortable thinking about it for long.

"Is there somewhere you've always wanted to go, something you've always wanted to do?"

Aveline swirled the paintbrush in the jar of water to rinse it before using another colour. "Edith was the dreamer, not I."

"Surely there is something you desire."

Luckily, Aveline had the canvas to hide behind. "I am just getting to know myself in truth for the first time. Sooner or later, desire will find me." *A different desire*, she silently corrected as a pair of brown eyes came to mind. "Perhaps I will become a professional painter." Society felt that it was ludicrous for a woman to never truly marry, and to instead pursue a career. But why would she let that stop her? She did not have to secure a match now; why not pursue something that would make her happy?

"You certainly have the skill for it." While Aveline tried not to preen at the compliment, Maud continued, "If you do leave, I hope you'll visit us often. This place wouldn't be the same without you."

"If that's the decision I make, I'll most certainly visit." Her throat tight, Aveline refocused on smaller details so she could keep those imaginings at bay for just a little while longer. A future without them could loom on the horizon, but she would bask in the sun anyway, for as long as possible.

"You don't have to leave, you know."

Aveline flinched, causing paint to smear. Releasing a soft hiss between her teeth, she dabbed at the section with a cloth. She supposed she could make the background a little darker to hide the mistake if necessary.

"Aveline, I mean it. You don't have to leave if you want to stay."

She remained behind her canvas, only able to see Leo's face and part of Solas's back paws from this angle. Yet there was enough of Maud painted that it seemed like she was staring at her anyway. "Thank you."

"But?"

Carefully setting the paintbrush on the easel, she clasped her hands together in her lap. "But I don't know if I'll be able to."

Amidst the prolonged pause, Aveline considered resuming her painting, but then Maud said, "If this is about Sebastian—"

"What about me?"

The women turned to see Sebastian standing in the open doorway.

CHAPTER 35

HE WAS MY FRIEND...

Sebastian cocked his head to the side, looking back and forth between the two of them. "Seems I startled you—my apologies. I thought I'd make myself known before I overheard something I wasn't meant to." His brow pinched as he focused on Aveline, who couldn't find it in herself to break eye contact or school her expression.

"If only Leo would pick up your good habits instead of my bad ones." Maud sighed. "You look as though you're feeling better."

It was true: his cheeks held a little more colour, and he stood taller, shoulders not so slumped. It didn't escape Aveline's notice that he wore a cloak. Was he headed somewhere? At least his shirt was a brighter tone today, meaning, Aveline had learnt, that he was in a better mood. She decided that the green suited him—but so had red and purple and blue. And black. His white shirt as well.

She peeled her gaze away from him and resumed her painting.

"Thank you, I do feel somewhat better." He moved past her, and her back tingled. In her peripheral, she saw him kneel beside the bed and murmur something in Leo's ear. He placed his hand on his forehead, earning an incoherent mumble from the boy, and then stood. "I mended his fractures a little. I should be able to completely heal him in the next few days."

Maud *tsked*. "You recover your magic faster when you give it more than a few hours of rest at a time."

"I cannot bear the thought of leaving him in pain longer than I have to." Sebastian adjusted the blanket so that Leo was completely covered again, and when Solas nosed at his hand, he scratched under his chin. "I see you are painting Maud, Aveline. It's coming along beautifully."

"You can't keep changing the subject when things don't go your way," Maud griped, her words carrying no sting to them.

"You are next," Aveline reminded him, eyes trained on the canvas even as he drew closer.

"Did Meredith turn down your offer?"

"I still need to confirm with her. If she declines, you are next. Also, I concur with Maud: you need rest."

"I'm finding it difficult to sleep, given the circumstances."

"Understandable, but rest doesn't always mean sleep." Maud whistled, making the hounds' ears perk up. "Come along, you two. When was the last time you were outside?" Solas and Luna hopped off the bed and trotted along behind her as she exited the room.

"Perhaps I should help her." Aveline made to stand, but Sebastian stopped her with a hand on her shoulder.

"No need. I made small doors especially for them; all they have to do is push to go out and back in."

Again, he had thought of nearly everything to make everyone else's lives easier while neglecting his own. Each scrap of magic replenished was instantly used again—

Realising the dull ache in her ribs was easing, she pulled away from him. "Stop."

"Stop what?"

Aveline threw him a judgmental look. "I know you're trying to heal me. You and Leo need the magic far more than I do."

"Aveline..." Sebastian reached for her; she stood so fast that the chair toppled.

"No, Sebastian. I appreciate that you want to help me, but I'll not accept it at your expense." At his wounded look, she softened her tone. "You have given so much already. It is good to take a little time for yourself."

Slowly, he lowered his hand. "But I want to help."

"You cannot help anyone if you cannot help yourself. We will be fine, I promise. Leo isn't in any danger. I'm not in any danger. But *you* are in danger of exhausting yourself." She cupped his cheek, ran her thumb over the stubble. He leant into her touch. "We care about you, Sebastian. *I* care about you. We want you happy and healthy just as much as you want those things for us."

With a small, bittersweet smile, Sebastian kissed the heel of her palm. "There is something I must tell you."

"What is it?" she breathed.

"Bash?"

They jumped apart like children getting caught pilfering biscuits when they were supposed to be in bed.

"How are you feeling?" Sebastian knelt beside Leo.

"Awful." The boy blinked, expression sharpening as if coming out of a daze. "You killed Titan." He pushed himself up and away from Sebastian, hissing and clutching at his arm. "How could you?"

"He was a threat, Leo—"

"He was my *friend!*"

"He hurt you and Aveline. I couldn't risk anything else happening."

Leo halted, his fury melting into shock as his attention shifted to Aveline.

"I'm all right," she said. "Just some aches and bruises."

Tears welled in the boy's eyes. "He was my friend..."

Aveline went to console him, but Sebastian had already climbed onto the bed. "I know," he whispered, pulling Leo into his arms and pressing a gentle kiss to the top of his head. "I'm so sorry, *moy mal'chik*, I'm so sorry."

With a patter of paws, Solas and Luna bolted into the room and leapt onto the bed, licking and nuzzling Leo's tear-streaked face. Maud remained in the doorway, watching with a pained, helpless expression until Aveline hugged her.

Maybe we are a family, Aveline thought. *No matter how difficult the circumstances, we endure them together.*

AVELINE HAD HOPED THERE WOULD BE A MOMENT FOR SEBASTIAN TO resume his confession, but she couldn't bear to break up him and Leo, not when they were mending the hurt between them. She and Maud gave them privacy by taking a walk through the castle.

"I told him Leo would forgive him," Maud said. "But I understand how horrible it feels when a child says they hate you."

"That does sound awful." Although the silence of the castle was a nice change of pace, it left an uncomfortable knot in her stomach, waiting for a cry or scream or for the walls to shake. Normally clean, a thin layer of dust covered the floor at the bottom of the stairs, where they had huddled together while Sebastian redirected the castle. *He must be the one who cleans everything... He keeps up with too much using magic.* "He admitted he doesn't feel like a good parental figure."

Maud huffed. "That man puts too high of a standard on himself. He's raised Leo since birth—even helped with the birth itself."

Aveline blinked in surprise. Of course it made sense that Sebastian had helped her, but she hadn't imagined it. Every time her mother went into labour, all of the children had been brought to another part of the house while the midwife and doctor did what was necessary. Only once had Edith talked her into sneaking in to see what was happening, but they hadn't even made it to the door before their mother's wails inspired them to hightail it back to their rooms. They never saw what exactly happened (Aveline was given a basic understanding when she became an adult), but their mother always recovered. Maud had not. Sebastian had been there to witness Leo's birth and Maud's death within a short time span...

The two of them walked into the garden, but not even the fresh air cleared the dark imaginings plaguing Aveline's mind. If she had lost her mother... would she have been able to forgive her youngest siblings?

She greatly doubted her mother would have stuck around as a ghost, not when they were so widely believed to be nothing but scary stories.

"I suspect he still blames himself," Maud said. "But, truly, there was nothing he could have done without risking his own life. I've told him repeatedly, as much as I wish I could be human again, I consider myself lucky that I can at least be a part of my son's life and watch him grow up, if only as a ghost."

"That's a bittersweet thought."

They stopped in the middle of the greenery, high hedges hiding them from the sunlight and obscuring their view of the castle. Aveline had to focus to see Maud, the faint lines of her almost blending into their surroundings.

"I've had far worse. The bitterest of my thoughts is that, while I am the ghost, my son is the one haunting me." She reached out to pluck a rose, and sighed when her fingers went through it. "What I would not give to be able to hold him someday."

Heart twisting, Aveline suggested, "Perhaps Sebastian will find a way."

"...Perhaps. But it is the least of our worries." With a sad smile, Maud turned to walk back, but Aveline grabbed her hand.

"Your desires are important, Maud."

For a few seconds, they stared at one another. Aveline could have sworn Maud regained a little colour, the edges of her more defined.

"Yours are as well." Smile brighter, Maud led her back inside, and Aveline was content to not have to respond. "We should probably give them a bit more time. Is there somewhere you'd like to go, something you'd like to do? It's rather unfortunate we left your painting supplies in Leo's room."

"Actually," Aveline replied, "I'd like to pay Meredith a visit."

Her brows shot upwards. "The crotchety old woman seems to have taken a liking to you, or at least tolerates you more than the rest of us."

"You don't like her?"

She chuckled. "I didn't mean that in the least. I actually hoped we could become friends, but she's far more interested in her books and consolidating information on her genealogy. By the time she was starting to get to know me, I had Leo, and I don't think she's yet forgiven him for drooling on and ripping a few pages out of her *Lineage of the Blaise Family* tome."

"I can only imagine how horrified she was. When we were young, Edith tried to dye my hair with ink because I'd accidentally ruined her favourite book with spilt milk. Our father caught her in time, so I only had to have a few inches of my hair cut off."

Maud shook her head. "Ah, the insanity of children. When Sebastian had finally convinced Meredith to allow Leo to visit the library again a few years later, he swiped one of the books and tried to take it to his room. She wasn't pleased in the least, and even more so when he broke the spine."

Having arrived at the library, Aveline knocked. "Meredith? May Maud and I enter?"

"Does she have her imp with her?"

"No."

"Then you may enter."

Aveline skirted around the dozens of neat stacks placed about the room. She eyed the titles but had no idea what *Love the Heartbreak* and *Histories of Burketon* had in common that would clue her into what organisation method Meredith was trying to incorporate.

"I am sorting them by level of tragedy," the ghost librarian explained, guessing correctly what she'd been wondering, "coupled with how easily crises could have been avoided if someone had had a lick of sense." Based on how few of the shelves housed books, Aveline assumed it was taking more time than normal to categorise them properly. "What are you two doing here?"

"I thought we might stop by for a visit," Aveline said.

Meredith adjusted her thin-framed spectacles. "Where is your imp? Not intending to jump out from behind one of the bookshelves in an attempt to scare me, I hope?"

"No," Maud confirmed. "He's bedbound at the moment. Sebastian is taking care of him."

"I did wonder if something happened, given the horrible ruckus when the castle moved. Somehow more horrible than usual. Anyway, I hope he recovers soon."

Maud's lips parted. It took her a few seconds to reply, "Thank you."

Meredith smirked. "You thought I couldn't stand the child? True, all children are wild animals, but you're raising him well enough, given that you're stuck in a castle. And as a ghost. If I am to wager a guess, Sebastian is helpful but probably spoils him far more often than he should."

"I... Well, he doesn't spoil him too much, but often enough that it does get on my nerves at times."

With a sympathetic look, Meredith patted Maud's arm. "I can only imagine trying to raise a child in this form. I was not one of the most involved mothers either; the nannies and governesses did most of the work while I tried to handle my husband. Bitter old cad was intent on going to the grave early, leaving me with young children to raise and a castle to run." She waved her hands and returned to sorting through books. "Enough about that. Aveline, how is your practise coming along?"

"I haven't practised since we teleported," she admitted. "A ghoul attacked, and while I'm not seriously hurt, it seems injuries keep me in corporeal form. However..." She linked her arm through Maud's. "I have found I can still interact with ghostly presences."

Meredith shelved one more book before coming to investigate. "Fascinating." She took Aveline's extended hand. Neither of the women gave off sensations other than slight pressure and perhaps a hint of a chill, but Aveline could touch them, nonetheless.

"I have to wonder..." Meredith began carefully "...if, perhaps, you are changing this curse into a gift."

"I've... never heard of something like that. Is it even possible?"

"I'm certain there are many possible things of which we've never heard."

"Can you not touch people?"

She re-adjusted her spectacles, pushing them further up the bridge of her nose. "I may have led Leonard to believe so to inspire better behaviour, but no, I cannot." She released Aveline. "It seems like you are making progress regardless of intention."

A curse turning into a gift? Aveline scoured her memories of Edith telling stories about curses. None of them had anything like this. Either the curse consumed them, or they broke the curse before it could, usually through True Love's Kiss or passing a series of tests to prove their worth. "I will return to practising," she said, unsure what else there was to say on the subject when her mind was swirling, trying to process the implications of such a theory.

"Let your body recover first, then return to practising." She resumed her organising.

Maud threw Aveline a questioning look, but Aveline was not quite ready to leave yet. "Meredith, do you know why some stay as ghosts and others do not?"

Any nervousness about upsetting her dissipated when the ghost librarian replied without a hint of emotion, "It depends on the person, from what I have studied. Most stay because of unfinished business, or they have too great a tie to something or someone in this world that prevents them from moving on."

"I think I would have stayed as one regardless of whether Sebastian tied me to the castle," Maud chimed in. "I would have wanted to stay to see Leo grow up."

Like he bound me to himself to keep me here. What had made him so desperate as to tie her to himself, when he had used the castle before? Was it that the attic ghost was being driven mad? Maud did not seem to be, and she had been like this for years.

"Did Sebastian bind you here as well?" Aveline dared to ask.

"No. I died when he was younger, before he grew into his powers. He might have been able to had he known to try, but I stayed because I feared that how my son was running everything was going to mean the end of our lineage."

"The end?"

"I had two sons, one who died shortly after his father. His grief drowned him." Meredith focused on sorting through the books, but Aveline caught the hard set to her jaw. "I pressed Reginald to marry and sire a child before I could lose him as well. There were many he could have picked, but he chose Sebastian's mother, knowing she already had a son. Some thought he was smitten with her, but really, I think he liked having something to lord over her, a secret he could use to control her." She sighed. "Instead of the son he wanted, she suffered through many miscarriages before she bore him Lila, and he hated that she loved Lila and Sebastian equally. He had a son by marriage but not by blood, and a child by blood who was not a son, therefore not a true heir in his eyes.

"I, too, ignored Sebastian at first, wanting our line to be strong." Meredith huffed a laugh. "Reginald would roll in his grave with the knowledge that Sebastian has inherited the castle. Perhaps that is why he did not become a ghost."

The more I hear of him, the more I detest him. "You believe there is something you can do?"

"Originally, I stayed to see potential future grandchildren. Lila was but a babe when I passed, and I thought Reginald and Julianne would have more, or that my daughter would have... but she passed away from illness not long after she married. Now, I see that Sebastian, blood or not, is family. He is my grandchild, and he will carry on an even greater legacy, I believe. As long as he can put this castle to right and preserve our history."

"He may not like it, but he is well-suited for the task," Maud agreed.

"Indeed." She offered them a polite smile. "I would like to return to organising these books before we teleport again, but please visit again soon."

CHAPTER 36

I'M JUST LIKE BASH!

Maud and Aveline replaced Sebastian so that he could rest. Keeping Leo bedbound was no easy task, but Aveline found him a sketchbook to draw on while she painted. He slept a lot still, and it was in those quiet times that Aveline finished painting Maud and moved on to Meredith. She'd considered asking her again, but after hearing her talk about keeping family history alive, Aveline knew she had to do it—the series wouldn't feel complete otherwise. She may not have said it aloud, but it was obvious that she didn't want to be forgotten.

Who would?

Leo woke once more, grumbling as he attempted to use the charcoal stick with his right hand.

"Are you left-handed?" Aveline asked.

"Yep, like Bash. But he doesn't have much of a choice."

"Leonard," Maud hissed.

"What?"

She turned to Aveline. "He's ambidextrous in most things but tends to prefer his left hand because he wants to be like Sebastian."

"Isn't that what I said?"

Sebastian knocked on the open door. "How is everyone doing this morning... afternoon... whatever time it is?" He peeked out the window. Still wearing a cloak, he seemed much more energised than before, a bounce in his step and sparks in his eyes.

"I'm trying to draw with this hand," Leo announced, waving it in the air. "Look, Bash, I'm just like you!"

Sebastian paled, smile faltering.

"Aveline finished the portrait of me," Maud cut in, gesturing towards the canvas resting against the wall. "It almost looks like me when I was human."

"It does. This is beautiful." He gave Aveline a nod of approval. "You are very talented."

"Do you think I could be as good as her?" Leo piped up.

"If you practise a lot." Maud hovered her lips near his forehead. He leant into her despite knowing they could not touch, and Aveline caught the hint of disappointment when they didn't.

"I can give you some lessons if you'd like," she offered.

Leo beamed. While he chattered about art and how to hold the charcoal to his mother, Sebastian said to Aveline, "I was hoping I could speak with you in private."

Her pulse leapt. Unable to form words, she nodded.

"We will be back shortly," Sebastian informed Maud and Leo as they made their exit.

"Take your time."

Does she know what he wishes to speak with me about?

They walked side by side but did not hold hands. Aveline hoped she was finally about to get the answers she truly craved but decided to keep the questions to herself. Getting ahead of the situation wasn't going to help.

To her surprise, he brought her to his room and shut the door behind them. Nowhere to sit but the bed, she remained standing.

Slowly, he faced her, expression pained and raw. "I told you previously that... that there was something I must tell you. I thought I should do it now before I lose courage again."

Aveline swallowed. "Sebastian, if you're not ready, you don't have to—"

"But I do. I've been selfish for far too long. I thought I had enough magic to keep up the illusion and manage everything else, but it's making me weaker, all because of my pride. I've been so afraid of what you'll think of me, that I..."

"You don't need to be afraid of what I think of you, Sebastian. I like you."

His smile was faint. "I like you as well, Aveline. I told you that I'm not good at being vulnerable, so here is my attempt to fix that. To let you know me without any illusions."

Her insides knotted. She knew he had one illusion, but were there more? Maud and Leo must have known what he truly looked like, and they didn't fear him, they loved him. So why was he fearful?

With shaking fingers, Sebastian undid the clasp of his cloak, letting it fall and pool at his feet. At first, she stared, trying to figure out what she was supposed to be seeing. But then she noticed the empty sleeve hanging off his right shoulder.

"I wanted to tell you sooner, I just... didn't know how."

Aveline drew her gaze up to his, her heart twisting. She wanted to quell his fears, but no words came to her. All this time, he had been compensating with magic. How much had he spent trying to hide this from her?

His throat bobbed. "I can... put the cloak back on if you want. Once my magic is—"

"No, no no no." Aveline took a clumsy step towards him, realising she had moved before she'd decided what she wanted to do. Hug him? Squeeze his hand? It all suddenly made sense, how he always wanted her on his left side, how he struggled to play piano like he used to, how his penmanship had been barely legible...

His focus pinned on her, expression and stance tense. "If... If it does bother you, or you need time, it's all right."

"No," she repeated, reaching for his hand. "You don't have to pretend around me. I'm honoured that you trust me." The furrow in his brow softened but didn't quite smooth out, so she added, "It was a shock, but I promise you, it does not bother me in the least."

His rich brown eyes danced back and forth between hers. "It's silly," he confessed, "but I thought you'd see me differently."

"I wouldn't say that I see you differently, but I think I understand you better now." She offered a small, fragile smile and was happy to get one in return, tentative as it was. "I'm sorry you spent so much magic trying to make me feel more comfortable."

"Well... like I said, it was more of a pride issue than anything else. People tend to treat me differently when they see I've only one arm." Sebastian grimaced. "Besides, the King has been wanting to force me into servitude for a long while, and I don't want him catching wind of this and thinking his wizards have a shot at overpowering me."

"This castle would fall apart without you."

His thumb stroked her knuckle in small circles. "There are too many people I care about in these walls for me to abandon it."

I think you would stay for just one person you cared about. "Even if King Byron sent his wizards, they'd be no match for you."

"I appreciate the confidence in me," he said with a hint of satisfaction, "but it'd only be a matter of time before I lost."

"How have you kept out of his grasp for so long then?"

"Tricks, mostly. While there are some powerful wards around the castle, there are some illusion spells and enchantments meant to cause confusion to anyone not permitted on the grounds. He's tried to come after me a few times, but the war efforts have his attention at the moment. He cannot spare any men."

Aveline's eyes widened. "Wizards have died trying to get through your spells?"

"No, nothing like that. A few have been temporarily blinded or left in a daze—I think the most amusing was the one who could only speak in animal noises. I'd imagine that got wildly frustrating until the charm wore off or they found a way to dispel it."

A giggle escaped her, and his smile returned. "Aveline, are you certain this does not bother you? I must admit, you are taking this much better than I expected."

She clasped his hand between hers. "I promise, it does not bother me. I will admit to having questions though."

"That, I was expecting. What can I answer for you?"

Aveline chewed the inside of her cheek. "Would it be terribly insensitive of me to ask how it happened? I assume it has to do with the monster attack I caught a glimpse of in your memories..."

"Not insensitive," he said. "I don't mind talking about it. A ghoul went insane, and it mauled me while I was trying to protect Maud. I was so worried about her and her unborn child that I got distracted. By the time I managed to kill it, there was little left of my arm to salvage. Maud did what she could." He unbuttoned the collar, exposing the scars and knotted flesh along the right side of his neck that disappeared under the shirt.

"I'm sorry," she said, at a loss for a better response.

"Don't be." Sebastian rebuttoned it with one hand, fingers moving with practised ease. "While I wish it hadn't happened, I'd much rather that outcome than any involving harm to Maud and Leo."

"I assume it would've taken too much magic energy to heal yourself?" Aveline could only imagine the toll. Sebastian was exhausted trying to heal Leo's injuries, which were far less severe.

"I'd lost too much blood. Even if I'd had the semblance of mind to know what spells to cast, the cost surely would have killed me. Maud stitched up my side and tried to save my arm, but in the end, it was better to amputate what remained." His eyes glazed over. "It's been nearly nine years, and I still have trouble with some things. I thought my magic would compensate, and it does in some ways, but not all."

"Like playing piano?"

He nodded. "That takes finesse and precision that's hard to replicate with magic."

If Aveline were in his shoes, she would have had a difficult time adjusting to everything, especially painting with her left hand. Would she have kept trying or just given up? "What about a prosthetic?" she asked carefully, studying him for any signs of irritation. "Would it be easier to manipulate that than pure magic?"

Sebastian ran a hand through his hair. "It would. I've been playing around with that idea for a long time, but I tend to get distracted by one thing or another. Leo has drawn up designs over the past few years, and I'm sure he'd be ecstatic to collaborate if given the opportunity."

"Is it something you actually want?"

It was hard to read his expression with all of the minute shifts. "I do. I think I would like to try, at least."

"Then let me know if I can help."

"Thank you." This time the smile reached his eyes and warmed her chest. "I do have a silly request, if you don't mind."

Hoping intrigue didn't colour her tone too much, Aveline asked, "What is it?"

"Would it be all right if I... hugged you? Without an illusion, that is."

While she wasn't sure what she'd been expecting, that was definitely not it. "Of course." Trying not to grin too wide, she stepped towards him, prepared for it to be quick, but he held her tightly.

"You can hug me back," he whispered. "You're not going to hurt me."

Despite this, she was still gentle as she wrapped her arms around him and placed her ear against his chest, like there was some phantom pain she might trigger if she weren't careful. After a few moments, she relaxed into him.

This is Sebastian—no walls, no illusions, just him.

Eyes closed, Aveline listened to his heartbeat, strong and fast. Understandable, that he'd be nervous after having shared a major secret. A step in the right direction was usually a scary one. "Sebastian?"

"Yes?"

"You can be yourself with me."

He rested his cheek atop her head. "I know."

CHAPTER 37
IT WOULD BE SO MUCH EASIER IF YOU WERE NOSY, JUST THIS ONCE

"Oh! We could add some light sticks here so you wouldn't have to conjure one or hold a candle!" Leo scribbled on the sketchbook propped up on his knees. Sebastian lounged beside him, the hounds resting at the foot of the bed. For the first time since Aveline had known him, Sebastian seemed completely relaxed: no illusions, no tense jaw, and he was even snuggled up beside Leo on his right side, leaning over to point and make suggestions.

Aveline and Sebastian had returned to Leo's room hand-in-hand, exchanging bashful smiles along the way. While Maud had quietly nodded in approval, Leo had burst, "Finally! I don't like keeping secrets."

As Sebastian had predicted, the boy was enthralled with the idea of creating a prosthetic arm for him. While the two of them dreamed and planned, Aveline resumed her painting.

"I'm glad things went well," Maud said in a hushed tone.

"I'm honoured he trusts me." Aveline grinned as Leo giggled at a joke Sebastian made.

"We all do."

She froze. They trusted her with what, secrets? To stay? They called her family, and yet she planned on leaving. Was working towards it, in fact. After the curse was broken, she could not imagine living here, not if Sebastian only wanted to be friends. Jeanette's observation stuck with her—no matter how many times Aveline tried to reason her way out of it, there was no denying that she had feelings for him. It would be unfair to both of them if she stayed.

Would they be heartbroken, saying goodbye? Would she be all right with just visiting every once in a while?

He could feel the same way. But even if he does, could I imagine this being my entire life? Could I get over feeling guilty for leaving my other family behind for this?

She continued painting.

"You know, I saw Meredith leave the library for the first time since I've known her."

Aveline looked up at Maud, then back at the ghost librarian coming to life on her canvas. "She did? Did you see where she went?"

"To the gardens, from what I can tell. It was brief, and I didn't want to intrude. That's the first time I've ever seen her leave the books, and she didn't even bring anything back with her."

The only part of Meredith Aveline had finished detailing was her eyes, and they bore into her.

"That is interesting," Sebastian said. "I've not seen her leave it once either, not since becoming a ghost. I wonder what inspired that outing."

"Maybe she's thinking of organising other parts of the castle," Leo suggested.

"Then you'll have nowhere to hide from her. Better be on your best behaviour."

"I can't be *all* of the time. That sounds too exhausting. I'm good half the time, at least."

"That might be a bit generous," Maud muttered with a crooked smile.

The boy opened his mouth to protest but was cut off by the sudden appearance of a letter and token falling into Aveline's lap. The token slipped and clinked onto the floor, rolling towards the bed, but she managed to snatch the letter. Sebastian retrieved the token and was at her side by the time she had broken the crown seal.

"Who is it from? What does it say? I want to see!"

"Stay," ordered Sebastian, and Leo sat back, pouting with crossed arms.

"It's from my sister Jeanette." Aveline scanned the fine-quality paper and impeccable penmanship. "She's arranged to have our whole family meet at a house they're using just outside of the city."

"When?"

"Hush," Maud said to her son.

"Four days from now." Aveline double-checked the date in the top right-hand corner. "She's asking for us to send a response so she knows we can make it."

"We're all going?" Leo asked excitedly, making the hounds' ears prick up and tails wag.

"Not all of us." His mother sighed. "We're not leaving this castle, child. If anyone goes with Aveline, it'll be Sebastian."

"But I want to go…"

"It's not safe." She crossed the room, continuing to speak in a quieter tone that made it hard to overhear.

"You really want me to come?" Sebastian questioned.

Aveline smiled up at him. "I do." There was little doubt in her mind that Jeanette would tell their family all about Sebastian, if she hadn't already, and it would be much easier to have them meet him themselves instead of conjuring false impressions based on her sister's wild imagination and fears. She couldn't imagine a scenario where they wouldn't find him charming. They deserved to know where she'd disappeared to for all of these months, and to meet the man who saved her life—more than once.

He dipped his head. "Then I'll be honoured to accompany you."

AVELINE PENNED A RESPONSE TO HER SISTER, WHICH TOOK A BIT longer than she anticipated: her hand kept fading, taking the pen with it, and then rematerialise suddenly, blotching the ink. She felt Sebastian's eyes on her as she hunched over his desk for her fifth attempt with a fresh sheet of paper.

"You must be healing," Sebastian mused aloud, "if you are slipping back into being a ghost. I'm glad." When she raised a questioning brow, he tacked on, "Not glad that your curse is affecting you, glad that you're healing."

"I assumed. I was just teasing you." She signed the letter *Addy the Lion Tamer*.

"If I may ask, what is the story behind that title?"

"Nothing interesting, I'm afraid." Aveline folded the letter. "Jeanette couldn't pronounce my name for the longest time, so she called me 'Addy'. We used to play circus, putting on shows for our parents. Edith was the ringmaster, I was the lion tamer, and poor Lottie was the lion. Reserved and timid, it didn't take much to tame her. I thought we should have made her Jeanette's assistant so the spotlight wouldn't be on her."

"Jeanette's assistant?" He readied the wax for her, carefully pooling it in a small circle on the envelope.

"Jeanette named herself a master magician. I think she would've made a better lion, especially since she accidentally set a few things on fire. There is still a scorched spot in the lounge carpet to this day. Fixing it wasn't in the budget, so the housekeeper rearranged the furniture."

"It sounds like your family had lots of fun together."

"We did. Did you and Lila ever play games?"

His expression dimmed. "Yes, but not often. There were a lot of years between us, and her father thought she should be associating with her equals."

"He sounds like someone I wouldn't have gotten along with." She pressed the seal harder than intended. When she lifted it away, the Blaise family sigil was there: a rose surrounded by thorns and vines.

"There were very few people he did get along with." He pressed the letter against the token and murmured something incomprehensible. They disappeared without a trace, presumably to go to her sister, and he reached past her to put away the seal. When he straightened again, Aveline noted how tall he was; he could have touched the ceiling if he stretched, maybe having to stand on tiptoes. He moved with greater ease and comfort than before.

"What is it?" Sebastian cocked his head to the side, with a look that danced the line between curiously amused and slightly concerned.

Her face flamed. "You look like you're feeling better." She stood quickly, making the chair scrape across the floor. He caught her elbow as she tripped over her own feet.

"I am," he confirmed, tone thick with restrained laughter. "But are you feeling all right?" His grip softened, and as he made to let go, she took hold of his hand.

"Sebastian, I..." Her mouth had gone dry. What was she doing? Was she willing to risk their friendship, of potentially going backwards by having him put distance between them again? There was a part of her that had to know, too afraid of going the rest of her life wondering *what if*.

As she gathered the remnants of her courage, he waited, patient as always. He wouldn't push her; if she wanted to, she could drop the whole thing now, and he'd leave it alone, no questions asked. *It would be so much easier if you were nosy, just this once.*

Aveline opened her mouth, but the words refused to come—at least, not in a single, organised thought, but a jumble of ways to start and no endings to match...

The floor pitched beneath their feet, throwing them against the wall. Aveline collided with his chest, and together they slid to the floor.

"It's too soon." Sebastian scrambled to his feet, pulling Aveline up with him. The window rattled worse with each increasingly strong tremor.

Too soon. They'd just sent a letter saying they'd come, but if they didn't make it back to the right point in time...

He raced to the door and flung it open. Bits of the ceiling sprinkled down, coating his hair. "I have to get Leo."

Running was out of the question for the injured boy who could barely walk. Aveline could worry about her other family later. *This* family needed her right here, right now. "I'm coming with you."

He gave no argument. Hand in hand, they sprinted to Leo's room, stumbling and helping one another during the stronger shockwaves that ripped through the castle.

"How is it happening this soon?" Aveline shouted over the howling shrieks.

"I don't know." His jaw tensed.

A sconce fell and bounced along the floor, flame sputtering. Sebastian flicked his fingers, and the light went out before it lit the carpet.

"Bash! Aveline!"

"Leonard, there is no reason to panic. They know this is happening and will be here when they c—"

Their entrance cut off the end of Maud's sentence. The hounds barked and jumped as if begging them to be quick. Sebastian hurried to the bedside, but Aveline stopped him short. "Let me carry him. You focus on redirecting the castle."

After a split second of hesitation, he nodded.

"I can use the crutch—" Leo started, but Maud interrupted, "No, sweet. There isn't time. Let Aveline carry you."

Another quake nearly brought her to her knees. "Come on now, I've got you, Leo."

The boy wrapped his good arm around her neck and she cradled his lanky form. A bit heavier than expected, but nothing she couldn't handle. She could do this. She had to.

The hounds circled her legs until Sebastian whistled and pointed out the door. Everyone rushed out, Aveline keeping close to the wall in case she lost her balance. Leo buried his face in her neck, whimpering as the shrieks became ear-piercing. "We'll make it," she murmured, trying not to grunt when her shoulder bumped the wall and her knee hit the floor. Sebastian was with them in an instant, hauling her onto her feet, keeping his hand at her back even when she was steady once more. His fingers trembled and twitched and his brow furrowed, already fighting the invisible battle.

"Why is it happening already?" Leo gripped the collar of Aveline's dress.

I wish I knew. She refused to look up at the swinging chandelier as they made it to the foyer. The hounds pressed against her skirts, but she couldn't reach down to pet them, not with Leo clinging to her like a lifeline. She took solace in feeling Sebastian against her back, in seeing his arm raised towards the ceiling, and fought the urge to lean into him. Maud grabbed Sebastian's shoulder with one hand and made a motion over Leo's hair with the other, as if smoothing it back, all the while whispering in his ear things too quiet to catch over the screams and the wind and the rattling. The tempest picked up, trying to rip Leo from her arms, but she held him tighter despite her burning muscles. *Just a little longer...*

It all ceased abruptly. Aveline collapsed to her knees, still clutching Leo. Whining, the hounds licked at the child. Sebastian knelt too, and rested his head against Aveline's. She relaxed into him. The key on his necklace dug into her back with each heaving breath he took, but she didn't bother to move. They'd made it, if only barely, and that was all that mattered.

"It wasn't supposed to happen yet," Leo said quietly, but it sounded far too loud in the silence the chaos left in its wake. Far too heavy, far too real. Aveline kissed his brow and held him close, her free hand squeezing Maud's.

They huddled together, silently commiserating their worries. If they had moved in time and space this quickly, who could say when the next time was, and if Sebastian would be recovered enough to handle it? She hated how long it took for him to catch his breath, how long it took for him to stop shaking.

It was hard for Aveline to stress over making it back in time to see her parents and siblings when there was the possibility that they might not make it back at all.

CHAPTER 38

HE'S COME FOR ME!

When they eventually rose from the floor, Aveline strode to the window, just as curious as Leo to see where they'd ended up.

"There's another castle over there, just like this one!" He pointed, leaving a fingerprint on the glass.

"That is because it's this castle, but in the past," Sebastian explained, leaning against the wall next to them.

"Are you going to visit Lila again?"

Aveline glanced at Sebastian. She wondered how difficult it would be for him to see his deceased sister—and how odd it was to chance running into a younger version of himself. If he was comfortable with it, she'd go with him, if only to see him as a child. Even the risk of running into Reginald was worth it—and hadn't Sebastian mentioned he'd met her when he was a child?

"No." There was no room for argument in his tone. How, then, was she to meet young Sebastian and say the words that made him remember her all these years?

"I thought you missed her." An innocent statement from an innocent boy, yet Aveline saw the spark of pain burn in Sebastian's eyes before he turned away.

"We should get some rest," Maud suggested. Sebastian left without replying.

Leo held onto Aveline as she carried him to his room, trying her best not to flinch at the sobs echoing down the stairs.

"I didn't mean to upset him," Leo said glumly, resting back against the pillows.

"I know you didn't." She patted the bed, and the hounds hopped up to join their master. He wrapped an arm around each of their necks, pulling them close.

Should I check on Sebastian, now that Leo is safe and Maud is with him?

"A little more rest, and you'll be able to walk without much pain," Maud said. "Maybe then you can start working on his prosthetic arm."

The boy's frown softened. "That might make him happy. Do you think he'll forgive me?"

"Of course he will, love." His mother continued to speak, but Aveline left the room, intent on finding the man they were discussing. He'd been so hurt that she had to see if she could help him somehow, whether it be a hug or a listening ear or a shoulder to cry on. She was heading to his room when she noticed him coming down the hallway towards her. All black attire and a downcast face, he could have been the Grim Reaper in one of Edith's tales. *How he would hate that job, being something people fear.*

Sebastian stopped a few steps away from her, gaze slowly meeting hers, bearing the weight of a soul crippled by grief. *Is the black attire meant to be for mourning Lila?*

"Are you going somewhere?" Aveline asked.

"Yes. But not to visit her. Or anyone. There is a magic artefact here that might help our situation. I realised it when we were here last, but there wasn't time. Now..." His focus flitted upward, like he was trying to look upstairs through the ceiling. "I don't know how much time we'll have if I don't get it."

"Do you want me to come with you?"

She tried not to show her disappointment when he shook his head. "Thank you, but not this time. If everything goes according to plan, I shouldn't be gone long."

"All right."

"I'll find you when I return. There's more we need to discuss, but..." Sebastian paused as the wails grew louder, then quieted again into moans of distress. His expression hardened. "I'll be back soon," he promised.

You had better. Aveline squeezed his hand. "I'll look after the others."

"Thank you."

She watched him march towards the front door, steps heavy, purposeful. Determined. She waited until he was gone, then waited a few minutes more, before she went to the kitchen to make food for Leo. Now that the adrenaline from earlier had worn off, she imagined he was probably hungry. She should've been as well, but the tightness in her chest prevented her from feeling much else.

He will return soon, he will be fine...

It grew increasingly difficult not to check the clocks every few minutes. Aveline refocused her efforts on cooking, deciding to slice a few carrots from the garden. The sound of the knife methodically tapping a cutting board filled the kitchen, reminding her of home. She wondered how many new recipes Timothée had created since she'd seen him last—he was the reason their father had been forced to let out his trousers and shirts, and why none of them minded when they couldn't afford a cook anymore. Timothée had been more than willing to take over the job, seeing it as a challenge when he had to get creative with the limited ingredients they could buy or grow. Sometimes he let her help, correcting her technique and warning her that she'd hurt herself if she weren't careful. "I know from experience," he'd say, showing off the scars on his hands from cuts and burns. All small, most unnoticeable unless you were looking for them. Easily covered with gloves.

As much as those repetitive corrections irritated her, Aveline resolved to make another meal with him the first chance she got. She doubted there would be time with the meeting happening in a few days...

If we even make it back. Would it be worth the risk, if they did return? What if the castle decided to leave again while they were gone?

The hounds scampered past her mid-cut, jolting her. She inhaled sharply as the knife came down at a different angle than intended—

There was no pain. Gathering her courage, Aveline looked down. Her hand was on the board, solid, the knife through her thumb—straight through it, translucent and incorporeal. No cut, no blood. She lifted the knife. Sure enough, it was a ghost of itself, and yet she was completely human. The moment she set it down, it returned to its tangible form. Aveline picked it up again, and this time it stayed physical, weighted. She stared, willing it to shift. It flickered like it was fighting with her, tired of playing this game.

Solas and Luna rushed past the kitchen again. White-knuckling the handle, Aveline put the knife back down. *Another oddity to mention to Meredith.* But first, she wanted to finish the painting.

When the meal was prepared and the kitchen cleaned (she refused to give Sebastian another opportunity to waste magic), Aveline carried the tray of food to Leo's room.

"Aveline!" He rocked back and forth from his heels to his toes. "Look! My legs are doing a lot better. Still hurts a little, but Mum says—"

"Sit back down," Maud ordered, rubbing at her temples. "The pain medicine has kicked in, and he thinks he's invincible."

Aveline bit down a chuckle, thinking Sebastian was probably very similar as a child. "I made food. Would you mind if I ate with you?"

"Of course! Come, sit." Leo hopped back into his bed and the hounds crowded him, wide eyes trained on the meal. Ignoring the stew, he went for the butter biscuits instead. "You should look at my drawings. I've a lot of good ideas for Sebastian's new arm! He told me that he has to regen... reneg..."

"Regenerate," Maud supplied.

"Yes! That word." He swallowed and smacked his lips. "He has to re-gen-er-ate his magic, so I thought maybe we could add something to the fake arm—"

"Prosthetic."

"—*pros-the-tic* that can hold onto some spare magic for him." He tapped the page, smearing the corner with butter. Aveline couldn't make heads or tails of the scribbles but nodded along anyway as she ate.

"That sounds very helpful," she said when the boy was through with his presentation. "Has he any idea when he'll start working on it?"

"I'm hoping when he gets back."

Aveline tried not to look surprised. Of course they knew Sebastian would leave the castle—just as he always did—and they trusted that he would come back—just as he always did.

They finished their lunch, and then Aveline said, "Come along, hounds. Time to go out."

"They just went out not too long ago, before you came up here," Leo told her.

"Ah, I should have remembered that." She rubbed the back of her hand.

"They are smart enough to take care of themselves in that regard," Maud explained.

"They're very smart!"

Maud raised a brow. "Then why don't they always listen?"

"That's because they don't want to."

"Just like a boy I know."

He grinned.

After they were done, Aveline settled back into her chair and resumed her painting. Leo had fallen back asleep, and when she started to move him into a more comfortable position, Maud insisted that she leave him be.

"I hope his neck won't be sore, sleeping like that."

"He's a child—he'll be fine. I've found him in worse positions: once he napped curled up in a small box under Sebastian's desk. He hardly fit. If I'd managed that, I'd still be trying to recover from a stiff neck."

Aveline smothered her laughter with the back of her hand. Minutes dragged by as she worked on the portrait, gaze constantly drawn to the timepiece on the mantle. She wished she had her ring, so she could feel Sebastian's heartbeat.

"He'll return soon," Maud said. "It may feel like an eternity has passed, but Sebastian never leaves us waiting too long."

She could only manage a dip of her head in acknowledgment. The food in her stomach soured more the longer she waited, so she tried distracting herself by shifting the paintbrush back and forth between tangible and not. A drop of paint fell before she could turn it incorporeal, spattering her skirt. She swore under her breath, garnering a chuckle from Maud.

"What are you doing over there?"

"I was trying something and got paint on my dress," Aveline answered with a sigh. "I should have worn a smock. My mother would have said something about pride coming before the fall, putting too much faith in my abilities."

Maud shrugged. "We all make mistakes. The portrait is coming along well. I don't know how you manage to capture the essence of someone in your art, but you do. I'm impressed."

"Thank you. Meredith's is about done, and then hopefully I can get Sebastian to sit still long enough for me to do his."

"Best of luck."

They shared an amused look. "I ought to change so I can have a prayer at getting this stain out," Aveline said, excusing herself. She hadn't been thinking when she forewent the smock, especially when using a dark brown colour for Meredith's eyes—very obvious on Aveline's light grey dress, which wasn't even hers to begin with. *This is what happens when you worry too much—you make silly mistakes that could've easily been avoided.*

Aveline had barely made it halfway down the hall before a bloodcurdling scream unleashed: "THE MAN IN BLACK! HE'S COME FOR ME!"

She froze in place. The screams continued, sometimes with coherent words, other times a mess of guttural sounds rooted in terror. The castle rumbled and shook, then ceased abruptly. A split second later, Sebastian appeared at the end of the hallway in a whirl of colour, which disappeared like a morning mist, leaving just him, shoulders hunched, panting, face twisted.

Aveline rushed to him, checking for signs of injury, but he cut her short, embracing her, burying his face in the crook of her neck. The corner of whatever was in his hand dug into her side, but she wrapped her arms around him, stroked his back. "What happened? Are you hurt?"

Sebastian released a shuddering exhale. "It's my fault," he said, as though that answered any of her thousand questions. "I did it to her. It's all my fault."

Sobs wracked his body; together, they sank to the floor. Words failing her, Aveline smoothed his hair, even dared to kiss his head, all the while keeping him close, hoping to bear the weight of whatever had gotten to him. Had he seen his sister? Had she seen him? Or was it something to do with his mother? Hundreds of scenarios flashed through her mind, each more horrible than the last, most involving Reginald taking out his anger at Sebastian on Lila or their mother.

Aveline wanted to give him comforting words, wanted to tell him that she was there for him and everything was fine, but *was* everything fine? Without context, the words seemed unhelpful at best and insensitive at worst.

"I'm sorry," he whispered hoarsely, and pulled away.

"Don't apologise." She wiped at his cheeks, her heart twisting at the hollowness of his eyes, at how deeply the pain had burrowed into him. "I'm always glad to be here for you, Sebastian."

His voice gave out as he replied something along the lines of "thank you". He stared down at the item in his grasp: a simple box, small and inconsequential, with no markings other than the initials *LVB* on the top.

Sebastian cleared his throat. "I have much to tell you, if you are ready to hear it."

"Of course," Aveline said. "Whatever you want to say, I'll listen."

Eyes closed, he took slow, deep breaths. Then he stood and helped her up, cradling her arm against his side as he took her to his room. Her eagerness to have answers diminished as she mentally prepared herself. At the soft click of the door shutting behind them, Aveline looked up at Sebastian, waiting for him to show how he wanted to proceed.

"We should sit." He placed the box on his nightstand. Once they were seated on the edge of his bed, Sebastian sighed heavily, running a hand through his hair. "None of what I am about to tell you is happy or good," he warned, making eye contact with her. "If you want to leave after you hear all of this, I will not blame you. You've made enough progress in breaking the curse that I can separate us as well, if that is what you want."

"Sebastian, how could you think I would want to be separated from you?"

His throat bobbed. "Just... wait until after I am done explaining, then make your decision."

I am not leaving you. After all they had been through, what could he possibly think would make her want to flee from his presence?

One more breath, then Sebastian finally confessed, "The ghost in the attic is my sister, Lila."

CHAPTER 39
I CAST THE WRONG SPELL

Sebastian paused, watching her reaction. Aveline had no idea what her expression looked like, especially given the mixture of emotions tumbling through her. If she thought about it, it wasn't surprising—it made perfect sense that he'd want to keep his sister with him. And yet there was a twinge of horror that dug its claws into her: What went wrong to have her be in such a manic state? Why was the castle reacting to her?

"I should probably explain." His hand twitched, reaching for hers, but stopped short. As he retreated, Aveline took hold of it and gave a reassuring squeeze.

"Lila and I were inseparable for a long time," he told her. "As much as we could be, anyway. Her father found excuses to keep me isolated, didn't want me to have relationships with anyone in his circle since I'm a bastard and a secret rogue wizard, but he especially didn't want me influencing Lila." Sebastian said her name tenderly, like he had it tucked into his heart. "When she turned fourteen, Reginald sent her to a school for ladies, knowing that was his best chance at keeping us from spending time together. He knew he couldn't send me away because our mother would leave him—their agreement was that she would do anything he asked, as long as I lived with them and was taken care of as a member of the family. But Lila, well... Mother couldn't argue about Lila being accepted into such a prestigious school. It would all but guarantee her a worthy match and excellent reputation, which the family sorely wanted to maintain.

"With what magic I knew, I gave Lila a protection charm, something she could wear at all times without being suspected, and I was pleasantly surprised when it seemed to work. Lila gifted me one of her favourite hair ribbons in return, and I kept it around my wrist. While she was gone, I wrote her letters but quickly realised that Reginald was throwing them into the fire instead of mailing them."

"How awful." *I wouldn't describe King Charles as kind, but at least he brought me that letter from my mother.*

"It was. So, I sneaked out a few times to visit her, never staying long. I saw how miserable she was and thought I could help; since I had to keep my magic a secret, most of my learning was self-taught with practise and any books and scrolls I could find, but I'd heard rumour of a magic-user who lived on the outskirts of town and would help people for a price. So, I risked it... and met The Heart Thief."

The mention of the witch settled in Aveline's bones like a biting winter chill.

"She wasn't well known then... She'd not had enough victims yet to earn her that title, and she seemed like just a beautiful middle-aged woman at the time, albeit unsettling, the way she knew things without explanation and never seemed to have a shadow. But her knowledge was valuable to me, and she was eager to help, her price nothing more than Lila's hair ribbon. I did find it odd that that was all she wanted, but I had little choice, seeing as The Heart Thief was thoroughly disinterested in the gold I'd brought to pay her."

Power and chaos are the only things I can see that witch desiring.

Sebastian lifted his chin in the direction of the nightstand. "I gave Lila that music box the last time I visited her. With The Heart Thief's help, I enchanted it to play her favourite song, thinking it would alleviate her homesickness." He swallowed.

"Take your time," Aveline said, scooting close enough for their knees to touch.

A ghost of a smile touched his lips, then faded. "Reginald received a letter from the headmaster, informing him that Lila was unwell and being sent home immediately. She gave details of Lila's outbursts, that she was seeing things that weren't there, screaming about a man in black coming to get her."

Aveline tensed.

"Reginald blamed me and my magic, saying that it had filled her mind with nonsense and broken it. He kicked me out before Lila arrived, threatening to kill me if I ever came back." Sebastian spoke quickly now. "My mother was too stricken by what was happening and didn't find out I was gone until days later, as far as Meredith has told me. I lived on the streets for about a year, surviving and trying to figure out a cure for Lila."

She tried to imagine it; surely that was when he became a street performer, to make barely enough money for a meal. Had he gotten so desperate as to steal? Where had he slept?

"In that time, I couldn't find The Heart Thief, no matter how hard I searched for her. It was as if she'd never existed; no one had any recollection of her. One day, my mother had men track me down and beg me to come home—Lila was dying, and Mother was certain I was her only hope.

"Reginald found out I was there, but Mother locked him out of Lila's room so he couldn't interfere. My sister was so still, so lifeless when I finally saw her again. She looked tiny, eyes dark and unseeing. She didn't even recognise me when I spoke to her." He sniffed, and inhaled shakily. "I'd set up a magic ward around Lila's room while I attempted to save her, but I couldn't figure out what was wrong—without a diagnosis, I had no real starting point I could go off of, and so I had to spend magic trying to understand what was killing her. Every so often, she would twitch or cry, and she'd talk about things that weren't in the room..." Sebastian squeezed his eyes shut; tears rolled down his face. "As I tried to heal her, she had a seizure. I could feel her soul trying to detach from her body, and in desperation, I bound her here...

"Even with proper training, I've never heard of someone successfully stopping death by reconnecting a soul to its body. But I was determined to try—instead of binding her soul to her body, it attached to the castle. It took so much of my energy that my ward spell slipped, and Reginald broke through the door, gun in hand." His breaths came in shudders, but Sebastian soldiered on. "I heard... I heard... I heard the shot, and when I turned around, I saw my mother bleeding out on the floor... Reginald was staring at her in shock... then he raised it at me, cursing me, but the amount of magic I'd used drew ghosts and ghouls and monsters and they... they ripped him to shreds."

Aveline covered her mouth, her gut twisting.

"I barely had the presence of mind and strength of spirit to protect myself, my mother, and sister. My mother died within minutes, and Lila was already a ghost. It took days to re-ward the castle—I was forced to confine Lila's ghost to the attic so that she didn't have as much control over the castle and didn't call every magic-connected being to us. I spent weeks purging it, getting rid of most creatures and letting the castle be a sanctuary for a few.

"That's when The Heart Thief came, when I had little to nothing left. I can only assume she'd used the ribbon to track down Lila; her appearance was different then, much more monster than human, which makes me think that, in that time, she'd traded her soul for greater magic. She tried to take Lila, but the enchantment in the charm I'd given her somehow protected her even as a ghost; she could not be harmed or taken by anyone except those she let close to her. In a rage, the witch went after me. I thought it was my end—I almost welcomed it, might have if I didn't still have hope that Lila could be saved. But the witch changed her mind at the last second. She said the link between us was strong, and that alone was shielding my sister from her. So, she cursed the link: As long as there is a connection between us, I am drawn to the city, unable to stop myself from roping others into this menagerie of tragedy."

Aveline's attention drifted to the music box, then snapped back to Sebastian as he continued, voice raw, "When the witch left, I buried their bodies in the garden. It would've taken too much energy to maintain Lila's body in hopes that someday she'd accept it again—but I've been collecting magic artefacts ever since, trying to find something that would fix her mind and possibly make her human again. I know it sounds impossible, but I have to try."

Gradually, he lifted his gaze to meet hers, eyes red-rimmed, tear tracks running down his face. She could see the sharp, broken edges of his heart etched into the harsh lines of his pained expression. As one might approach an easily spooked animal, Aveline embraced him. "It's not your fault."

"But it is," he argued, amidst a fresh wave of tears. "I'm the reason she went insane. If I'd only left her alone, if I hadn't made a deal with The Heart Thief, she might have been fine, but I couldn't help visiting her—"

"You didn't cause this. You were a boy wanting to see his sister—"

Sebastian grabbed her arm, grip borderline painful; Aveline jolted but didn't yank away.

"I'm not talking about then. I'm saying *now*. Present me caused this. By letting her catch glimpses of me when I go back in time, I broke her mind."

"Oh, Sebastian..." Her eyes welled. "She couldn't understand? Couldn't handle the idea of you being from the future?"

"She didn't recognise me. She thought I was a monster, come to hurt her. And her music box..." He glared at it. "I cast the wrong spell. Instead of making her happy, it amplifies emotions, feeds off them, replays them. I thought it would remind her of our happiest moments, but instead it replayed the worst ones." Sebastian bit his bottom lip so hard Aveline was sure he'd draw blood. "It reflects what's already there. I had no idea how much she was suffering, and then... I added to it. It kept playing her fears... She was terrified of me."

Aveline didn't know how long ago it was, or how old Sebastian was either. She'd assumed he was somewhat close to her age, given the amount of rumours still circulating about him, the castle, and the Blaise family. He must have changed a lot in the time between when Lila knew him and now if she didn't recognise him. Sebastian had said she only got a glimpse of him... Why had she thought he was going to hurt her?

The intensity with which he stared at the music box set Aveline on edge. "Sebastian..."

He didn't look at her, didn't even flinch. "I have to see what happened." His voice was barely audible, raw and rough, dotting her arms with goosebumps. With a strange sort of calm, Sebastian turned to her. "You don't have to come with me, but I'll admit I'd like you to."

Warnings stuck in her throat. Who was she to tell him not to? Certainly, this would cause him pain, but what if it unlocked part of the mystery of how to save Lila? Or, at the very least, helped him find closure and start to forgive himself? It was not her choice to make—it was his.

"I'll come with you."

CHAPTER 40

I'M HERE

Sebastian and Aveline went to an empty room on the second floor—no decorations, no furniture, not even drapes over the windows. It was as if it had never been inhabited, except for the nicks in the wallpaper and grooves in the flooring.

"I don't know how it'll react after this long. When I'd tested it, it was happy, but it might have morphed since feeding off of Lila's emotions."

"Is there something you want me to do?" Aveline offered.

"For the moment, just stand behind me, closer to the wall. Once I open it, I'll be able to give better directions."

Following orders, she skirted behind him, attention pinned on his back. Sebastian's stance was all tense lines as he eased open the music box. Aveline held her breath, steeling herself for whatever horrible reaction the item would have…

A slow, sweet song played. She craned her neck to sneak a peek over his shoulder, barely catching sight of a twirling ballerina dancer, its arms raised high and leg extended gracefully—

He staggered backwards, music box slipping from his hand. Aveline lunged, but before she could reach him, it hit the floor, the impact scattering the notes in a dissonant array, like the pieces of the now broken figurine. It still spun in the box, just a head and torso holding on by one leg. Sebastian trembled, jaw clenched. Aveline grabbed his hand—

The room melted away, replaced by a brighter one, full of furniture and lighting and artwork. It might have once been a happy, lively room, but all of it was overshadowed by the man towering over a dark-haired adolescent, foot winding backward yet again.

"Stop it!" screamed a little girl in the doorway. "You're hurting him! Leave him alone!" A slender woman appeared behind her, expression instantly falling.

"Reginald, please—" She grasped his shoulder; he shirked away, shooting a rage-filled glare at her. The woman flinched, taking a couple of small steps back. "Please," she implored again, eyes glistening. For a few horrible, elongated moments, nothing happened. Then Reginald stormed out, spitting, "He'd better not be here when I return." The little girl—Lila—darted out of his path.

Sebastian's grip tightened on Aveline as his mother sunk to her knees in front of the younger version of him, whispering in a language Aveline didn't understand. His mother smoothed his blood-matted hair, her tears falling onto his bruised face. "*Moy mal'chik...*"

"Bast," Lila cried, trying to hug him, but pulled away when he grunted. Weakly, he offered his hand and she clutched it.

"We have to get you out of here," their mother said. "Can you walk?"

Face gone white, adult Sebastian watched in stony silence as his mother half-carried younger him out of the room, his tall, lanky frame leaning heavily on her. "This is what she saw... I'd forgotten she was there that night. He was usually more careful about letting others see."

Disgust and horror roiled in the pit of her stomach. "Sebastian, I'm so sorry."

"It didn't happen often."

"That still does not make it any better." Aveline leant into his side, and he wrapped his arm around her, as if grounding himself in the present.

The scene bled and morphed into Sebastian's study, only the

younger version of him was nowhere to be found. Instead, Reginald sat behind the desk, with a young girl approaching him.

"What is it, Lila? I'm busy," he stated, not bothering to look up from the documents and letters littering his desk.

She lifted her chin and squared her shoulders. "Mother said you plan on sending me away to finishing school." Her voice trembled infinitesimally, yet her face remained calm and collected.

"I do. You are leaving in three days."

"But I am close to a match. Nolan Hillbrook has shown interest in me, and once I'm officially out in society—"

Reginald abruptly stood, knocking papers onto the floor. "You think to make a mockery of this family by settling for someone as lowly as he?" Lila began to stammer, but he continued, "The reason you have had no worthy interest is because you continue to associate yourself with that half-blood brother of yours, drawing rumours and suspicion."

"Sebastian is not—"

Pointing at her, he stalked around the desk. "You are not the son I was promised. Your worth to this family is contingent on marrying well, and I will not let you drag our name through the mud."

She swallowed hard. "I will go, but I have one request."

"You do not get to make requests," he growled, but she ignored it, saying, "I will go, but you will treat Sebastian well, or leave him alone, at the very least. You are not to hurt him again, or you can bid your family legacy farewell."

As if she could hear him, Sebastian whispered in warning, "Lila..."

Reginald drew closer, like a predator approaching its prey. Fear flickered in Lila's eyes, but she held her ground.

"I will make no such promise," he sneered. "But I will promise that if you are anything less than perfect, he will suffer the consequences of your actions. This is *our* family legacy you are threatening. Choose wisely, *daughter*."

Sebastian tensed; Aveline hugged him tighter.

The scene shifted again, but before it came into focus, it changed... and changed... Colours writhed and bled in a dizzying circle, quick-ening every few rapid heartbeats. Screams, cries, Sebastian's name, pleas for it all to stop—

For a second, it did, giving the serenity of blank darkness, a brief breath before they were plunged back under again.

Thrashing limbs and a guttural cry. Aveline fought the urge to look away as the monster tore at Sebastian's arm. Maud frantically sought something to use as a weapon. Then blinding light exploded, disintegrating the monster to ash, leaving nothing behind but a pale Sebastian lying in a pool of his own blood, a mangled mess beside him.

"I can help you," Maud said over and over, waddling as fast as she could. She tore at her skirt hem, creating a tourniquet, and struggled to tie it, her fingers slipping. "You're going to be all right. I can help you. Stay awake, Sebastian."

Then Aveline and Sebastian were suddenly in Leo's room, but there were no toys littering the floor, and it was Maud on the edge of the bed, sweat-soaked and screaming.

"You can do it," Sebastian encouraged, awkwardly squatting below her, hand extended like he was getting ready to catch. Fresh bandages covered his shoulder and side.

"You're... not... helping..." Maud panted and gasped, tears streaming down her cheeks. Red painted her legs, dripping onto the floor. This time Aveline hid her face in Sebastian's side, didn't check to see if he was still watching.

"Sebastian," she said, "these aren't Lila's memories anymore. We can stop."

A wail pierced the atmosphere. Aveline whirled around to see Sebastian cradling a messy infant against his chest. "Maud, he's beautiful." His burgeoning grin shattered the moment he looked up. "Maud?" He stumbled as he stood, luckily keeping hold of baby Leo. "Maud?"

The woman stared up at the ceiling with sightless eyes, motionless.

"Sebastian," Aveline said again, gripping his shirt, "please, let's go. You don't have to relive this. Punishing yourself isn't going to change anything."

He wouldn't acknowledge her, murmuring things in the same language his mother had. Everything transformed again, turning into a whirlwind. She caught a glimpse of Maud turning into a ghost, of Lila's final breath as Sebastian knelt over her, weeping—

Then Aveline saw her own face, and the scene came into focus, bringing them into the castle gardens. She collapsed against him and he lowered her to the ground, checking her in a panic. *The demon snake bite,* she realised.

Aveline stepped in front of the real Sebastian, cupping his face so he'd look at her. "I'm here," she stated. "I'm right here, and I'm all right. None of this was your fault."

He rested his forehead against hers and closed his eyes. Bit by bit, everything melted away until they were back in the empty room, the final note of the music box dying out.

"I'm so sorry," she murmured. "That is so much weight to bear."

"...I'm so tired, Aveline..."

She wiped the tears from his face. "You don't have to hold onto them. You can let yourself start to heal, if you're ready."

He was quiet for a long time. "You aren't afraid of me?"

"Not in the slightest. You are the bravest, most selfless person I know. I..." Aveline swallowed the next words before she could utter them. How they nearly slipped out, especially in such a time as this, was beyond her. *Don't be so careless.*

"I'm supposed to be the one helping you, and yet here you are, helping me." He huffed a hollow echo of a laugh.

Of course he'd think that. "I'm not used to letting people help me either. Perhaps we can be content with helping one another."

"That isn't a terrible idea," he conceded, pulling back far enough to lock eyes with her. "Thank you for facing that with me."

"You are welcome." She paused. "Are you all right?"

"No," Sebastian said without hesitation, voice ready to crack again. Gently, Aveline tugged on his hand. She had no idea where to go; she only knew that they had to get out of there, away from the shattered pieces. Instead of asking questions, Sebastian let her lead. It was so eerily quiet and still as they walked that Aveline could actually hear the soft padding of their footsteps. At the bottom of the stairs, she halted, frowning at the sight of the darkening sky through the windows.

"What's wrong?"

Aveline shook her head. "I was hoping it was still day. I think we could both use some sunlight to brighten our spirits."

Sebastian scanned the dim foyer, candlelight from the chandelier and sconces barely making their mark. Something minuscule shifted in his expression, too small for her to read, and this time he led without explanation. Normally, she would have had a number of questions flooding her mind, but she found she did not care where they were going, as long as they were together.

THEY DID NOT STOP WHEN THEY WERE OUTSIDE, NOR WHEN THEY reached the garden. Sebastian kept walking, and Aveline was content to be alongside him, trying to make out colours of flowers as the shadows turned them into silhouettes. Chilly breezes nipped at her skin and toyed with her hair, signs of impending winter. That brought to mind her family: Timothée's freshly made hot cider; snowball fights with the twins; snuggling by a warm fire with her siblings as their parents recounted their childhood stories, their father having grown up in the very house they lived in. Had they done it last year, with Edith and Aveline gone? Would they do it this year, with Jeanette gone as well?

Would she be able to return?

Sebastian brought her to a tree. An orb of light sparked into existence, floating in front of them. Aveline squinted, taking a moment to adjust, and noted that Sebastian had conjured it without releasing her hand.

The light did not drive away much of the darkness; long shadows sharpened the contours of his face, making him seem to be an entirely different person. In that moment, Aveline caught a glimpse of The Magic Collector that belonged to the rumours. It swiftly passed—the longer she studied him, the more evident it became that it wasn't anger or rage in his expression, but grief. This was still Sebastian, just a layer so deep that she could see his bleeding heart that was usually hidden behind determination, responsibility, illusion, and theatrics.

"This was one of our favourite spots to play and have picnics."

Aveline followed his line of sight. Etched into the bark of the tree was *Lila*, no honorifics, no surname, no moving words. Yet each letter was carved with great care, smooth and graceful in its loops. Her focus dipped to the earth at their feet, at the small mound at the base of the tree.

"I probably should have buried her elsewhere—in the cemetery with the other Blaise family members would have been prudent—but I couldn't, not when she made me promise not to. She hated the idea of being stuck with the others when Reginald swore he'd have me buried in an unmarked grave in the middle of nowhere."

How long had he held onto that promise, perhaps hoping that it would be a way to bring his sister back to him? How long had he waited before he buried her, giving up on the idea of reconnecting her spirit with her body?

"I want to help her," he whispered, "but I don't know if that's even possible anymore."

The words settled as a heavy weight around them. As far as Aveline knew, it had been at least nine years since he had started trying to bring his sister back. Such a long time, but... how far would she go for one of her family members?

"I'm sure there are still other artefacts out there. There might be something..." She trailed off as he shook his head.

"Artefacts, tomes, my own magic—nothing has helped. Every time I think there might be a lead, it only serves to enrage her more." The muscles in his jaw clenched. "Every time the castle moves, it's her, trying to escape. How long until she gets loose and does to us what Titan tried to do to Leo?"

"That was different—"

"But it wasn't. Honestly, it wouldn't surprise me if she was the reason Titan lashed out..."

Aveline placed a hand on his chest; Sebastian closed his eyes. "I'm not sure how much longer I can try, how much more I can risk."

"I wouldn't decide anything tonight," she said. "Let your heart and mind rest, and come back to it again in the morning."

Instead of looking at her like she hoped he would, Sebastian looked up at the night sky, at the few visible stars amongst the clouds. "You're right. You can return indoors, if you'd like, but I want to stay out here a bit longer."

"I'll stay too." Aveline rested against him, and he wrapped his arm around her.

CHAPTER 41
THERE'S THAT WORD AGAIN...

Aveline stirred when something wet sniffed her face. Her eyes fluttered open, and Luna barked, tail wagging. "What are you..." Aveline trailed off, taking in her surroundings: The morning rays of sunlight dusting the sky with pinks and oranges, she sat with her back against a mighty tree, snuggled against Sebastian.

"Good morning," he greeted. Remnants of the previous day's revelations clung to him in the dark circles under his eyes, but his smile still set butterflies loose behind her ribcage.

"Good morning." She sat up, fussing with her hair and clothes. "Um, how... how long have you been awake?"

"I'm not sure I slept much at all, if I'm being honest."

Her cheeks flushed as she noticed the small wet spot on his rumpled shirt; she wiped at her mouth. "You could have woken me."

"You were peaceful. Waking you would've been cruel."

"And forcing you to stay up all night in an uncomfortable position wasn't?"

Half-heartedly, he snorted. "If I was really that uncomfortable, I would've done something about it."

"Doubtful."

He raised a questioning brow.

"I'm just saying that you're... Oh, never mind."

"No, what were you going to say?"

"Nothing important."

"Aveline."

Her name should not have had such an effect on her as it did when it came from his lips. She sighed, settling back down beside him so she could stare out at the sunrise lighting the mountain peaks. "I was going to say you're as stubborn as I am," she relented. "We sacrifice our own well-being for the sake of others'."

Luna and Solas sniffed around a bit more, then decided to return indoors, no doubt to leap back onto Leo's bed.

"Is that such a bad thing?"

"That's the root of what I've been struggling with." She hugged her knees. "Helping others is praiseworthy, something to always strive for, but there are times when I've become bitter for it. I am the one who offered to step in on my sister's behalf, to play the role of princess to save our family from financial ruin, and yet I hated all of it. I was bitter towards my sister for deciding she wanted to take care of herself, I was bitter towards the rest of my family for letting me make the sacrifice... and I was bitter with myself for being so unhappy with the situation when I was the one who suggested it in the first place. I should have been happy to do something so important for them."

It wasn't until Sebastian brushed at her cheek that Aveline realised a tear had slipped. "I'm sorry," she said. "That was insensitive of me. You have much more pressing problems, and here I am blathering about nonsense."

"Your feelings and experiences are not nonsense, Aveline."

No matter how much she longed to, she refused to look at him. Her eyes stung and her nose was starting to run—seeing him pity her would make her lose the last bit of resolve she had.

"And we are not in competition. What you've endured—and are enduring—is just as valid."

Sniffling, Aveline took a deep breath. "What I meant to say before I started rambling is that... Well, you and I seem to do a lot for everyone else, but you are much more selfless about it."

"There's that word again..."

"What word?" She peeked at him as he shifted, sitting up a little straighter and crossing his ankles.

"'Selfless'. You've used it to describe me before."

"Because you are."

"If you saw the reasons behind some of my 'selfless' actions, I think you'd change your mind."

"Like what?" she challenged.

"Well... like my arm, for example. I could say that I kept up the illusion to keep you from being uncomfortable, or to protect myself from others finding out my weakness, but really, I was terrified of how you'd view me after you found out."

The risen sun cast warm tones across his skin and lit the inner circle of his pupils in a golden amber hue. Aveline gently took his hand. "I can understand that, but you really had no reason to worry."

His expression softened. "I see that now."

Aveline didn't know who started leaning first, she or Sebastian, and her mind was too muddled to figure it out. She could count his eyelashes if she wanted, but was mesmerised by the way his eyes danced across her face, dipping towards her mouth.

"Aveline!" Leo's voice rang out. "Bash! Are you out here?"

A sigh escaped her, and she was relieved to see that Sebastian hadn't noticed, already standing and trying to help her up. "We're over here, Leo." Then, with a furrowed brow, he asked Aveline, "Is that paint on your skirt?"

Looking down at the grass and dirt stains, she chuckled. "You're worried about paint on my skirt?"

Before he could respond, Leo hobbled over, one arm in a sling, the other clutching a walking stick. Maud floated behind him and the hounds ran around, giving Leo a wide berth so as not to trip him.

"I was worried when we couldn't find you, but Mum said you probably wanted your privacy," Leo said, to which Maud grimaced. "Can't want privacy if you're outdoors."

His mother sighed.

"Well, we're here, so nothing to worry about," Sebastian told him, a hint of pink creeping up his neck. Aveline was certain her face was bright red. "How are you feeling?"

"A lot better!" He shifted from one foot to the other and winced. "But it's still painful."

"There was no way to convince him to stay in bed for one moment longer." Maud's shoulders slumped in defeat.

Sebastian knelt in front of the boy. "Let's see what I can do to help."

Aveline was suddenly a child again, watching her father tend to her brother's scraped knee. Only instead of using a cloth and medicine, Sebastian placed his hand on Leo's leg, which straightened, the swelling going down. After a few moments, the boy hollered in excitement and dropped the walking stick so he could dance around unencumbered.

"Just a moment, don't you want me to help your arm too?"

He dashed back. "Thanks, Bash."

"Don't thank me yet. I don't have enough to completely heal your arm right now, but I can take some of the pain away. You'll have to be extra careful with it: no climbing or carrying anything. Got it?"

"Aye!" After the wizard was done, Leo threw his good arm around his neck. "You're the best."

Aveline couldn't help but smile as Sebastian's tension melted and he returned the hug. Then he stood and cleared his throat. "We should make some breakfast."

"Oh! There's a recipe I want to try!" The boy and his hounds sprinted back towards the door, Maud following behind at her leisure.

"Of course there is." Sebastian shook his head with a grin, watching Leo disappear back inside. "I think he's completely forgiven me." A light breeze tousled his hair, the strands not quite reaching his eyes as he faced her.

In a desperate attempt to ignore the pang of longing in her heart, she managed to smile back and say, "Of course he has. Children may have moments where they think they hate you, but they know who is truly there for them."

Drawing close, he intertwined their fingers, his warm palm pressing against hers. "I was terrified when I realised Maud had passed away," he whispered. "I hadn't had a friend in years, and when I finally made one, we had such a brief time together, and then she... and there was nothing I could do to stop it. I held a newborn as I stared at her lifeless body, and all I could think was 'I can't do this alone.'" His throat bobbed. "I've hated myself for years over not being able to save Lila, for binding her here as a ghost. And yet, when I was put in the same position, I did it to Maud too. I panicked over the thought of being alone, of raising an infant alone..."

Aveline embraced him; he let out a deep exhale.

"It was selfish, bringing her back as a ghost, but I was relieved... and full of guilt. Maud thinks I indulge Leo because I have no willpower, but really... I do it because I'm afraid he'll come to despise me when he understands why I kept his mother here."

After a brief pause, she replied, "I don't think anyone wants to raise a child alone, Sebastian. From what Maud has told me, I think she wants to be here. But either way, I think you should talk to her about it, clear the air."

For a few minutes, neither of them said anything. Fear pricked the back of her neck as she worried she'd said too much.

"I think you're right," he said, interrupting her barrage of self-doubt. "It's been far too long." He stepped back but kept hold of her hand. "Leo will come looking for us soon if we stay here any longer."

AFTER A BREAKFAST OF EGGS AND HALF-BURNT TOAST THAT required lots of milk to be able to swallow, Aveline told Leo, "I have a special errand I'd like you to help me with." As she suspected, he required no convincing to lure him away from Maud and Sebastian. "I'll give you a small break" was the only explanation she gave. Whether or not Sebastian was going to broach the subject was up to him, but she thought that finding a good time for it might be more difficult with Leo around.

"What is the special errand?" the boy asked, his grip on her hand tightening. "Do I need my tools? Lockpicks? Bash said not to climb, but I think I can manage if I just—"

"No, none of that. We're going to make a delivery." She walked carefully, trying not to step on the eager hounds accompanying them.

"A delivery? To who?"

Aveline ignored her mother's voice in the back of her head correcting him: *To whom.* "I have a gift for Meredith."

Leo frowned as they approached his bedroom. "I don't think I have anything she's going to want—Oh, wait! You were painting her, right? Did you finish it?"

"I did." Aveline wriggled her hand free of his so she could remove the dust sheet covering the canvas.

"Wow! You made it look just like her! You even got the wrinkles around her eyes and mouth."

"Thank you... I think we should take it to her now, see if she likes it."

He hesitated in following her to the door.

"Leo? Is something the matter?"

The hounds looked up at him as if they were wondering the same thing. Inhaling, Leo said, "Well, I think she'll like it fine. I just don't think she'll be too happy about me going in there. And she definitely won't want Luna and Solas."

That should have occurred to me. "She and I are becoming good friends. I'll ask if she can make an exception. But," Aveline warned with raised brows, "that means that you have to promise me that you'll be on your best behaviour when we visit the library. No tricks. Show her you're old enough to be trusted to visit every now and again."

He puffed out his chest. "You can count on me, Aveline!"

She swallowed her laughter and shook his extended hand. "Good!" The two of them began walking towards the library. Aveline adjusted her grip on the canvas once, twice... "If I should become a ghost again..." She glanced at the sling holding Leo's arm. "Well, I don't know what we'll do."

He scanned her up and down. "You look pretty human to me. Too solid to be a ghost."

I don't always feel solid. "Well, we'll worry about that only if necessary, then." She could try changing it to a ghostly form, but she feared the possible repercussions that would have on the paint. The rose hadn't changed any and neither had she, but the worry niggled at her regardless.

"All right." Leo marched beside her with his chin raised, going much slower than usual.

"I thought you'd have sprinted to the library already."

"I've gotta show how grown up I am so Meredith'll trust me, right? She won't take me seriously if I'm panting or sweaty."

Aveline decided against commenting on the dirt smudges on his pants and the small leaf caught in his hair. "That is wise of you."

He dipped his head, his movements rigid as if his idea of being trustworthy meant that he had to emulate a mechanical soldier, like the wind-up toys her brothers used to leave out for others to trip over.

"I was thinking," Leo said, "I need to have a nickname for you, since you're part of the family. I call Sebastian 'Bash', and Luna and Solas are 'Lulu' and 'Sol', though I don't call them that often. Mother has all sorts of names for me, and I call her 'Mum' or 'Mummy', but if I really want to butter her up, I call her 'Mother Dearest' or 'Lady of the Wild Lands'."

"Why Lady of the Wild Lands?" Aveline curled her fingers, digging her nails into the wood frame. A small part of her had hoped for a splinter to prick her finger on, but no such luck. She'd have to focus.

"Because Mum says the wilds call to her, that they mean freedom. I tried calling her 'Queen of the Wild Lands' but she said she isn't interested in ruling anything—she has enough on her hands trying to keep me in line."

"I can imagine her saying exactly that." Aveline was starting to smile when everything went numb. The canvas slipped from her grasp; Leo halted, turning, hands reaching—

She snatched it. The painting shifted instantly, a translucent version of itself. Meredith's painted eyes stared at her in judgement.

"Woah! How did you do that?" His mouth hung open as he looked up at her.

"A new trick I learnt recently but haven't quite mastered." Aveline scrutinised it, checking for flaws in her work. After all of the hours she'd spent, she'd loathe spending more fixing it, or worse, starting all over again. She was finally supposed to be moving on to Sebastian's...

She shifted back to her corporeal form, the painting following suit. The tightness in her chest eased when she saw it hadn't been altered in the slightest.

"That's neat! Can you do that with anything? Oh! Or anyone? Can you turn me into a ghost?"

She blinked, slowly meeting his eager gaze. "No, I do not think so."

His mood dropped instantly. If she'd not been holding the painting, Aveline would've hugged him. Who could blame the boy for wanting to have the chance to be like his mother?

"So," she said, hoping a subject change would help, "what were you thinking of calling me?"

Thankfully, he let the topic go, and continued walking alongside her. "Well... I hadn't come up with anything yet. Did anyone else ever have a nickname for you?"

"Well, my siblings call me 'Avie' sometimes."

"Avie," Leo repeated. "I like that. How many siblings do you have?"

"Six."

He sighed. "I wish I had siblings." Aveline scrambled for an answer, but he continued, "Oh! I'll have them when you and Bash have kids. Not that they'll be my siblings exactly, but it'll be close enough! Can you imagine the games we could play? And I could teach them my tricks! And..." Leo turned around, realising that Aveline had stopped. "Are you all right? Why is your face red?"

Of all the things that he could say. Aveline slammed the door shut on those thoughts before her imagination could run wild. "I'm fine. Care to knock for me?"

Straightening his posture, Leo knocked.

"Who is it?"

"Aveline, and Leo is with me. He's promised to be on his best behaviour."

Meredith took her time in responding, "He'll have to promise me that if he wants to enter this sanctum."

"What's a 'sanctum'?" the boy whispered out of the side of his mouth.

Aveline bit back a chuckle. "She's saying this place means a great deal to her, so you'd better promise her you won't cause trouble or ruin anything."

Taking a deep breath, Leo projected with great fervour, "I, Leonard, son of Maud, resident of this castle, owner of Solas and Luna, here do so swear that I will neither cause trouble nor ruin anything." At Aveline's surprised expression, he asked, "What?"

"Where did you learn to speak like that?"

He beamed. "Stories Mum tells me. We like to reenact them sometimes. I'm a knight, and she's—"

"Do you swear no shenanigans?" Meredith's voice boomed from the other side, making Leo jump.

"I do."

"And no deviousness?"

"None whatsoever. If I break my vow, you can dangle me from the balcony by my toes."

"That is quite the punishment. I highly suggest you do not break your vow. Come in."

With a dramatic bow, Leo opened the door. "Ladies first."

"Thank you, kind sir." Aveline stepped through to see that there were no books lying about; everything was organised.

"Did you bring me my cake?" The ghost librarian eyed the canvas with barely contained curiosity.

"There's supposed to be cake?!" he hollered in excitement.

Aveline refrained from saying a few choice words she wouldn't dare utter in front of Leo. "I apologise, Meredith, I'd completely forgotten."

"How could you forget cake?" He clutched his chest like he'd been shot through the heart.

"How, indeed." The corner of Meredith's mouth twitched upward.

"We can make you a cake. If you just wait—"

"Next time, little one." She surveyed him. "Seems more time has passed than I thought. Either that or Sebastian is lacing your food with a growth potion. How old are you?"

Leo rolled his shoulders back. "Eight."

"Sebastian was a little younger than you are now when I passed away. He used to come here for solitude, a safe haven away from my son." Leo opened his mouth to ask a question, but Meredith pressed on, saying, "You are a handsome boy. What would you like to be when you grow up?"

Aveline lowered the canvas so that the bottom edge rested on the floor. She thought wistfully about the painting supplies she'd left upstairs, and how she wished she could paint this scene. There was something in the way the young boy and the ghost woman looked at each other that she itched to capture.

"Well," Leo answered, "what I want is to be a wizard like Bash, but he says that's not safe. So, I guess I want to be an entertainer."

"An entertainer? Why is that?"

"I want to make people happy, whether it's as a street performer or an actor or the ringmaster of a circus! But not a travelling one, not unless I could take Mum and Bash and Aveline with me." He paused. "And you, too, if you'd like to join us."

"What a magnanimous offer," said Meredith. "You remind me a bit of Sebastian when he was your age."

"Really?" Leo dropped his serious facade. "I want to be just like Bash!"

"Well, you're off to a good start." She turned to Aveline. "What did you bring?"

Aveline turned the canvas around. "A gift."

Whenever she showed someone a painting, it was always nerve-wracking, especially when it was a portrait—but normally, she could read something in their expressions or body language that clued her into whether they liked it or not. Meredith said nothing as she drew closer, her face a stony mask, her eyes scanning back and forth with intensity.

"Well?" Leo urged. "What do you think? Do you like it? Aveline's a master artist, isn't she? She did mine and Mum's too, and she's going to paint Bash next."

"It is impressive," she said in a hushed tone. When she didn't say anything else, Aveline told her, "We'll hang it in the hall with the others."

"So we can show we're a big, happy family!"

"A family," Meredith murmured, fingers hovering over the canvas.

Then she turned to Leo. "How would you like to stay for a little bit? We can exchange stories."

"I'd like that very much." He grinned.

"I'd like that too." She gestured towards the desk. "Aveline, set the painting there and come with us. We have stories to tell."

CHAPTER 42
WE HAVE TO PICK THE RIGHT MATERIAL

"And Meredith said there was even one tale where a princess kissed a frog and it turned into a *prince*!" Leo stuck out his tongue. "I wouldn't kiss a frog. Never ever ever."

"That is quite the tale." Sebastian smiled. "I'm glad you had fun. I didn't expect you to be gone for that long."

"I didn't expect Meredith would let me in, but Aveline asked her nicely."

"All I did was tell her you'd behave," Aveline corrected, taking a seat in one of the chairs near the fireplace in Sebastian's study. Even without the fire, the atmosphere in the room was so cosy that it would be easy to nap if she wanted. "Which I greatly thank you for doing."

"You, behave?" Maud butted in. "When does that ever happen?"

"Like you say, only once in a great while."

The adults chuckled, while Leo looked the wizard over. "Are you feeling better yet?"

Lounged in his chair, Sebastian almost appeared to be a normal man enjoying a lazy afternoon. "A bit, thank you for asking, but it will take a little while before I am completely back to normal. I've spent far too much magic trying to keep up the illusion for my arm."

"You've had plenty of other things to spend your magic on as well," Aveline pointed out, garnering a tired smile from him.

"I suppose you're right."

The boy's focus darted to the empty sleeve draped over the arm of the chair. "Are you ready to make the fake arm now?"

"Prosthetic," Maud said with a hint of an edge to her tone.

"We could start working on it. Why don't you fetch your drawings?"

By the time the words had left Sebastian's mouth, Leo had scampered off, and his mother went with him.

"You know," Sebastian said, propping his chin on his fist, "I wasn't planning on speaking with Maud about such a sensitive matter so soon, but then I supposed it was as good a time as any, given we've avoided it for eight years."

Aveline replied, "I can't quite say I'm sorry to have orchestrated it. How did it go?"

"Just as you suspect, I'd imagine: She told me it was ludicrous to have felt guilty about it for all of these years, that if I would've let her pass on without becoming a ghost, she would've found a way back to us just so she could haunt me, and that she cannot believe that I hadn't cleared the air sooner." He gave a quiet chuckle. "Although she, too, had some worries. She was terrified I held a grudge against her for leaving me with her infant son to raise, and that she could do little to help with him... Oh, the ridiculous things we worry about when we could just ask."

Aveline ignored the skip in her pulse. As much as she wanted to ask about his feelings, she could hear Leo's footfalls resounding. *There will be time later.*

"Bash!" Leo bounded in, waving his sketchbook. "Look! I added some more ideas."

With a smile, she watched the two of them study the scribbles and notes.

"You have a lot of good ideas, *moy mal'chik*," Sebastian said, "but first we have to pick out the right material."

"I was thinking we could use metal, like armour!"

"Well, that is one option, but it'd have to be the right kind of metal for me to use magic with, like all of the things you are suggesting."

Leo scrunched his nose. "What do you mean? Your rings are all metal."

"All metal can be a conductor for magic," Aveline said, chiming in, "but there are some metals that are more suited than others."

They stared at her, and Aveline could see out of the corner of her eye that Maud was as well.

"How do you know that, Avie?"

Sebastian cast a puzzled look at the boy. "Avie?"

He raised his uninjured shoulder in a half shrug. "I have nicknames for you and Mum. Had to have one for her too—family rule."

"Fair point." He turned back to Aveline. "How did you know that? I didn't think polite society cared to teach—or even know—about wizards and magic."

"Normally, no," Aveline conceded, smoothing her skirt. "I do not pretend to know much, but since my home country is the source for nickerite, it stands to reason that I know a little."

"Ah, yes, you did mention that, I apologise. Accessing the nickerite mines was the reason King Byron agreed to you marrying his son."

"No need for an apology."

Leo's jaw dropped. "You have lots of nickerite? That's the metal that's stronger than anything else, right, Bash?"

"Stronger, and melds well with magic." Sebastian's response was calmer, albeit no less excited by the sparkle in his eyes.

"King Byron wanted to secure access to the mines before Katin did, to make sure they had ample materials for wizard rings before the worst of the fighting started." She clasped her hands together to keep from fidgeting too much. "That is the most important part of the agreement, from what I gathered."

The room grew quiet; Aveline fought the urge to squirm under Sebastian's ponderous gaze.

"There's going to be fighting?" Leo asked, breaking the silence. "Are we going to be called to join the army? Are you going to be one of the King's Wizards, Bash?"

That tore Sebastian away from his train of thought. He squeezed the boy's shoulder. "There is bound to be fighting, but I plan to take no part in it." Standing, he suggested, "Why don't we inspect the knights at the entrance, see what kind of metal armour they are wearing?"

"You could use it for your arm!" he squealed, rushing out of the room. Maud and the hounds kept up with him, but Sebastian walked slowly beside Aveline. Her pulse quickened; her mouth went dry. Was he upset that she hadn't told him about this sooner? She didn't think it was important, not when her extent of knowledge on the subject was so limited. Or was he hoping she could take him to one of the mines to get a supply of nickerite for new, more powerful rings? That would certainly help if he wanted to continue evading King Byron, as well as have a chance at breaking The Heart Thief's curse on him.

"I didn't mean to say that that's the only reason Prince Alexei agreed to marry you," he said. "I apologise if it came across that way."

Aveline blinked, and tried to smother a surprised giggle with the back of her hand, but failed miserably. Her cheeks flamed as she snorted. How more ridiculous could she be? Here she was worried that he wanted something from her or was mad at her, and he was worried about how he might have offended her.

Sebastian's brow pinched slightly. "I'm not sure what I said was funny."

She cleared her throat. "Oh, I'm sorry, that was... that was not what I thought you were going to say."

He stopped and tilted his head to the side. "What is it you thought I was going to say?"

"Well... Given the previous conversation, I thought you might have wanted to ask me if I could help you get to the mines for nickerite."

"Oh. I still don't understand how what I said was humorous."

Aveline sighed. "It was me, not you. Your statement was sweet but wholly unexpected." *And my nervous energy had to go somewhere.* "As I said before, there was never any sort of feelings between Alexei and me; we were marrying out of duty, nothing else."

No doubt processing what she'd said, Sebastian stared at her. Colour had returned to his cheeks, and his movements were no longer rigid and heavy, but the tired lines in his face were not quite gone. By the soft cries coming from the attic and the rattling of the walls,

Aveline judged Lila's next outburst would be soon. He'd need to take every opportunity to rest between now and then.

We might return in time to see my family, Aveline thought selfishly.

"Are you coming?" Leo's shout echoed down the hall.

"We are!" Sebastian offered his hand, and Aveline took it. "I do have a few questions, if I may."

"Go ahead." How could she refuse him, after how vulnerable he was with her?

"How was your sister chosen to be the original bride?"

A fair question. "King Charles's daughter died of illness just a few weeks before King Byron paid a visit to extend the offer of marriage. Fearing for the safety of our small country, he pretended that his daughter Gwendoline was elsewhere, visiting friends. Us, really. Gwendoline was not our friend in truth, but we kept up appearances of friendship as many nobles do. There used to be talk of her brother Prince Ivan marrying Edith, but there was never a serious proposal, which was fortunate for our father, who was more than happy to offer Edith's hand, letting her pretend to be a princess."

"It sounds exhausting, being royalty. So many games to play and lies to remember."

"It is. The worst secret—the one I'm not sure we'll be able to keep for much longer—is that our mines are nearly empty."

"Empty?"

She nodded. "My family owns more than most, and since we have very few magic-users in our country, we export the metals all over the world. Everyone always wants more, but the earth only has so much to give. It is possible there are veins deeper in the earth, but the deeper you go, the more risks you take of losing men." She'd seen the haunted look in her father's eyes too many times after reading through reports. To have the weight of it all on his shoulders... *I am glad I will never become queen.*

"Are the other mines empty too?"

"The others are running low, as far as we can tell. Royals always do their best to keep up appearances, remember?" She halted when Sebastian did, and peered back at their interlocked fingers, then up at him.

"May I make a confession?"

He was hoping for metals... "Yes, of course."

Instead of speaking, Sebastian took one step, then two, and suddenly they were so close she was afraid he could hear her heart trying to pound its way out of her chest. "I am grateful that King Byron followed his greed," he said, "and I am grateful your sister followed her heart."

It took a few tries for her to manage, "How is that selfish?"

He raised her knuckles to his lips. "Because if they hadn't, I would not have met you."

Sebastian resumed walking. Aveline let him lead her, his words nestling deep in her soul.

CHAPTER 43

DO YOU NOT LIKE KISSING IN BOOKS?

"I have the sugar!" Leo attempted to sprint to Sebastian, but Aveline snatched the jar, stopping the child abruptly.

"That is salt," she informed him. "Try the other jar."

"Or, better yet, we could pick berries to add to the top," Maud proposed.

"Good idea, Mum, that sounds grand!"

As he scampered outside, Aveline turned back to Sebastian. He'd switched between stirring the bowl with his right and left hands multiple times in the past few minutes. It had taken a bit of tweaking to fit the arm from the knight's armour to Sebastian's shoulder, the only thing truly keeping it in place being a couple of belts that went up his chest and back, securing together beside his neck. Bulky and awkward, Aveline had expected Sebastian to take it off right away, but seeing how happy Leo was at rigging it together, he'd said nothing so far.

His right hand slipped, nearly knocking the bowl onto the floor; he swore between gritted teeth. Aveline righted the bowl and reached towards his neck.

"What are you doing?"

"Helping you take it off. It's clearly leading you down the road to insanity." *And it's making you spend the little magic you cannot afford to lose.*

Sebastian caught her wrist. "I just need help adjusting it again."

She paused, choosing her next words carefully. "Do you want to wear it?"

"Aveline—"

"Do you want to wear it?"

"Leo would be—"

"Do *you* want to wear it? It doesn't matter what any of us think, Sebastian. If you're unsure, take it off for a bit, and we'll try again later. Or you never have to put it back on again if you can't stand it. Leo doesn't care about you wearing it unless it's helping you." She swallowed, realising how close she'd gotten to him. In a gentler tone, she added, "I can help you take it off if that is what you want."

He hesitated, then nodded. "Thank you."

"You're welcome." Aveline stood on tiptoes and Sebastian stooped so she could reach the buckle. It took a few tries for her to get it loose, revealing a splotchy red patch underneath. Refraining from making a comment, she eased the armour away from his shoulder, which he rubbed at with a grimace.

"It's not the most comfortable prosthetic, but not a bad starting point. Leo has some good ideas, but I need much more magic replenished for them to help."

"Understandable." Aveline finished stirring in the final ingredients and set it in the oven, all the while fully aware of Sebastian's eyes on her. "You should wear it for you, not for anyone else. We l..." She cleared her throat. "We care for you as you are; neither decision will change that."

"And if I don't know what to think yet?"

Wiping her hands on her apron, she faced him. "Then take your time deciding. There is no reason to rush it." His smile set her heart aflutter; she hurried to clean their utensils and the flour Leo had managed to make rain over parts of the kitchen.

"I could clean it with magic."

Aveline threw him a glare. "Do not waste your magic. It's not a horrible thing, having to clean."

His chuckle came out as a half-sigh. "At least let me help you without magic, then."

"There is not much to do." Besides, she wanted something to keep her busy, to distract her. "Though if you are insistent, bring me Maud's medical supplies, and I can put a salve on your neck and shoulder."

She'd expected an argument, but he slipped away without a word, leaving her to exhale in peace. *This is not the time to bring up the topic of feelings... but when is there a good time? Am I willing to stay, to make this my life? If not, shouldn't I keep them to myself?*

"I think that bowl is plenty dry," Sebastian teased when he returned. Aveline flinched.

"Oh! Yes, sorry, I suppose my mind got away from me." She accepted the salve. "Do you mind opening your shirt?" Her cheeks flamed.

With an amused smirk, Sebastian unbuttoned the collar and pulled it aside, exposing the raw skin. She dabbed at it. "Sorry, I'm not trying to hurt you," she said when he closed his eyes.

"You're not." He peeked at her from under long, dark lashes. "And stop apologising. You are literally apologising for helping me."

"Sor—" Aveline caught herself, shrinking back at the playful scowl he shot her. "Oh, never mind. How does that feel?"

"Better, thank you."

"Do you want me to bandage it?"

"No, it's fine, I'll just leave the collar open."

"Very well. Umm... Do... do you want some on your..."

Shaking his head, Sebastian put her out of her misery by answering the half-spoken question: "I already put some on my shoulder, but thank you for your thoughtfulness." He took the jar back, peering down as if trying to read it, even though it had no markings at all. Aveline started to ask what was wrong when Leo burst back into the kitchen with a basket.

"I got the blueberries!" He popped a few into his juice-stained mouth, which matched his purple fingertips. "They're ripe—perfect timing!"

"Wonderful, thank you." She patted the counter. "Set them here for now. It'll be some time before the cake is out of the oven and cool enough for frosting and berries."

"How much longer?"

"Long enough that if you keep eating them, there will be no more left for the cake." Maud raised a brow. "This is for Meredith, not for us."

He sighed. "I know... and she did see the basket, so she knows there'll be berries."

"You visited her in the library again?" Sebastian inquired.

"No, she was in the main hall, looking at the portraits Avie painted. She seemed kinda sad, but she smiled when I told her we're making her cake."

She left the library again... There is always hope.

Leo spotted the makeshift prosthetic lying on the counter. Aveline held her breath as the child's lips parted, then clamped shut again. He set the basket beside it and wiped his hands on his pants, much to Maud's dismay. "Since we have to wait, want to see my new trick?"

The tension in Sebastian's stance vanished. "Of course!"

"Careful," Maud warned for the fourth time, to which Leo snapped back, "I'm being careful!" as he shifted his grip on the cake yet again. One of the berries rolled onto the floor, which Sebastian scooped up.

"Everyone ready?" Aveline asked, then knocked. "Meredith, may we enter?"

The door swung open. Meredith scanned them with what could almost have passed as a grin. "Well well well, someone finally remembered the cake they promised me."

"It's vanilla!" Leo announced, proudly lifting it. "I frosted it and put the berries on myself!"

"Ah, I'm surprised there's any on it given how much juice is on your face. Thank you for the treat. Come in."

They made their way inside, stepping around stacks of books. "Did you change your mind on your organisation strategy?" Aveline inquired.

"I did. I thought perhaps this time I would arrange them based on how strong the family ties are." Meredith scooted a few stacks out of the way so they could reach the sitting area near the stained-glass window. She aided Leo in setting the cake on the table, and Aveline put the plates and utensils beside it. "And, if they have no family ties to speak of, then based on friendships, which can be just as important." The woman settled into an armchair, back straight and chin lifted high, the picture of ghostly royalty. Despite Meredith's light-hearted demeanour, Aveline did not quite find herself at ease: The woman's appearance was faint, more spectre-like. She could barely make out her edges, and she'd seemed to have lost almost all colour. Even the myriad of reds and greens the sunlight cast through the window were unable to touch her.

"Sebastian, child," Meredith requested, eyeing the cake, "would you do the honours?"

"Yes, *Babushka*."

As he sliced the cake, she said, "I see you are no longer hiding yourself."

Sebastian started to look towards Aveline but seemed to change his mind. "I have no reason to anymore."

"I am glad to hear it."

"So am I," Leo chimed in. "It was a hard secret to keep!" The hounds sat at either side of his chair, eyeing the dessert.

She even let the hounds into the library.

"I am impressed," Meredith said. "Well done, Leonard. You are growing into a fine young man."

He sat up straight and puffed his chest out; Maud pressed her lips together to keep from laughing.

"Are you going to have a piece?" the boy asked Meredith, snatching the one Sebastian offered to him.

"I am afraid not, dear. I may be able to have some effect on the world, but I am still a ghost. No treats for me."

He blinked, holding his fork halfway to his mouth. "Then why'd you ask for cake?"

"I am not entirely sure. Perhaps I just wanted to see one, since it's been so long. Go on, eat it."

Not needing to be told twice, Leo wolfed down the cake, "accidentally" letting a couple of crumbs fall, which the hounds gobbled up before anyone could stop them.

"You eat as though we starve you." His mother sighed; the others chuckled.

Aveline took a bite, caution fading at the sweetness of the flavours. She had, indeed, caught Leo just in time, before he'd added things he wasn't supposed to. From the corner of her eye, she saw Sebastian's brows lift. "This is delicious, Leo," he complimented, managing to keep the surprise out of his voice.

"Isn't it?" Licking his plate, he halted rapidly when Maud cleared her throat. "I mean, thank you, Bash." He wiped his face with a napkin.

"I take it you did an excellent job, Leonard," remarked Meredith. "I'm honoured to have such a cake made on my behalf. What other talents do you have?"

"I can do tricks! Not real magic like Bash though. Would you like to see?"

"Nothing with fire," Maud ordered.

His shoulders slumped, and it was his turn to let out a mighty sigh. "Fine, I have plenty of others."

The adults watched as Leo the Fantastical (as he presented himself) performed a wide variety of tricks, some including the hounds, who were much more likely to listen when they saw he had a couple of stale biscuits in his pockets. Then he moved on to showing off his gadgets made up of bits of wood, stones, and metal pieces. He had long, fun-sounding names for each that he announced with great pride, but Aveline had little to no idea what any of them were supposed to do. One shot marbles into the air, causing Maud to demand that he switch to the next act before he hurt anyone or himself. The boy huffed but obeyed, extending a metal pole with a couple of hooks on the end: "A Dog Scratcher!" he called it, but when he reached for Solas's back with the invention, the hound fled behind the chairs with his tail between his legs.

"Next one," encouraged his mother.

Sebastian scooted to the edge of his chair and brushed his knuckles against Aveline's. With a shiver she hoped no one noticed, she wound her fingers with his. They exchanged a brief smile before turning their attention back to Leo, who was shakily attempting to walk on his hands. After a few steps, he remembered how much his arm hurt, and luckily had already fallen back onto his feet when the castle trembled. They all went still and silent. But nothing else occurred, so Leo persisted in his entertainment.

Once his antics wound down, Meredith said, "How about I read you a story? It is a personal favourite of mine."

"That sounds wonderful!" Leo cuddled with the hounds on the couch, eyes never straying from her. She projected with confidence, adding voices that had him giggling, and even sang a few sections that the princess was supposed to sing to her beloved.

"Does this book have a lot of kissing in it?" he questioned.

It might have been her imagination, but Aveline could have sworn Sebastian's grip tightened.

"It has some." Meredith cocked her head at him. "Do you not like kissing in books?"

After a moment of thought, he shrugged. "As long as there's not too much."

Standing near the edge of Leo's seat, Maud snorted. "And how much, child of mine, is too much?"

"I don't know, but we need to have some good fight scenes in there, too."

Despite the fading sunlight being unable to touch Meredith, her eyes gleamed. "Oh, there are some wonderful ones in this. Do you like pirates?"

"I love pirates! They always have good fights. All right, go on."

Meredith returned to narrating the story. Aveline imagined that this is what Edith would be like when she was a grandmother, although with more flair. Her heart pinched, and she was almost gladdened to feel a small rumble beneath her shoes. There was still a chance for her to see her family before Jeanette got married.

And maybe a chance to attend the wedding, if they were extremely careful.

Sebastian squeezed her hand. She looked at him, catching his expression, a silent question of *Are you all right?*

Aveline gave him a small smile, although she had no idea what he'd read into it, not with her flurry of emotions. She wanted more than anything to see her family, but why did it feel like if she did, she was going to end up saying goodbye? If not to them, then to Maud, and Meredith, and Leo... and Sebastian.

I understand you now, Edith. For him, I might have left everything behind too.

But she couldn't stay, not when there were too many variables, too many unasked questions that demanded answers—

"And they lived happily ever after." Meredith closed the book with great care. "The End."

Candles lit their small part of the room, and despite the unending darkness in all directions, the only word Aveline could have used to describe the atmosphere was cosy. Leo had fallen asleep, his mouth ajar, drooling on the arm of the couch.

"Leo," Maud called.

Sebastian let go of Aveline and stood. "Don't wake him, I'll take him to bed. He's had an eventful day."

The hounds moved out of the way as he gently picked up Leo. The child snored and murmured something unintelligible, wrapping his arms loosely around Sebastian's neck.

"We should have him entertain us more often if it'll tire him out," Maud joked. "Thank you, Meredith. Today was lovely."

"It was," she agreed. "Thank you all for coming."

CHAPTER 44

I WISH I WOULD HAVE SAID SOMETHING SOONER

Aveline couldn't sleep, not with the way her mind refused to settle. It jumped and spun in all sorts of directions, dancing around one thing: Sebastian. True, he was her husband for the time being, but how had he become so intertwined in her thoughts and emotions and, most importantly, her *decisions*?

To make matters worse, the castle creaked and groaned like a child complaining of a belly ache, and Lila's sobs grew louder.

Of course the first time I manage to stay corporeal overnight by myself, sleep is out of my reach.

Giving up, Aveline threw off the covers and put on a simple gown. Perhaps she would just wander the castle for a while, or visit Meredith, or...

She paused as she finished brushing her hair. Was there a chance that Sebastian was awake and that he'd be willing to discuss feelings? Was it possible that this marriage felt as real to him as it did to her?

The first rays of dawn sneaking in through the window, Aveline could barely make out her own features in the vanity mirror. It was like looking at someone she knew from long ago, the small details somewhat familiar, but time had transformed them into a stranger. The face and body were undeniably Aveline, but there was a difference in the way she held herself, in the determination of her expression, in the spark in her eyes. The person who stared back at her was no longer the person who arrived here, trembling and fearful, worried of what the future might hold. That person had lived her life in submission to everyone around her, hoping to appease all, a ragdoll giving away pieces of herself until there were only frayed strings left.

She set the brush down and leant forward, gripping the sides of the vanity. "I am Aveline," she declared to her reflection. Three words that encompassed so much, a colourful, vibrant series of paintings she would never be finished with.

And that was all right, being perfectly imperfect. It didn't matter if she didn't have all of the answers, it only mattered that she *tried*.

Her bare feet brought her to the door before she fully processed her decision. She broke into a run the moment she stepped into the hall, her heartbeat drowning out Lila and the castle, but she listened, hoping for a sign that he was awake, like him playing the piano...

Nothing. She peeked her head into the music room, then hurried to his bedroom when she found it empty. What if he was still asleep? Could she really wake him?

She halted at his door, which was cracked open. Knocking quietly, she called, "Sebastian?"

It creaked open, revealing no one was inside. She was about to leave when she saw the curtains fluttering, the double window wide open, letting in the morning breeze. *I should probably shut that for him in case something tries to fly in,* Aveline decided, even though she wanted to scour the rest of the castle for him. Where could he have gone? Leo's room to check on him? The library to visit with Meredith some more?

Or had he changed his mind and went to see Lila? She couldn't blame him, not when he missed her so much. Wouldn't she do the same in his place, if one of her sisters were, in all ways that mattered, deceased?

The thought sobering, Aveline reached out to grab the window handles, then stopped as she caught sight of Sebastian in the garden, eyes closed, face turned towards the rising sun.

Latching the windows, Aveline raced downstairs, narrowly avoiding the wobbly bottom step by catching the bannister at the last second.

She recovered and broke into another sprint, all but throwing the door open when she made it outside.

Sebastian turned, surprise turning into a mixture of concern and happiness that re-sparked her hope. "Aveline, good morning."

I must look wild, she realised, having burst outside without shoes and breathing heavily. But it didn't matter—what did was that she had to tell him now, before she lost the nerve again. Because with his dark chocolate eyes pinned on her, all of the words she'd been crafting in her mind jumbled together. "Good morning," she managed, tucking a strand behind her ear.

"Is something wrong? You seemed upset last night. I was going to find you after I put Leo to bed, but you had already gone to sleep."

He had been looking for *her*. She could have grinned, had her stomach not been doing somersaults. "I... I wasn't sleeping."

Sebastian's head tilted to the side. "Are you all right?"

Had he always been this tall? The sun at his back gave his silhouette an ethereal glow, as if he were a fantasy creature come to life—one that she would paint later.

"I... Yes, I'm all right," she said, which did little to ease the lines in his brow, "but I have something to tell you."

"Should we go indoors, to have a more private conversation? I'm not sure when Leo will wake, but given how early he fell asleep, I'd assume soon."

"Oh, no, I think it should be fine out here." *Do not give me another excuse to delay, I beg of you.* She locked away the memories of their almost kiss before it could snatch the last of her resolve. It didn't have to end that way again. She'd tell him, and then he'd respond. There would be no almosts this time.

"Very well." His throat bobbed.

Where to begin? "I know you and I have only known one another for a short time, but... Well, we are technically married, but that was to save me from fading—I understand—yet I cannot deny that, at least on my end, there is something that makes it feel real to me, and I..."

He did not speak, did not move.

"I'm not making any sense." She sighed. "What I mean to say is that, I don't know if you feel the same way, and I'm so sorry if you don't, but I have to tell you…" Aveline tried to inhale, but could only take half breaths. Fear and anticipation climbing their way up her throat, carrying a thousand heavy what-ifs, she managed, "I love you."

Even the chirping of birds ceased. Sebastian stared at her, expression unreadable.

What have I done? How could I possibly have thought there was a chance that he—

Sebastian crossed the distance between them in two long strides. She dared to look up as his hand cupped her face, and caught a flicker of intensity lighting his eyes before he pulled her to him.

"Sebas—"

He cut her off with a kiss that sparked fire in her veins, making her gasp. He moved back, and she grabbed his shirt, trying to find the words to tell him not to stop. But she had no words, no coherent thoughts, just a scramble of overwhelming emotions begging to continue. There must have been something in her expression that he understood, because Sebastian started to lean towards her again, but this time Aveline pressed her lips to his, wrapping her arms around his neck. He melted into her, holding Aveline as if he wanted to make her his anchor, the one steady constant in the torrent of craziness and uncertainty life would bring.

She would gladly be that for him, to weather whatever storms would come their way.

Their frantic intensity slowed to a pause, their faces still so close that they shared breaths. Aveline considered that he might want her to let go, but she couldn't bring herself to, not yet. Instead, she played with his silky hair; his eyelids fluttered.

"I probably should have said it first," he murmured, touching his forehead to hers, "but… I love you too."

Somehow, her heart soared even higher. "I wish I would have said something sooner."

"I'm just as guilty. I almost let you kiss me the day you cut my hair —I wanted to kiss you, but…" He shrugged his right shoulder, empty sleeve fluttering in the light breeze. "I wanted you to know that first, in case it changed your mind."

"Not in the least."

They shared a grin, and a few more kisses, these slow and intimate, savouring the moment like they had all of the time in the world.

"Mum, they're *kissing!*"

Sebastian and Aveline jolted but kept hold of one another, turning to see Leo hopping just outside of the doorway, pointing at them.

"Look! They are in love, I told you! She is too part of the family!" he shouted. "You're staying with us, right, Aveline? When you see your other family, you're coming back?"

"Leonard," Maud hissed, looking as if she wished she could yank him back inside with her.

Sebastian's hold on her loosened. Aveline looked down at the boy with the big blue eyes, brimming with vulnerability and unrestrained hope. He had been worried she wouldn't return? Had they all been worried?

They want me to stay.

"Of course I will return," she promised. "You are my family too."

Leo threw his arms around her and squeezed tightly. She ruffled his hair.

Even if they made it back in time for her to see her blood family, she would not leave any of them behind. They were just as much a part of her.

"Leo," Maud interrupted, "how about you and I make some breakfast for everyone?"

"Or we can all make it together," Sebastian said.

Disappointment welled inside of her at the loss of extra alone time, but Sebastian did not meet her gaze, instead hurrying indoors.

DID I SAY SOMETHING WRONG? AVELINE REPLAYED THEIR interactions as they cooked and ate breakfast. Sebastian didn't keep away from her, but he also didn't look at her for more than a split second at a time. Was he embarrassed at being caught kissing?

The castle rumbled and quaked.

"Finish quickly," Maud urged. "We may be moving again."

Sebastian examined the ceiling, where a crack was forming. "Agreed."

"Do I have time to grab my light stick?" Leo white-knuckled the edge of the table.

"If you go now and don't dawdle," Sebastian answered, and the boy dashed away.

"I'm going with him." Maud excused herself. "We'll meet you in the foyer."

He dipped his head in response and set about gathering the dishes. Aveline hurried to help. Judging by the gradually increasing volume of Lila's cries, they still had a little time, but not much. Sebastian must have come to the same conclusion, because he didn't even try to use his magic to clean the dishes and put them away, instead wiping them with a rag by hand.

Tentatively, she sidled up to him. "Sebastian, are we all right? If I said or did something earlier—"

"You didn't do anything wrong." He locked eyes with her. "Leo reminded me of things we need to sort out about our future, if we are to have one together."

Aveline welcomed the trickle of relief. She didn't do anything wrong, and he wasn't having second thoughts about his feelings. "We should talk about that," she concurred.

The tremor pitched them forward, and they gripped the edge of the kitchen counter.

"...But perhaps we should wait until after we teleport again."

He nodded his agreement, quickly dried his hand, and took hold of hers. Together, they rushed to the meeting spot. They made it a few seconds before Leo, Maud, and the hounds, the boy clutching his light stick.

"Just in case!" he shouted over Lila's wails and the boisterous winds clawing at their clothes and hair.

Aveline pulled him close, and put her other arm around Sebastian. "Use my strength when you need to," she said in his ear, hoping he couldn't feel her shake. *Home,* she thought. *We're going home, and I might be able to make it in time to see my parents and siblings—*

The winds stung her eyes and made them water. Even if she couldn't see what Sebastian was doing, she saw the effects of it, the way the spiderweb-thin cracks spreading across the ceiling suddenly slowed. The wood around them splintered, but it stopped a couple of feet away, as if there were an invisible barrier.

The candles sputtered out, a few falling to the floor. Leo kept the light stick close to his face, but the black swallowed up its glow. Aveline could make out the edges of Sebastian's profile, sharp with determination. She pressed her side against his. *Don't be stubborn, take my strength.*

Something sparked in her chest, hot and urgent. Aveline closed her eyes, imagining a small fire trying to grow. "Take what you need," she whispered, then gasped as the heat flooded her senses. The torrent's biting chill could no longer touch her. With an almost smile, she opened her eyes once more, lips parting at the sight of an iridescent brilliant blue light clashing and wrestling the darkness above their heads. A translucent version of that magic surrounded them, unshakable against the tempest that rattled the floorboards and slammed against the barrier. The darkness was all shapes, reminding Aveline of The Heart Thief's shadow monsters. Every time it started to form into beasts, Sebastian's magic sliced through them, scattering the shredded bits. When it regrouped, it was smaller, thinner, less opaque, with gaps in its smoke-like being.

An enraged, guttural scream tore through everything. Sebastian's grip nearly crushed Aveline's knuckles; his magic exploded in a blinding light that swept across the room. The darkness reeled, its pieces tumbling through the air, then slowly slinked back upstairs. Sebastian's magic dimmed and paused, waiting like guards. Once the darkness disappeared, his returned, melting into his skin. The barrier dissipated, and the spark vanished, leaving her insides feeling like they'd been scraped out. Her eyelids drooped; Aveline could have taken a nap right there on the floor.

"Are you all right?" Sebastian murmured, pressing a kiss to her temple.

She nodded, leaning into him. Was this how he always felt? How could he handle this deep ache and exhaustion?

Leo cracked one eye open, then the other, the tautness in his stance slowly unwinding. "It's getting worse, Bash."

"I know, Leo. I'm sorry."

"It's not your fault."

Sebastian didn't argue. He pulled out his pocket watch, and the lid flipped open to reveal a normal clock face with multiple smaller circles with various symbols and numbers. "We returned just in time," he announced with a weary smile. "We'll be able to visit your family tomorrow night."

Since when did smiling take so much effort? Aveline wondered. Then again, just standing there was sapping the last bits of her strength. "Wonderful."

"I'm going to play outside! Want to come, Aveline? Bash, I know you're usually too tired, but you can come, too, if you'd like!" Leo stashed his light stick in his pocket. Sun rays streamed through the windows, making her think it was probably around noontime.

"I think we need some rest," Sebastian replied, "but thank you for the offer."

Maud hastened after her son and the hounds. When Sebastian tried to lead Aveline towards the stairs, she looked up at the askew portraits she'd painted. "Wait, I want to check on Meredith first."

"She's fine," he assured her. "You know she'll just want us out so she can reorganise." At Aveline's hesitancy, he added, "We can check on her when we wake. I think I took too much from you, and I want you to recover."

"We both need to." Her eyes slipped shut as his lips touched her forehead.

Aveline didn't quite remember the journey to her bedroom, only that partway up the stairs, Sebastian carried her, and she rested her heavy head against his shoulder and breathed him in. She mumbled something about wasting magic, but he dismissed it. When he set her down and started to leave, she asked, "Stay... please?"

The mattress shifted, and she rolled into his warmth as sleep overtook her.

CHAPTER 45
YOU LOVED WELL

Dreamless sleep gently ushered her back to the waking world by the chirping of birds at the window. It took three tries for her to open her eyes, and a few seconds for her vision to focus. Soft light bathed the room, telling her it was either close to night or early morning. She was resting on Sebastian's chest, his arm cradling her, his soft breaths ruffling her hair. His heartbeat was slow and steady, nearly luring her back to sleep.

Meredith. Aveline tensed, stopping herself from jarring him awake. As horrible as she'd felt earlier, she couldn't imagine how much more rest he needed. With stiff limbs, she slipped out of bed, fighting her desire to remain. After their last interaction with Meredith, surely she would be appreciative of Aveline checking on her. She'd seemed so melancholy when they'd arrived, and Aveline hadn't had the chance to ask why.

I'll be back if you don't wake soon, Aveline silently promised Sebastian as she studied him, dark hair splayed across the pillow, arm still out towards her side, fingers twitching like he was seeking her. She'd asked him to stay, and he had, she mused with a grin. Selfishly, she hoped he didn't wake quite yet, that way she could climb back into bed for a little more peaceful rest, just the two of them.

Before she could change her mind, Aveline left, keeping the door cracked open. *Just a quick visit. Meredith probably won't open up to me, but at least she'll know she's cared for. I wonder what organisation strategy she has this time.*

At Lila's whimpers, Aveline couldn't help a shiver, rubbing her arms. *Do not move the castle at least until after Jeanette's wedding, please. I will never hear the end of it otherwise.* She padded down the stairs as a list of decisions flooded her mind: If she did go, she'd have to either wear a disguise or face an onslaught of questions about her disappearance, and even if she did manage to come up with a satisfactory explanation, how was she going to protect Sebastian? Would they know who he was if he used the surname Blaise? Would it raise suspicions, since they knew the Blaise family owned this castle and they were presumed murdered by The Magic Collector?

If Meredith doesn't want to talk about her problems, I might seek her advice on mine. On her way to the library, Aveline peeked into the kitchen but saw no sign of Leo, Maud, or the hounds. Out the window, the sky appeared to be the more pastel colours of morning than the darker tones of evening. *We did sleep quite a long time then. I hope we didn't overdo it... No, Maud would've woken us.*

Aveline examined her hands; she'd remained in her corporeal form for far longer than she'd anticipated. She could share that with Meredith too—it might be worth risking an impromptu practise of her strange powers.

The sconces in the hall were unlit, but she could see well enough to make it to the door and knock. "Meredith?"

No answer.

"Meredith, it's Aveline. May I enter?"

Nothing.

Had she decided to take a walk through the castle again? Unlikely but not impossible. Hesitantly, Aveline eased open the door. "Meredith, I—"

A gasp caught in her throat. Half of the bookshelves had toppled over, the floor covered in strewn books, pages bent and spines cracked. The vase that had sat atop the desk was mere glass fragments alongside scattered rose petals.

"Meredith?" She rushed inside, doing her best to avoid stepping on the books. "Meredith? Are you hurt? Please, say something." *You can even berate me for entering without permission, just say something!*

Had a creature sneaked into the castle? Ghosts could be harmed, too, as Sebastian had warned Aveline what felt like a lifetime ago. Something she knew firsthand. With Sebastian sleeping, magic nearly spent, something could have found a crack in the defences, made its way inside...

She ran, tripping and sliding and swearing when she banged her shin on the corner of a fallen bookshelf. "Meredith, where are you?" There were more books on the floor than on the shelves, and the couches they'd sat upon had been toppled as well. *It was teleporting that caused all of this*, Aveline told herself as her heart thudded painfully. *It's just getting worse, more powerful, like Leo said, and maybe Meredith got overwhelmed and decided to go outside...*

Aveline made her way back towards the door, but stopped short at the sight of a piece of paper near the rose petals. Avoiding the glass shards, she picked up the letter when she saw her name.

Dearest Aveline,

For a long time, I had thought the Blaise family was lost, and the only way to keep our proud memory was through these books. I was taught as a little girl that our family name was the only important thing, and that letting it be forgotten was worse than a ruined reputation.

My parents were only half right: family is important, but not the name. While these books are valuable and we should never forget the past, the present and future will just as easily slip through our fingers if we are not attentive to be a part of it. I was grieving a life I thought I'd lost, and yet the Blaise family lives on—in Maud, in little Leonard, in Sebastian, and in you.

Thank you for returning to me the hope and peace I thought had died when I did, and for teaching me that true families do not have to come from the same bloodline. Take care of them, especially Sebastian, and make sure to raise your children to bring the same light into the world as you brought into my life.

All My Love,
Babushka

Through blurred vision, Aveline poured over the words again and again as if they would change. They could not be a farewell—she refused. They had only just begun to bond, had only just begun to get to know one another. This was not the end, it just wasn't.

"Aveline?" From the doorway, Sebastian surveyed the scene, his eyes gradually finding hers.

"She can't be gone," Aveline choked out, shaking the letter. "She can't be, she can't—"

He read the letter, expression growing grimmer. Then, with calm reverence, he set it down on the desk and embraced her. She gave into the sobs then, clinging to him like he could keep her heart from crumbling. But she felt his small shudders, heard him sniffle, felt the weight of him against her. The grief was not hers alone to bear.

Finally, when the tears had been wrung from her and she could manage half a breath, Aveline whispered hoarsely, "She's gone…"

"I know."

"Why?"

His response was delayed. "She must have felt it was time to move on. Ghosts only remain while they want to, when they feel there is something they still need to remedy." He took a deep breath, and sighed. "At least we can take solace in the fact that she made this decision herself, that she finally found what she was looking for. After twenty years of seeking, you finally helped her move on." He kissed the top of her head. "You helped her find peace."

Without letting go of him, she shook her head. "I did nothing extraordinary."

"You didn't have to," he said gently. "You loved well. That's all it takes."

MAUD AND LEO EVENTUALLY FOUND THEM, LEO KEEPING CLOSE TO the door, eyes wide as he took in the destruction. "Where's Meredith? We'd better clean this up before she sees this and thinks I did it."

"Leo—" Aveline started.

The boy carefully picked up the books. "She was in such a good mood, and this will put her into a foul mood—"

"Leo—"

"Then she won't want me to visit and show her my new tricks and—"

Sebastian knelt in front of him, gripping his arm. Leo looked at Aveline, then back to him. "Bash? What's wrong? Why are you crying?"

His throat bobbed. "I'm sorry, *moy mal'chik*, but Meredith is... gone."

Maud's hands flew to her mouth; Leo's brow furrowed. "She's gone? Where did she go?"

"She passed on."

"But... why?" His eyes brimmed with tears.

Setting the books aside, Sebastian smoothed the boy's hair back. "It was her time."

"But it wasn't!" Leo insisted, voice starting to give out. "We just became friends, and she was going to be my *babushka* too."

Aveline moved closer, ready to hug him, but Sebastian beat her to it, cradling his head.

"She didn't have to go!"

"She chose to," Sebastian said. "Ghosts stay until they find contentment. You made her very happy; she was finally at peace, ready to move on."

Sniffling, Leo turned to his mother. "Are you going to do the same?"

"No!" Maud answered immediately, hand reaching out. Leo tried to touch her fingers, to no avail. "No, my darling," she said again, more tenderly. "I will not leave you, not for a long time. I will stay your whole life through, if I can."

He wiped his nose on his shirtsleeve. "Promise?"

"I promise." At his nod of acceptance, she put on a small smile. "Come now, we have to help Aveline get ready to see her parents and brothers and sisters."

"But what about Meredith's books?"

Sebastian squeezed his shoulder. "I think, for now, we need to leave things where they are. We'll clean this up and organise another time, then have a proper goodbye."

With a heavy sigh, Leo picked up the small stack he'd gathered and reverently took them to the desk. He stared at the stem and petals on the floor. "We should bring flowers. Meredith liked roses."

"That is a good idea."

"And we could have a cake, just like we did before." Leo hung his head and plodded towards the door. Maud walked beside him, murmuring something that Aveline couldn't quite catch.

Wordlessly, Sebastian extended a hand. After taking one last lingering look around the room, Aveline accepted it. Meredith was right: whether she was there or not, the world would move on without her. But that didn't mean she would be forgotten.

Aveline would make sure of it.

CHAPTER 46

I'M SLIGHTLY TERRIFIED, NOT KNOWING WHAT THAT EXPRESSION MEANS

Aveline and Maud exchanged very few words as they picked out what she was going to wear for the evening. Sadness clung to everything, tingeing the world in hues of grey, even dampening the brightly coloured gowns in the closet. Not that she was in a mood to wear a bright colour anyway, pushing them aside in favour of the darker tones. She inspected the sleeve of a simple black gown. Where gems or intricate embroidery decorated the others, this had nothing but a matching black veil. Not very festive, and it would draw more questions from her family than she wanted to answer.

"You could wear that, if you wish," Maud suggested after the silence had drawn out so long it felt ready to snap.

"I could," Aveline agreed reluctantly. "Although I feel as though Meredith would say that she'd died a long time ago, that it's no use mourning her, not when she is at peace. She chose this, so what right do I have to feel sad?"

She flinched as Maud unexpectedly touched her shoulder. *I wonder if it works both ways... but only for me? She still cannot touch Leo...*

"You have the right to feel whatever way you wish to. Being sad that she is gone means that she meant a great deal to us. We can be happy that she is happy but also sad that her choice took her away."

Aveline hugged Maud, and noted how much thinner she felt, like she could pass right through her if she were not careful. "Are you feeling all right? Did you spend too much energy when we teleported?"

"Possibly." She shrugged. "I've been quite tired as of late, but we all have. One way or another, we survive together."

The declaration should have bolstered her spirits, but it got snagged on her train of thought. *Maud looks more ghost-like than I've ever seen her. I know we just teleported, but what if it happens again while Sebastian and I are gone? Lila's outbursts have become more frequent and erratic— Maud wouldn't have the power to stave her off...*

"Enough worrying," Maud ordered, gesturing at the closet. "If you want my opinion, I think you should go with the dark red one. It'd suit you well."

Aveline admired the black lace on the bodice and skirt. "It's beautiful, but it might be a tad too fancy for a visit with my family. My *other* family," she amended.

"I think seeing them for the first time in a long while is cause for celebration."

"You make a good argument. All right, it's settled then." Aveline stepped behind the screen to change. She undressed easily enough, but it took a minute to put on all of the under layers of the evening gown. Plus, with this type of bust, she'd have to wear a corset. Stifling a sigh, she wished Maud could help her. They could try holding hands, see if she could help Maud affect the physical world...

"So... I noticed that Sebastian spent the night in here."

Aveline made a strangled noise as the corset laces slipped from her fingers. No, she wouldn't ask Maud for help and risk giving her the satisfaction of seeing her blush. She could manage by herself.

"Have the two of you... finalised your marriage yet?"

"Maud!"

"What? The way you two moon over one another, it wouldn't have been surprising."

"If Leo had asked that question, you would have scolded him."

"He is also eight years of age."

"When he says things like that, just know where he gets them from." Aveline tied off the corset and stepped into the skirts.

Maud chuckled. "I know very well where he gets it from. The boy was supposed to get all of my good traits and none of my bad. Apparently he took a decent mix of both."

She refrained from asking if he'd taken any traits from his father. Whoever he was, he clearly didn't matter anymore, not to Maud. The man had never met Leo, and there was a good chance he knew nothing about his existence. Instead, she lifted the heavy skirts into place and said, "Some of his traits come from Sebastian, so you're not the only one to blame."

"True, true. Little goblin is too clever for his own good. Makes me wonder how much mischief Sebastian got into when he was a child, God bless his mother. From what little he's told me, she raised him alone for a decent amount of time before she married his stepfather. And he had magic to learn all by himself! I'm very grateful Leo doesn't have magic, or I'd be driven mad with frustration and anxiety. He gets into enough trouble as it is, and doesn't need any help getting bruises and scrapes."

"I can imagine." Aveline finished dressing and stepped out from behind the divider. "How does this look?"

"Perfect. Now—"

A knock interrupted her. "Aveline, may I enter?"

Maud snorted; ignoring her, Aveline gave Sebastian permission.

"I left Leo in the garden with the hounds. If we're to be punctual, we need to leave right..." The moment he laid eyes on her, he stopped, the door only halfway open.

"I told her that dress would suit her," Maud said with a smirk.

"It does." Sebastian took a tentative step towards Aveline. "You are beautiful."

"Thank you. You look dashing yourself." She eyed the suit, stain-free and tear-free, complete with a glove, an overcoat, and a top hat.

"I wanted to make a good impression."

"You certainly will."

Maud cleared her throat. "Before you two lovebirds get carried away with compliments and flirting, might I suggest Aveline tie up her hair?"

"I rather like it down." Sebastian playfully tugged on a strand. Aveline couldn't help grinning—and blushing.

"That may be, but you two are attending a dinner as guests, and her family is high society. On the off chance anyone else sees you, you should at least look presentable."

"She's right," Aveline admitted with a sigh, hurrying to the vanity to tie up her hair into a stylish bun. "Now, shall we?" She put on a shawl and looped her arm through Sebastian's, but he didn't seem quite as eager, turning towards Maud.

"We shouldn't be gone long. If something should happen—"

"Nothing will happen—"

"*If* something should happen, Leo has a bauble I told him to break. It'll let me know to return immediately."

Pressing her lips together, Maud nodded. "Do be careful not to overdo yourself."

"I'll only use magic when necessary, I promise."

"See to it he keeps that promise!" she called to Aveline as they left.

TRUE TO HIS WORD, SEBASTIAN DIDN'T EVEN TELEPORT THEM TO their destination, opting to use an open carriage. "I'd use a motorcar, but I'm afraid I never quite grew comfortable with driving. I gave up on the notion completely when I lost my arm; if anything goes wrong, it's much easier to soothe a beast's mind than figure out what spell to use on a machine. Far too many parts for my understanding."

"I honestly don't mind the carriage, as long as it doesn't move at a snail's pace. Grand Duchess Katarina Lestat always insisted we use hers, and I hated that it took an eternity to get anywhere. I think she just wanted everyone to see her carriage and remember she was still alive and in power."

The sun made its descent towards the mountains, leaving a chill in its wake. Aveline scooted closer to Sebastian as she scanned the horizon, taking in the countryside's transition into winter. Soon, there would be snow snatching the last of the vegetation colours and baring the trees.

"This might not be as fast as a motorcar, but it's suitable for our needs. We should make it there with a little time to spare."

"Perfect. Then would you like to continue our earlier conversation, the one about our future?"

Sebastian stared straight ahead, the muscles in his jaw flexing.

"Is something the matter?"

"I don't think now is the proper time for this discussion."

"Why not? For once, we don't have a castle or Leo to interrupt us."

Unfortunately, her jest only earned her a hint of a smirk that rapidly disappeared. "That's not what I'm thinking."

"Then what are you thinking?" she asked.

"That you should see your family before you make a decision about us that could irreparably change your life."

"I think my life has already been irreparably changed, Sebastian, and for the better, I might add."

"I count myself lucky that you see it that way."

"However?" she pressed.

"However... a life with me is not an easy choice, Aveline, and I would hate to have you live with regrets. The curse is lifting—you've more control over it than the other way around, I believe—so you can return to your family, your way of life. Not that you'd marry the prince, but you could be with whomever you desire, go where you please, all without risking your life on a daily basis. The castle is not a safe place to call home." He glanced at her. "Your turn to speak. I'm slightly terrified, not knowing what that expression means."

"Stop the carriage."

Sebastian followed orders, pulling them off to the side of the road. Tenderly, Aveline cupped his face and kissed him, the knot in her chest unwinding as he reciprocated, soft and sweet. When she pulled back, he waited, watching her with an unspoken question in his dark eyes.

"I still don't know what that expression means," he said huskily, "but it can't be all bad."

"It means that I cannot believe you think I would so easily be able to walk away from you, Sebastian Aleksander Blaise." Aveline traced his bottom lip. "I've seen the dangers the castle has, and I've survived them. I've made my choice: I want to be with you, for as long as you want to be with me."

Sebastian pressed her palm to his mouth. "I would have you with me forever if I could."

"Then do it. We are already married."

"It is not a true marriage, Aveline."

"Why not? You said it is. That is what bound me to you, what kept me here when I was going to fade away." She pulled her shawl tighter as a breeze passed through.

"I misspoke... Of course you're right, it is a true marriage, but not one I expected you to want to keep. I don't want you feeling trapped. It could easily be annulled, given we have never..." Slowly, he lowered her hand.

"Do you not want it to be true?" Aveline whispered, ignoring the way her eyes stung. She would not cry, not now. She didn't want him to feel guilted into telling her what she wanted to hear.

"I do. More than anything."

"Then why are you trying to push me away?"

Sebastian interlaced their fingers and pulled her hand against his chest. "I'm not, I promise you. I just want you to think through the decision before you make it." Aveline opened her mouth to argue further, but he cut her off, saying, "See your family tonight, enjoy the time together, and afterward, when we return to the castle, you can tell me your answer. All right?"

This is not a decision to make lightly, her mother would have said. *Consider the consequences, the risks.* Aveline had done that her entire life, and now she felt much more like Edith, wanting to rush headlong into this. Visiting her family would not change her mind, of that she was certain. But the sun was sinking in the sky, and they had little time to lose before they ended up late.

"Very well."

CHAPTER 47

I AM GLAD TO SEE THAT YOU AND I ARE OF A SIMILAR MIND

Although still technically in the country, the cottage was much closer to the city than Aveline anticipated. She could see the main gate in the distance, the long line of people trying to get in even though the sun was still an hour from fully setting.

Sebastian helped her out of the carriage. "I just realised I'd quite forgotten to ask if you think I need an illusion for my arm. I'd considered the prosthetic, but..." He offered a sheepish expression.

"Not at all, unless you are worried about King Byron getting word."

"No. It's just for one dinner, and I'd rather your family get to know the real me."

"Good, because I like the real you."

They shared a smile that was interrupted by a boy shouting, "Aveline!"

"Amos! Alan!" She barely had time to open her arms before they barrelled into her, almost knocking her over. "Have I been gone for months or years? You two will be taller than I am in no time!" They were little boys when she'd left, and now they were just shy of reaching her shoulders.

"We've some time yet, don't rush them." Timothée chuckled.

"Easy for you to say." She poked him in the ribs. "You shot up like a weed! Are you taller than Father?"

"Nearly."

"Is she here?" their mother shouted, rushing outside.

"Yes, Mum!" The twins shifted so she could join the group hug, bringing with her the scents of vanilla and jasmine. Tears pricked at Aveline's eyes as all the time spent yearning for their reunion resurfaced.

"My darling!" Her mother peppered her cheeks, forehead, and nose with kisses. "I prayed every day that I would see you again."

Aveline swallowed, but the lump in her throat remained, rendering her unable to speak. Beaming, her father and Lottie calmly approached, reaching past the others to touch her cheeks and smooth back her hair. Lottie took Aveline's hand; her heart cracked, seeing the woman her youngest sister had grown to be. *I have missed so much,* she lamented.

Their mother let go, wiping away her tears then Aveline's. "I knew we would be reunited again," she declared. "All of us."

Aveline stilled. Jeanette would arrive soon, but that left...

Two more people exited the cottage. She didn't recognise the man in the back, but her knees almost buckled at the sight of Edith. The rest of the family stepped aside. Aveline could barely hear her sister's footfalls on the stone walkway over the pounding of her heart. Her boyish haircut had grown to her shoulders, and there were fewer sad lines to her face.

She stopped an arm's length away and said in a faltering voice, "Hello, Aveline."

When had her sister ever shown anything but confidence, even in her recklessness?

Edith offered a tentative smile. "It's good to see you. I—"

Aveline embraced her like she was the only thing that could keep her from falling to pieces. It wasn't a dream. Edith was real and whole and safe and unharmed, and most importantly, she was *here*. Unable to hold back any longer, she sobbed onto her older sister's shoulder. Edith whispered something, but was too choked up to be articulate, and finally gave up and cradled the back of her head.

No, Aveline decided, it did not feel like she was falling apart. It felt like the final piece of her heart was being put back into place.

WHEN THEY EVENTUALLY CALMED DOWN ENOUGH THAT THEIR father could shuffle everyone inside the small, homey cottage with barely enough standing room, Edith stepped beside the stranger, a broad-framed man with a kind face. "This is Maurice," she introduced. "My husband."

Old me would have judged her before, Aveline thought. Back then, she would have seen him as the man who took their sister away from them. But she found only genuine happiness as she said, "It is a pleasure to meet you."

"You as well." He bowed his head. "Edith speaks highly of everyone, but you come up more than anyone else."

"For good reasons, I should hope."

"Mostly." Edith winked. "Now, who is your handsome stranger? Jeanette told us some of what happened, how you disappeared, but I can't say we quite understand the details."

It hadn't escaped her notice that all eyes kept straying to Sebastian. He took it in stride, seeming perfectly comfortable other than the fact that he had to duck under the doorframe. How was she going to explain their relationship when they were still sorting it out themselves?

"They do sound a little too fanciful." Timothée crossed his arms as he leant back against the wall. "But you know how Nettie likes to embellish."

"Embellishing details makes a good story great!" argued Edith, to which Timothée rolled his eyes with a grin.

"Go on, everyone sit where you can," their mother interrupted, motioning them towards the assortment of chairs and stools near the fireplace. "I had the boys set up the seating."

"I thought we were having dinner." Aveline chose a chair opposite the fireplace, where Sebastian would have more leg room. *I feel a little overdressed for chatting by fireside.* But as she took in her family members, she noticed that they, too, were dressed up—even the twins had their hair slicked back, not a dirt smudge or tear to be found on their clothes.

"We'll get to all that." Their mother waved her hand dismissively as she sat down. "We had you arrive early so we'd have plenty of time. Come, tell us all about what happened."

"I can take your coat," offered their father.

"Ah, thank you..." Sebastian faltered.

"You may call me Raphael, and my wife, Colette."

"I am Sebastian." He shrugged off the coat; the house went silent. Aveline was just about to say something when her father smiled and extended his hand. "It is a pleasure to meet you, Sebastian."

Aveline exhaled quietly as they shook hands and Sebastian took the seat beside her. "I must say, you are all taking this quite well. Jeanette was almost offended to find out I had disappeared and showed up with a stranger." She winced the moment the words left her mouth—to her relief, Edith snorted.

"Wouldn't be the first time one of us did that." She laughed, squeezing her husband's arm. "Although out of all of us, you would have been my second-to-last guess. Lottie being last, of course."

Dipping her head in agreement, Lottie folded her hands daintily in her lap. If any of the Clément women could have earned Grand Duchess Katarina's approval, it would have been their youngest sister, with her gentle, ladylike demeanour and reserved nature. The nobility would have swallowed her whole, without any fight.

"Jeanette filled us in on what she could." Raphael settled next to his wife. "As Edith said, not a lot of it made sense, but she did emphasise that Sebastian has been helping you."

"And that you are married!" squealed Colette. "Oh, I am so happy for you, darling, although I wish we could've been there for the ceremony. Perhaps we can host a couple of private ones for you and Sebastian and Edith and Maurice. Maybe back home, in the garden? But—"

"Dearest, if we want answers, we should let Aveline talk."

"You're quite right, I'm getting ahead of myself. Go on, love."

At least they are supportive of my decision. Thank you, Jeanette, for giving them time to process this. "Well, yes, we are married." She met Sebastian's gaze, and smiled at the tinge of pink in his cheeks. Concisely, Aveline told their tale, the bare bones that hopefully made sense. She kept Sebastian's secrets to herself, and even without them, she had a captivated audience, the twins included.

Towards the end of the story, her father stoked the fire, adding another log. Why only one when there was a large stockpile in the corner, she had no idea; were they possibly renting the cabin and trying to limit their use of the resources?

"You don't look like a ghost." Alan scrunched his nose.

"We all hugged you," Amos said. "Does that mean your curse is broken? How'd you do it?"

Aveline inhaled, glancing at Sebastian as if he could somehow inspire the explanation that she didn't quite understand herself. "Well…"

"I bet it was his magic." He pulled his knees up to his chest. "Nettie said you're called 'The Magic Collector', that you're a rogue wizard."

"Amos, we do not put our shoes on the furniture." Colette swatted at his knee. The boy scooted out of reach just in the nick of time, and put his feet back on the floor with a scowl.

"That's something we have to keep quiet," Timothée warned, with a finger raised to his lips. "People around here don't take kindly to rogue wizards."

"They didn't back home either," Edith pointed out, "but they're rare enough anyway. No one wants to stay in Arreth, just visit to drain us of our metals."

"That's quite enough." Colette raised a brow at her eldest child, who blatantly ignored her.

"There's no pretending," she continued on. "What with the war on our doorstep, everyone wants our resources to make rings for magic-users. It seems almost silly to mass produce guns and swords when what it's really going to boil down to is who blows up whom with the strongest spell."

"Edith!"

"I commend you for staying clear of it, Sebastian. Don't let them use your magic for destruction."

Sebastian dipped his head. "I am glad to see that you and I are of a similar mind, Edith."

She raised her chin with a gratified expression, but when she looked Colette's way, she sighed. "Oh, Mother, unclench. I promise to behave at the wedding tonight, but right here and now, I'd appreciate being allowed to be myself."

Her family continued to talk over one another, but Aveline caught none of it. "Tonight?" she tried to ask, but could not find her voice, could barely move her lips.

"Pardon me," Sebastian said, "but did you say that the wedding is tonight? We were told it was not for another few weeks or so."

To Aveline's surprise, he caught their attention. Raphael said, "That was what the entire kingdom was told. We had no idea until this morning that it had been secretly changed." He put an arm around his wife, pulling her close to his side as if to effectively dispel any lingering chance of the argument between her and Edith sparking anew.

"After what happened with Aveline disappearing," Timothée clarified as he rested his elbows on his knees, "King Byron wanted to be certain that no one else could interfere with another wedding."

"No one else? Does he think someone kidnapped me? I thought the rumour was that I fled."

"That is the most popular rumour, unfortunately," Colette confirmed with a heavy sigh. "But there are some who believe our enemy sent someone to kidnap you to prevent the wedding, although they were rather baffled that there was no ransom demand."

King Byron wouldn't have cared if there were. Aveline was nothing but a tool to him, and if he had another one easily accessible, then it was no use spending time and resources to find her. "If I'd known, I wouldn't have... well, worn this for starters." She picked at the black lace.

"We can find you something to wear, dearest."

"No. I mean, yes, thank you, that is kind, but... I suppose the major issue isn't what I'm wearing, but rather, the fact of... well, what we were just discussing. I am not just a random attendee, Mother.

Someone is bound to recognise me the moment I step foot inside the castle." They'd somehow forgotten her name when the curse was placed on her, but no one else had a difficult time knowing exactly who she was so far. She had a much better grip on the curse now, and while she wanted to be there for her sister's big day—*night*, she silently corrected, peering at the darkening sky outside the window—Aveline would be loath to cause a scene. Or worse, put anyone in danger. While she didn't have significance to King Byron, he was a prideful man, and might take her sudden reappearance as mockery.

There was Sebastian's cover to think about as well. If anyone figured out who he really was...

"Not to worry, not to worry." Colette crossed the room so she could pull Aveline to her feet. "Jeanette said she would take care of everything. Now, we should get everyone ready since Jeanette's attendants are certain to be here any moment to fetch us."

CHAPTER 48
I WAS AFRAID I HATED YOU

Just as her mother and sisters had been fighting over what to dress Aveline in and how to do her hair, Jeanette had arrived, surprising everyone. She ignored their plethora of questions, instead ordering them to get into the carriages she'd brought with her, which were large enough to seat six people apiece. Drivers and footmen helped them make haste—Aveline was certain that *someone* knew Jeanette was missing from the palace and would be looking for her. Not quite Queen—or Princess—yet, and already doing whatever she wanted.

"Are you certain you wouldn't prefer a lighter colour on Aveline?" Colette asked as Jeanette ushered her sister into her carriage.

"Aveline looks gorgeous, Mother."

"What about her hair?"

"I'll fix her hair," Edith assured her, stepping into their carriage as well. Sebastian and Maurice followed suit, and then they were on their way, heading towards the palace as the sun dipped low in the sky.

While Edith brushed her hair, Aveline studied Jeanette. She wore subtle cosmetics, but her strawberry blonde hair was twisted and pinned into an elegant updo that must have taken hours to achieve, especially with the gemstones adorning it. No doubt the court-bound magic-users had put enchantments on her like they had Aveline.

"Hanna is stalling for us, but I guarantee there'll be a fuss when we arrive. The driver is going to let me out at the back entrance so I can sneak into my room." Jeanette smoothed the front of her simple gown, one Aveline guessed belonged to the handmaiden.

"I bet there are hundreds of secret passages throughout the palace." Edith caught a snag in Aveline's hair and instantly apologised.

"Yes, and Alexei knows them all." She stared out the window, eyes glazed over.

"You risked a great deal by sneaking out," Aveline said. "While I'm glad to see you, I'm worried you'll incur the wrath of the King."

"Let him be angry. He will not do anything, not when he has a war to focus on. Since he wants his nickerite, he is willing to concede a few things."

Edith snorted; Aveline asked, "Like letting me attend the wedding?"

"Yes, like letting you attend."

"Will that not cause tension and drama?"

"Royal life *is* tension and drama—I'm sure you got to see that for yourself. Edith, Mother gave me these for Aveline's hair." Jeanette handed over three rose pins that matched the shade of her dress. "Avie, please don't look so concerned. I wouldn't have invited you if I thought you were in danger." She lowered her voice. "If it makes you feel any better, the King will be too concerned with his own welfare to worry about you attending."

"Why?" Aveline asked, feeling Sebastian tense beside her.

"We are keeping it hushed, but King Byron may not live to see another month."

Edith dropped the last pin. "What happened? Is he ill?"

Maurice stooped to pick up the pin for his wife, closing her hand over it when she was too distracted to take it.

"No, not ill. He was wounded in the last battle by an explosive; not close enough for the blast to mortally wound him, but his court-bound wizard claims it had magical properties that are turning his own body against him." She shuddered. "I only got a quick peek, and what I saw...

Suffice it to say that he will be wearing an illusion tonight, so as to not cause alarm. Alexei thinks we will need to rule soon, and with a war on our hands... As much as it pains me to say it, I think you would be safer to flee the kingdom after tonight. We have the magic-users to protect the palace, but even so, I'm not sure if you would be more protected in the city or far away."

Sebastian handed her a handkerchief, and Jeanette dabbed at her eyes. "Thank you. I will inform you all of what I think would be best for you when Alexei and I have a better idea of what is going on with the warfront."

Had Aveline married Alexei, those heavy burdens would have been hers to bear. Would she have been able to handle being Queen?

"But do not worry about that." Jeanette handed back the handkerchief. "Sebastian, King Byron knows that you are Aveline's husband—Gwendoline's, as everyone else knows her—but he remains unaware that you are a rogue wizard. Can you hide your magic?" She blinked, just then noticing his dangling sleeve, her expression blank as she drew her line of sight back to his face.

"I can," he confirmed. "I've removed illusions, and will only use magic if absolutely necessary."

"Good. Aveline, can you refrain from turning into a ghost?"

"I will do my best."

"Ah! We didn't talk much about you being a ghost," Edith interrupted. "What's it like? Also, describe the castle for me, will you? Is it like the ones in a fairytale? Are there others living there?"

They passed the remainder of the carriage ride with her asking a barrage of questions while Sebastian and Aveline answered them. She preferred to let him talk, enjoying the small details she hadn't thought to question, like if any of the plants in the garden carry natural magic qualities, or if the ghosts ever tried to move the suits of armour at the front of the castle. He was surprisingly relaxed, as if there were not half a dozen topics to carefully avoid. Out of anyone in her family, Edith would have been the one to take it all in without judgement, but Aveline respected Sebastian's choice to keep secrets.

"This is where I must leave you," Jeanette said as the carriage came to a halt. She kissed her sisters' cheeks, lifted the hood of her cloak, and exited. Aveline barely caught sight of her sister's skirts disappearing through the doorway as they pulled away.

Edith and Maurice moved to the opposite side of the carriage. Even though her husband's wide frame took up a large portion of the seat, Edith had plenty of room. Yet she picked at her nails, glancing out the window.

Gently, Aveline reached forward and covered her hands. "If there is something you need to say, you can. I'm not sure how much time we'll have with the ceremony and reception."

Edith wouldn't meet her gaze, but she did go still. "I was hoping for a more private moment, but... I think you are right." She cleared her throat. "I know you are mad at me for leaving, for abandoning the family when I was supposed to be the one to marry Alexei, and you have every right to be. While I will not apologise for following my heart, I am sorry that the burden was passed down to you."

The carriage swayed as they took a turn. Aveline kept hold of her sister's hands; she had never noticed how small they were, not when they were always moving, animating everything Edith said, especially when she told stories. Edith herself seemed smaller than Aveline remembered, like her abundance of personality made her appear bigger.

"I was angry with you, for a long time."

Reluctantly, Edith made eye contact with her, the blue in her hazel irises more apparent than usual.

"At one point, I was afraid that I hated you. But over time, I came to understand why you did what you did: You fell in love, and that is a precious thing no one should ever squander." Sebastian's hand at her back was a sweet reassurance that encouraged her to continue. "I also realised that, when I thought I was angry with you, I was really angry at myself. I had chosen to take your place, and yet I was bitter with everyone else for letting me do it. I wanted someone to release me from the burden." She paused, gathering her thoughts. "Neither of us wanted that life, and I am glad we didn't end up stuck in it. Jeanette seems excited to marry Alexei, and I am happy for her, as I am sure you are too.

"As for apologies... you owe me none. Just as I am happy for

Jeanette, I am happy for you as well. I no longer bear you any ill will. I love you, Edith, just as I always have and always will." Had the carriage been a smoother ride and less cramped, Aveline would have attempted to hug her.

"I love you too." Edith sniffed and wiped the corner of her eye. "You have changed much since we last saw one another. You're your own person now, not just my little shadow."

"The curse is partially to thank for that," Aveline said. "The more confident I've become, the less often I fade into a ghost."

The carriage stopped again.

"I'm not sure how Jeanette managed to sneak away to get us, what with all of the war chaos." Edith peered out the window. The sun was close to disappearing, yet there was plenty of light from the lampposts lining the cobblestone pathway to the palace entrance.

"Alexei must have been in on it," Aveline suggested. "He was kind to me, and I can't imagine he's found a way to say no to Jeanette, not when we've tried for her entire life."

She clicked her tongue. "Perhaps... And if he is a smart prince, these are no mere footmen and drivers, but also trained warriors, possibly even a magic-user or two."

"It wouldn't surprise me. Speaking of magic..." From his waistcoat pocket, Sebastian retrieved her wedding ring and the enchanted one that matched his. "Just in case," he whispered.

Aveline accepted them, taking comfort in the familiar pulse. "Just in case, but just so we're clear, I'm not letting you out of my sight."

He smiled.

"Neither am I!" Edith chimed in. "Sorry to break up the moment, but we're about to go inside, and I'm going to second Jeanette's request—you have to bid us farewell before you disappear again."

Aveline thought of the bauble Sebastian had given Leo in case of an emergency. *Everything is fine so far,* she reasoned. *Lila will not suddenly whisk them away. No sense in ruining the night by worrying.* "We will."

The footman opened the door for them, dipping into a low bow. "Welcome to Salise Palace, honoured family of Princess Maribelle."

It was time to don the mask of Princess Gwendoline once more, twin sister to Princess Maribelle, daughter of King Charles Allard of Arreth.

King Charles... and Prince Ivan... Just as they'd forgotten about her, she'd completely forgotten about them. What were they going to think about her reappearance? Surely, they would not risk their plans falling to ruins by making a scene.

Maurice stepped out of the carriage first, then helped Edith. Aveline was vaguely aware of their vacant seats, that it was time for her to exit, and yet she couldn't move. Sebastian leant forward. "What is the matter?"

Then Edith's attention was on her, as was her husband's, as was the footman's. *Move, Aveline. Do not draw suspicion.*

"My, how gorgeous the floral arrangements are!" Edith exclaimed. "And the lights! They are so bright I could have been tricked into thinking it was daytime. Is the entirety of the palace decorated for this special occasion?" She continued to pester the footman with questions, even going so far as to tug on the sleeve of his jacket to demand his focus.

"Aveline."

"I hadn't accounted for King Charles and Prince Ivan," she whispered, looking up at him. "What if they insist on knowing the truth?" There was a slim chance that they wouldn't recognise her...

"You owe them nothing."

Like a lock opening to release the chains, the weightiness slipped off her shoulders.

She owed them nothing.

"I'll be beside you the whole night," he promised, kissing her knuckles. "Princess Gwendoline."

"Are you sure you do not want to use an illusion?"

He shook his head. "Only minor ones to hide the rings. The more magic I use, the more likely I'll draw someone's attention." Seeing her gaze drift to his empty sleeve, he added, "Who would suspect someone like me?"

A choked chuckle escaped her. "If we make it out of this without being caught, I won't know whether to call it brilliance or luck."

"Perhaps a bit of both."

CHAPTER 49
YOU CANNOT HIDE FOREVER

Seeing the palace so bare surprised Aveline. There had been much more to hers, with all of the silk curtains, plush carpets spanning the halls, and the flowers adorning every table and chair. *This is supposed to be a secret*, she reminded herself. *The populace still thinks it won't happen for another few weeks.*

As one of the servants led them to the throne room, Edith cast her a reassuring look over her shoulder. They exchanged a quick smile, which dimmed the moment a group of women raised judgmental eyebrows at Aveline. She refused to lower her gaze, opting instead to keep her chin held high. She had special permission from her sister to wear something daring in a sea of pastels and subdued hues—what did it matter what they thought of her?

Sebastian leant close, lips brushing the shell of her ear. "It's all right."

Were her emotions that noticeable, or could he feel her heartbeat through the ring? His was faster than normal but steady. How could he not be nervous? One slip up, and King Byron would have him bound, stripped of his freedoms. What would become of Maud, Leo, and the castle then?

What of Lila?

I trust Sebastian. One slow breath in through the nose, then out through barely parted lips. Then a second, a third. By the fourth, they were approaching the double doors that led to the throne room, and Aveline caught some of the whispers about her, the Runaway Bride. Before the blow could land, it dissipated with a single thought: *I'd rather they talk about me than about him.* Either they hadn't noticed his missing arm, or had the decency not to say anything. It was much better that they mock her.

The last of the attendees to arrive, they were seated in the middle of the left section, a few rows behind Prince Ivan. There were far fewer people than Aveline's wedding; eyes shifted back and forth, accompanied by hushed conversations. *I wonder if they remember The Heart Thief coming here.* Probably not, she decided, given that they thought she had abandoned everything to pursue a lover. Even if The Heart Thief came again, she wouldn't come for Jeanette—no one had helped Sebastian, so she wouldn't curse them. Jeanette would go through with the wedding, not be a third runaway bride. Well, second, as far as they knew. Edith had left before King Byron had sent an entourage to bring her to the palace, leaving Aveline to go in her stead.

Sebastian laced his fingers through hers, and she had to stop herself from resting against his shoulder. She could practically hear Grand Duchess Katarina barking at her to sit up straight with her shoulders back, stomach sucked in. The crabby old woman sat in the first row in the other section, the long feathers in her stylish hat close enough to tickle the nose of the man behind her.

Conversations ceased when the music started, soft strings inviting the viewers on a romantic journey. The priest and Prince Alexei took their places near the throne, where King Byron sat with a stony expression. Aveline made a mental note to ask Sebastian later if he could see the illusions cast on the king. She would've had no idea how close to death he was, had Jeanette not said anything.

The music swelled; everyone stood as King Charles escorted Jeanette down the aisle. Eyes locked on Alexei, Jeanette beamed. Any lingering guilt that clung to Aveline disappeared.

King Charles handed her over to Prince Alexei, and the Crown Prince brought his bride up the stairs to the altar, where the priest and

Ralph, the King's personal magic-user, waited. Soon, Jeanette's and Alexei's souls would be bound together like Aveline's and Sebastian's.

She sneaked a peek at him, catching his ponderous expression. Before she could think too much about it, the priest launched into his speech about love and loyalty, that Alexei and Maribelle would be forever bonded. Months ago, she was in Jeanette's shoes about to have a panic attack, when The Heart Thief arrived and changed everything. Aveline held her breath, waiting for a chill, a tapping of the cane, of shadows to move on their own.

Nothing.

Sebastian squeezed her hand. As Alexei and Jeanette exchanged vows, Aveline forced herself to relax. Everything would be fine. The only people the witch was interested in were Sebastian and Aveline, unless someone else had struck a deal with her.

That was the one time Aveline hoped that Grand Duchess Katarina Lestat was correct: Polite society did not go looking for magic.

The vows finished, the priest stepped aside so Ralph could take his place. Gold and silver rings gleaming, Ralph cupped their hands between his. There was nothing for normal people to see, but the wizard stared intently, focused on the binding. She wondered if the magic looked like strings, a binding in a literal sense, or if it was just a shapeless glow. Neither Alexei nor Jeanette reacted other than a small, quiet inhale just before Ralph released them. The priest resumed his place, raising their clasped hands. "May I present Prince Alexei Voland and Princess Maribelle Voland!"

The crowd stood and applauded politely as the prince and princess shared a chaste, brief kiss. Aveline stamped down the urge to cheer, and almost laughed when she saw her parents cover the twins' mouths before they could hoot and holler like they did at every celebration.

At least there are some things that never change.

THE RECEPTION TOOK PLACE IN THE BALLROOM. AVELINE WISHED there were more guests, that way she could blend in with the crowd. Nowhere to hide from critical eyes, and not enough commotion to cover the quips about runaway brides.

"She gave up on Prince Alexei for *him?*"

If Sebastian overheard, he didn't react. He did, however, notice Aveline studying him. "Are you all right? You look pensive."

I would give up Prince Alexei and this life a hundred thousand times over just for the chance to be with you. "I'm more than all right."

"Good." He smiled, setting his glass down on a nearby table. "There are enough people staring at you already. Might as well give them a better view of your dress by dancing, wouldn't you agree?"

"I don't think they're still staring at my dress. Have you heard what they've been saying?"

"Yes, but does it matter? I've heard the runaway bride jokes, the scoffing of the colour of your dress, the fact that I am clearly not royalty and haven't properly styled my hair, and one rather bold 'gentleman' had the nerve to comment that I was a poor choice on your part because my handicap clearly shows that I cannot provide for you the way you deserve."

Aveline's jaw dropped, a rush of fury ready to spew out of her, but Sebastian said, "There will always be people who look down on us for one thing or another. It is our choice to either listen to them and let it shape what we think about ourselves, or ignore it because there is no point in caring what they think." Sebastian leant down so that their foreheads were nearly touching. "I love the colour of your dress, because I, too, like wearing bright and bold colours—they make me and others smile. I don't care what they think about my handicap because I am who I am, and even though it came from tragedy, all of the highs and lows brought me to where I am today, with you. And although I do not like that you were cursed, I am happy that it brought you into my life for however long I may have you." He kissed her knuckles. "Selfish as that may be."

Despite the butterflies in her stomach, Aveline raised a judgemental brow that made him chuckle.

"Say whatever you like, but the way I love you makes me feel like the most selfish person alive. I don't want to share your attention with anyone."

Aveline grinned, leaning even closer, noses brushing. "Then I suppose we're both horribly selfish," she murmured.

His pupils dilated. Aveline moved to close the small distance between them, but he caught her chin. "Not here."

As her spirit sunk, the voices and music became more apparent to her again, reminding her of where she was. She had been about to kiss him in the middle of the ballroom without a second thought about what high society thought, something the previous Aveline would never have considered doing.

The disappointment melted under the heat of her cheeks as Sebastian whispered in her ear, "Later tonight, when we're alone."

With a mischievous hint to his grin, he stepped back and extended his hand. "So, what do you say? Will you honour me with a dance?"

Aveline nodded. Then she found herself amongst the dancers, her hands on his shoulders while his was on her low back. A welcome shiver rolled up her spine; somehow, she stumbled into the correct steps. Sebastian tweaked their position slightly before another couple bumped into them.

"You're a wonderful dancer," Aveline complimented. "When did you learn?"

"Lila had to learn, and insisted I be her partner." His grin dimmed, the bittersweet fondness in his expression fading as the song ended and switched to a more upbeat one. They hopped and twirled, splitting apart and coming right back together. With each rotation, Aveline searched for him, as if he would suddenly vanish in the growing crowd. She caught sight of Edith and her husband, Jeanette and Alexei, their mother and father—

And King Byron. His icy stare pierced her, and she tripped, falling into Sebastian. With a grunt, he caught her elbow.

"Leave if you cannot dance," hissed a woman near them.

"I'm sorry," Sebastian said. "I didn't mean to pull too hard, I got overzealous—"

"It wasn't you." Aveline urged him to leave the dance floor, ignoring the glares and snide remarks. He went with her to the refreshments tables without hesitation and accepted the drink when she offered him one.

"The King is watching me."

Lifting the glass to his mouth, Sebastian furtively checked out of the corner of his eye. "It could be either of us. We could've adopted an inconspicuous profile, but I thought he might be more suspicious if we were hiding off to the side."

She took a step closer to him, letting his scent calm her nerves. Hopefully, onlookers would think that they were murmuring sweet nothings to one another. "He knew I was coming," she processed aloud. "I doubt he's happy with my presence, given the circumstances. Do you think he suspects you at all?"

"If he does, we'll have to make a quick escape." He took another sip, his wedding band gleaming in the light. To her eye, that was the only ring he wore—was the illusion strong enough that it would get someone's attention? He might have fooled the novice wizard that guarded the upper city, but she spotted at least ten wizards stationed about the room, and they assuredly would have at least four rings apiece, silver and gold. *How could I get so wrapped up in what others were thinking and saying that I didn't think about the bigger problem at hand?*

Because she was trying not to let herself, lest she bolt from the palace and never return. Her heartbeat pounded in her ears as she saw King Charles and Prince Ivan in her peripheral. King Charles bowed his head to King Byron, then started stalking their way, Prince Ivan and a magic-user at his flank.

"We should leave," Aveline whispered in a strained voice.

"Any quick exits will draw attention and confirm what I am. We need to wait until no one is watching us."

"What if that opportunity doesn't come?" How could she be so selfish, bringing him here? He'd agreed to it, but she should have insisted that he remain at the castle, or at least outside of the palace walls.

Did that shadow move of its own accord? Gooseflesh covered her skin as she scanned the wall. One of the statues had a darker shadow than the rest. *Do not become paranoid...*

The dancers gave King Charles and the others a wide berth,

dipping their heads in respect and slipping right back into the dance. Inhaling as deep as she could, Aveline steeled herself, turned—

—and found herself in the arms of her sister.

"I did it, Gwendoline!" Jeanette squealed. "I am a married woman!"

Doing her best not to sag in relief, Aveline returned the hug. "I am so happy for you."

The trio of men halted, avoiding stepping on the bride's beaded train.

"I am so overjoyed that you are here! It is good that we could celebrate as one big, happy family. Isn't that right, Father?" She cast a questioning look over her shoulder at King Charles, then gestured at Prince Ivan. "The three of us children, you... the only person we're missing is poor mother, God rest her soul. Although I am sure she is with us in spirit." She made a religious motion over her heart, a silent prayer that they would see their deceased "mother" once more.

King Charles's cheek twitched. "Yes, darling, you are quite right. Now, if you'll excuse us for a moment, I have not seen your sister in quite some time and am curious to meet her..." His focus alighted on Aveline's ring. "...husband."

Panic crept over her like a wintery night chill, slowly stealing the warmth from her bones. He dared not make a scene in front of everyone, but if they went with him somewhere more private, there was no telling what he would say or do. The fact that he had brought a magic-user with him—one of King Byron's personal wizards—did not help matters.

"Father," Jeanette pressed quietly, leaning as though she were about to hug him, "must we do this here and now? Surely this can wait until after the festivities, so that we do not risk ruining them."

With a sickeningly sweet smile, King Charles said, just loud enough for Aveline to hear, "You have tried both His Majesty's patience and mine long enough. We upheld our end of the bargain by allowing them here, now you uphold yours."

Aveline was pinned to the spot. How could Jeanette not mention an agreement? He had to be lying, trying to get into Aveline's head so that he could have absolute obedience.

"You said I could be there when you spoke with them."

"But King Byron made no such promise." He straightened, a glint in his eyes. "It will take but a moment, my sweet. I just want a word alone with my daughter and son-in-law."

Her hand found Sebastian's. After being out of the political world for so long, she had forgotten how treacherous the game felt: one wrong step, and she could plummet to her doom. There were already curious eyes on them; if they made a quick escape, it would expose Sebastian. But what if they already suspected and wanted to capture him? *No, I think they'd have done so already if that were the case...*

"That is not a problem, Princess Maribelle," Sebastian interjected, speaking with a cheerier tone than Aveline was prepared for. "It will be but a few moments, and we will return to the party soon."

Edith wove her way through the guests, her husband behind her. They would catch up momentarily, drawing even more attention and getting themselves looped into something Aveline would rather they steered clear of.

As Sebastian said, every high society gathering has its share of drama. Plastering on her polite society smile, Aveline said, "Of course I am delighted to speak with you, Father, after having so much unexpected time apart."

King Charles's brow ticked upward. He gestured towards one of the side doors, unfortunately not one that led outside as she'd hoped. "Come, we will be able to better converse this way."

She barely had time to squeeze Jeanette's hand before following behind King Charles like a dutiful daughter. The tapping of Edith's heels was drowned out by the music and conversations, which had picked back up with extra fervour as the spectators watched the group exit the ballroom. *They wanted enough of a scene to show there are still consequences for not letting the Kings get their way,* Aveline thought, *but not enough that their subjects would know what is happening.*

Something moved near the far wall; a chill snaked down her spine. By the time she glanced at the empty corner, there was nothing noteworthy.

I should not have brought Sebastian here.

A soldier dutifully closed the door behind them the second everyone had stepped through. The lock clicked. *Breathe. Do not let the mask fall.* She schooled her features to resemble the subservient woman she'd once been.

It was a small room, void of windows and comfortable seating and, with the five of them, not much space to move. Aveline was grateful that there were no statues with sharp edges to prick her back. Had these rooms been here the whole time? She'd seen people go into them and not return, and had neither the courage nor the time to find out what they were meant for. Now, she had no desire to.

"Aveline..." King Charles scanned her with a scowl. Prince Ivan was much more interested in studying Sebastian, the same harsh lines etched into his expression. "To where did you disappear on the day of your wedding?"

The magic-user stood off to the side, head bowed, but she could tell by the way his eyes moved back and forth across the floor that he was listening intently. Three rings on one hand, four on the other, one gold and the rest silver. Formidable, but no match for Sebastian. Maybe they hadn't figured out his secret after all. If she continued to play her part, she might buy them time to slip out unnoticed by most.

"I succumbed to the panic," Aveline answered, deciding that drawing on a bit of truth would aid the act. "The idea of becoming Queen overwhelmed me. I knew you would not approve, but I decided I wanted to be in love with the man I married. You will probably never forgive me, and I do not expect you to. We had an agreement, and I—"

"Enough," King Charles growled. Behind him, the wall slid open, allowing King Byron and a few more magic-users in. The sconces dimly lit, too many harsh shadows sharpened the angles of King Byron's face, and his cloak hid his body. She straightened, pressing her nails into her palm.

"You do not expect us to believe you left because of love," King Byron rasped, as though the vocal cords were grating on one another. "You disappeared without a trace, in front of everyone. There had to be magic involved."

"I have no magic," she managed to state in a neutral tone.

"I was not talking about you." He took a wheezing breath. "I was talking about him."

CHAPTER 50

IS HE GOING TO LET HER OUT?

"Have you come to steal something else from me?" King Byron's eyes flashed as he tilted his head. "Was my Conqueror's Sword not enough for you, Magic Collector?"

To anyone else, Sebastian might have seemed unaffected, but Aveline caught the slight shift in his demeanour. If he used magic now, he'd confirm who he was—and all Aveline could do was turn into a ghost and flee in hopes of finding help, but she couldn't leave him. She wouldn't.

"I beg your pardon, Your Majesty, but I believe you are mistaken," Aveline said. If she'd learnt anything from living with royalty, it was that making others doubt put you in control—they had done that to her enough. A longshot, but if it gave Sebastian time to formulate a plan...

A wintery breeze snaked through the tiny room, coiling around them. From the corner, a shadow rose, forming into the shape of a woman. Her long, red hair and pale skin stood out in the dim light.

"Is the King mistaken?" The Heart Thief clicked her ashen tongue. "Aveline, I thought I taught you that no good comes from helping The Magic Collector. Certainly, by now you have seen what remains of his sister."

No one showed any alarm as she drew closer, the edges of her skirts like wisps of smoke. *Can they not see her?*

"Leave them to me," demanded King Byron. "You still have the castle to conquer, witch."

A wicked grin split her lips. "Yes, I do, Your Majesty."

"We have to teleport," came Sebastian's voice in her head. Aveline blinked, seeing a vision of herself standing in front of her, teary-eyed, smiling bittersweetly, her hair windswept, her dress torn and covered in dirt and... spattered with blood?

"They'll know who you are."

"That doesn't matter as long as you're safe."

"You had better be coming with m—"

"Seize them."

At the King's order, the magic-users retrieved silver manacles from their satchels. The door was locked from the outside—could Aveline turn into a ghost to slip out and unlock it before anyone saw her? With her terror so palpable, she never felt more corporeal in her life, stuck in her human form.

"Hold your breath," Sebastian warned as something exploded in a cloud of sparkling dust. She closed her mouth too late, the dust coating her tongue, leaving a fuzzy sensation. Her knees buckled. The others hacked and gasped, and someone collapsed, landing on Aveline's leg. Her eyes burned and her limbs grew heavy—

Sebastian yanked her upward, and then the colours twisted and writhed and bled into black. There was a moment of weightlessness, of feeling like nothing was tangible except for Sebastian's embrace. A second later, they stumbled across the foyer of the castle and landed in a heap, tangled in one another. The floor trembled erratically, as if struggling to hold them up.

Aveline's eyelids drooped. They were home, safe. But now King Byron knew Sebastian's face, knew that he was The Magic Collector.

And he was working with The Heart Thief.

"Are you hurt?" Sebastian pushed himself onto his knees so he could examine her, brushing the loose hairs away from her face.

Shaking her head took far more effort than it should have. She pressed his hand to her cheek before he could pull it away, enjoying the coolness of his touch on her flushed skin.

"You breathed in some of the sleeping powder."

"Sleeping... powder...?" Her attempts to keep her eyes open failed.

"I'd let you sleep, but I need your help." He pressed tender kisses to her brow, her cheekbone, and then lingered on her lips. A pleasant tingling warmth spread through her, revitalising her. She breathed him in, winding her fingers through his hair. At his low moan, a thrill shot up her spine. Wanting to hear it again, she slid her hands down his back—

Sebastian broke the kiss, panting as he stared down at her, eyes so dark they no longer looked brown. It was then she noticed the sparkles on his cheek, his nose, his jaw, his hair... She started to wipe them away, but stopped short as she realised that she, too, was covered in them.

"Glitter from the sleeping powder bomb," Sebastian explained, clearing his throat. "Won't harm you, but it's annoying to get rid of. Leo's idea. He helped me put them together."

"That doesn't surprise me."

He paused, gaze dipping to her mouth. "I need your help," he repeated, as if reminding himself, and stood, helping her up.

"With what?" she asked, hoping he hadn't spent too much magic dispelling the effects of the sleeping powder. He held her as she swayed.

"We have to be ready for when they come."

Aveline blinked, the fog lifting from her mind. "They are coming here..." King Byron working with The Heart Thief was just another way the Grand Duchess was wrong: Polite society would seek out magic when it suited their interests. "I shouldn't have brought you. I'm so sorry." She hugged him tightly, hating that she'd almost lost him—could still lose him.

"I'm not. I would've done nothing but worry if you'd gone alone. Besides, I finally got to dance with you."

She placed a hand on his chest, her thumb bumping the key under his shirt. "As much as I liked it, I loathe that King Byron knows who you are now—knows about your arm—and is working with that witch."

"He would have found out either way: It would be a waste of magic to use an illusion during a fight."

She chewed the inside of her cheek. They'd left her family behind without so much as a goodbye, not that they'd had much of a choice. If fate was kind to them, maybe she would see them again...

Sebastian tilted her chin upwards so she'd meet his gaze. "I'm sorry," he said softly, tone full of remorse. "I thought we could get through tonight unscathed and that you'd still have a choice, but I don't know if it would be safe for you to return to your family anymore, not unless you flee with them out of the country. Your father said you cannot go home, not with King Byron's soldiers taking over the mines. You might be safe in—"

She grabbed his wrist. "I don't want to leave."

"It's never been safe here, but now it's more dangerous than ever, with Lila going mad and the chance of King Byron's men coming after me..."

"I'm not leaving you."

The muscles in his jaw relaxed. "Then I'd better re-strengthen the wards around the castle."

"How much time do we have?"

"A day or two, if we're lucky. It all depends on how long that powder lasts."

"How do you want me to help?" She hated the exhaustion wearing him thin, having to protect them from outside attacks as well as inner, with Lila's frequent outbursts. There had to be some way she could be useful.

"Help keep an eye on Leo, and get some rest." He gave her a peck on the forehead, and as he started to step away, she caught the tips of his fingers.

"Will you find me after you're done?" she asked, a tad shocked by her own boldness. If he was right and King Byron would send wizards their way, who knows how much time they had left? She had no choice but to be bold. "Come to my room, that is. Now that we know that my choice is certain, we could finish that conversation..." *And make our marriage official,* she had almost said, but the words stuck in her throat, realising the implications. She'd meant that they would live as a true married couple, but it hit her what he'd meant was the final step now that they'd given their hearts to one another. Her cheeks flushed, and she smiled as his did as well. With Alexei, that unknown had seemed scary, but with Sebastian, there was no fear. He cared about her thoughts and feelings, and he only wanted to make her happy.

"I—"

An ear-splitting shriek punctuated a quake that nearly knocked them to their hands and knees. "Help me!" wailed Lila. Aveline rushed after Sebastian, gripping the bannister. She pitched this way and that, banging her elbows and knees. More sure-footed, Sebastian reached the top by the time Aveline was halfway up the second set of stairs.

"We didn't know you were home yet," Maud said as Aveline joined them below the circular stairway leading to the attic. Broken glass lay at Leo's feet, and with a snap of Sebastian's fingers, what remained of the bauble disappeared.

"HELP ME!"

Leo covered his ears. The hounds whimpered, tails tucked under. "We're moving again?!" the boy exclaimed. "We just got back!"

"Go back to bed. I'll calm her down." Sebastian rushed up the cramped stairway, until only his boots could be seen. "Lila, I'm here."

The sobs continued. Maud suggested they listen to Sebastian, but it took Aveline gently tugging on the boy's arm to get him to move.

"Is he going to let her out?"

"No, little cub," Maud said as Aveline tucked him back into bed. Solas and Luna cuddled beside him, focus pinned on the door.

"What if she breaks out and hurts Bash like Titan did?"

"She won't."

"But how do you *know?*"

Maud knelt beside the bed, hand hovering over her son's hair. "Do you trust Sebastian?"

"Bash is the most powerful wizard to ever live," Leo declared with conviction.

A doubtful expression flitted across Maud's face, one that he didn't catch. "Then don't you think he can handle the situation?"

Mouth pressed into a thin line, he nodded solemnly, clenching the blankets in his fists.

"Good. Then go to sleep, and all will be well when you wake."

"Are you going to stay, Mum?"

"Of course. I'll be right here the entire time."

"Avie, can you check on Bash? I think he's sad when his sister is upset."

"I will." Aveline kissed his forehead. "Good night, Leo."

"G'night, Avie."

She made sure to shut his door before she returned to the stairwell. It wouldn't keep Leo from hearing Lila, but it'd at least muffle her cries and screams. She'd be impressed if he could actually fall asleep.

Having returned to the iron stairwell, she debated if she should check on Sebastian, his boots still the only things she could see of him.

"It's me, Bast," he said, his words barely audible over Lila's wails. "I'm here, I—"

"He did this to me!"

"I know... I am so sorry..."

"Let me out!"

"I... I can't... Lila, I wish I could. I'm trying to find a way to save you, I want—"

"LET ME OUT!" The plea repeated over and over, the stairwell vibrating. "LET ME OUT!"

"Sebastian?" Aveline tried calling to him.

"I'm so sorry, Lila... I tried saving you..."

She took one step, another, then halted at the sound of Sebastian crying.

"I don't want to give up hope that I can save you, but I don't want to lose everyone else in the process."

Her chest ached at his despair. She wanted to go to him, to wrap him up in her arms and never let go. But this was a private moment, something she needed to let him deal with himself. Reluctantly, Aveline made herself go to her room, pulling the covers up tight under her chin as Leo had.

Don't forget that I'm waiting for you, Sebastian. I'm here, even if you only want me to hold you while you cry.

Dreaming of screams and blood and crumbling castles, Aveline woke from a fitful sleep by a knock.

"I'm awake," she assured Sebastian, seeing his silhouette in the doorway. When he didn't move, she opened her mouth to repeat herself, but then he approached the bed, sinking onto the edge of it. A candle wick sparked to flame, casting a small, dim glow that left room for plenty of shadows to stretch along his features.

"Are you certain you want to stay?" he asked, voice hoarse, eyes red-rimmed.

Aveline scooted close enough to make out the tinier details of his face: the thin scar on his nose, the freckle on the right side of his jaw, his long eyelashes… "More certain than I have ever been of anything," she answered. "I want to be with you, Sebastian, for as long as you'll have me."

"We may only have tonight…" He traced the side of her face, leaving her stomach twisted in unbearable anticipation, and yet she didn't want to move away from his touch. "…but I'd have you forever if I could."

"Forever it is then," she managed, almost inaudibly.

Sebastian closed the distance between them, kissing her with renewed fervour that made her head spin. Had he not been holding her when he broke the kiss, she might have fallen back against the pillows.

"Are you certain this is what you want?"

In her daze, it took her a few seconds to answer; at first, she thought he'd meant to question her about maintaining their marriage, but then it clicked, seeing him blush. "Yes."

He went rigid.

"…What is it?" The heat in her stomach cooled. *I went too fast, I scared him, I—*

"We don't have to…" Sebastian swallowed.

"Do you not want to?"

"I do, but..." He shrugged his right shoulder. "It's not... sightly. There are lots of scars, and not just on my shoulder. If you want, I can create an illusion to—"

"No," Aveline interrupted, then softened her tone. "If you want to wait, we can, but I want to be with you, not an illusion of you. No magic."

Easing off the bed, he fumbled with the buttons of his shirt. Aveline forced herself to stay where she was. If he wanted help, he'd ask her.

After one more moment of hesitation, Sebastian let the fabric fall to the floor. Silvery scars and twisted flesh made up the right side of Sebastian's body, starting at the bottom of his ribcage and ending between his shoulder and neck. Aveline could only imagine the pain and suffering he went through, and she wished she could have been there to prevent it, or at least help him heal. But Maud was a healer by trade, and it was impressive how much she had saved, even if he had lost the arm.

Aveline gently placed her hands on his chest. He trembled.

"Are you sure you don't want an illusion?"

"I am sure. No magic. I just want you."

His smile gave her heart wings. He ran his thumb across her knuckles. "Then you have me. Forever."

"Forever." She sealed the promise with a searing kiss. They clung to one another, hands wandering, tracing lines, curves, and scars, committing them all to memory as they fell back against the rumpled sheets. Tender kisses and quiet murmurs of consent, the darkening of the room as the candlelight flickered out.

Even when sleep eventually came to claim them, they were inseparable, a tangle of limbs and shared heartbeats.

CHAPTER 51

YOU DON'T HAVE A BAD SIDE

Waking snuggled up with Sebastian was its own sort of heaven, Aveline decided. Chaos was bound to be at their doorstep soon, and that would be one of the few things that would convince her to leave the bed.

"Good morning." He kissed her forehead.

"Good morning."

"How did you sleep?"

"I haven't slept this well since... well, I can't recall." She inhaled, relishing his warmth. "Although I might've moved in the middle of the night. I think I fell asleep on your other side."

Sebastian grimaced. "I might have moved you. Didn't want you on my bad side."

"You don't have a bad side."

"Aveline..."

She propped herself up on one elbow so she could look him in the eye. "If you prefer me on this side, I will stay here. But you ought to know that, for as long as I live, I will never find any part of you bad." Thoughts niggled at the back of her mind, reminding her that their time might be severely limited. She could see the same thought forming in his eyes, darkening them, so she added in her best teasing tone, "Well, apart from your insistence that you are not selfless, but I've resolved to prove to you how wonderful you are."

His throat trembled. "Thank you."

"You don't need to—"

"Oh," he said, his hand skimming across her back, "but I do. I need to thank you and all of the stars for bringing you to me in the first place."

She smiled, tracing the side of his face with a fingertip. Who would have thought a curse would lead her to everything she never knew she wanted? Or allowed herself to want, for that matter. By releasing him from the police motorcar, she had unwittingly changed the course of her life forever.

Aveline paused, her thumb on his jawline.

"What is it?"

"When we mind-spoke at the palace, what memory of mine did you see?"

"You were fixing Edith's hair after she chopped it all off. I'm amazed how well you did with it after it was sticking out every which way."

She chuckled. "It took quite a bit of work."

Curiosity lighting his eyes, he asked, "And which of my memories did you see?"

"Well... I think I saw a glimpse of when you first met me, back when you were a child. What did I say to you that made you remember me?"

"I... think I'll keep that to myself, lest I change what you say."

She pursed her lips. "Then when does it happen?"

"Soon, if I had to hazard a guess. You looked much the same as you do now... Gorgeous."

They shared a slow, lingering kiss. Aveline temporarily tucked her questions away, too invested in knowing these secret parts of Sebastian that were hers alone. If she had known marriage would feel like this, she wouldn't have had a single worry... and she might have spoken up about her feelings sooner.

Sebastian pulled back with a sigh. "As tempting as it is to stay in bed with you all day, I should recheck the wards."

Swallowing her protests, Aveline studied his back as he dressed. He moved with more confidence, but she noted the taut set of his shoulders. The chain of his necklace disappeared as he pulled his shirt collar into place and began buttoning it up.

"I'm sorry your conversation with Lila didn't go well."

He stopped mid-button. "I am too. I'm... As terrible as it is, I'm afraid she's no longer herself."

Aveline refrained from commenting that he'd voiced that fear previously.

"I might have to let her go."

She wished she could give him hope, but it would be empty. After a decade of trying to bring her back, after potentially hundreds of magic items tested, Sebastian would know better than Aveline if there was any hope left to be found.

He leant over the bed so he could cup her cheek. "I can't keep risking my family's wellbeing." His kiss was sweet, full of emotion. "And speaking of family..." Sebastian retrieved the wedding ring from his pocket, slipping it on the same finger as the enchanted band. "I'm honoured to officially call you my wife."

Feeling like her chest was about to burst with joy, Aveline would have yanked him back into bed had he not sneaked a kiss and stepped out of reach.

"I'll meet you in the kitchen for breakfast after I check the wards," he promised.

HAVING BRUSHED HER HAIR AND DONNED A PERIWINKLE DRESS MADE of a lightweight fabric, Aveline all but skipped her way down the hall, humming one of the previous night's songs. But it didn't cover Lila's sobs, or make her forget about the way the castle rumbled. She stayed light-footed in case they grew stronger, and paused at the bottom of the stairwell. If she didn't know it was a ghost in the attic, she might have thought that there was a woman trapped up there and been convinced to set her free.

Aveline frowned. Releasing Lila was out of the question—she wouldn't be able to, not without Sebastian—but there had to be something she could do. She hated seeing the haunted lines in Sebastian's face, the shadows in his eyes.

Her feet were lead as she ventured up the cramped stairwell, white-knuckling the handrail. At the third step from the top, she halted. "Lila?"

The sobs hushed slightly.

"My name is Aveline. I'm your brother's wife… which makes us sisters." She made to touch the door but hesitated. If she wanted to, could she turn into a ghost and go through the door? No, certainly whatever magic Sebastian used to keep Lila contained would prevent Aveline. Besides, he'd warned her that ghosts could hurt one another; if she didn't recognise Sebastian and wanted to hurt him, why would Aveline, a complete stranger, be any different?

"He misses you." She then recalled Lila's nickname for him. "Bast is doing everything in his power to bring you back. He doesn't want you to suffer."

Lila sniffled.

"We want you to get better, that way we can have our family happy and whole."

The castle fell still and silent.

"Wait a little longer," Aveline implored her. "We're trying to find a way." The quiet should have given her at least a modicum of hope, but it was smothered by an eerie chill pricking the back of her neck. Had the castle ever been this cold?

Imagining Lila could somehow feel it and take the gesture as comforting, Aveline touched the door. A shock jolted up her arm, causing her to stumble backwards into the railing. Stars danced in her vision as she clutched her arm to her chest, teeth gritted against the pain still sparking along her veins.

"Let me out!" cried Lila. Aveline flinched and barely caught herself from falling further. "LET ME OUT!"

Done tempting fate, she sprinted to the kitchen and, panting, rested against the doorframe.

"Are you all right?" Maud asked, making Aveline jump.

"Yes, fine, Lila just frightened me as I was coming down the stairs." She smoothed her dress, ignoring the dull ache up her arm. "Where is Leo?"

"He decided he wanted blueberries on top of his porridge." There was a sparkle of amusement in Maud's eyes. "So, I saw Sebastian leaving your room this morning."

Despite her stinging cheeks, Aveline couldn't suppress a smile.

"Should I take it your marriage is... 'official'?"

She cleared her throat and walked to the stove to stir the bubbling porridge. "Yes."

"At the risk of sounding like my son, *finally*."

Shaking her head, Aveline scooped portions into bowls.

"I told him it would help your curse in the beginning. Keep you more corporeal. I mean, you look more human than I've seen you."

When was the last time she'd been in her ghostly form? "I've been human for days," Aveline said as much to herself as to Maud, examining the back of her hand. Gripping the serving spoon, she focused, willing it to turn incorporeal. At first, nothing happened, and then it shifted, along with her hand. She turned things back to normal and faced Maud. "But I do not think it was our being... *intimate* that made the curse lose its hold on me."

"I didn't think it cured you of the curse entirely, just that it helped."

She considered Maud's words carefully. "The witch said that my greatest desire is to be seen and loved... So she made me unseeable by most. No, I do not think it was necessarily any physical affection between Sebastian and me that weakened the curse's hold on me. I think it was learning to love myself, and allowing myself to be loved."

With a smile, Maud covered Aveline's hand with her own, her touch so faint it was nearly indiscernible. "We are all grateful to have you as part of our family, Aveline. We love you dearly, and I've never seen Sebastian so full of life. All of these years searching and spending magic to no result, losing those who help him... You rekindled his hope."

Aveline started to say that she didn't think Sebastian ever truly lost it, when Leo burst through the doors, Solas and Luna barking emphatically. Blueberries tumbled out of the basket as the boy skidded into the kitchen. "The King's wizards are coming this way! There's a lot more of them than he normally sends!"

Her heart dropped into her stomach. They'd waited until the bride and groom had left on their honeymoon, and then immediately came here, she was sure of it. King Byron had to have everything—and everyone—under his control, including The Magic Collector. "We have to warn Sebastian."

"I'm sure he already knows if he's checking the wards," Maud pointed out.

"I'll go get my weapons!" Leo bolted out of the kitchen.

"No, Leo, stop!"

Aveline took off after him, catching his sleeve. She gripped his wrist before he could wriggle out of her grasp.

"Just my powder bombs and gadgets—they won't hurt, but they can be helpful!" he protested. "I can—"

A high-pitched whistle cut through the air. The castle shuddered, debris sprinkling from the ceiling. Aveline yanked Leo to her, protectively cradling him. Lila wailed as though someone had hit her.

"The next will strike true, Magic Collector," boomed a voice that had to be using magic to project that far. "Undo your enthrallment on Princess Gwendoline Allard and bring her outside, both of you unarmed. One way or another, you are coming with us. Come peaceably, and you will not be harmed."

They thought she was a captive, under some sort of spell. Whatever magic they had thrown had not only affected the wards, but also the castle itself. How many magic-users had King Byron sent? How long could Sebastian hold them—and The Heart Thief—off with his tricks?

"Stay here with your mother," Aveline ordered Leo, giving him a no-nonsense look before she sneaked towards the entrance to see for herself what they were dealing with. As she peeked through the heavy curtains, she smothered a gasp.

The Heart Thief was accompanied by thirty wizards.

CHAPTER 52
WHAT FOUL PRICE DID YOU REQUIRE OF HIM FOR THIS?

The witch's red hair resembled a living flame, bright against the snowy landscape. She stood beside the leader of the magic-users, like she could be considered his equal.

Sebastian strode towards them, making footprints in the fresh snow. *No, what are you doing?* Aveline leapt to her feet and sprinted outside, only to realise that he had stopped a few feet away from the castle, leaving room between himself and the others, the garden and gate still in the way. Without the Sight, there was no telling how much damage had been done to the wards.

Instead of answering the leader, the one who gave the warning, Sebastian addressed The Heart Thief: "You are not welcome here."

"And yet, here I am, at the request of the King. I do find it amusing how even those vehemently against wild magic beg for its aid when the situation becomes dire." Her obsidian eyes pinned onto Aveline, one brow flicking upward. "Interesting, how your pretty little pet has lasted longer than the rest."

"Hand over Princess Gwendoline," ordered the leader, who now Aveline could tell was Ralph.

Sebastian kept his sights trained on them. "She is free to go if she wishes, but The Heart Thief is to do nothing else to her."

"By order of King Byron, the witch is to undo any enchantments you've placed on the princess, as well as aid in your capture."

Aveline positioned herself beside Sebastian, catching sight of the muscle twitch in his jaw. From what she could tell, he bore no illusions, his empty sleeve fluttering in the breeze, his expression carved stone. There was to be no more running, no more hiding. Any remaining tricks would take care of some of the wizards—at the very least slow them down—but that would still leave plenty for them to fight. Even if Aveline gave herself over, it would do them no good, since Sebastian was who King Byron truly wanted.

"What foul price did you require of him for this?" Sebastian questioned.

The witch raised a thin, bone-white finger to her lips. "It is not proper for a businesswoman to reveal the contents of an agreement."

"There is nothing here for you to claim."

She threw her head back and cackled. "Oh, you poor naive boy. Long have I waited to claim what is mine, and I sense that Lila is ready to let go of your bond and accept me at last."

His hand curled into a fist.

"We are here for Princess Gwendoline," snapped Ralph. "Your Highness, do not be afraid to come with us. Your father, brother, and sister are anxious to have you back safely."

"I am safe." Aveline side-stepped closer to Sebastian. "Tell your King that, if he is so concerned with the well-being of his senseless war, he should focus on that instead of sending his best men on a doomed quest."

Ralph shifted his scowl from Aveline to Sebastian. "Last chance, Magic Collector. Release her and come with us."

"No."

An ear-splitting shriek resounded; the earth shuddered, bringing a few wizards to their knees. The Heart Thief's grin grew wider, teeth sharp as a wolf's. "She is breaking free of your restraints, boy," she taunted. "Can you contain her and stop us?"

Grabbing Aveline's hand, Sebastian rushed back inside. The door slammed shut behind them, and Lila screamed, sending violent quakes throughout the castle. Aveline stumbled; Sebastian pulled her back to her feet.

"What's happening?" Leo shouted, kneeling in the centre of the room, arms around the hounds.

"Trouble. Stay here with Aveline and your mother." Sprinting up the stairs, Sebastian grasped the bannister as the quakes grew more ferocious.

Another explosion collided with the wards, rattling Aveline's teeth. She hugged the whimpering boy.

"Where is he going?"

"I don't know," admitted Aveline, "but we can trust him." She clung to that statement as tightly as she did the boy, the only things keeping her from following Sebastian. One look at Maud told Aveline that she, too, was considering doing the same.

A bloodcurdling scream ricocheted. Aveline's paintings wobbled and fell off the wall. At Sebastian's yelp, she was instantly on her feet—

The third explosion sent Aveline to her hands and knees, banging them on the edges of the steps. She caught a bannister spindle before she slipped too far back down. She couldn't hear Sebastian over Lila's wails, but he wasn't all right, he needed her.

Gritting her teeth, Aveline stumbled up the staircase, shouting for him even though she knew it was futile.

He came into view, making his way back down, limping.

"Se—"

A whistle, a boom, a shower of debris. Flat on her stomach, face in the carpet, Aveline coughed and wheezed, tasting copper and dust. With great effort, she lifted her head enough to see Sebastian pinned to the stairs by fallen beams. Snowflakes swirled downward through the hole in the roof, landing on his head to mix with the blood trickling down his face.

Aveline failed to get up, also caught under the rubble. "Sebastian. Sebastian, wake up."

Panic tore at her insides as he didn't so much as stir. "Sebastian!" Coughing, she attempted to reach him. He had to be alive—the ring still pulsed. If she could just grab his hand, shake him awake…

"Aveline!" Leo yelled.

"Don't come up here!" she managed with a hoarse voice. "Sebastian, please, wake up." Her fingertips barely missed his. In frustration, she hit the floor, as if its tiny vibrations could compete with the waves of earthquakes rocking the castle. "Sebastian, please!"

Maud appeared beside her, and gasped. She touched his back.

"He's alive," Aveline said, unsure whether it was a statement or a question.

Sombrely, she nodded. "He's alive, but I don't know how to wake him."

A bright light exploded above them, raining down smaller bits of the roof, the walls cracking. Aveline covered her head as best she could.

"Can you turn into a ghost?"

Aveline closed her eyes, willing herself to shift. All she felt was the adrenaline, the fear, the desperation, tethering her here. "No, I can't."

"Mum, they're breaking through the gate!"

"Hide!" Maud ordered, and cast a conflicted look at Aveline. She grabbed her hand, coolness seeping into Aveline's skin...

Aveline remained corporeal. "Go to him," she insisted. "Show him where to hide so we can find him after we get out."

Maud pressed her lips together into a thin line. "I'll be back for you," she promised, then disappeared through the floor.

Aveline shook the snow from her hair, and winced at another scream from Lila. "You're not allowed to die, Sebastian. We have forever together, remember?"

No reaction.

"I'm not giving up on you, just like you never gave up on me." Awkwardly angling her free arm, Aveline manoeuvred her hand between the floor and her chest, fingertips straining towards her heart. Staring at his unconscious form, she called, "Sebastian."

He vanished, the beams sliding down the stairs, and reappeared beside her, as limp as before. The chain around his neck slipped from his shirt, the key exposed on the ground.

By the chill creeping up her arms, she knew The Heart Thief was close—they'd gotten through the wards. Time was a luxury they did not have.

She murmured his name, kissed his face, tried to wipe away the blood but only smeared it. "I need you," she choked out, eyes stinging. "You cannot leave me."

Yet another spell collided with the doors, briefly muting the shouted commands and battle cries; Lila's answering scream resounded. Aveline's ears rung. A crash shot pieces of splintered wood down the stairwell.

The key shattered into sparkling dust as black as a moonless sky.

A fresh wave of fear hadn't quite crashed over her by the time a dark form spilled down the stairwell like fog. Its pace quickened as it reached the middle steps, then fell through, landing in a heap. Dark tendrils writhed and shivered, slowly rising into the form of a young woman.

"Lila," Aveline breathed, her throat tightening. This is what she'd imagined a ghost to look like before she'd become one herself: stringy hair that half-covered her soulless, hateful eyes; a pale complexion; a small, sharp frame. Her dress—if it could be called that—hung off of her in mere rags, the tattered skirt exposing her bare feet and shins.

A far cry from the Lila in the paintings.

Lila's head jerked to the right. Her onyx eyes bore into Aveline, who snapped her mouth shut, afraid a scream would escape.

Then her focus shot to Sebastian. She took one shuffled step forward.

"He's your brother," Aveline said in desperation. "He's Bast." *Don't hurt him.*

Lila's cracked lips parted to reveal broken, rotted teeth and a shriveled tongue. Her inhale was but a rasp. The castle trembled and creaked.

"Break the doors, the windows, I care not—just get inside, all of you!" Ralph barked over a series of yelps and shouts. "These are but tricks, they'll wear off!"

Lila hissed in their direction; the chandelier chain snapped, the crash echoing. Aveline took solace in the fact that Leo was not there, but in hiding.

Maud, I may need you to return. She couldn't fight Lila as a ghost, not when she was struggling to shift into one, not when she didn't have a connection to the castle like Lila did.

Or Maud.

With Lila distracted by them breaking in, Aveline seized the opportunity to shake Sebastian's shoulder.

"THE MAN IN BLACK!" Lila shrieked, and lunged at them. As though she could protect herself and Sebastian, Aveline threw up a hand, and Lila collided with it, flying backward, hitting the ground with a loud crack that jolted through Aveline's body. A now corporeal Lila groaned and her head lolled to the side.

Aveline whispered, "Lila?"

The entrance doors exploded, followed by triumphant cheers and snapped orders. Determination renewed, Aveline tried to wriggle herself free. "Sebastian, I need you to wake. Please." Even if she could get free, how would she escape? She'd have to carry him, and where could they possibly hide?

A couple of pieces on top of her shifted, one nicking her leg. Blood trickled down her calf.

Lila's groan turned into a growl. She leapt to her feet, shifting back into a ghost. A deep inhale, and then she unleashed a scream that created shockwaves, further cracking the floor. More of the ceiling caved in above the entrance.

The temperature plummeted. A layer of frost formed over the bannister and stairs, inching towards them. Aveline's breaths came out as white puffs of air; her mouth and throat felt like they were being scraped by tiny ice crystals.

"Lila, my darling," crooned The Heart Thief from downstairs. "It is time to join me. Bring me your brother and his beloved."

Lila jerked her head towards the voice, an unreadable expression crossing it. Curiosity? Concern?

"Bast loves you, Lila," Aveline dared to speak, flinching as the woman's dark gaze switched to her. "He wants to help you." *Please recognise him.*

Lila stared, unblinking, her completely black eyes like The Heart Thief's, making it difficult to tell exactly where she was looking. But Lila's hesitation sparked a flicker of hope in Aveline. Now that she could see Sebastian for herself, could she put together enough pieces of her broken mind to remember him?

Aveline lifted Sebastian's face to give his sister a better view, dirt and blood streaked as it was. "Bast loves you."

"Do not keep me waiting," warned The Heart Thief. The frost reached them, clinging to Aveline's fingers and dress and lashes. Since there was no sound coming from the foyer, she assumed all of the wizards were frozen, just as the witch had done at Aveline's almost-wedding. They had been just an excuse to get in so she didn't have to spend her magic until it mattered. A few tears trailed down Aveline's cheeks, freezing over before they could fall to the snow-covered floor.

Breathing was laborious now, nigh on impossible with the cold seeping into her. "Lila," she wheezed. "He..."

"Bring. Them. To. Me."

With a snarl, Lila bared her teeth and sprung at them. Aveline gripped Sebastian's hand and buried her face in his neck. *I'm sorry I couldn't save you.*

The blow never came. Aveline peeked to see Maud wrestling Lila, all limbs and awkward grabbing before blows could land. The castle creaked and leant and trembled as they rolled, then disappeared through the wall.

"Aveline?"

Her heart skipped a beat. "You're awake."

Coughing, Sebastian pushed himself up onto his feet. With a grunt, he lifted the largest piece of rubble pinning her. She crawled out, teeth gritted against the pain and stiffness, and he let it drop again. "What happened?"

"Lila—"

"I grow impatient!" The Heart Thief's voice boomed as she floated up to their floor. Along the walls, the shadows skittered, gnashing their teeth and swiping their claws. Sebastian and Aveline moved to the centre of the hall, clutching each other.

"The floor is about to fall apart," Aveline said, but didn't know if Sebastian heard her, not when his attention was on the witch hovering just outside of the bannister. The castle quaked, but Sebastian held fast, keeping Aveline up with him.

"Lila broke free." The Heart Thief clucked her tongue. "And here you thought you could keep her from me. That you could *save* her." She tilted her head to the side, red hair rippling as if she were underwater. "That you could save anyone."

"He saved me." Aveline straightened as best she could despite her protesting back.

"Did he?" An unsettling smile teased her lips. "My curse still has a hold on you, child. It is not gone." Her gaze drifted back to Sebastian. "Your castle is in ruins, the King's wizards are here to make you as enslaved as they are, and..." She looked pointedly at the empty chain he wore. "...your connection to your sister is broken. The one thing that protected her and you."

He grabbed at the chain. Aveline searched for the dust remains, but the snow had covered everything, leaving no trace.

"She escaped..." His wide eyes scanned the bits of wood scattered about the stairs and floor.

"You cannot keep those you love caged like a wild animal, Sebastian." The witch *tsked*. "You made her hate you."

"Don't listen to her," Aveline begged, tugging on his shirt. "You made mistakes, but you've been trying to help her."

Sebastian wouldn't look at Aveline. "You're right," he said, shoulders slumping. "I should have had the strength to let her go."

Aveline opened her mouth to protest, when Maud and Lila tumbled back into the hall in a frenzy. The shadows jittered like they were itching to join in.

"Enough!" A blast of wind shot from the witch's raised hand, knocking Lila and Maud apart. "Time to bring this accursed castle to the ground and end this."

Aveline cried out as the cracked floor began to split apart; Sebastian yanked her to him and Maud, still trying not to get too close to the shadows hungrily prowling back and forth.

"Hold onto me and don't let go," ordered Sebastian. Torrents whipped about, stirring up snow and frost that stung her face. With each quake that further split the castle, Aveline squeezed her eyes shut and prayed to whomever was listening that Leo was safe, wherever he was hiding. Through icy lashes she saw Maud placing her hands on

Sebastian's shoulders, ready to lend her strength. She felt the familiar draw of power, and a shred of relief that Sebastian was not too proud to rely on them in this moment.

Please be enough.

Her vision changed, allowing her to see the spells battling in bursts of black and blue. The floor shook and began to mend, the sides drawing together, reaching for one another like long-lost lovers. Then Lila shrieked and stamped her foot, and the gap widened again.

"You cannot hope to win," sneered The Heart Thief. "When you lost your sister's love, you lost entirely."

Hand still raised as he kept up his spells, Sebastian made eye contact with his sister. "I'm sorry, Lila."

The harsh lines of her fury eased slightly, briefly. Then the earthquakes resumed with renewed fervour. Lila screamed at the top of her lungs.

And hundreds of voices screamed in answer.

CHAPTER 53

AH, MORE'S THE PITY

The swarm of spirits, ghouls, and demons flooding the castle blotted out what little sunlight remained, swooping downward like a flock of birds descending upon their prey. Sebastian's blue magic retreated to form a bubble around himself, Aveline, and Maud. The hallway split completely, and a scream almost tore from Aveline's lungs as she clung to Sebastian, steeling herself for the fall. But they floated down instead, passing the floors, the devastation. Winged creatures snapped at the bubble and jolted away, hissing. The witch's shadows scurried between the broken walls and floors, jumping off to tear at the newcomers. Just as the trio almost reached the second floor, The Heart Thief unleashed magic in all directions, at anything attacking her.

They passed Sebastian's music room in time to see the ceiling cave in and smash his piano. He winced, refocusing on lowering them down to safety, his fingertips shimmering with the magic powering their protective barrier. They drifted like they were in a balloon that was slowly losing its air, returning to the earth.

Aveline rested her ear against his chest, letting his heartbeat ground her amidst the ice, fire, and destruction around them.

Fire.

She peered over her shoulder to see the unfrozen wizards battling the creatures, some spirits, others beasts like Titan. Demon snakes slithered across the floor, latching onto any unfortunate soul too distracted to notice their presence. Their victims instantly collapsed, one then trampled underfoot by a ghoul who stepped backwards to avoid a fire spell a wizard cast. It shot through the wall and set the dining room ablaze, where the frost had not travelled.

The split grew, leaving only the front parts of the castle still connected. The floor and walls rippled with the aftershocks of magic.

"I need you to find Leo and the hounds and run," Sebastian said, snapping Aveline's attention back to him.

"We stay together."

"I have to stop Lila. The castle is ready to teleport again, and we won't be able to stop it."

Aveline bunched the back of his shirt in her fists as she struggled to come up with an argument, a reason against splitting up.

As if reading her thoughts, he pressed a quick, meaningful kiss to her lips. "Get him to safety, and then come find me, if you must." His teasing smile fell flat.

"I assure you, I must."

They landed on the bottom floor hallway. Even the ground beneath the castle was gouged, pulling apart, and a wizard that tripped fell into its depths, crying out for help.

The bubble dissipated. Aveline reluctantly released Sebastian, losing her Sight. With only a glance back at her, Sebastian sprinted to the entrance. Lila threw a spirit trying to bite her neck and flew after her brother.

"Leo is this way." Maud took Aveline's hand. Fighting the desire to run after Sebastian, she let Maud lead her through the smaller, intersecting halls, away from the heart of the chaos. The sounds grew quieter the further they ventured, and familiarity itched the back of her brain as they turned the final corner.

The storage closet, where she'd found the hidden paintings.

"Leo." Aveline jiggled the doorknob. "Leo, it's me, Aveline, and your mother is with me. Please open the door."

"How do I know you're not a magic-user come to trick me?" Leo asked, his voice as muffled as the hounds' warning growls.

Any other time, she would have been proud of his caution. "Leo, I—"

Maud interrupted, "You know because I am Lady of the Wild Lands, not Queen, because all I ever want to be in charge of is you."

With a click, the door eased open, and Leo flung his arms around Aveline's waist. "I've been terrified! What's happening?"

"We'll tell you later," Aveline said, taking his hand, noting that his other one clutched a broken piece of wooden frame like it was a sword. His light-stick dangled from his belt, along with an assortment of powder bombs, or so she guessed. "Right now, we have to run. Don't look back, don't try to fight, just hold my hand and run."

"Okay." He swallowed hard.

"Maud, which way should we go?"

"Out the back. I think I know a passageway that should help us avoid most."

"Most what?" Leo asked in a small voice, but neither woman answered. Gripping his hand and Maud's, Aveline hurried forwards, trying not to let her imagination run wild with the sounds of battle.

He's alive, she assured herself, focusing on the pulse the ring provided. *Sebastian is alive and going to make it.* He had to.

The narrow passageway required them to walk in a single file line. Aveline scraped her knuckles against the stone wall, but the stinging was rapidly replaced with numbness from the cold. After what felt like far too long, it eventually opened up to a large room filled with beds and dressers pressed up against the walls.

"Servants' quarters," Maud explained. "It has passages that lead to the main parts of the castle so that the servants could travel quickly without mingling with the upper classes. Fortunate for us, but for them..." She shook her head and pointed to the opposite end of the room. "Looks like the split affected here as well."

Frigid winds from outside swept snow onto the wooden floor.

"This way." Maud tugged on her arm. "Sebastian thought the servants' quarters would be the smartest place to hide his collection of magic artefacts." Leo's eyes lit up. His mother lifted a brow at him and said to Aveline, "If the protective ward is down, I can slip inside, but you're the only one who might be able to get in and bring something back out. We need some sort of protection if we're going to survive. He's already taken the curses off these, but I'd still be careful."

Aveline walked towards the unremarkable wooden door in the corner. This was where Sebastian hid them? Was it a supply closet? Was it warded? Maud mentioned being able to enter, but Aveline still had to mentally prepare herself.

"I don't know if I can shift back." She hated the distant sounds of bloodshed and death, hated the consistent tremors beneath her feet and the way the castle continued to break.

"You can."

Aveline closed her eyes. Took an uneven breath, and slowly released it. Another. And another.

Then she opened her eyes and stepped forward, tensing as she walked through the wall. It resisted her at first, like trying to run underwater. She expected a spark of pain, a block, something to keep her from passing unhindered, but she managed, falling onto her hands and knees in corporeal form on the other side.

Torches lined the walls, burning with blue fire, the same shade as Sebastian's magic. Only one was unlit, where the crack in the wall had broken the circle. There was nothing else in the room but the artefacts, some made of precious metals, and others made of wood or stone, common-looking items she'd never suspect were enchanted. Vases, books, toys, scrolls, jewellery, boxes, clothing—

A sword with an ornate golden hilt leant against the wall at an angle. Although she knew little about swords, it appeared more ceremonial than battleworthy, like the ones she'd seen King Byron and King Charles—even, at times, her own father—wear on special occasions.

Is this the Conqueror's Sword King Byron was referring to? It seemed to be an unlikely thing to bring Lila's spirit back to her body, but in Sebastian's position, she would've been willing to try anything as well. She hesitated in taking it—a sword might not be enough against the witch or any of the creatures, but a magic sword? It might stand a chance.

Far too heavy to hold for long, Aveline shifted it into its ghostly form after a few attempts, and sought out what else they could use. The tremors reminded her that their time was limited; there was little in the way of weapons to sort through anyway, most of the artefacts baubles and trinkets. She snatched a cloak and a dagger, and scanned the room one last time.

"Aveline!"

Panic flooded her veins. She rushed back through the wall, barely catching her footing as she shifted to human faster than she intended. A lion-like beast swiped at Maud and Leo, the tip of its claw catching Maud's shoulder. She stumbled backwards, stepping through Leo, who recoiled, head whipping around to see where his mother went. The hounds lunged and jumped back, avoiding the beast's mighty paws. Leo swung his makeshift weapon, and yelped as Luna bit the back of his shirt and snatched him out of harm's way.

Dropping the other items, Aveline gripped the hilt with both hands and tried to lift it up in an arc so she could bring it down on the beast's head. She barely got it off of the ground before it fell back, tip thudding against the wooden floor. With a snarl, the creature whirled on her, snapping its jaws. Aveline dodged, and turned the sword to its ghost form so she could bring it up, returning it to physical on the downward arc. The skull cracked upon impact, the vibration shooting up the weapon and her arms. She nearly dropped it, but managed to keep hold until the blade was engulfed in flames that overtook the creature. Aveline fell, trying to get away as sparks jumped at her skirts. With a pitiful cry that ended abruptly, the beast collapsed into a pile of ashes. The sword clattered on the ground, the fire disappearing instantaneously.

"Whoa," Leo breathed as Luna and Solas howled. Aveline gaped at the wind-stirred ashes scattering across the floor. The hilt hadn't been hot, and somehow she'd avoided catching herself on fire.

"More are bound to come," Maud warned.

On shaky legs, Aveline stood, retrieving the other two items. Realising she'd shifted the cloak back halfway through the wall and gotten it stuck, she remedied it, making sure it was undamaged before clasping it around Leo's neck. The end of it dragged across the floor, but it would do for now. She hoped it had magic properties that would protect him, but she would settle for keeping him warm as wintery day was fading to wintery night.

Facing Maud, she tried to turn the dagger to its ghostly form. "Don't give it to me. Leo needs better protection than a broken piece of wood."

"But, Mum, you should have a weapon too."

"I'll be fine, dearest. Get rid of that and take the dagger from Aveline."

The boy frowned, and reluctantly tossed the makeshift weapon aside. Aveline closed his hand around the dagger hilt. "Only use this if you have to."

Leo nodded. Cautiously, she picked up the sword once more and changed it to incorporeal for easy carry. "Now where to, Maud?"

"If we can make it outside—"

Aveline slipped as ice coated the floor, but caught herself on the wall. The hounds growled, hackles raised as they positioned themselves at their master's sides.

"There you are." The Heart Thief floated in via the wall the split had broken. "Thought you could avoid the fun?" Shadows followed suit, slinking towards them. Aveline regripped the sword as she checked that the ring still showed a pulse. Sebastian was still alive—was the witch leaving Lila to deal with him?

"Come no closer." Aveline lifted the ghostly sword in what she hoped came across as a threatening stance, or at least a defensive one, trying to remember what she'd overheard from her brothers' fencing lessons.

The witch's eyes glittered with malice and amusement. "You think to stop me?" She snorted. "I will admit curiosity... that you, out of all who helped him, are the only one to survive this long. To have fought your curse... and to use it to your advantage. You might have made a formidable witch, had you the interest."

"Never."

"Ah, more's the pity. Although... would you be interested in a deal? Before you reject it, it would benefit you to hear the details."

Scowling, Aveline bit back, "I have witnessed the destruction your deals bring."

She quirked an eyebrow. "This is because of your lover's foolhardiness, trying to keep what is rightfully mine from me. No, dear child, this deal would save him from all of this destruction and turmoil."

Against her better judgement, Aveline bit her tongue. She needed to think, to figure out how she could possibly get them out alive. Keeping the witch talking gave her that extra time, but... What could she do? There was no escape but through the opening behind the witch. "Let Maud, Leo, and the hounds go free, and I'll stay to listen to your deal."

Her laugh rumbled, sending shivers through Aveline. "I think not. You will be much more receptive with their wellbeing hanging in the balance." The shadows made a half circle to block the exit.

Aveline clenched her jaw, her thighs beginning to burn as she maintained the stance. "Well? What is your deal?"

"I will let Sebastian go free—and these two and Lila as well—if he gives me his magic and I take you in Lila's place."

CHAPTER 54

AND BEYOND THAT, IF IT IS POSSIBLE

Listening to a witch, especially this witch, was foolhardy. Aveline knew that. Yet she didn't respond right away, the implications playing out in her mind. Sebastian would finally be free of the curse, no longer worried about drawing others into this mess, and would have his sister safe from The Heart Thief. That was all he ever wanted...

But he wouldn't have his magic. He wouldn't have Aveline. And he wouldn't truly have his sister either, unable to save her without his magic. It didn't take much imagination for her to know that he'd turn down the offer.

"Aveline, reject the deal!" Maud urged. "Sebastian will hate it if you accept."

Her lips parted, a counteroffer on the tip of her tongue.

"Those are the terms," the witch snapped. "I will have no bargaining. A soul he loves is an equal trade for another soul he loves—and I will not have him coming after me with his magic to try to free you. You will belong to me for all eternity, however long you last. Your marriage bond will be severed; he will be unable to track you, even if he employs a powerful enough magic-user to help him." She took half a step forwards, and Aveline tensed. "But you will have given him one of his greatest desires: to have his sister back. Is that not what you humans think love is, an ultimate sacrifice for someone? Is it not a holy and noble thing, a story that minstrels will sing your praises for even after a thousand years have passed?"

"Avie..." Leo whimpered.

The witch drew closer. "Isn't that what you desire as well? To be seen and loved for who you are. Everyone will know your name and sacrifice for generations to come. You will not be forgotten."

Her heavy arms lowered the ghostly sword; her tongue felt thick as she tried to speak. She couldn't even turn her head to look at Maud, Leo, and the hounds, who had gone suspiciously silent.

The Heart Thief stopped in front of her, the shadows at her heels, gradually closing in. Her bony hands cupped Aveline's face, their chill seeping into her skin. The sounds of fighting seemed too far away—was it ending? Or was the newly formed ice wall muting them?

"You know what decision you have to make," the witch murmured, like a mother to a child. But what was the correct decision to make? What if there wasn't one? What if Sebastian hated her for choosing herself over giving them a chance to escape? If they even survived for him to find out...

"This is your one chance to change your fate, Aveline. Do not squander it."

Fate had brought her here, but Aveline had taken it into her own hands, making choices that changed who she was for the better. She could have given up and succumbed to a curse that she was unfairly given, but instead she'd made the power her own. It was hers. *Hers.*

Staring directly at the witch, Aveline managed to smile, imagining she was looking into familiar warm brown eyes. "I am seen and loved," she whispered. Confusion crossed The Heart Thief's features. Gathering what remained of her strength, Aveline thrust the ghostly sword upwards. It shifted to metal, and Aveline willed herself to keep hold, even as the flames sprang to life, catching first on the shredded tulle of the Heart Thief's gown. Gasping, the witch tried to step away, but Aveline moved with her. The shadows writhed at their feet, pooling into shapeless beings. Flames licked at Aveline's hands with blistering heat. She squinted as they consumed the witch, her head thrown back, her mouth ajar in a silent scream. Bits of her fell away, mingling with the snow coating the floor. Even though her cheeks and hands burned, Aveline didn't let go until the witch's form collapsed into a heap of ash and the shadows dissipated.

With a thud, the sword slipped from Aveline's shaking hands and the fire went out. She fell to her knees, the winds scattering the remains across the floor.

Aveline had killed someone.

She could not look away. Her mouth went dry; her ears rang, muffling the words spoken to her.

She had taken a life. A witch, yes, but she was *someone*. Edith's stories praised those who slayed villains and monsters, so why did she feel anything but victorious?

Tears streaming down her face, she retched, dry heaving when what little was in her stomach was gone.

A gentle hand settled on her shoulder. "Avie?"

Wiping her mouth, Aveline reluctantly looked up at a concerned Leo, Maud standing just behind him.

"You saved us." He threw his arms around her neck. Feeling like she was not quite in her own skin, it took Aveline a moment to pat his back. She met Maud's gaze over his shoulder, and barely heard her say, "It had to be done."

Unsteadily, Aveline pushed onto her feet and retrieved the sword. "We have to keep going, before the others find us." *I don't know if I have it in me to do that again.*

Maud gestured at the iced over wall. "We may have to find another way outside."

"I'd rather not backtrack if we can avoid it." Aveline slammed the hilt into the ice. The cracks spread in a web-like pattern, and by the third blow, it gave way, a big enough hole for them to get through. Spell explosions, battle cries, dying shrieks, they all reverberated in a cacophony of tragedy that had Aveline focusing on the ring, her one lifeline to Sebastian.

"Watch your step," she said to Leo, extending a hand.

"What about Bash?"

Hoping her voice wouldn't falter, Aveline promised, "I'm going back for him, but we need to get you to safety first."

After another moment of hesitation, the boy clasped her hand.

Lila's scream pierced through everything; the castle broke apart completely. Aveline and Leo tumbled and skidded across the floor, narrowly missing the hounds, whose claws did little to keep them in place. Then the castle tilted back the other way, towards the edge, the gouge in the earth that was growing wider by the second. The sword skittered past her, falling into the abyss. Ice shards cutting her palm, Aveline scrabbled for purchase with one hand, gripping Leo with the other. Her feet caught the bottom of the ice wall, and Leo slipped past, dangling over the gorge, sending a jolt up her arm. The hounds whimpered and barked, sliding towards the more intact parts of the wall.

"Don't let go!" Aveline ordered, muscles straining. Leo clutched her wrist, eyes wide. If she could turn him into a ghost, she could pull him up, get him to safety. But that was beyond her capabilities, and she was terrified of accidentally dropping him if she shifted without shifting him as well.

"Sebastian is trying to mend the break!" Maud shouted. "Hold on, don't give up! I'm going to help!"

The cracks spread under Aveline's feet. Even if she could pull him up, would his extra weight be the breaking point? *Think, think, think.*

Inching closer, the hounds peered down through the hole, yipping and whining. Her palm grew slick, their grip waning. There was no time for what-ifs.

"I'm going to pull you up, but I need you to grab the edge so I can get a better hold on you. Ready?"

"Ready!"

Gritting her teeth, she yanked with all of her might. But the edge was just out of reach, and his clammy, sweat-soaked hands slipped—

The castle fell back into place, tossing them the other way. Leo landed beside Aveline with an "oomph!" that resounded in the suddenly silent room. Their panting breaths far too loud, she broke eye contact with Leo to look around. They had landed on broken pieces of floor that were covered in scorch marks and ash—which was on top of normal, unblemished wood, the rest of the room in perfect condition. The hounds ran over, tails wagging, to lick Leo's face. With a grunt, she sat up and inspected the intact wall behind them. No sign of any split or fight, not even distress cracks.

Her hands were blistered and raw, the fabric of her dress singed and dirty. Had Sebastian managed it? Had they won?

"Who are you?"

Aveline jumped to her feet, then relaxed when she saw it was a normal young woman, dressed in servant attire. She carried a basket of freshly folded sheets. "Forgive me, Miss," the servant said, bowing her head. "But you cannot be in here. 'Tisn't proper." Her lips parted when she saw the rubble, but she didn't question them; that was not a servant's place. "I can show you to the healer's quarters."

Leo stood, drawing the attention of the servant. The cut of her dress was different than what servants would normally wear. No, this was a style that reminded her of a simplified version of her mother's old dresses, the ones that were tucked away in the closet.

We travelled in time... but how far? And why are there people here? In the heat of battle, Sebastian must have been unable to direct the castle while also attempting to mend it.

She cleared her throat. "We were trying to go outside. Can you show us the nearest exit?"

With a puzzled frown, the servant pointed at the room where Sebastian stashed his magic artefacts. Or, rather, would in the future. "If you go through the laundry room, it'll lead outside, Miss."

"Thank you." Aveline took Leo's hand again. At least she hadn't transported with the sword, causing even more alarm. She could only imagine how they appeared after all they'd been through.

Solas and Luna followed closely as Aveline and Leo walked through the laundry room. Steam flooded her senses, the warm air melting the remaining ice crystals that clung to her. The servants threw them odd expressions, obviously debating if they should say something or keep to themselves. Aveline strode straight through the back door, and shut it behind them when the hounds made it out.

Instead of a snowy landscape, green hills and wildflowers greeted them. She inhaled the fresh spring air.

"Where did we end up?" Leo asked quietly, despite there being no one around.

Aveline turned. The castle was completely whole, with no signs of magic or magical creatures. There should have been some sign of distress by now, someone screaming at the spirits and ghouls that suddenly filled the halls. Where were Maud and Sebastian?

"I'll hide, you count!" called a little girl's voice from nearby. Aveline furtively checked around the corner. A young boy with black hair sighed as the girl fled deeper into the gardens.

"All right." He leant back against the tall tree, crossing his arms as he began to count. Both of his hands bore rings, a few of them catching the scraps of sunlight streaming through the branches.

Aveline hid behind the castle, her heart beating faster. Was it possible? Was this the meeting Sebastian hinted at but refused to tell her any details about? She imagined she looked just as wild as she'd seen in his memory... There was only one way to find out.

"Stay here with Solas and Luna," she said. "Only come get me if someone tries to talk to you. I'll return shortly."

"All right, but where are you going?"

She didn't answer, gradually entering the young dark-haired boy's line of sight. He stared up at the tree boughs, not noticing her presence until she was about ten feet away. His brown eyes focused on her, and she couldn't help a small smile. It was him. There was no mistaking it.

"Are you all right?" he asked with a furrowed brow. "You look like you're hurt, Miss."

"I'm all right, Sebastian. Thank you for asking." She studied him, appreciating all of the small movements and features that he still bore as an adult. Another painting for her to create when all of this was hopefully put to right.

The furrow deepened. "Are you Lila's new governess? Is that how you know my name?"

"No. My name is Aveline..." she trailed off. He'd known her real name, not as someone married to him, when she had first met him. A small detail that had made her curious, had made her eager to trust him. And if she told him that she was his wife, would that affect their future? He had chosen her of his own free will, not because of what she told him.

Starting again, she said, "My name is Lady Aveline Clément. You are going to know me in the future."

"You're visiting me from the future? Why?"

"I have something very important I need you to remember for me." A weight settled on her chest as young Lila peeked from behind a bush. The future Sebastian had said Aveline's words were important, that he'd held onto them for a long time. Could she give him a clue about Lila, tell him he had to let her go? Or to keep fighting, and never lose hope?

Sebastian, what did I tell you? What is it you need to hear? All of the times he helped her, were they affected by this moment? If she told him everything and he believed her, would it rob them of the future they built together? Would he avoid hurting Lila and still find Aveline, some way, somehow?

Sebastian hadn't risked affecting her decisions by telling her what she said. He hadn't influenced her choices, making sure that she was certain every step of the way. He had been there for her, in times of both joy and sorrow, accepting it all for what it was instead of what they wished it could have been.

"Remember what?" young Sebastian pressed eagerly, pushing off of the tree and moving closer.

This was a young boy who knew nothing of the sorrows to come, yet she couldn't bring herself to steal his free will away, not when he hadn't taken hers.

Tears lined her eyes. "Remember that some decisions are difficult to make, and sometimes there is no 'right' choice. But no matter what happens, I will be by your side, until the very end. And beyond that, if it is possible." She smiled at him, at the way he tilted his head as he processed her words. Still determined to find a way back to him, a thought formed in the back of her mind: If this was the last time she'd see him, there was something poetic about it being both their first meeting and their last.

Swallowing the urge to tell him that she loved him, Aveline dipped her head in farewell and returned to Leo, equal parts relieved and disappointed that young Sebastian did not follow.

CHAPTER 55

IT IS DONE

"Who was that?" Leo questioned, craning his neck, but Aveline pushed him back into the castle's shadows.

"I'll explain later. Right now, we need to get back to Sebastian and your mother."

"How?"

How, indeed? She could call him with her hand over her heart, but what if that broke his concentration or pulled him away from a vital moment in battle?

The ring pulsed and shimmered. Last time, it had guided her to Sebastian, but he'd been not twenty feet away from her then. Could it help? Knowing it only needed an intentional thought to activate, Aveline said aloud anyway, "Bring us to him."

She waited for the knowledge to come to her, to tell her what to do, but got nothing. Were they too far away, split by time? Had Sebastian and Maud stayed behind?

Light radiated from the ring, forming a swirling iridescent oval slightly taller than she was.

"What is that? Do you have magic, or did Bash give you something?" Leo squinted, straining to get a better look at the ring that was now obscured by the light.

"Sebastian gave it to me." Aveline grinned, hope fluttering in her chest. "When we walk through this portal, it will take us back to him."

"I'd better be ready to grab my dagger then. Once we land, that is. Don't want to risk losing it in the portal."

"Sensible."

They exchanged approving nods, grabbed hands, and stepped through. "Come along, Lulu, Sol!"

The hounds barked, and when she turned to check on them, they were bounding on nothing but air. Everything was pure sparkling white, with no shadows to define parameters. She looked down, then right back up as her stomach twisted at the nothingness under her feet. It was better to just keep moving.

"What is this place?"

"I don't know. Perhaps a place between places."

"Between space and time?"

"Something like that." It didn't matter, as long as Sebastian and Maud were waiting for them on the other side.

A dark dot appeared in the distance. Aveline tried to run faster, but the dot grew at its own pace, regardless of her speed.

"We're almost there!" Leo cheered, pumping his fist in the air. "We're coming home, Mum! We're coming home, Bash! We're going to help you save the castle!"

Or, at the very least, escape. But his excitement was infectious, and she stuffed the sombre thought deep down. She had to think positive, had to hope.

The dark dot grew until it was a door, which opened by itself. Their first steps onto the floor of the grand entryway were unsteady, reacquainting themselves with solid ground. The light and door vanished the instant they stepped through, and a flood of noise assailed their ears: wizards yelled at one another to flee while they still had their lives; the castle creaked and groaned as pieces of it fell to the floor, which was covered in bodies and broken glass from the windows; creatures hissed and shrieked and roared as they sprinted away from the still-growing chasm. They were on the opposite side of the castle now, Aveline noted, the other side halfway sunken into the earth.

There, near the edge of the chasm, Sebastian stood before Lila. For once, she was silent, but Aveline couldn't see her face. Maud hurried to them.

"What is happening?" Aveline questioned loudly.

Maud shook her head. "Now that The Heart Thief is gone... Sebastian wanted to speak with Lila alone. He said this is his burden to carry."

Aveline pressed her lips together. Everything in her wanted to go to him, to see if he was hurt and to be there as emotional support.

This is his decision.

"I'm sorry," she heard him say over the rush of winds and rumbling quakes. "I shouldn't have tried to keep you here. I thought I was helping, but... I wasn't. I should have let you go, knowing you wouldn't have wanted to be kept here, not like this." Sebastian embraced Lila, and she went rigid. He said more, but the words were too faint to overhear as the last of the spirits, creatures, and wizards scrambled away.

Lila suddenly relaxed, her eyelids slipping closed. The tremors lessened to a standstill. Bits of her skin and hair floated, drifting away to nothing.

"Is he doing to her what he did to Titan?" Leo asked in horror.

Sebastian's name caught in Aveline's throat. *His choice,* she silently repeated to herself. As those pieces of Lila peeled away, they revealed another form underneath, a translucent one made of light instead of shadow. Sebastian's shoulders shuddered and he hunched over, gripping her tighter. Lila hugged him back, her face now in full view. That was the woman in the paintings, the one she'd caught a glimpse of in the past just a few moments ago. Her sleek dark hair reached her hips, her cheeks were rosy, and her fair skin glowed softly. A pale pink spring dress replaced her dingy rags, the skirt brushing the tops of her bare feet.

"She looks like an angel!"

"She is beautiful, isn't she?" Maud said to her son.

Aveline blinked to clear her teary vision. After all of this time, after all of the sacrifices and risks, here Lila was. The true Lila.

Her lashes fluttered as she opened her warm brown eyes, looking directly at Aveline. Lila smiled contentedly; Aveline smiled back. Then she closed her eyes again, and murmured something into Sebastian's ear. He shook as he pressed a kiss to her temple. When he let go, she disappeared.

Head in his hand, Sebastian's knees hit the floor. Aveline ran to him, hugged him, but he didn't hug her back. "It is done," he rasped. Tears wet his cheeks, silent and heavy. No sobs, no cries, no shrieks or screams.

"I'm sorry." She cupped his face, wishing she could take the pain from him.

His jaw tensed. "It's time for us to go."

"But what about—"

"There is nothing left for us here." He stood, lifting Aveline, and a piece of the ceiling struck the floor beside them. The tremors returned with force, nearly bringing her back down.

"We have to leave before this place falls apart." Sebastian beckoned Maud and Leo, who did not need to be told twice. All of them hurried outside, stumbling and sliding. Aveline was grateful the front door was broken open, as was the gate. Nothing to impede their escape. They were free—

Sebastian halted. Aveline turned, and her heart sank. Maud stood on the steps of the crumbling castle, so faded that Aveline couldn't quite make out her face.

"Mum? Come on, the gate's right here." Leo strode to her. "Hurry, we have to go now, before…"

"I can't," Maud choked out, voice faint. "I'm sorry, I… Without Lila's help to hold the castle together…"

"Bash, you've got to do something! Please!"

"I don't know how to transfer a bond," Sebastian said. "Can you take control of the castle, stop it?"

"I tried, but I can't. It belonged to Lila long before I was bound to it."

"You have to try something!" Leo pleaded. "Anything!" The hounds howled and barked.

"Can we take a piece of the castle with us?" Aveline asked. "Until we can figure out—"

"I cannot leave. This is as far as I can go. The castle is dying without Lila, and I am at its mercy." With a shuddering inhale, Maud's nearly invisible hand reached towards Leo. "I'm sorry, my lion-hearted boy. I wish I could have had longer with you."

"You're not dying!" He attempted to grab her, like he could save her with sheer willpower. "You have to stay with me! We're a family! We stay together!"

A sob escaped her. "I'm sorry, Leo, I'm so sorry. I love you, my dearest—"

"No goodbyes! You're not leaving!"

Sebastian pinned Leo in a hug. The boy kicked and squirmed and fought, then burst into tears. "You can't... We're a family..."

Aveline clenched her fists at her sides. It was wholly unfair, to have come this far and have to say goodbye to two family members within minutes of each other.

"I'm sorry..."

"Bash, we have to do something, please!"

"Leo," Sebastian said, "we can't. There's nothing I can do. I wish I could, but I can't."

"But I can." Aveline grasped Maud's hand. She felt too soft, like smoke slipping between her fingers. *We cannot lose you too.* Tightening her grip, Aveline pictured the woman she'd seen in Sebastian's memories, the woman she'd caught glimpses of, full of life and spunk and determination. "This family's ties are not so easily broken."

Everything around them shook and rattled, yet Aveline held her ground. If she could get Maud to connect with her enough to materialise, maybe she could be her anchor to this world. Mustering all of her remaining strength, Aveline yanked Maud into her arms.

They collided and fell to the ground in an awkward heap. Wind knocked out of her lungs, it took Aveline a few tries to breathe again, coughing and gulping air.

Maud was atop her. Corporeal. Solid. Flesh. The woman sat up, staring at her trembling fingers. "I am... here..." Rolling a strand of her hair between her finger and thumb, she beamed in wonder.

"Mum?"

She looked up at her son, who stared at her, eyes welling. Sebastian let him go, but Leo stayed where he was.

"I'm here." She jumped to her feet and opened her arms wide. A moment more of hesitation, and then the boy launched himself at her. Face buried in her shoulder, Leo's words were muffled, but it didn't matter—Maud could hear him. She smoothed his hair, kissed the top of his head, held him tight. "My sweet boy, I have you," she repeated, her voice thick with eight years' worth of longing. "I'm here."

Sebastian helped Aveline to her feet, and kissed her temple. "Thank you," he said quietly, to avoid interrupting the scene unfolding before them.

"No thanks necessary. She is my family too." Half leaning against him as fatigue weighed upon her, Aveline embraced Sebastian, thankful for the physical reminder that they had survived, that they were all right, even if it would take time for the emotions to heal.

"How did you manage it, if I may ask?"

"I honestly haven't a clue. I've done it with inanimate objects, and I hoped the principle transferred to ghosts." She noticed a spire starting to sway. "But the castle is still crumbling, and I fear it'll come down on us, or the chasm will catch up to us."

"Without Lila, it shouldn't grow, but we should leave. There is no reason to stay, as long as Maud is strong enough to come with us."

"You're strong enough, aren't you, Mum?" Leo clutched her hand between his.

"As long as I have you," she said.

They raced past the trampled and scorched foliage as the castle caved in, sending out one final quake like a death rattle. Aveline stopped at the gate, gazing upon the remains of what she'd begun to consider her home. Broken pieces littered the ravaged landscape, the only testament that a castle had once stood there at all.

"Where do we go now?" asked Leo.

They all looked to Sebastian, who stared at the wreckage. "Wherever we want," he answered. "We can build a new home wherever we want." He wrapped his arm around Aveline. "As long as we have one another, that is all that matters."

CHAPTER 56

NOT WITHOUT ME

Since the carriages were destroyed during the chaos of the battle and the castle splitting in half, the six of them were left to walk to their destination, which they decided should be Aveline's family's cottage, at least until they figured out what to do. The hounds happily ran around and sniffed every rock along the dirt road, while the humans trudged through the snow, shivering. All but Leo, who seemed completely unaffected by it, other than a slight redness in his nose and on the tips of his ears.

At least Leo kept the cloak, Aveline thought, smiling at the sight of him holding hands with his mother. The first few steps past the castle gates had been nerve-wracking, but they'd passed without incident, other than the colours of Maud's hair, skin, and dress lightening slightly, like a painting being faded by the sun.

"Are you all right?"

"As well as any of us can be," Aveline said to Sebastian. "I think I may have spent too much energy, bringing Maud back, but a good night of sleep should help, I think. Maybe two or three." She glanced sidelong at him, inspecting the way his head was bowed and his eyes were darker than usual. "You could use some rest as well. You spent too much magic."

"Perhaps. But I think we will survive."

"We will," she agreed, squeezing his hand.

The sun beamed high overhead. It was strange to think that so much had happened in one morning, and it was just now noontime. If they could manage to keep pace, maybe they would make it to the cottage by nightfall.

Maud and Leo chatted about anything and everything, sometimes singing and skipping and running. They had to take frequent breaks because she became winded easily.

"Maud is growing far too pale," Aveline commented. "She seems to be shifting back into a ghost."

"My guess is that is because Maud is a ghost," Sebastian said. "She no longer has a human form of her own. You gave her a temporary one."

"I'm glad I could, but I don't understand why I am still affected by the curse when The Heart Thief is gone."

"You've taken control of the curse, turned it into a gift. You're its master, not the other way around."

She grinned. "I rather like the sound of that."

"You're stronger than you give yourself credit for, Aveline."

"Like someone I know."

He rolled his eyes, but the brief smirk told her he was more amused than annoyed. "I was referencing the way you slayed The Heart Thief. Very impressive."

"How did you know about that?"

"I saw it in Maud's mind as she lent me her energy to try to save the castle."

"Then you also saw that I used a magic sword, so it's less impressive."

"I disagree. It may be magic, but it draws its power from the inner strength of the wielder." He paused. "A fact you might find amusing: that sword was one of the magic artefacts I stole from King Byron. Someone told him it was the Conqueror's Sword, and that it would ensure his victories in battle."

"I had a feeling that was it. No wonder he's livid about it being gone, especially in a time like this." She wondered how many of the wizards survived, and what tales they would tell when they returned to the palace. Would King Byron punish them for failure? *He should count himself lucky that he doesn't have to hold up to his end of the bargain with The Heart Thief...*

"Let him be livid. War holds no joy, and having that sword in his arsenal would only add to the tragedy."

She recoiled at the thought; Sebastian offered his arm, and she accepted it. Here he was, still processing the loss of his sister, and he was worried about Aveline. Unsure if it was too soon to bring up Lila, she said, "I finally met you as a child."

"Oh? I felt the castle trying to go back in time, but I thought I'd managed to keep it here."

"I somehow went back with Leo and the hounds. We confused a lot of servants, showing up in their quarters."

"I can imagine."

"What do you recall of that day?"

His eyes hazed over in remembrance. "It was an unseasonably warm day in early spring. Reginald was still upset at us for being too unruly for the previous governess, so Mother sent us outside to play."

"I cannot imagine you being unruly," she teased.

"I was about eleven years old then, and all boys that age are unruly. Just wait until Leo reaches it." He nodded at the boy, whose brow furrowed slightly as his mother's hand slipped through his. Leo peered over his shoulder at Aveline.

"She's not going anywhere," Aveline assured him.

The frown didn't quite leave, but Maud managed to coax him back into conversation.

"I remember you surprised me," Sebastian continued once Maud and Leo were chatting again. "I didn't expect to see an unfamiliar woman in the garden, especially one so beautiful."

"Charmer." She nudged him with her elbow.

"It's the truth! I thought you were beautiful."

"I'm dishevelled! My dress is torn, my hair is a mess, and I'm covered in dirt and scrapes and bruises."

"That doesn't make you any less beautiful."

"Well, I can't argue that. What else?"

"I wrote down your name, committed it to memory. You'd told me that I'd know you in the future, and I was very curious about how that was going to happen... and who you'd be to me." Sebastian let out a deep exhale. "I suspect all that's happened will take a good long while to heal, and I know you're worried about me. I won't pretend to be all right, but I will say I am glad to still have you by my side through these tough times. I'm not quite ready to talk about Lila yet, but when I am, I'll tell you."

He gave her a brief kiss, and then they continued their journey in comfortable silence.

Not long ago, she had been a lady pretending to be a princess, ready to shackle herself to the Crown Prince and the political games of court life, all for the sake of provision and safety for herself, her family, and her country. Now, she was the wife of a rogue wizard, with no future plans or even a place to call their own.

She would not have traded it for the world.

Unable to help herself, Aveline peeked over her shoulder for one final look at the place that had irrevocably changed her life forever. All that she could make out of the castle was dark rubble, a stark contrast against the snowy landscape. It was naught but ruins, but for some reason, Aveline had half expected to see it just as it'd been before, travelling through time to tempt them back again.

No more time travelling, Aveline thought bittersweetly. *No more dark halls, no more vicious creatures, no more echoing screams...*

Suddenly, she could no longer feel the frosty air biting at her face, her ears, her fingertips, nor the wetness of her slush-soaked shoes and socks. An eerie feeling hovered around her, ready to sink its teeth in and drain her of the bits of happiness she'd managed to gain.

Noticing she'd stopped, Sebastian did too, taking in her ghostly form. Just as she was about to give into despair, he reached out and said with an exhausted half-smile, "You're not allowed to go anywhere, not without me."

Her fear vanished as she took his hand. "I wouldn't dream of it."

EPILOGUE
ARE YOU...?

Aveline wiped the sweat from her brow as she strolled through the gardens with Sebastian. Carefully pulling out weeds, Lottie was hunched over the carrots, Timothée beside her, talking about all of the new recipes he wanted to try.

"Your family has adjusted well," Sebastian said. "I think they're happy here."

"I think so too."

In the distance, Leo ran with Amos, Alan, and a few ghost children, who squealed in delight as the hounds playfully chased them. Smiling, Maud watched from close by.

Sebastian halted and sighed, looking down at his untied shoelaces. "Can't quite get the hang of this; never tight enough. Mind waiting a moment?"

"Not at all."

He fumbled with the laces. The new prosthetic was metal, made from what nickerite Aveline's father could get. There had still been some in other mines in Arreth, and it made the prosthetic much more lightweight and manoeuvrable than the one Leo had come up with. Sebastian only wore it about half of the time, but he tried a wide range of things with it. Recently, he'd taken up piano again. She sat with him as often as she could, letting the music inspire beautiful imagery in her mind.

She'd finally painted him, not just once, but time and time again, hanging some of them, and keeping the rest to herself. She loved the way his eyes lit up each time she showed him a new painting, seemingly humbled that he was often the subject. It had taken months for the shadows of his grief to stop clinging so tightly to him. She doubted they would ever truly leave, but they had gotten lighter over the past year.

He'd had no qualms with her hanging recreations of their family portraits in the main entryway of their new home. Not quite large enough to be considered a castle, there were still plenty of rooms for guests, whether they were human or ghost. Sebastian had plenty of wards up for safety, but so far, they'd proven unnecessary: The only spirits and ghosts visiting had either been curious or in need of help. The majority of the ghosts were because of the war, and many had either already left or found their inner peace, passing on.

At one point, there had been so many that Sebastian had joked that, instead of collecting magic items, they were now collecting friends, humans and ghosts alike.

"There, that should hold, at least for a bit." Sebastian stood and nodded triumphantly, taking Aveline's arm again so they could resume their stroll. "Now, what was I going to say...? Oh, yes. We have a bit of a full house—when are your mother and father returning?"

"In a few days."

"Is Edith coming with her husband and child?"

"I assume so. With the war finally over, Jeanette and Alexei might visit too, although I doubt they'd stay overnight."

He tapped the ends of his mechanical fingers as he counted under his breath. "We ought to clear three or four rooms then, and I can put wards up so none of the ghosts enter by accident. Maud does a good job of keeping them in line, especially the little ones, but it's better to be safe than sorry. Don't want to give anyone a fright."

"That is a good plan... although I will say we might want to clear one more room, preferably the one beside ours."

Sebastian's brow furrowed. She could almost see the gears working in his head as he recalculated, trying to make sure he didn't miss anyone. "As you wish. Who will that one be for?" He turned to face Aveline as she gently moved his hand to her stomach. She beamed as his jaw dropped, eyes sparking with hesitant hope.

"Are you...?"

"Yes." She squealed as he picked her up and spun her around. When Sebastian stopped, he kept a tight grip on her, not quite letting her feet touch the ground, and rested his forehead against hers.

"I love you, Aveline. So much more than you'll ever know."

"I have an idea," she teased, kissing him. He melted into her, slowly letting her back down. But just as she wrapped her arms around his neck, he scooped her up and started hurriedly walking. "Where are we going?"

"Inside," Sebastian said. "We have to prepare for our next grand adventure."

ACKNOWLEDGMENTS

When I was finishing up *The Fox and the Briar*, I'd intended to go directly into the next fairytale retelling—I had artwork done of the next fairytale couple, finished an outline, had even started writing it! But then, as strange as it sounds, I had a nightmare, and when I woke, ideas spilled out of me faster than I could write them down. Thank you (and sorry!) to Kate and Lydia for how much I rambled about it. I'm glad I pursued this story because, as with all of my books, it revealed some things about myself that I need to work through. Like these characters, thankfully I have loved ones to help me on the journey of healing.

As with any project, I could not do this alone! I am so grateful all of these wonderful people:

Nicole Scarano: The interior is gorgeous! I'm grateful for all of your creative ideas on how to make this book shine.

Lydia Russell & Katherine Macdonald: There aren't enough words to thank you for everything you help me with. I treasure our friendships and feel absolutely blessed and lucky to have met you. I wouldn't be half the author I am today without you lovely ladies!

@stephydrawsart_ and @WinterMaiden11: Thank you for the artwork! You helped give my story an extra bit of magic.

All of my Betas: My thanks for all of your super helpful feedback. This book is so much stronger for it!

Neil Infalt: My love, I didn't realise how much of you I put into Sebastian until I started editing. Thank you for encouraging me to be me, for reminding me not to care what everyone else thinks, and for helping me heal. I love you!

Charlie & Maximus: My adorable fur babies, I love that your favourite room in the house is my office/library. Thank you for keeping me company throughout the entire process, especially those gruelling edits!

Sienna Schilling: Thank you for always being excited for my books and for telling everyone about them. You are the best sister anyone could ask for.

Lastly, I want to thank my readers: These stories and characters are precious to me, so thank you for taking the time to read my books and leave reviews.

Much love,
Chesney Infalt

ABOUT THE AUTHOR

Chesney Infalt has been writing stories since she got her first notebook at the age of six. While those are under lock and key, her books *The Magic Collector, The Heart of the Sea, The Fox and the Briar,* and *A Different Kind of Magic* are available now on Amazon.

www.chesneyinfalt.com

For Signed Copies:
chesneyinfaltbooks.etsy.com

All socials:
@ChesneyInfalt

Made in the USA
Columbia, SC
03 September 2024